Heard It All Before

Heard It All Before

Michele Grant

KENSINGTON PUBLISHING CORP.
www.kensingtonbooks.com

DAFINA BOOKS are published by

Kensington Publishing Corp.
119 West 40th Street
New York, NY 10018

All Kensington titles, imprints, and distributed lines are available at special quantity discounts for bulk purchases for sales promotion, premiums, fund-raising, educational, or institutional use.

Special book excerpts or customized printings can also be created to fit specific needs. For details, write or phone the office of the Kensington Special Sales Manager: Kensington Publishing Corp., 119 West 40th Street, New York, NY 10018. Attn. Special Sales Department. Phone: 1-800-221-2647.

Dafina and the Dafina logo Reg. U.S. Pat. & TM Off.

ISBN-13: 978-0-7582-4219-8
ISBN-10: 0-7582-4219-0

First Kensington Trade Paperback Printing: January 2010
10 9 8 7 6 5 4 3 2 1

Printed in the United States of America

This book is dedicated to my late father, Dr. Frank William Thompson, Sr., who infused me with a thirst for knowledge, a strong sense of self, and a bit of a princess complex. Only now do I fully appreciate his brilliant choice of life partner, dedication to discipline, trailblazing ambition, ability to laugh at any situation, and unconditional devotion to family.

I know you are chilling:

Holding court with all the cool kids, telling a really bad joke, sippin' on two fingers of scotch, smoking a Cuban, listening to jazz, and occasionally doing that terrible dance.

We were loved; you are missed.

If someone tells you who they are, believe them.

—Maya Angelou

ACKNOWLEDGMENTS

I've never been that girl who just opens up and shares every little thought and emotion. Though it's odd for a writer, I tend to show my feelings with actions, not words. Maybe I'm saving it all for the plots. . . .

However, every now and again even I have to acknowledge and thank those who have hung with me on this journey. And, yes, it has been a journey.

First and foremost, I must acknowledge fam. Nellie Mae (otherwise known as Hat-Wearin', Bridge-Playin', Grammar-Correctin' SuperMom), Errington, Melissa, and Frank II have been patient cheerleaders who remained optimistic long after I threw up my hands. Yes, E—I'll try and get a Maui run out of this. Yes, Misa—I'll try and get a Bali spa run out of this. Yes, Jr—tequila and a poker game. Womb to tomb, people.

A moment for my godparents, the esteemed Melvin and Rita Reddick, who teach by example, are faithful and true, and just flat out are the best people I know in the world.

For my Dallas and Bay Area crew: Sheri, Jenn, Juevette, Shirley, Tami, Cyn. For Christopher and even MEH (holding it down for the Y chromosome). I appreciate the steadfast support, unwavering loyalty, 2:00 A.M. conversations, and rum drinks.

To Pastor Paul and the entire ALCF congregation, thanks for keeping my head right and my soul ready.

Thanks to my editor, Ms. Lena, for recognizing, and to my agent, Ms. Katie, for fighting.

For all those mentioned and to cover those I didn't name directly who have walked with me and talked with me along the way, you are appreciated. More than you know, more than I can say.

Heard It All Before

1

The Kleenex, the Prince, and the Rose?

Jewel—Friday, May 18, 8:00 p.m.

"Chivalry is dead and Prince Charming fell off his charger years ago, you hear me?"

I heard her.

"I know what you want, Jewel. You want some tall, fine, intelligent, sensitive, heterosexual, drug-free, financially stable, Christian, chocolate god over the age of thirty with a great sense of humor to come knock-knocking at your door!" Renee paused. "Don't you?"

When she put it that way, it *did* sound kinda pathetic.

"Well, *don't* you?"

"He doesn't have to knock on my door," I protested weakly.

Renee snorted in disgust. "And where, exactly, are you going to find him? You go to work; he's not there. You come home; he ain't here. You go to church twice a month, slide in the side door five minutes before service starts, and slip out the back before we've sung the last Amen. So if he's there, you'll never see him. You work out at an all-girls' gym. That leaves the grocery store and the cleaners." She snorted again. "You think Mr. Wonderful is hanging out at Martinizing or Safeway?"

I threw my hands up. "Okay, okay. You're obviously trying to tell me something. What is it?"

"Actually, I'm trying to tell you a *few* things, Miss Capwell. Number one, even Cinderella had to dress up and go to the ball to find *her* prince. Number two, life is like the last Kleenex in the box, so be careful how you blow it. And number three, you've got to gather your rosebuds while you still can!"

At this point, I was starting to get mildly annoyed with Renee. Only mildly because I was somewhat confused over all these mixed metaphors. The Kleenex, the Prince, and the rosebuds were throwing me off. What were we talking about?

Okay, see, I invited Renee over for *dinner.* How this turned into a "let's talk about what's wrong with Jewellen's life" thing, I'll never know. But that was Renee for you. Renee and I met freshman year in college. She took one look at me and decided I was an uptight princess; I took one look at her and decided she was ghetto fabulous without the fabulous. We kept running into each other on the campus of the University of Texas in a series of catty exchanges that culminated in an epic battle for the last chocolate pudding pop in the all-girls' cafeteria. On a campus that was only 2 percent African American, we decided it was better to be allies than enemies. When all the dust settled, we discovered we somehow clicked.

I had grown up a bit sheltered. My mom was a bank manager, my father an investment specialist, and prior to their divorce, we had been one unit. I have an older sister and a brother. My sister, Stefani, got married about three years ago before moving to Alaska with her husband. I never could understand moving way up there to the frozen tundra, but that was where Lamar got promoted, so Stefani went. She loved it. Of course, none of us have been as close as we used to be since Mom and Dad's divorce and subsequent remarriages. Mom moved to Denver. Dad moved to New Orleans. My eldest sibling, Ross, got his international law degree and had been globe-trotting ever since. At Christmas, we all get together in a neutral city. Last year it was Miami. This year we're going south of the border to Cancun. I talk to them once a month or so. Since college, Renee, my former roomate Stace, and the gang have been my immediate family.

Renee, on the other hand, had grown up way before she should have. Her mother had Renee at age fifteen, so they kind of grew up together. Her mother was that unfortunate woman who could not be without a man. Renee grew up with a large group of random "uncles." After watching her mom get dogged by player after player, she developed a kill-or-be-killed attitude toward dating. By the time I met her, she had decided that if no one else would love you, you'd better love yourself . . . a lot. She was determined to get the best of everything and the better of everyone. Somehow this translated into convincing herself that the world was as in love with her as she was with herself.

When we started this conversation, she was telling me about the latest love of her life. No exaggerating, Renee Nightingale was the most in love person I knew. She was in love with her job as promotions manager for Royal Mahogany Cosmetics. You know, one of those new spin-offs a white cosmetic company puts out now that they've finally realized that, yes, black people need makeup and hair and skin products of their own! God bless them and I bear no grudge, but I've yet to meet a white person who truly understands the terrifying concepts of ashy legs and nappy hair.

But back to Renee. She was in love with her lazy dog, a froufrou little white chow named, of all things, Peaches. I told her to get another and name him Herb; she didn't take my reference.

Renee was also in love with some new man she met about a month ago. Yes, I said one month. Renee fell in love like other people washed clothes, regularly and in cycles. This cycle, she was into the "Corporate Self-Made Black Man." You've seen him. That swaggering, overconfident, look-what-I've-made-of-myself buppie with the round tortoise-shell glasses, navy Armani suit, Polo paisley tie, Dior white shirt, and Cole Haan leather tassel loafers, don't you know? I think this one was named Gregory.

But most of all, God love her, Renee was in love with Renee. She loved the way she talked, which was rapid and often around the girls, slow and sultry around the boys, and a fascinating combination of both in mixed company. She loved the way she moved, which was exactly how she talked. She loved the way she looked, which I had to admit was pretty damn good. Skin the color of rich, dark chocolate, smooth as silk, and crystal clear. Your basic African American wide brown eyes, gently sloped nose, and a perfect bow mouth.

She had short jet-black hair, and it was *always* whipped up. I mean, I'd known her for ten years, and even first thing in the morning, the clever pageboy was *on*. Sometimes curly, sometimes wavy, sometimes straight but always on. And the makeup, which she actually does change for morning and evening even if she stays at home, was flawless. She kept her manicurist on speed dial.

Her clothes? The woman planned her outfits every Sunday evening for the entire coming week, down to exercise wear and undies. She was 5'6", a size 8, not real big but adequate on top, and was in possession of a true sister's ass and thighs. She had fretted and sweated since "the ass" really kicked in at about age twenty-two but to no avail. I kept telling her nothing short of liposuction was going to rid her of it. And in all truth and fairness, she looked good with it. Only occasionally did I raise my brows when she tried to stretch some Lycra or knit across there. If you asked me how she caught half these Mr. Could-a-Been-Mr.-Rights, I'd say with her smile and that ass. Okay, not my point. I was reflecting on Renee's narcissistic ways. So, back to my growing annoyance with her little diatribe. Nine times out of ten, Renee talked to hear herself talk. Unfortunately, she was talking about me.

Where did she leave off?

Oh, yeah. "Cinderella met her prince at the ball with one Kleenex and a rose?" I muttered. "Girl, what the hell are you talking about?"

"You, girlfriend." She pointed a finger with a red-lacquered nail at me. "You've gotta get out there. Mohammed ain't making his way up this mountain, okay? I've decided it's time to hook you up."

I didn't even try to hide the dismay on my face. "Hook me up?" I shook my head rapidly from side to side. "Ah, hell to the no. You remember the last time you tried to hook me up? I didn't get rid of him until I moved away! You hear me? I had to change *area codes* to get rid of that psycho!"

She had the good grace to look chagrined momentarily. "Oh yeah, him. Well, who knew he was obsessive-compulsive with an Oedipus complex. Is it my fault you reminded him of his mama? Hell, at least he was fine!"

That year she considered minoring in psych obviously didn't do a thing for her. She skipped right past that obsessive-compulsive thing. "At least he was FINE? That was his redeeming quality?" I asked.

She waved that away dismissively. "Anyway, that's history. This time, I don't have anybody specific in mind; I just want to get you out into the proper arenas so you can see the available players, that's all."

Ignoring the sports imagery, I sighed my deepest, weariest sigh. "Renee, let's not do this, really. I'm happy enough with my life. And if the Lord intends for me to have a good man and a good relationship, then I'm sure one will come my way."

Renee shot me a look of stunned disbelief. "What way is that? Safeway?" She leaned forward, warming to her topic. "Listen, sugar, the Lord helps those who help themselves; you hear me? Sitting in this house waiting for something to happen . . . I just can't see that as being the good Lord's plan. You're thirty years old, you own your own house, you run your own company, you're in possession of a decent bank account, you have good sense in your head, and when you give a damn, you look good! All we've got to do is enhance your marketable traits, camouflage your flaws, and present you to a wide and appreciative audience." She sat back with a flourish and a smile.

I raised a brow. "Oh, so I'm your latest marketing project?" She started to speak, but I held my hand out to stop her. "No, no, a thousand times no. My life is fine. Or, here, in words you'll understand—if it ain't broke, don't fix it!"

She turned her nose up and tilted her head to the side. "How ya know it ain't broke? When was the last time anyone turned it on, took it for a test drive? Hell, even kicked a tire! And since you like things in plain English, I'm asking you flat out—when was the last time you had some? Okay, no . . . We don't even have to go all there. When was the last time you had a date?"

Uh-oh, she had me on that one. "A date?" I stalled, trying to think back that far. Could it have been that long ago? Maybe I was getting a little stale?

She smirked. "Yeah, honey, you know the thing . . . when a man asks you out, you go somewhere together merely for the sake of being together, he brings you home, he makes a play, and knowing you, you send him home. A date."

"Well . . ." I squinted up at the ceiling, determined to recall one. Let's see, we're in May, and there was that one guy I went to that concert with. . . . Was that Thanksgiving? Couldn't have been too memorable since the whole experience was a distant blur in my mind.

"You can't remember, can you?" Her expression was irritatingly smug.

"Yeah, yeah, just gimme a minute." Surely I'd gone out over Christmas? No, went to visit my sister's family. New

Year's? No, went to the candlelight service at church. Valentine's Day? No, watched the *Flava of Love* reunion show with a bottle of wine and a gourmet pizza. Ah, shit. This *was* just sad. I had some male friends; could I count lunch with them as dates? My brother and I were at the mall last week, and some guy came up and offered to buy me a smoothie—that's sort of datelike, isn't it?

Truthfully, since Patrick (the ex-fiancé) and I walked away from each other without a backward glance about two years ago, I can't say as I've felt motivated to dive back in the deep end of the dating pool. I was comfortable here in the shallows. A mocha here, a movie there . . . I was all good, right?

Renee was shaking her head. "You don't need a minute. I'll tell ya. Your last date was that jazz concert downtown over the Thanksgiving weekend with that tall boy with the bad haircut. What was his name?"

"It was Richard or Roland or something." What *was* his name?

"Umm-hmm." She said nothing else, just sat there with that know-it-all smirk on her face.

"Okay, okay! So I haven't exactly been the social butterfly lately. I'll start dating again." I shrugged. How tough could it be?

Her eyes narrowed. "How, who, when? You don't go anywhere to meet anybody!"

I rolled my eyes. "Oh, I guess I'm supposed to break out the leather miniskirt and the pumps and start hitting the club scene? No way. I outgrew that six years ago and didn't like it much then. I don't mind going out to cut a step every now and again, but, uh-uh, I'm not getting back into the meat-market scene. No way." All that smiling and posturing and tell me your life story and I'll tell you mine—who wanted to go through all that? Standing around in killer stilettos pretending not to care if anyone looks at you or not . . . yeah, I sure miss that.

"Who said you had to, Miss Priss? I happen to know of a

dozen places to go to roll up on some brothers, not one of them 'meat market' in the least!" She sounded sincere, but Renee always does.

I was suspicious. "Oh, yeah?" I was torn between the desire to be among single men and the deep-rooted belief that Renee was up to something for her own good.

"Yeah. Now, why don't you do something with that hair tonight? We got places to be tomorrow." She drained her glass of wine, stood up, and looked at her watch. "Gotta late date. Gotta shuffle. Thanks for the grub." She strode toward the living room. Girl never wasted a minute, always on the go.

I got up slowly, trailing behind her, still suspicious. "Okay, but where is it that we're going? And what do *you* mean when you say 'roll up'?"

Slinging her $400 Dooney & Bourke over her arm, she looked back at me with a sigh. "Jewel, even *you* know what 'rolling up' means." She headed down the hallway to the front door.

I pursed my lips. "Listen here, Ms. Nightingale. I know how to roll up on a brother. But somehow I feel like my roll and yours are two different things. *Where* did you say we were going?" I stood in the doorway of the kitchen, waiting for my answer. Renee can come up with some wild-ass schemes.

At the door she turned. "To a b-ball court. Got invited to watch a game." She opened my front door and stepped outside. "I'll call you 'round noon. Dress accordingly—the court's kinda up in the hood." She shut the door and made tracks to her car.

I hopped forward, ran to the door, and whipped it open. I caught her fumbling for her keys, thereby foiling her smooth exit. "Excuse me, Miss Thing, did I hear you say we're going to the *hood?* And can you tell me why?"

"Jewellen Rose Capwell," she scolded with one foot in her new Lexus SUV, "you can't be afraid of your own people." She shut the door, turned on the ignition, and whipped out of the driveway.

"Oh, sure I can," I said aloud before closing and locking the door. I walked to the back of my safe little house and turned on my safe little alarm.

As I cleaned away the debris from dinner, I shook my head repeatedly. The hood. Color me snobbish, but I was always scared as hell of the hood. Hey, color me wimpy too. I grew up in Far North Dallas. The farther north the better.

I went to private school with two other blacks in the entire school; that meant in grades K through 12, there was a total of three. After my parents' divorce, I went to public school in one of the richest, whitest suburbs in the city. I thought a fistfight by the bike racks after school was gang violence. Caught a couple kissing under the stairway and I thought that was indiscriminate premarital sex. What did I know? You grow up and realize that the news doesn't tell the whole story, that the Northside was not without crime of its own. I also realized that guns belonged to folks of all color. Nonetheless, I always felt more in my comfort zone north of downtown.

Probably stems from an experience I had when I was sixteen. Just hanging out at a football game on the Southside with some friends. Next thing we know, someone rolls up to do a drive-by and we're literally sprinting for our lives. Spent an hour and a half hiding between a Dumpster and a parked car before we got the all clear. For weeks afterward, I was terrified that one of the shooters had seen my face and was hunting me down. Melodramatic, yes, but also terrifying. Since then, it took a major event and arm-twisting to get me south of downtown.

Don't get me wrong, I hang with "my own people." I like the music, can speak the lingo, rock the attitude, the whole nine. I can go to a Metallica concert Friday and a 50 Cent concert Saturday and never confuse the two. I watched reruns of *Friends* and *Girlfriends*. I had a lot of black friends but quite a few white ones too. I was equal opportunity.

Even dated one white boy for a little minute until I realized that my natural inclinations simply attracted me to tall Nubian princes, as Renee would say. So what if I met a great white guy and fell madly in love, I wouldn't be with him? Not sure, it would be a decision. Not that any of this matters; it had been so long since I met a male of any color that attracted me, I'd forgotten what it feels like. Apparently it was time I got out and saw what was out there . . . again.

I went upstairs, entered the bathroom, and began pulling out all the various paraphernalia I'd need to resurrect this hair and face before morning. I caught a glimpse of myself in the mirror as I turned around to look for my intensive conditioner and almond-peppermint mask.

Pausing, I took stock of what I saw. Medium complexion, somewhere between butterscotch and caramel if I was forced to narrow down the color. Features set in an oval-shaped face that has too often been called "cute." Large brown eyes with lashes that appreciated a volumizing mascara. Button nose and medium-lipped mouth that was a little wider than I would like. Shoulder-length chestnut brown hair parted sensibly on the side. It was currently in need of a trim and conditioning rinse. Usually curled under and tucked practically behind my ears, which were pierced once and usually adorned with a simple hoop or a diamond stud.

I turned to the side and shifted my shoulders back to see how the silhouette was holding up—5'7" on a tall day. Size 8 from the waist down, 10 across the chest. I inherited my grandmother's body—small bones, top heavy, narrow waist, no hips or ass to speak of, thighs that required weekly aerobic maintenance atop admittedly great calves and size 7 feet. Speaking of feet, it couldn't hurt to touch up the toenail polish and do a quickie manicure.

It was entirely possible that I had let a few things slide during my dating hiatus. How did I let Renee sucker me into this mess? I had about ten hours to turn myself from Hilda the hausfrau to Fiona the fly girl. It ain't gonna be easy.

2

Let the Games Begin

Renee—Friday, May 18, 8:45 p.m.

I was gonna fix that girl up whether she liked it or not. It was just pitiful the way she sat up in that house just wiling away her life. And she had so much to offer a man! Jewel was a cute girl. She just bought herself a perfect starter home. A three-bedroom, two-bath, two-story, Mediterranean-style in gray stucco with a semi-circular driveway. Classy with a little flavor—described Jewel to a T. She owned her own business, a temp agency that just got recognized as one of Dallas's most promising new small businesses by the Small Business Association. I talked her into letting that old Chevy Cavalier go, and she was now rolling the new Lexus coupe. To top it off, she loved cooking and did her own gardening too. I came by and watched her plant the gardenia bushes and crepe myrtle in the front lawn. She actually enjoyed all that domestic shit. I believed in writing a check to have someone come and do those things for me.

But that's my homegirl. She was gonna make somebody a good little wife. Hell, ain't none of us getting any younger. If anyone had told me ten years ago that I'd still be single at thirty, I'd have laughed and called them crazy. Who was crazy and laughing now?

My cell phone rang, and I hit the hands-free Bluetooth button on the dashboard. "This is Renee," I said in my softest, I'm-here-for-you-baby voice. Turned up my R. Kelly jam a touch so I could influx a little musical ambiance. Atmosphere was *so* important!

"Renee, it's Gregory." Damn right it was . . . Mr. Greg with a rich baritone that sent a shiver down my spine. My current fresh fish, trying to hook him for real, doncha know?

"Hello, Gregory." My tone was welcoming but not overeager. Gotta play a brother a little, you feeling me? Especially his kind. The kind that wanted me to call him Gregory while his boys called him "G." Daddy was a lawyer; Mama was a CPA. He grew up in private schools, graduated from a big public college for the "exposure," then went on to Ivy League for the MBA. Raised in the burbs and planned to settle there soon. The kind of guy Jewellen's parents probably invited over for pool parties and shit like that.

Pool parties were not a realistic part of my upbringing. We were more concerned with paying to keep the water on, not swimming around in it with twenty of our bestest friends. Private school was a place rich people on TV went to. My daddy was the quintessential rolling stone, and my mom was a receptionist on a good day. What she gave me were life lessons and a will to do whatever it took to not live like that . . . ever again. So I made the grades, won the scholarship, got the education, and maneuvered my way into this career. All I was missing was the long-term brother to fill in the last few blanks. Yes, I knew exactly how to play to get a Gregory kind of guy.

He was the kind who expected me to be impressed by all that he was, is, and will be. This was a man who knew he was a catch and wanted you to act like you knew it too. So I acted like I didn't realize he was a cut above any disposable Buppie. I never did the expected. Hell, I knew what he was and where he was going. That was cream of the crop and straight to the top, and damn skippy, I'd like to be along for the ride. Yes, I had a great job and a great future of my own, but do you really think I *wanted* to work seventy-hour weeks for the next thirty years of my life? Hell no! I had been searching for a Gregory for a good long time. Someone I could pool my resources with for the next few years, traveling and getting a nice house and some stocks here, an IRA there. Then, after I had the two kids, he'd say, "Honey, why don't you stay home with the kids for a few years?" BINGO! That's what I was talking about. After the kids hit high school age, I would open up a little fashion-consulting business. About ten years after that, Gregory would be ready to retire and we'd travel for a few more years before settling down to live out our twilight years around family and friends, involving ourselves more and more with church activities and our grandkids. Oh yeah, I knew exactly who Gregory was and exactly how to play him, and that was as cool as the other side of a six-hundred-thread-count pillow.

"So tell me," he damn near growled in that rich, sexy way brothers had of talking when they were on the prowl, "are we still on for tonight?"

"Well, I don't know, Gregory. What did you have in mind?" Like I didn't know. When a brother made a date for any time after 10:00 p.m., what the hell was that but a booty call? I smiled and tapped the brake as a gray-haired lady cut me off on the tollway.

"Renee—" he made my name sound like a hot, wet kiss on a cold winter night—"I just thought I'd come by and spend a little time with you." Ah, the deliberately vague ploy.

"That sounds nice," I purred, noticing as I whizzed past the woman that she was shooting me the finger. "I guess we could watch a movie or something."

"Um-hmm, or something," he repeated like I was a fool. He had a plan, and I had one too. Mine involved cinema. His . . . didn't take much to figure out.

"Okay, I'm about to pass Blockbuster. What would you like to see?" How I loved to call a bluff.

"Oh well, listen, baby—you don't have to go through all that trouble. Let's just find something to watch on cable." I had to hand it to him, the brother was smooth.

"I don't know." I bit my tongue to keep from laughing. "Cable's kinda iffy. If there's nothing on, I'd hate for you to sit there bored."

"Are you doubting your ability to keep me entertained?"

Ouch! Brother was smart too. Time to change tactics. My voice went silky. "I'm sure if we put our heads together, we can come up with *some* way to pass the time—don't you think?" Dangled the promise out there, let him think what he wanted.

"I never doubted it." Ah, there it was . . . the smug, satisfied voice of a man who thought he had reeled in the catch of the day.

I had no intention of being Gregory's damn catch of the day or freak of the week. If he wanted this fish, he was going to have to reel slowly—I planned to stay caught for life. No way was he getting by with a hot and sloppy affair. Pulling up to the security gate of my apartment complex, I flashed my access card across the beam and waited for the gate to open. Behind me, I noticed a black BMW that looked familiar.

"Is that you behind me?" I stared at the phone. Modern technology played with my timing—with a brother calling me cell to cell, how was a woman to prepare for that? I should have checked the caller ID.

"Yeah, incredible timing, hmm?" There was that catch-of-the-day tone again.

For one second, I struggled to recall whether I was playing him or whether he was playing me. Then I thought about it. Hey, he was *chasing* me, but I would be the one *catching* him.

"Um-hmm, incredible." I shot through the gates. "Follow me up." I hung up the phone and pulled in front of my building. I never looked back, just climbed out of the car and headed up the steps. I heard him behind me and put a little more wiggle in my walk. That confident, I-*know*-I-look-good walk. Purple knit shirt, fitted black jeans, tight stiletto peep-toe heels—fly. I smirked, knowing what kind of view he was getting. Ass Almighty, as my mama would say. Ass Almighty and Thighs Everlasting in tight black denim. I reached the third floor and glanced back. Yep, his eyes were on the ass.

I opened the door, turned off the alarm, and flicked on the lights. As always, I spent a minute looking around to make sure everything was still in its proper place. Peaches jumped off the sofa and slunk over to her bed and lay back down. If I may say so, my joint was live. The entire place was done in black leather with ebony and pastel accents. I had a pretty good collection of African figurines on my mantel and in a display case by the far wall. Bold abstracts, African artifacts, and tropical plants completed the look. The place was two bedrooms, two baths, and perfect.

Gregory had come to pick me up before but had never come inside. He was standing in the doorway, trying not to take inventory. Did I mention that Greggy's in banking? So he couldn't help thinking in dollars and cents . . . my kinda man. While he was scoping out the place, I was scoping *him*. About six feet even, milk chocolate, bow-legged, long-legged, and lean. He moved like a cowboy, a kind of smooth-flowing action with an economy of motion. Does that make sense? Whatever, the boy looked damned fine to me. Close-cropped afro, preppy glasses, and all. The buppie look was in full effect tonight—light green long-sleeved polo, straight-leg button flys (could I get an Amen, all praises to Levi Strauss), woven leather belt, Cole Haan loafers, no socks. Umm, umm, good.

"Why doncha take the tour while I make some popcorn?"

"Thanks." He threw me that much-obliged-ma'am grin that I was fairly sure had melted many a heart through the years. Hell, I thought mine even skipped a beat or two. He patted Peaches on the head as he passed and went into my spare room first. It was sort of a catchall: a computer, an exercise bike, a small pullout sofa, and a sewing machine I hadn't touched in years. As I heard him go farther down the hallway toward the master suite, I held my breath and waited.

"Holy shit," I heard him say, and I released my breath on a laugh. He'd seen the bed.

He came back out to the kitchen with what I'd have to call a predatory gleam in his eye. "That's some bed you got there."

I smiled. That bed was a study in decadence. It was king size and made of heavy ebony wood, canopy style with sheer silk drapings in peach, black, and purple. The bed was elevated, so you had to jump or take the steps. The comforter and sheets were rich peach and black satin. Pillows of all sizes in a million colors created a plush mountain at the head of the bed. "You like?" I asked, very tongue in cheek.

"I certainly think I will," he replied solemnly. "Tell me, what possessed you to create such a wonder?" He stepped a little closer while he waited for my answer.

"Well, I think the bed is the most important piece of furniture in the house. Did you know that a third of a person's life is spent in bed?"

"Is that right? All that time in bed? How very interesting."

Something in his tone compelled me to look up and meet his eyes. His deep brown eyes were framed with long, almost girlish lashes. Damn. Pure, unadulterated sizzle—I have always been a sucker for sizzle. I could feel that electric live wire of sexual awareness flashing from him to me and back again. I didn't know how long I stood there staring at him while my body temperature elevated.

Forcibly, I took a breath and started talking to myself in my head. *Buck up, Renee. Don't give in or you'll blow it. Look at the big picture!* I dropped my eyes back to the popcorn. "Sleeping, that is. You want this au naturel or with butter?" There, my voice sounded normal. I was in control. Now, if he would back up a step, I could breathe again.

"Butter it up—the slicker the better." Need I describe the inflection, the tone of his comment?

Now, what was a girl to say to that? A smart one says nothing. My mama didn't raise no fools. "Why don't you settle in on the sofa and start flipping channels? I'll only be a second." I smiled my best hostess smile and turned to the refrigerator. It was a full minute before I heard him move away and was able to get all systems back to normal again.

He was good at this game. A smoldering glance here, a caressing tone there, innuendos running amuck, and all the while, my raging hormones were playing snap-crackle-and-pop with my nerve endings.

Okay now, Renee, you've doctored this popcorn as much as you can. Get it together and get in there!

I tossed a couple Cokes on the tray with the popcorn bowl and some napkins, took a deep breath, and headed out to the living room. There he was. He sat comfortably on my sofa, like he belonged there, the remote control in his hand, his eyes following my every move.

I placed the tray on the sofa table and sat down a substantial but not prudish distance away from him. "Hope Coke's okay?" I gestured toward the tray.

"Fine, thanks." He picked up a can, popped the top and took a sip before speaking again. "Like you said, there is not a lot to choose from"—he inclined his head toward the TV—"but there's an old Clint Eastwood coming on if you like his movies."

I started to smile, at ease for the first time since he entered my apartment. "Yeah, I like Clint. Which one is it?"

"*The Outlaw Josey Wales.*"

He smiled; I smiled back. Harmony reigned. I picked up the popcorn and inched a little closer to him. "Let's see it."

Believe me, I was surprised. We were actually enjoying just watching the movie. We were having intelligent conversation and laughing together. He had a funny way of finding an obscure moment in the film and making it hilarious. During a commercial, he took the empty cans and bowl to the kitchen. Yes, the boy voluntarily did a domestic thing, a novelty among the men I'd dated before. We laughed about Peaches, the world's laziest dog, who hadn't moved the entire night.

By the time the movie wrapped, I was curled up by his side with his arm draping lightly around me. I was relaxed and secure. It was nice to spend some time with a guy and not have to plot, plan, and wonder what he really means every time he says something. All that gets exhausting. I allowed myself to relax and enjoy the time off.

My relaxed state ended abruptly when he clicked off the TV, hoisted me onto his lap, and laid those sexy lips against mine all within a one-minute time span.

He stunned me with the suddenness of it, but his kiss was so subtle that I was lulled into a false sense of security. He wasn't even opening his mouth, just pressing light angel kisses on my lips and face. It was sweet and at the same time strangely sexy. I had to admit, he was playing me like a piano and hitting all the right notes. Who opened their mouth first, him or me? The next thing I knew, I was flat on my back with all six feet of fineness atop me. The kisses were wet and sloppy; I could hear us slurping like cats with bowls of milk. As to be expected, Gregory took control and kissed as he wanted to kiss. For once I let someone else drive while I rode eagerly in the passenger seat. His technique was, of course, flawless, managing to infuse passion, tenderness, and authority into every lick and nibble. He was quite good at this—too good.

He untucked my shirt from my waistband and slid his hands slowly up my spine. Then he did this slithering thing where he brushed the entire front of his body up and down the entire front of mine. No lie, I damn near lost it. I would've lost it too, but right then he reached for the snap on my jeans.

Warning! Danger dead ahead! Point of no return! Do NOT yield! My brain finally flashed signals through my passion-fogged senses. Damn, I wanted that boy! But I had to remember the game; I had to stay cool.

"Greg." I put my hand on his wrist and deliberately shortened his name.

He instantly stilled and raised his eyes to my face. When had he taken off his glasses?

"No?" he asked softly, making it oh so easy on me. Or was he?

"No," I answered just as softly.

"Not yet, huh?" Damn. I really *could* love this boy. He made it sound more like a promise than a question.

"Not yet."

He sighed, started to ease off me, and then paused for a minute. "Could I change your mind?" He should register that voice as a lethal weapon, really he should.

"Probably." I gulped. "But I wish you wouldn't." I hoped that sounded firm.

"All right." He got up, put on his glasses, and helped me up. We stood there holding hands and staring at each other for one of those minutes that felt like an hour before he dropped my hand and picked up his keys from the table.

"Thanks for letting me come over so late—the movie and all. I had a nice evening." His mama raised him well.

I walked him to the door and opened it. "Thanks for coming over. It *was* nice." Damn, we sounded like a chapter from an etiquette book: "How to Say Good Night to Your Date."

He leaned over and kissed me lightly. "I'll see you tomorrow?"

"I'll be there." If I had to walk across the burning plains of the Serengeti, I would not miss his game in the morning for any reason short of death. This was *the* man for me. Mine.

"Later." He turned and was gone.

At the sound of the closing door, Peaches finally roused enough to bark once. I went over, and she climbed into my lap and looked up at me. "Woof?"

I smiled down at her. "Yeah, I know. I'm in deep shit with this one."

My brilliant dog nodded, said, "Woof," and settled back down.

Gregory—Friday, May 18, 12:15 a.m.

Climbing into my ride, I decided that I have changed and wondered if that was a good thing.

Back in the day, I'd've been *in there*, no matter what. Hell, I guess I was getting mature or some shit, because two, three years ago, *nothing* could've gotten me to leave that apartment without getting the drawers.

Renee had it going on. Wasn't just that she was crazy fine, though heaven knew she truly was. Renee was that rare combination of feminine intrigue and masculine ambition wrapped up in a beautiful mahogany package.

I first saw Renee about a month ago at this bullshit Young, Black, and Professional thing my boy Aaron dragged me to. She came in late and alone, wearing a long, tight, red silky thing. Baby knew how to make an entrance. Every guy in there had both eyes on her, and I'll be damned if she didn't know it.

Anyway, after the meeting, I saw her talking to Rosaline. Rosaline was a pain-in-the-ass chick who worked at the bank. She had swiftly slept her way through all the execs at the bank, and I supposed I was to be next on her hit list. But I was never one to take a number and wait in line, you feel me? It took me all of one lunch to charm Renee's name, number, and some pertinent info out of Rosaline.

On the surface, Renee seemed real bourgeoisie and uptown. You'd never know she came up on the Southside just one generation out of the projects. She was putting her younger brother through college and paid half the rent on the condo where her mother and aunt live in Phoenix. She had a marketing degree from University of Texas and climbed into management in only four years. No doubt, she had a reason to walk around like respect was her due.

After hearing all of this, I knew I had to roll up on Renee smooth. The Renees of the new millennium are used to brothers sweating 'em and sweating 'em *hard*. So I arranged a few casual meetings. Arranged a little coincidental sighting at the soup and salad spot where she ate at least two times a week. A waving drive-by as she strolled from her building to her parking garage. Things like that.

I was building up to the 'how-about-some-lunch' call when *she* came to see *me* at the bank. Waltzed into my office looking good as hell and said, "Hi, I'm Renee Nightingale, and I was wondering if you'd like to take me out sometime?" WHOA!

My kinda woman.

Now, no need to trip. I *did* know Renee thought she had some sort of game running. That was fine; I did too. For every action, there was an equal and opposite reaction. For every line she threw, I had a lure of my own in waiting. Player to playette—the game was on. For every step, a countermeasure. I saw this like a game of chess; strategy was everything, and once you captured the queen, the game was pretty much yours.

Pulling up in front of my condo, I smiled. Now, wouldn't it be great if we both won the game?

3

Meet-'n'-Greet

Jewel—Saturday, May 19, noon

"I got it already, okay!" I threw my hands up in frustration. "I'm not a child who needs to be tutored every step of the way. I think I know how to behave at a simple basketball game." I was looking directly at Renee, because to be truthful, I didn't wanna watch the road. Her driving scared the shit out of me. Acceleration, never braking. Swerving, never turning. Offense, no defense. Made me downright prayerful.

Renee clucked her teeth and shot me a look out of the corner of her eye. "I don't know—you don't spend too much time in the hood."

"Because I choose not to," I bit out, "not because I'm afraid of making some faux pas against ghetto etiquette." We hit the off-ramp without slacking off of seventy. I wondered if I remembered to put Rolaids in my purse as I gripped the door handle.

"See? That's exactly what I'm talking 'bout. Don't nobody know what the hell *faux pas* means over here, and if they do, they ain't bragging about it."

I rolled my eyes. "Now who's stereotyping? I mean, what do you think—I'm going to stroll around and accidentally drop my Gold Card?" I laughed. "Who cares anyway? No one is going to pay any attention to me with you in that outfit."

She looked over quickly. "What's wrong with my outfit?" She had on a clingy, green, camisole-style bodysuit with a short denim wrap skirt and strappy, green eelskin sandals. She'd switched to the green Dooney and put the green wristband on her Gucci watch, had on a perfect face of complimentary makeup, and, as expected, the hair was whipped. My girl looked good, as usual. I forgot that Renee, for all her showboating, was insecure about damn near everything.

I patted her thigh. "Girl, you know you look good." We shared a smile. "I guess I'll get to meet the oh-so-wonderful Gregory?" I looked at her, and I swear I saw her blush. I couldn't be sure, but she looked damned flustered. "Throwing you for a loop, is he?"

Miraculously, she slowed for the last turn toward the MLK Recreational Center. "It's hard for me to fathom, girl, but the brother could have me straight feenin'. I was damn near off my game last night."

I sucked in a surprised breath. I had watched Renee run many a game, and even when the boy was a flat-out *dog*, she still came out with the winning game plan. Always walked away like she'd planned all the shit from the beginning. Personally, I never understood why she couldn't just meet somebody, let things happen, and go from there. But, no, she always had a master plan, a scheme, a game. If this Gregory had her turned around this early in the match, I *definitely* wanted to meet him. But all I said was, "Hmmm."

"Actually, I can't wait to get your impression of him; he's really more your type than mine."

Here we went with this shit again. I rolled my eyes. Renee had no idea what my type was. Hell, if truth be told, *I* had no idea what my type was. She assumed that every brother from a professional family with a degree and a professional job was my type. So why was she the one dating and I was sitting at the house testing out new recipes for one? More of that type-casting, stereotyping shit. I actually never cared WHAT a man did as long as he DID something, you know? The title, the car, the trendy condo—that was her kick, not mine.

I decided her comment was rhetorical as we pulled into a parking space. I took the opportunity to look around. "Isn't that Roni Mae's car?"

Renee nodded. "I called her. And, Jewel, could you *please* remember to call that girl Veronique?"

I opened the door and climbed out. "Shit, Veronica Mae Jackson is the girl's name. Has been the girl's name for as long as I've known her. Her mama calls her Roni Mae. Just because her voice is on the radio five nights a week don't make her Veronique to *me*!"

"Jewellen Rose!" she scolded.

"Yes, Darnella Renee?" I returned, and laughed. "Fine, I'll call the girl Veronique . . . for now." I never understood why people get a little paper in their wallet and tried to forget who they are. Roni Mae had been perfectly happy for thirty years being Roni Mae. Someone gave her a paycheck with a comma and some zeroes, and suddenly she morphed into Veronique.

We walked inside the rec center and followed the sounds of screeching high-tops and booming Li'l Jon to the courts. We stepped through the gym door and over to the bleachers. I stopped dead in my tracks. A couple of games seemed to be going on at once. I counted at least twenty mighty fine specimens of manhood sweating and running in shorts and tank tops. I saw a lot of brothers, a few Hispanic-looking guys, and even a white boy or two. God bless America, home of the fine and free.

"My, my, my," was all I could manage. I did need to get out more often. For the scenery if nothing else.

"What'd I tell ya?" Renee grinned. "High five for fine brothers playing basketball."

"Amen, sister." We shared a high five.

"There is quite the ho fest going on in here, though," she mentioned as she tilted her head toward the bleachers.

There was, indeed, your standard assortment of Lycra-wearing, lollipop-sucking, crimped and finger-waved, nose-ringed, blond-weave-wearing, round-the-way girls lounging about. "Why you gotta call 'em hos, Renee?" I said wearily. We'd had this argument before. "They're just girls in trendy hip-hop, urban gear. How does that make 'em hos or hoochies or bitches? I just call 'em fly girls."

"I call a spade a spade and a ho a ho," Renee persisted.

"They could all be as pure as the driven snow for all we know." I really hated broad-sweeping generalizations of an entire group of people we'd never met before. Then again, I *was* the one who thought everything south of downtown was nothing but a cauldron of crime. But I was working on that—after all, I was here, wasn't I?

Renee shrugged. "Yeah, yeah, and I'm the Virgin Mary."

"Jew-Ro, Nay-Nay!" a voice screamed at us. I looked over to see all 5'10" of Veronica Mae Jackson hopping up and down, waving at us from the first row.

Renee and I looked at each other. "And I can't call her Roni Mae?"

"Shit, call her what you want." Renee shot a look at the court. "I can't believe she called me that here!"

"Believe it," I muttered as we headed over. "Which one is Greg?"

"Gregory," she corrected, "is the one in the navy Nike stuff."

Gregory, not Greg. He was THAT guy. Got it.

We reached the bleachers. "Hey, Roni Mae." I greeted her, sat down, and feasted my eyes on the sights before me. Gregory was indeed a sight to see. He was perfectly coordinated, I noticed, and I didn't mean just his moves on the court. Brother was sporting navy Nike tank, navy Nike baggy shorts, navy and green biking Lycra shorts underneath with the Nike swish showing. White socks with a blue Nike swish and, of course, Air Jordan high-tops in white with a blue swish. Just swished all up one side and down the other. I'd lay odds that the navy Nike gym bag in the far corner with the navy and green sports bottle was his. He was intent on the game, aggressive but not pushy, vocal but not loud. He moved well, not really fast but with accuracy. He was an intelligent ball player—not a street player. All in all, he looked good.

I decided to reserve judgment of him until after we met and I had a chance to hear him speak and look him in the eye. The eyes told a lot. I turned my attention back to my girls. "What's been up, girl?" I asked Roni Mae. I hadn't talked to her in a while and wanted to catch up. She was one of my oldest and closest friends, even if we didn't hang as tight as we used to. People grew up and learned you didn't have to live in each other's back pockets morning, noon, and night to be friends.

She answered in her patented voice. "Living for work and working for a living." She had the best voice I'd ever heard, as smooth as whiskey and sweet as molasses. Took her a while to realize she could make money off that voice. Then she put her hand to her hair—or, rather, the hair atop her head—and asked, "You like?"

I sighed. I'd been diplomatic in not mentioning it before, but it was my belief that black women should *not* be blond, for any reason. No, not even Beyoncé. Now, I spoke up when Roni Mae first got this weave. One day, she was sporting a microshort natural; the next thing I knew, she had long wavy hair halfway down her back. I asked her why she couldn't have eased into the weave in stages. At least pretend to fool somebody. Now she was long, wavy, *and* blond. Well, at least it matched the purple (oh, I'm sorry, violet) contacts.

Roni Mae looked a sight. She was a big woman, about a size 22 and damn near six feet tall. She had a beautiful face, but she kept it obscured with the hair and outrageously huge earrings, and for some reason, we couldn't seem to make her let go of that Tropical Sunset (orange) lipstick. Roni Mae was not dark or light; she was kinda in between, with an olive tinge to her skin. Back before she became Veronique, night personality for one of the black radio stations here, she was starting to get it together. She went down to about a size 18, the hair was natural but she could wear that (not every sister can!), her eyes were the deep brown the Lord meant them to be, and she smiled a lot. She had a sweet man around, and she seemed real happy doing voice-overs and other commercial entertainment work. Then she became K-Soul's "Mistress of the Dark"; the man left and she morphed into Veronique. Her 10:00 p.m.-to-2:00 a.m. segment was called "Midnight by Candlelight," specializing in baby-come-to-bed songs mixed in with an on-air *Love Connection*-like game and talk show. Her show was consistently one of the highest rated in the state. Not to say success did not become her . . . or maybe that was exactly the thing to say.

"Well, Roni Mae, it's blond." I settled on that as the best answer I could give, because, after all—who was I to tell her how to look? One of her best friends, that's who. But sometimes you had to pick your battles. I wasn't about to start arguing over Roni Mae's ghetto-ass do. I let it go.

"Sho nuf iz." She giggled. Behind me, I heard the loud thudding sounds of heavy feet pounding the ground and the distinct swishing sound of a ball sailing through the basket. Cheers rang out on both sides of the gym.

"Roni, why?" Renee was not so subtle. "Why in the hell is your hair ass length and blond?" She had one eye on Roni and one eye on Gregory; he was traveling but there were no refs to call it.

Veronica shrugged. "I wanted a change. I'm going to catch me a man with this hair, girl."

"And that outfit, too, I suppose?" Renee asked.

Gregory missed the rebound.

Roni Mae had on a catsuit (yes, a catsuit!) of bright purple with a crochet batwing overtunic in multicolors. She had on multicolored snakeskin pumps to match. She looked like a big round rainbow. "Well, do you like it? It's part of my new look."

"It does go with the hair," I answered. Always the diplomat when what I wanted to say was, "How did you put that shit on, look in the mirror, and *still* allow yourself to leave the house?" Or, "How did you BUY that mess and spend legal tender for it?" But I let it go. I was good at that . . . letting shit go.

"Girl, you look ridiculous. You do realize that just because it comes in your size, doesn't mean you should buy it . . . or wear it." Renee came out with it, bluntly. She hasn't mastered the whole let-it-go thing.

Instead of looking hurt, Roni Mae looked amused. "You just don't understand where I'm going with this whole new me."

I couldn't help myself; I was curious all of a sudden and couldn't let it go not one more minute. "Where *are* you going, Veronique? Where have you *gone*, Roni Mae?"

Before she could answer, there was more screeching of shoes on rubber, and the sound was closing in. "Watch out!" I heard someone say, and I turned around in time to see a big mass of flesh flying toward me. I shrieked and tried to jump out of the way, but there was nowhere to go. I instinctively put my hands out and braced myself. So when the boy flew into me, I somehow caught him neatly in my arms, and we ended up flying off the edge of the bleachers, where we landed in a tangle on the ground. The hard, unyielding ground. We both grunted upon impact. It hurt.

"Ah, shit," a deep voice said by my ear.

"Uh," I grunted again. I hurt a lot. Whoever was on top of me was big. Big and heavy. Big and heavy and sweaty. Big and heavy and sweaty and smelly. And muscled, not an ounce of flab anywhere on him by what I could feel—and that was plenty. We were sandwiched together from chest to toe. I opened my tightly shut eyes to see what hit me. From the patch of skin I could see, he was cocoa-colored. I always loved cocoa.

I felt him moving. It was weird because it all felt like slow motion. He put his hands on either side of my head and raised himself up, like a push-up. Add good-looking and strong to the list. Okay, very good-looking. His face was a sculptor's dream, chiseled, manly, and strong. One of those rare faces where everything was in perfect proportion, except the lips. His lips were . . . I guess juicy was the word to use. Not huge, just full and juicy. His hair was curly, naturally not processed, and his eyes weren't exactly brown. Maybe gold? He had a real Cajun look to him.

"Hey, miss, you okay?" Definite Cajun ancestry—that light sprinkling of patois was right there in the voice. He looked down at me with a slight smile. Hmm, a polite and educated brother whose eyes were hypnotizing me. Who wasn't a sucker for pretty eyes? Okay, okay, they were regular eyes, for Christ's sake; I just couldn't figure out what color they were. It was for some reason monumentally important to figure it out, since they were staring right into mine. Most unnerving. Quite unsettling. But oddly exciting.

"Yeah, I'm all right." Damn, I sounded breathless. Well, shit. I was breathless! The impact from my body hitting the floor and his body hitting mine pretty much took all my wind. We hadn't moved yet. He needed to move first. He didn't appear to be in a hurry. I can't say I was rushing him much.

"Y'all okay?"

"You all right?"

"Is anyone hurt?"

The questions came one after the other, and still we lay there looking at each other. It seemed like forever. It was one of those moments when you're glad to be a woman, and you can tell he's glad too. That man-woman thing. It made you uncomfortable, but you liked it anyway.

"If you're okay, Ro, let's finish whippin' some ass up in here." Ro? Roland? Roderrick? Rowen? Ro-what?

"Jew-Ro, you gonna make it, girl?" I shut my eyes for a second. Did Roni have to call me that? It was like a dash of cold water. Maybe I would thank her before I kicked my shoe into that ample rear. I looked away from him and shifted a little to let him know I was ready to get up. It was time, unfortunately.

"Ro, you can hit on them hoochies later!" Some ignant ass called out from the floor.

He frowned. I frowned. He vaulted to his feet gracefully, with a fluidity of motion. He put a hand out. I took it and let him pull me up. He didn't let my hand go. "Sorry 'bout that, miss." I had a feeling he was apologizing for his friend's "hoochie" comment rather than the careening-to-the-floor thing.

"Jewel," I corrected. "It's all right . . . Ro?" Color me smooth, sister was trying to get some 411.

He smiled, beautifully I might add. "It's Rome. You sure you okay?"

I nodded, ignoring the little twangs and twitches from all my jarred nerves and muscles. He dropped my hand. "Cool." He turned back toward the court and strode away. Um, poetry in motion. He had to be about 6'3", 210. Broad shoulders, lean hips, ripped abs, buns of steel. This was a man who knew his way around a gym. Moved like an athlete. Smooth skin the color of milk chocolate stretched across his large-boned frame. He was a man's man. The kind other men admired and women hungered for. I had to keep myself from licking my lips, and I was sure my stomach growled.

Halfway back to his position, he looked back and pointed a finger at me. "See ya round, Miss Jewel."

I pointed back and nodded before turning away coolly and easing my bruised bones back onto the bleachers.

"Well *who* and *what* was *that*?" Roni Mae asked.

Renee giggled. "One of her wildest wet dreams!"

I just smiled and said nothing. Shit, it was true. If the brother had any kind of résumé to speak of, we were gonna have to spend a little time together. It was not every day you came across something like *that.* All of a sudden, I had a much clearer picture of what my "type" was, or at least what he looked like. I made a mental note to get Renee and Roni to check the brother's references at first opportunity.

Oh, Renee could have her games. I liked to break down the important shit. Résumé and references. What do you do, who do you know, who knows YOU, and is the blood test in order? Blame it on my profession—I liked to get a background check. Facts, the faster the better and keep 'em coming.

Rome—Saturday, May 19, 12:20 p.m.

I was playing hoops, but my mind wasn't really in the shit. Me and the fellas played here every Saturday unless that's the Saturday when I was over at Graham's getting a clip—'cause you can't let the head get too shaggy. Anyway, I knew I had never seen that girl here before. I'da remembered.

I saw her come in earlier. I was doing one of my Air J moves with the pivot and the hook when in she came . . . she and her girl. Her friend looked good, too, but it seemed to me like there was something phony about her. I'd seen her round here before. She must be hooked up with one of the boys on the other team; if one of *my* posse was on her, we'd've heard about it before today. But back to Miss Jewel, back to Miss Jewel . . . um, um, um. Sure was something about that girl.

When she rolled in and I got an eyeful, I thought, *Baby fine.* She walked with her head up, shoulders back, and that chest out. Good God Almighty was that chest out and saying, "Pow! Bam!" You had to sit up and pay attention to a chest like that. 'Course, where the Lord giveth, he also taketh away—barely any ass on that girl at all. But you didn't really need ass on a girl like that—kept a man too busy.

What ass she had was packed into that little skinny jean skirt proper. She had on one of those clingy knit shirt things that comes down into a V in front in a dark red kinda color. Was a V to make a man's mouth water.

She was a healthy girl, not big but not tiny, either and soft where she should be, ya know? Came to a little below my shoulder—guess that'd make her about 5'7 or 8". She was easy to pull up, so I could lift her if I wanted. Beautiful girl, got a face to stop traffic. Round, with a little nose and pouty-looking lips. Big brown eyes. Either real good perm or good hair, didn't matter which as long as it looked good and felt soft. She wore it normal, too, not all kinked or crimped up—just sorta straight, then tucked under at the bottom, ya know? It hung down to her shoulders, light brownish. She spoke real soft and uptownlike. Didn't seem stuck-up or fake. I can't stand phoniness!

See, that was all I asked for, a sister who at least came to my shoulder, someone you could pick up without too much strain, a face I wouldn't wince at first thing in the morning, a sweet voice, good sense in her head, and a job of her own. I didn't know if she had the last two, but I would bet my Duke Ellington original vinyl collection on it—and that's serious!

"Ro, look alive, boy!" Darren yelled at me as he ran past.

"Sorry, dude." I looked over at Miss Jewel one last time before the ball shot at me from nowhere. I yanked it out of the air, bounced it behind my back before dribbling forward. I bumped Aaron out of the way, turned, jumped, and shot. *Swish!* "Two!" I gave Darren a high five and looked over at Miss Jewel. She smiled and clapped for me. I took a little bow and went back to guarding Aaron. I'd catch up with Miss Jewel later.

4

Return of the Mack

Renee—Saturday, May 19, 12:30 p.m.

I got so wrapped up watching Rome watching Jewel and watching Jewel watching Rome that I almost forgot to watch Gregory. I had seen Rome around; he was a Southside brother. But I couldn't remember hearing anything about him. I would have to pull Aaron aside and ask about him. He might have looked tasty, but if he was about them streets, Jewel wouldn't be falling for his play. That girl had always been scared to death of the hood. Don't get me wrong—she had dated the ruffnecks before, but as you can see, they didn't make it. She had this fear that she'll end up living in the projects on welfare with six kids and an abusive husband someday. Which killed me, as she had never so much as stepped inside a project home in her life. Even if she lost her car, her business, and her house today, she'd still just move in with her folks or me or somebody. What did she think, some man was going to sweep her off her feet and force her to live in the hood? Hell, half my family came from the projects; a few of 'em still up in there. Besides, projects didn't make up all of the black neighborhoods.

I kept telling her, "Your life is what you make of it, and no man can take you where you don't want to go." Well, if this Rome even got the digits out of her, it should be interesting to watch.

Rome was wearing an old Cowboys sweatshirt with the sleeves ripped out; he had great arms on him. Gray shorts, great legs. The boy had great everything on him. But looking around the courts, there was a lot of greatness out there. Gregory looked predictably good. I was still trying to keep it all together about him. I knew Jewel thought I needed to quit planning, maneuvering, and game playing, but the girl had no comprehension. I was trying to get somewhere *with* somebody. And I needed to be in control to do it.

See, I was not content to just sit back and say, "The Lord will provide." Fine, he had provided me the opportunity to land Gregory, and I planned to do it. Amen.

"You go, boy!" Roni Mae was screaming at Rome, who had just stolen the ball from Aaron, Gregory's friend. Lord! Roni Mae looked ridiculous in that getup. She was jumping up and down, and she looked like a big kaleidoscopic marble bouncing through the air.

"Go for the dunk! Go for the dunk!" she screamed, and I looked back at the court. Rome had indeed sprinted down the length of the court and was going for the dunk. He went up over everyone's head, came down for the two-handed slam, and hung on the rim in a fairly decent Kobe imitation before landing with his arms out in a "Don't you just love me?" gesture. The bleachers went wild. He looked right at Jewel and raised a brow as if to say, "How ya like me now?"

She smiled, raised two fingers, kissed them, made a dunking action in the air with them, and placed them over her chest in a be-still-my-beating-heart motion. He smiled and turned to jog back up the court.

I looked over at my girl with my mouth hanging down. Jewel was flirting. No, Jewel was getting her mack on! Had the mack kicked up to full throttle! Jewel never macked a day in her life. She was one of those women who never looked for a relationship; they just sort of fell in her lap. Granted, her lap had been empty for a little while now, but check this! My girl was the mack!

"What?" She smiled at me when she caught me staring.

I reached over and knocked on her head. "Hello, is Jewellen Rose in? Some fly girl mackin' mama has taken over this body!"

She swatted my hand away. "Let Mama handle her business, baby."

A cheer from the court preempted my answer . . . the game was over. Rome's team was victorious; Gregory's team had lost. Gregory gathered up his navy gym bag and came straight over, even though he hadn't looked over or acknowledged my presence for the past half hour. I sat up and decided to smile casually. Like a friend greeting a friend.

He stopped right in front of me. "Hey."

"Hey, yourself." My, what repartee. For the first time in I don't know how long, I was not exactly sure what to say or do next. It was totally against my nature to sit and wait for someone else to make the next move. But wait I did.

He looked straight at me for a minute, no glasses on today. Then he did that man thing I've never decided if I liked or not. That thing where they drop their eyes all the way down your body before pulling them all the way back up. Then they smiled and looked you right in your eyes. When I was younger, this used to fluster the hell out of me or really piss me off. As I got older, I took it in stride and more often than not, I returned the look. Today, it kinda left me dazed and tingling. I was losing it.

"You look nice today. Do you mind?" Gregory asked me.

"Mind wha—"

His lips cut off my question. Hot damn, there he went again with a sneak attack. His hand was on the nape of my neck, moving slowly up and down in rhythm with his tongue in my mouth. My arms reached for him, and I sighed the little air I had left. How did he do that? How did he take a seemingly simple gesture and shatter me into pieces?

"This must be Gregory." Roni Mae's smooth voice cut all into my moment.

I felt his lips curve into a smile before he pressed one last oh-so-sweet kiss on my mouth and lifted his head. I dropped my arms to my side, still unable to figure out what to say. He turned to look at Roni Mae, and I took the opportunity to collect myself. To Gregory's credit, he didn't wince or blink when he saw Roni Mae in all her glory (or whatever).

"With that voice, you must be Veronique from K-Soul. I fall asleep to your 'Midnight by Candlelight' segment every night." He put his hand out. "Gregory Samson, pleased to meet you."

Roni Mae actually blushed before composing herself and shaking his hand. "Why, thank you, Gregory. I do love to meet fans." She gave him the eyelash flutter and hair toss before launching into her practiced getting-to-know-you routine.

Jewel and I rolled our eyes behind Roni Mae's back. She was in her Veronique mode, and there was no stopping her. She and Gregory talked some more, but with Gregory's hand still slip-sliding up and down my neck, I couldn't say as I was paying them much attention. Eventually, Roni Mae excused herself and went off to talk to someone she knew across the gym. She was off to get her network on. Every occasion was an opportunity to network as far as she was concerned. Usually, Jewellen was right behind her with the business cards and recruiting spiel going. Personally, I only networked with people I KNEW could do something for me. I tuned back in at the sound of Gregory's voice.

"And you must be Jewel." He turned his suave smile on Jewel.

I snapped out of my lethargy in time to watch Jewel's reaction to "the Gregory Look." God bless my homegirl, she was no pushover. She raised a brow and looked at him assessingly. Taking his hand, she gave it a brisk shake. "Must I be?" She pulled her hand away and waited.

"Aren't you?" The boy had a comeback for everything.

She shrugged. "So it seems." Ah, one of the things I alternately loved and hated about Jewel—she always wanted the last word. She looked at him square in the eye before dropping her eyes to where his hand still rested against my neck.

Gregory wasn't fazed. "Listen, I've got to tell you—we used some of your people during our changeover from Dallas Republic Savings to Nationwide United Bank earlier this year, and I was impressed by how quickly and easily they were able to pick up our operation and help out." There he went with the business schmooze. He leaned into me a little closer, and now just his thumb stroked lazily along the column of my neck. It was hell on my jumpy little nerves.

"Thanks. At the Capwell Temporary Agency, we aim to please," Jewel quoted from her latest brochure. "I understand that you hired away a couple of my best." She raised her eyes to his again.

He nodded, at ease and never dropping his gaze. "I think we did. I know we tried to." She held his stare and nodded back; then they grinned at each other. They looked as though they'd reached some sort of nonverbal understanding.

"He's all right, Renee," Jewel said in an offhand voice.

"He is?" I asked her, dazed at her easy capitulation. It usually took weeks and weeks before Jewel even remembered the name of my latest, let alone give him a stamp of approval.

His thumb stilled. "Aren't I?" The look he give me was pure challenge.

I let my smile spread slowly and gave him back that up-and-down-every-inch-of-your-body look. "I guess you'll do." Didn't pay to let 'em get too cocky.

"Better believe it, baby." Too late on that cocky thing. Ah, the inbred arrogance of the secure black man. Who said real men were nowhere to be found?

"G!" Gregory's friend Aaron came over with another fella behind him. "D and I fittin' to grab some grub. You down?" Aaron wasn't the cutest brother in the world, but he was cut with a six-pack. He had a law degree that he didn't use, but he worked with the city manager's office. He was that brother all into politics and contacts. I'd never seen the brother standing behind him. He was dark, baby-faced, not terribly tall, but all in all okay-looking.

Gregory looked at me. "Wanna eat?"

I looked at Jewel. She was looking at Rome, who was standing across the way, drinking water. Jewel looked real thirsty too. "Jewel, wanna eat?" She jumped a little and turned back toward me. I smirked and she grinned. Roni Mae walked back over and sat down.

"Yeah, I'm *really* hungry." Jewel laughed.

"For food? Honey, I'm not sure we're gonna find what you want on any menu," Roni Mae drawled in her best K-Soul voice, and winked at Jewel. It was one of those girls' moments where we laughed and the brothers stood there looking at us like we really did come from Venus.

Aaron's head whipped around to look at Roni Mae. "You're Veronique, aren't you?"

Roni Mae went into the blush-and-simper routine. "Yes, I am. Pleased to meet you." She stuck her hand out, and I caught a glimpse of those acrylic claws she's calling nails painted in that same horrid tropical sunset.

Aaron shook her hand like it was the greatest moment of his life. "Aaron Paris, I'm honored." He turned her hand over, raised it to his lips, and kissed the back. I thought she'd faint. "Really honored. Would you like to join us for lunch?"

What happened to the homey rolling up with "wanna grab some grub?" Brother went real smooth all of a sudden.

"Lunch?" Roni Mae looked at me.

"Are we going?" Gregory asked me.

"Jewel?" I asked her.

"Haven't we done this already?" she asked. "Let's make tracks—you know I'm always down to get some food on." She hopped up and put her purse on her shoulder. She looked at the guy standing behind Aaron. "Hi, I'm Jewel." She waved at him.

The cutie smiled and waved back. "Demetrius." Obviously a man of few words.

Gregory looked at me. "And this lovely lady is Renee. Now that everyone knows everyone, why don't the fellas and I hit the showers real quick before we treat y'all to lunch?"

I beamed up at him. "If you guys are treating, take your time; we'll be right here." Was there anything more romantic than men opening their wallets with ease?

"Back in a flash," Gregory said, and finally took his distracting hands off of me. He grabbed his bag and walked away. Demetrius followed.

Aaron was still cooing over Roni Mae. They had eased over to the side a little bit, and he was still holding her hand. Jewel and I exchanged a glance; then we both looked at Roni Mae and blatantly eavesdropped on their conversation.

"So that's when I thought that radio should be a more spontaneous medium," she was saying.

"Exactly!" Aaron agreed. "With its uncanny ability to reach so many people, I still think radio is a more powerful source of communication than the TV or the newspaper. It's a far more personal media tool. Second only to the Internet. Of course, now that you can access radio off the Net, who knows where it can go?"

What *had* happened to Aaron's hip-hoppin' b-boy drawl of a mere minute ago?

Roni Mae lit up and nodded. "That's so true, Aaron . . ."

She broke off, suddenly realizing that Jewel and I were double-dipping all into her conversation. "You two are dippin' so hard, I hope you brought chips."

Aaron looked over at us as if surprised we were still there. "Where'd the guys go?"

"To shower?" Jewel said with a hinting inflection in her voice.

"Oh." He looked at Roni Mae and dropped her hand. "Guess I'd betta roll." The homeboy was coming back out in him. "Be back," he said, and raced toward the locker room.

"Well"—I looked at my girls—"this is certainly turning out to be some little outing."

Roni Mae flipped that godawful mane of synthetic hair and snickered. "I told y'all I was gonna catch me a man with this hair."

Jewel snorted. "That boy stood there for a full five minutes without so much as looking at your head, Ms. Jackson."

She blinked. "You think it was the catsuit?"

I rolled my eyes. "Doubt it, doll." I reached over and patted her hand. "Roni Mae, is it so difficult to believe that he's interested in *you*, not your hair, your eyes, or your nails?"

"This from Miss I-Can't-Leave-My-House-Without-Makeup?" Roni Mae asked. "You know that no man looks across a room and says, 'Damn, that babe looks intelligent as hell. I gotta push up on that!'"

Here we go with this argument again. Every so often, we had to have a men-only-want-looks-versus-men-really-crave-intelligence debate. "Okay, that's true, but do you really want someone who only cares about that?"

Jewel stepped in. "They want a woman with everything, and we want a man with everything. Eventually we all get real and take what we can live with. That's all you can hope for."

Roni Mae looked uncertain before shrugging it off. "Whatever. It was just a five-minute conversation and an invite to lunch; let's not whip out the wedding invitations."

Jewel looked at me. "Speaking of weddings—were those bells I heard going off during that steamy liplock Mr. Samson walloped you with?"

No use pretending I didn't know what she was talking about; the boy *had* thrown me for a loop. I'd underestimated him. He was playing games, keeping me off balance. I never knew what to expect from him; I couldn't read him. I hated that. It's not like I wanted to get inside his mind; I just wanted to know what the hell I was up against. I mean, what were we building up here? Were we just going to be bed buddies, or were we heading toward a commitment? I knew without a doubt that if I told Jewel what I was thinking, she would say, "Why not just take it as it comes?" So I didn't tell her; instead I smiled and asked, "You see what I mean about him?" Meaning, do you think I can handle him?

She nodded. "Good luck outmaneuvering that one." I guessed that meant no.

Out of the corner of my eye, I saw Rome waltzing over. "Good luck to you too. Roni Mae, let's go wait outside." I grabbed a reluctant-to-leave, nosy Roni Mae and headed outside.

Jewel—Saturday, May 19, 1:00 p.m.

He was coming over. Lord have mercy, here he comes. I wanted to be calm here. I just met the man, but then again, I didn't want to play games. I was definitely interested. Why didn't I follow my own advice and just go with the flow? I let out the breath I'd been holding and stood there with what I hoped was a nonchalant look. Was there a woman alive who didn't get slightly flustered around a really masculine specimen of manhood? If there was, I wasn't among her numbers.

"'Lo again, Miss Jewel." I wondered why he kept calling me Miss Jewel. Did I look like an old maid?

"Hello." Okay, so sue me for lack of originality; I couldn't think of anything else to say.

"Jewel short for Juliet?" He had a way of looking right at me that was really disturbing. Like he knew what I was thinking. Damn, what color were those eyes of his anyway, copper?

"Nope. Rome short for Romeo?" He smiled, full out, a damn dazzler it was too. There's a thing about great teeth, you know? Good teeth absolutely send me. And thighs. I forced myself not to look down at his. I felt like a tenth grader standing by the lockers when the new cute guy in school walked by. Kind of antsy, impressed, and really, really curious to know more.

"Nah." He stood there for a minute before continuing. "It's Roman. Roman Montgomery."

"Jewellen Capwell." We stood there for another minute—not awkward, just silent. "You've got some good moves." Oops, that was not how I meant to say that . . . was it? *Jewellen, speak like an adult!* I checked myself.

He put his hands on his hips—big hands, narrow hips—and grinned. "Beg pardon?"

I nodded toward the court. "The game." But my smile said "Any other moves you'd like to show me?" Might as well let a man know I was checking him out.

"Oh, yeah? Thanks." He looked around for a second before pinning me with that look again. "Ah . . . listen here. I'm just gonna come on out with it."

With what? "Okay." Whatever he said, I was ready.

"I'd like to give ya a call sometime, if that's all right with you?" I had the business card and the pen out before he finished the sentence. I scrawled my home number on the back and handed it to him. He pulled a card out of his wallet and reached for my pen. He scribbled across the back, and we handled the exchange solemnly. You take my card, I'll take yours. So different from the old days when you had a sweaty napkin that you penned your name and number on with an eyeliner pencil in a smoky club. Thank God for progress.

I looked down at his card. It was crisp and white, no-

nonsense. Black block lettering proclaimed him to be Roman L. Montgomery of Montgomery Design, architect, specializing in lawn, gardens, golf courses and planned community development. Architect?! *Thank you, Lord. Thank you, thank you. I swear I'll go to church early Sunday and stay the whole time. Just let this man be normal. Please don't let him turn out to be a total flaky dog.*

"Capwell Temporary Agency." He looked up. "All yours?"

I tried to nod modestly but gave up and grinned. "All mine!" I waved his card. "All yours?"

He didn't even try for modesty. "Down to every last paper clip." His own business too. God loved me. He would see me through this thing, whatever it was. I had that good feeling. Of course, I'd had that good feeling a time or two before, and that shit never panned out. But enough of that.

"Rome! Rome, you hear me talkin' to you, boy?" A little fly girl was standing near the entrance with one hand on her black-Lycra-clad hips and the other clutching the hand of a small boy.

He shut his eyes for a minute and looked to be in pain.

I looked over at her. "All yours?" I held my breath. Let him say no.

"Ya, half right," he muttered. "That's my ex-wife, Jaquenetta, and my son, LaChayse, but we call him Chase." He watched me closely for my reaction.

Damn, finally a man who interested me *and* made my mouth water, and wouldn't you know—a child *and* an ex-wife, named Jaquenetta no less. The baggage. I could feel it stacking up between us as I stood there. Resisting the urge to take the drama-free, easy way out and bail, I kept a neutral expression and struggled for diplomacy. "Oh, that's nice. LaChayse is an interesting name. How'd you pick it?" What I really wanted to ask was why a nice guy like him had to have an ex-wife like THAT?!

He searched my face before answering. "Old family name, my middle one."

"Rome, I ain't gonna call you no mo'!" Jaquenetta was getter louder.

"You did say *ex*, didn't you?" I had to ask. I really needed to know. 'Cause sister-girl was already on my last nerve.

"I surely did, Miss Jewel, I surely did." He looked at the pair by the door. "I gotta go."

"Yes, you surely do," I returned.

"I'll be in touch. Okay?"

I nodded halfheartedly. Did I want him in touch? He and his son and, damn, his ex-*wife*! God grant me tolerance. I studied him in silence. Ex-wife or no, child or no, there was something about him that clicked for me. "Okay," I said in a wispy little voice, and looked away, praying I hadn't just done one of the stupidest things in the world.

Demetrius came out of the locker room looking pretty nice in jeans and a long-sleeve polo. He walked right up to me like we've known each other for ages. "Ready for lunch?" He shot a glance at Roman. "Hey, Ro."

Roman looked from me to Demetrius and back. "What up, D?"

"Daddy!" Little Chase came running over. He was a cute little thing, the spitting image of his daddy. Roman reached down and picked up the child. "Can we go to McDonald's, Dad?"

"May we," he corrected.

"May we, Daddy?" the little sweetie persisted.

"I don't know—what did you do to deserve to go to Micky D's?" Not one chopped syllable in there! Um-hmm, I liked this guy.

"I pick-ted"—he paused at his father's frown—"picked up all my toys and put 'em away." This said, he turned in his daddy's big, muscled arms and looked right at me. He inherited that look for sure. Then he looked at Demetrius and grinned. "Hi, Demi."

Demi put his hand up. "High five." He slapped the child's hand.

Chase looked back at me. "Who's your pwetty gullfwiend, Demi?"

I beamed, so wise for one so young. "My name is Jewel, and I'm not his girlfriend." *I'd like to be your daddy's; could you hook me up? Stop it, Jewel.* I reached out and shook his little hand. It was real hard to be upset about his existence. He couldn't help if his mama was ghetto.

"Joo-well is a pwetty name," he said seriously.

"Pretty name for a pretty lady," Roman said. The boy was smooth. He put Chase down. "Let's go get your mama and go to McDonald's. Later, D." He turned to walk away before shooting me a lethal look over one shoulder. "I'll be seeing ya, Miss Jewel." A challenging promise if ever I heard one. He and Chase walked hand and hand to the door. Rome walked right past a furious Jaquenetta, saying little else but, "Come on." Then he was gone.

"So, what are you hungry for?" Demetrius asked in a friendly manner.

Something hot and Roman. I smiled at Demetrius. "Oh, anything. I'm starved." In more ways than one.

5

From Ex to the Next

Roman—Sunday, May 20, 11:30 a.m.

Damn, Jaquenetta was a pain in my ass. Not one to speak ill of no one else, especially not the mother of my only child, my *son,* but one day she was gonna push me too far. Always popping up like she got claims on me. I took care of my boy, spent time with my boy; it was her I had had enough of. More and more she has taking to turning up when it was my day for Chase. Used to be she'd just drop him off, and that suited me just fine. Now she wanna tag along, and I have to say, I didn't like it.

No need to pretty it up. I married Jaquenetta when and only when she turned up pregnant. Was no great love from the get-go. We were swinging an episode or two now and then. I was taking care of "thangs"; she *said* she was. But something must have . . . um . . . slipped, know what I'm saying? Yeah, seven months and fourteen days to the day I married her, along comes Chase. About a year after that, when I had my shit straight, my money tight, and my lawyer together, I bailed. Jaquenetta was a damn octopus and all eight of those arms clingy and money-hungry as hell. "Where you going? Who you seeing? Did you get paid? Did you buy me something? I want this, I want that." Lord, it's enough to drive a man out his mind.

Here was the deal: Jaquenetta never had shit, not even her daddy's name or her mama's love. I came up hard, but at least I had family, ya know? Pop and Madere slaved to bring me, my younger sister Kat, and my older brother Beau up right so we could get somewhere. We didn't have a lot of money, but we had each other. We may not have been given a lot of material things, but we were always told to hold our heads up high, be smart, and walk with some pride about ourselves. What we were raised with was beyond the monetary: love, values, morals, ambition.

When I started out, I was all about playing ball. Not that I wasn't smart or anything, but the athletics just came easy to me. Got a b-ball scholarship to Southern Methodist University, but believe me, I majored in the female of the species. Guess I minored in 'em too. Flunked out my second year and started cutting lawns, sweeping yards, and planting trees for a living. Next thing I knew, I was designing backyards for folks. Then I got a call from Racine-Verstat Architects downtown; they wanted me to come and work. They basically told me, "Rome, take your poor ass back to school; we gonna pay and you can come work for us." I was gone. Got out with the fresh degree, and after about a year or two doing time in corporate land, I struck out on my own. Brother was blessed at the right time with great opportunities and just enough smarts to take advantage of them. Started turning a little profit and building a real business.

I clearly remember my first big contract as an independent—a golf course community about ninety miles away. They wanted me to design the landscaping of the houses, the golf course, and the play area. Managed to clear a little profit and for the first time in my life, I had some change jingling.

Right about that time, yonder come Jaquenetta. I saw her

and thought, "Yeah, I could work *that* for a li'l minute!" Can't be noble about it; I was just looking to hit it and quit it without too much pause in between. Reckon she saw me and thought, "Paycheck!" Guess I got what I deserved, huh? Player got played! Had to turn in the player's card and get serious with the swiftness. Fatherhood broke me down for real.

Now get this straight—I wasn't ashamed of Chase. The boy had my heart, for real, no playing. But when I met Miss Jewel, I wanted to wait a while before bringing up the fact that I had a child and an ex-wife. You didn't just say, "Hi, I'm Roman. I have my own company, a four-year-old boy, and an ex-wife." So yesterday, when Jaquenetta came busting in like she was my mama sent to save my soul from the devil, I had no choice but to lay it all out on the line at once. I was watching Miss Jewel real close when I told her; she was cool, but for a second, she got that look in her eyes. That look women get sometimes that says, "Another shiftless brother."

Black men got it hard these days. If he was over thirty, single, successful, no kids, whadaya hear? "Must be a dog or someone woulda caught his ass." If he had kids: "Um, why every brother gotta have kids? Why can't a brother take care his business?" No job: "Why can't he hold no job?" Decent job: "Why don't he make mo' money?" No regular girl: "Must be gay!" Tried to play it cool: "Brother got an attitude." Tried to come clean: "Uh-uh, girl, something about him I don't trust." Either we're too short, too tall, too attitudish, too sometimey, too quiet, too poor, too ignorant, too nasty, or they thought they heard something about us from someone, somewhere. Had to drive the right car, live in the right place, say the right things, wear the right clothes, and always, always, do the right thang! Couldn't ask for sex too often but when you do, better make it last and make it good. Cook, clean, and wash clothes but don't make no mistakes; from now till doomsday, you'll be hearing about the time you turned her favorite bra gray or chipped her great-aunt's wineglass, for sure. Be proud, not arrogant. Sensitive, not wimpy. Good God Almighty, couldn't I just be me?

You always got the Jaquenettas trying to catch you and bleed you dry; then you got the ones who didn't wanna give you the time of the day. Lord, let a black woman make a little something of herself? Better not ask her to dance or buy her a drink. These were things she could now do for her damn self, and she will tell you about it with the swiftness. Those were the ones who just wanted a little bump and grind before they jet. But if you suggest a quick roll and run? BETTER NOT! Then you had the ones with PLANS (Plan to Land me a Negro Soon/Somehow). Date for two months, engaged for four months, married for two years, two kids in the next three, retire after twenty years . . . WHAT? Just lemme get to know you! That's what I said. Poor black man couldn't get a damn word in! If he took too long going from step A to step B, he might throw off the whole schedule.

I suppose if I took a sec and looked at this from the sisters' view, I could see where it gets kinda rough. A lot of the fellas I came up with were either six feet under or behind bars. A lot of my boys who escaped that life still ain't doing shit. And those who are doing a little something are packing major 'tude. Or they trying to be top dog in the pound. Lord knew, every dog had his day. But sooner or later, ya had to move beyond all that shit.

Back in the day, if the girl was looking right, I was down. I'd roll out my best flow and play the role I needed to play to get in there. If we really got along in the horizontal mode, I let her hang out for a little minute, ya know. When it looked like she was turning serious on me, I cut her loose. Then I got some bank behind me, and it seemed like the game changed. I couldn't tell if I was on the hunt or on the menu. I knew better but sometimes it seemed that some of these sisters wanted a man only for was his dick or his paycheck.

If I hadn't seen the way Pop and Madere still hang in there, I don't think I'd believe in love. I'd be one of those soulless brothers always talking about, "Just as long as I gets mine." Or maybe I'd be one of the brothers who decide that the sisters are too much trouble and get me a white woman. And don't get me started on those brothers on the down low. Can't go out like that.

I wasn't looking for the fly girl or Superwoman! I just wanted get along with somebody and start settling down. Lookie here, regardless of those women crying to Oprah, there are good black men out there looking to settle down. Hello. With one woman. Shit, now I was getting too old for this freak-of-the-week mess. I like black women no matter what all they do; nobody in the world can understand a black man better than a black woman, straight up. That's why I was about to give Miss Jewel a jingle. She clearly wasn't nobody's hoochie. Maybe she'd like to try and understand me, hmm?

I picked up my phone and checked my watch. It was late enough that I might catch her between early service and lunch.

One ring. Come on and be there.

Two rings. Come on, come on!

Three rings, then a click. Damn, voice mail. "Hello, this is Jewel. Sorry I'm not in to accept your call. Please leave your name, number, and a brief message at the tone and I'll get back to you at my earliest convenience. Thanks for calling. Have a nice day." Beep. Nice little uptown greeting.

Should I leave a message? Yeah, I'd better. "Hey, Miss Jewel. This is Rome. Rome Montgomery." Damn, now it sounded like a business call. Lighten up! "Enjoyed meeting you yesterday. Look forward to seeing you soon. Peace." Great, now I sounded like a rapper. I hung up and stared at the phone for a minute.

Chase came running out of his room with his hands full of

Legos. That boy was something else, always into something. I didn't even know where he got the Legos from. The only time he wasn't on the move was when he's asleep. "Daddy, did you call the pwetty lady?"

I looked down into his face. Kids these days know too damn much. "What pretty lady?" Like I didn't know.

"That pillow lady, Joo-well, with Demi yesterday."

"Pillow lady?" Where'd he get that from?

"She looked like she had little pillows wight here." He pointed to his chest.

I burst out laughing, couldn't help it. Her chest did look like something I wanted to rest my head against for an evening or two at least. "Those are her breasts, champ."

"They not like Mommy's." Poor little thing looked confused.

"No, they are not," I enunciated for him. "They come in all different shapes and sizes, son." He stood there looking at me like he couldn't believe it for a minute. "Did you come out here to ask me something?"

His face cleared and he jumped into my lap. "Can we go to the movies?"

"Alright, whatcha wanna see?" No need to remind the child that his bed time was in a half hour.

"Let's see the scary movie, Dad. The one we saw the 'mercial on." The one we saw the commercial on? Then I remembered. Almost five years old and my boy wanted to see the latest slasher film? Wasn't gonna happen.

"How 'bout the SpongeBob?" Rome bargained.

"How 'bout the scary movie?" Nothing if not persistent.

"How 'bout we watch the Disney Channel for a while?" He was about a half hour from falling out anyway. I had a pile of work to look over, and this could take the place of story time.

"Okay!" He jumped up and started running toward his

room again. Halfway there, he stopped and looked back at me. "Is Joo-well going to watch too?"

In a roundabout way, the boy had a one-track mind. "Maybe next time, son." I looked back at the phone. Yeah, maybe next time.

6

Getting Down to the Real

Renee—Monday, June 1, 10:00 a.m.

It was Monday morning, and I took the day off to sleep. Yeah, I did. Just didn't feel like playing the corporate bullshit game this morning. I had the ringer off, the voice mail on, and a little old-school Sade on the MP3 player. I was eating peanut butter and crackers in bed. Later I planned on sinking into my whirlpool tub and relaxing in wet, steamy, pineapple-mango-scented heaven. I knew this laziness was shameful coming right off a weekend, but I was beat. Gregory had been keeping me up nights. Oh, not that way, though I wished he would! Night after night, I had been lying awake rethinking my strategy, trying to map this whole thing out between Mr. Samson and me.

It had been two weeks since the basketball game, and that boy was driving me out of my ever-loving mind. Dammit, I knew when I was being played. And he was a maestro. Not so blatant that I could call him on it, mind you. Just ever so subtly sending me up a wall! He called, chatting about nothing for brief little moments during the day. He came over in the evenings, and we swapped life anecdotes, snuggled all up on the couch, and watched TV. He even cooked once. Brother who can cook scores many points. We've had a picnic lunch in Thanksgiving Square, dinner atop the Hyatt, a water taxi ride through the Las Colinas canal, hot dogs at a Rangers baseball game. We've been dancing, to movies, to the theater (don't ya love it!), to the mall, grocery shopping, bar-hopping, and to church (can I get an Amen!). Gregory was witty, urbane, sensitive, strong, masculine, even moody, all to the point of perfection. Gregory, I just figured out, was a big tease!

Little touches to help me out of the car, into a chair, up a stair, off a curb, for Christ's sake. Steamy glances by candlelight, moonlight, headlights, floodlights. Accidental brushes of the body as we leaned, reached, stopped, strolled. All of this I could handle. It was the Kiss. The single, solitary kiss at the beginning and end of each and every little excursion that was beating me down. Like that kiss at the basketball game a couple weeks back . . . only hotter. And that was it. That was apparently all I was getting.

My own damn fault; I was the fool who said, "Not yet." Actually, no, he said that; I just agreed. What was it I was waiting on again? Oh yeah, a commitment. Damn the commitment—it was time to get down and dirty. Look, if he had been building me up all this time for a weekend of frolicking and then planned to disappear into the sunset, there was nothing I could do about it. But I didn't think it would go down like that. I felt like I had been reading him a little better; I thought he was pretty into me. We had been hanging out for about two months now, and if a quickie hit-'n'-run was his goal, he would have been long gone, right? Was I rationalizing too much because I really wanted to do this or what?

I talked to Jewellen about it yesterday. She said I should go with my first instinct. My first instinct was to lure him to my bedroom and body slam him till I pass out. She laughed and told me to go for it. If he decided to sky up afterward, at least I'd have gotten two months' worth of first-class wining and dining and a much needed episode between the sheets.

My mind was made up as I sunk into my decadent tub of silky water. I opened the latest Sandra Brown novel and started reading. Thirty minutes later, I was overheating. The jets kept the water hot, and Sandra's book had me all aflutter. I wrapped up in a towel, padded to the fridge, and grabbed some juice. Whew, I was dying of thirst. That woman could write! She understood the South, Southern men, and sex; you had to respect a writer for that. Anyway, that last scene triggered a memory of one of her other books, and I'd formulated me an idea or two. Thought I'd slip on a little something and pay Gregory a visit at the bank. Two could tease, you know.

Now, you would think a man would know he was in trouble when a woman strolled into his office at two in the afternoon, at the beginning of June, with a trench coat on. This was Texas, the South—shit, it's hot outside, without a doubt. He was either a lot cooler or a lot dumber than I thought. After I quickly convinced his secretary to let me go in unannounced (no dummy, she knew it was ninety degrees outside), I expected some sort of reaction out of the boy.

I came in, shut the door, and locked it behind me. He was looking good and corporate, as usual. Charcoal-gray suit, flash of personality in the dark green paisley tie, and mint-green shirt. I dropped my purse, turned around, looked at him, leaned up against the door in my best seductive lounge, and what did he have to say?

"Hello, Renee. It's nice to see you feeling better. I called your office, and they told me you were ill." I could have strangled him. Did I look ill?

Instead, I smiled engagingly and said, "Hello, Greggy. I think I'm on my way to a speedy recovery." When I was teasing him, I could call him whatever the hell I wanted.

He raised one eyebrow over those Polo tortoise shells. "What can I do for you?"

Ah, my cue. I untied the belt, undid all the buttons (still

trying to look coolly seductive, mind you), and dropped the coat. His mouth dropped, the glasses tilted . . . finally, a reaction. I was laced into an emerald green teddy with matching four-inch peep-toe pumps, total. Matched perfectly thanks to the Victoria's Secret spring/summer catalog. Sorry, sometimes I got off on things like that. Back to the moment. In my patented, come-to-Mama-Sweet-Daddy voice, I said, "Come here, Greggy, and do for me." Good line, don't you know? It was one of many I practiced in the car on the way over here. This seduction shit had to be carried out perfectly. Couldn't be too bold or too shy. Gotta get the right words, the right tone, and by all means, the right lingerie!

He yanked off his glasses, vaulted over the desk (which was pretty impressive, as it was a big desk), and was standing in front of me in no time flat. "Is it my imagination or did you lock that door?" Um, he was working that baby-come-to-bed voice. He loosened his tie and threw it over his shoulder.

"I locked the door." I barely got the sentence out before he grabbed me and kissed me like he was walking the Sahara and I was a truckload of Evian. Wow—wait a minute! My plan, you see, had been to tease and leave. Drop the coat, swap a little kissy-face, then exit with a "See ya later, playboy." Just like he did. But, um, he had me backed up against the wall, and his hands were doing incredible things, and his kisses were . . . Whoa, boy! "Gregory!" This was one of those speak-now-or-forever-hold-your-peace moments.

"Hmmm?" He had the flimsy straps down my shoulders, and his mouth was sliding down my neck. I was fading fast.

"We can't do this here?" Damn, I meant to make that sound like a statement. His lips were introducing themselves to my breasts, and good Lawd! He had amazing technique. They were very pleased to make his acquaintance.

He turned me around and shuffled me backward before maneuvering us down on the sofa. "Oh, we're *going* to do this here." He whipped off his jacket and tossed it to the side. Without thinking, I started undoing his shirt buttons; mere seconds later, the shirt joined the jacket. He kicked off the loafers and turned his attention back to me. Easing down over me, he did that body-slithering thing I loved so. "We're gonna do this, Renee. Right here, right now," he repeated, making it sound like a definitive statement. *That's* what I was trying to do earlier.

That big hand was sliding up my thigh slowly, slowly—bull's-eye, like an old pro, he unsnapped the teddy and peeled it back. That was it. I was done for. Any plan I had of leaving this room with a kiss and a promise was GONE. Listen, this boy possessed *skills*. Perfect suction on the breasts, exquisite pressure right where I needed it, and those fingers . . . those long, thick, incredibly inquisitive and sensitive fingers with an impeccable sense of timing. This intense attack on my entire mind and body went on for I didn't know how long. I heard all these little gasping, groaning sounds and was shocked to find they were coming from me! I heard him chuckle, a deep, very macho, self-satisfied sound.

This was totally unlike me. Oh, don't get me wrong—I generally enjoyed sex, but I rarely surrendered myself totally to the pleasure of it. Just lying back and letting some man run amuck with my physical and emotional well-being? Never, not me. His mouth left my breast and started sliding down my stomach. I had to get a hold of myself; if I let him go where he was heading, I would never regain an ounce of control.

If I had ever been shy before, I gave up all pretense of it now. I shifted a little, reached down, grabbed his belt buckle, and dispensed with that. His pants were unbuttoned and unzipped hastily. "Get rid of those NOW!" It was a demand, nothing less. Shit, playtime was over.

His head came up and he grinned. "Impatient, are we?" Asshole. I felt his impatience lying against my hip. I reached down into his boxers and raked my nails lightly across the entire glorious length of him before holding the very pulse of it in my hand, stroking ever so slowly.

"Aren't we?" I countered cattily as he sucked in a breath and released it in what sounded pretty much like a moan.Yeah, there we go, player. Let me see you lose some of that Ivy League composure for a minute.

"Don't play, Renee." His thumb zeroed right in on the spot most likely to make me beg.

"Then come on with it." I refused to beg, but I could certainly make an urgent demand or two.

"Let's slow down," he said, and tried to back out of my hold. I tightened my grip.

"We've had two months of foreplay, Greggy." I pushed his pants and boxers down. "Now I'm telling you one last time—unless you want those beautiful pants hopelessly wrinkled, I suggest you get rid of 'em."

He slipped off his boxers and pants after digging that trusty Trojan out of his wallet. "Preparing to do work, are we?" he teased, and ripped open the packet.

I looked him up, down, and over before licking my lips. Yum-yum. Surely Adam didn't look this good to Eve in the Garden of Eden. He took care of the condom and slid back on top of me.

I put my hands on his shoulders and smiled. "Well, I'm planning on getting real busy, Greggy. I kinda hoped you could hang on for the ride."Yes! I was smooth and in control again. I brought his face close for a quick I-got-you-now-boy kiss.

"I'll try to keep up." With that, he raised up on his arms over me. "You ready?"

I rolled my eyes, thinking I'd hate to be much more ready than this. "Willing and able."

His knee nudged mine aside, and he was in in one smooth stroke. Damn, I should have known it would feel this way. I shifted my hips in anticipation of his first thrust. He didn't move, just lay there forcing me to bask in the knowledge of his possession. I shimmied around again, the combination of the reality of him inside me and the anticipation of more to come was making me lose it. His hand snaked down to that ever sensitive button and flicked across me, once, twice and I came apart into a million pieces. I was in a trance, under a spell, all of that totally bewitched stuff. Shit, I was still trying to put myself together when the master warlock spoke again.

"Now you're ready." He bent my knees up and started stroking. Slowly and continuously. I went off again, and I was pretty sure I was begging.

"Tell me you want me, baby." Not now with the macho shit, not now when I could barely remember my name.

"Tell me you want *me*." I was trying to hang on to the old, cool, controlled me, but she was slipping away fast. I couldn't think straight, catch my breath, or maintain my controlled façade.

"I want you—all of you," he answered seriously, sliding out of me. He went down and put his mouth to work. Oh, the wicked, wicked knowledge his tongue had. Whatever I had planned to say flew out of my mind like the wind. I called out his name. I think I wept. I was way over my normal threshold of pleasure by the time he raised up, gave me a tangy kiss, and slid back in, deep and full.

I didn't even try to recover. I just let instinct kick in, and I started matching his strokes with a few of my own, dragging him with me into this vortex where nothing but exquisite pleasure existed. There was no room for machismo or games—finally, it was real. Just him and me, together. It was real and it was right. We both knew it.

The tempo increased and we kissed wildly, raking our hands up and down each other, grabbing oxygen when and where we could. "Damn, Renee," was the last thing I remember hearing him say before we rolled off the sofa and got down to business in a serious way. Every touch was hotter than the last, every kiss sparked yet another nerve ending, and every stroke . . . every stroke was an erotic invitation to paradise. It was wild; it was primal; it was totally mind-blowing.

We were finally at the point at which it absolutely could not get any sweatier, any faster, any dizzier, any *better.* Gregory went absolutely still for a minute before withdrawing and coming back for the final slam dunk. I tried not to scream, but after he called out my name for the entire world to hear, I followed suit. What the hell? Over the edge we went, holding on tightly to each other. We laid there panting, stuck together and in shock on the rug.

"Jesus, girl, you trying to kill me?" He sprawled on top of me, breathing in my ear.

"Damn," was all I could muster up, willing my mind to quit spinning. *Control, control, control—get some control!*

"Renee?" He sounded so serious, I opened my eyes quickly. I thought, *Oh shit, here it is.* The thank-you-and-good-bye speech. Couldn't he have waited until I had the trench back on? I looked down and realized I'd never kicked off the pumps. I was surprised I didn't gouge his back out.

Never one to back down, I looked him straight in the eye. "Yes, Gregory?" We were back to Gregory.

"You realize what this means, now, don't you?" No, I didn't and wasn't sure I was ready to hear it.

"Do I?" He absolutely hated it when I answered a question with a question.

He took my chin in his hands. "You're mine now, Ms. Nightingale."

Whatever I'd been expecting him to say, this wasn't it! "Yours?" I knew I sounded as confused as I was. Lord, it had been years since I allowed myself to be this scattered over someone. Okay, so I never allowed myself to be this scattered over anyone.

He dropped a light kiss on my lips. "Mine, all mine."

His to do what with? His for how long? And did that mean

he was mine in return? Shit, I had to get my ass up off this floor and outta here so I could rethink everything. I had really done it now. Just jumped overboard without a life raft or nautical map. Whatcha wanna bet there are sharks in the water?

"What are you thinking about?" Gregory asked me. I wasn't about to tell him. I hopped up and put the straps of the teddy back on my shoulders. My damn legs were shaking; my thighs almost groaned. Then I tried to nonchalantly redo the snaps on the teddy. How did one calmly fiddle around with their crotch? "Need some help with that?"

I shot him a glance as I managed to get one out of three snaps done . . . good enough. "Got it; thanks, though."

He got up and started pulling on his poor clothes. They were hopelessly wrinkled from our tussle on the ground. That didn't stop him from looking real good in them, especially now that I knew what was under there. My mouth went dry, then started to water. I had to escape before I turned into one of those pathetic dick-whipped girlies I'm always dogging at the office. They go on and on about how great their latest was and how much they put up with from him because he knew how to do them right. I mean, these girls gave up their money, their families, their jobs, sometimes even their religion for some man who turned them inside out in bed and might not give a damn about them. Hell, until today, I had never been with anybody worth acting that much of a fool over. Don't get me wrong—I had had good sex before, even great sex, but this thing we just did? I couldn't even begin to categorize it. Let's just say that if I allowed myself, I could act a plumb idiot over this boy and still keep a smile on my face. It was only with God's grace and my willpower that I turned away and picked up my coat. Or maybe God had nothing to do with it all; this really wasn't his arena. Shit, I didn't even know what to think.

"Renee, I wish I knew what you were thinking." He was affectionate, he was tender, he was worried, and I was totally freaked out.

Hell, I wish I knew what I was thinking too! But until I did, I had to bounce. Still, the boy did just turn my whole world upside down, changed the entire way I looked at sex and the committed relationship. And he didn't look like he was sprinting in the other direction. I guess I could say something nice. "Greg, you literally knocked the thoughts right out of my head. I'm totally overwhelmed and I'm leaving." There, honest flattery if he cared to read into it.

He didn't. "Is that good or bad?"

Time for more confessions. "It's the best I've ever had, and I don't know if that's a good thing or not." I tied the belt on the coat, picked up my purse, and put my hand on the doorknob and fiddled with the lock. I waited for him to say something, but when I looked back, he was just standing there looking at me like he didn't know what to make of me.

"Later," I muttered, and yanked the door open.

"Wait!" He came forward and slammed the door shut. "Are we okay?"

Whatever the hell that meant. What is okay? "Uh-huh." I kept my eye on the doorknob. I was really afraid I was about to start crying—I never cry! And what the hell would I be crying about? I had to go.

"Babe, you look spooked as hell. We should talk, huh?"

I opened the door again. "Later, all right?"

"Yeah, later," he said as I pulled the door closed behind me.

Gregory—Monday, June 1, 3:40 p.m.

Now what the hell was that, I wonder? God as my witness, I'll never understand women.

First, she put me off. So I thought, okay, we'll do this her way, to my liking. I was taking it slow and easy, giving up just enough to let her think about what she's missing.

I was laying it on her with the entire Samson Romance Kit—the picnics, the theater, even church! Working that see-how-much-I-like-you, see-how-much-fun-we-have-together strategy. Then, at the end of the night, the kiss that said BOOM! "See how much *fun* we could be having, baby?"

See, you couldn't just run around plucking fruit from trees. You had to prime an apple. You fed it; nurtured it; gave it sun, moon, sustenance, and pleasant surroundings. Even fed it a little bullshit now and again. It grew ripe for you and began to sway on the tree. Just when you started losing patience, don't you know that succulent fruit fell right into your hands. So sweetly.

After all the effort you had put into this, you finally got to savor this fruit, careful not to bruise it; you enjoyed every rounded contour, every juicy bite, right down to the core.

But what apple, I had got to know, ever jumped up and ran away after this amazingly profound experience?

A green delicious apple named Renee.

She shocked the hell out of me with that lace thing and the pumps. Can't begin to tell you what pumps and lace do to me.

Anyway, then she shocked the hell out of me when she seemed almost shy for a second there. Almost unsure of herself . . . not Renee?

Then I thought maybe she shocked the hell out of herself. I guess she really didn't expect to enjoy herself quite so much. Maybe she thought I was only about the boardroom not the bedroom? Come on, now, men in the new millennium simply couldn't play like that. You had to be about handling business no matter what, no matter when, no matter where. Now, she had to know that rolling up to my office in the middle of day wearing one scrap of material and some do-me-baby pumps was going to set things off!

Okay, we were both shocked when I told her she belonged to me now. Truly, I couldn't say which one of us was more stunned to hear those words floating around in the air. That one slipped out before I really thought about it. Usually my game is tighter than that. So much for basking in the after-glow—more like quaking in the aftershock.

Clearly it was going to be up to me to make sure we make it out of this state of shock and onto some solid ground.

This could call for a whole new game plan.

7

Failure to Communicate

Roman—Wednesday, June 17, 5:10 p.m.

I stood in the hot-ass Texas sun basically stewing. Ninety-four degrees in the shade, and the client was tripping and changing job specs for the fourth time. This was off the chains ridiculous.

My client was LeeCom, a start-up wireless provider that wanted me to build an outdoor break room at its new corporate headquarters. No sweat. Originally, this was supposed to be a quick-n-dirty, pour some gravel, put in some picnic tables, slap up a basketball hoop, and dot some decorative trees and bushes around the place kind of job. Two weeks, tops. That was six weeks ago. Since then, Mr. Lee had bought more land surrounding the building and had added two water features feeding into a koi pond, a walking trail, and a rock-climbing wall.

So I took a moment at the end of an already too long day to drop by and check on progress. Here was old boy talking about a Zen garden with a meditation area. Uh-huh.

"Mr. Lee, we can certainly incorporate a Zen garden, but it

will have to be along the north perimeter. If you're thinking of adding Japanese maples, they really need morning sun and afternoon shade. Furthermore, to raze that area and build in the type of feature you're thinking about will significantly impact your budget and your timeline," I informed him with as much diplomacy as I could muster. I had two other jobs on hold just waiting for the crew that was trapped on this never-ending job. This would have been okay if Mr. Lee wasn't funny with the money. He had champagne ideas on a beer budget.

It had been years since your boy had been suckered into a just-send-me-the-invoice move. I was strictly cash on delivery or CFO-approved purchase order these days. I had twelve people on my payroll, and I preferred to pay the bills on time.

"Well now, Roman, let's talk about that. Can you give me an estimate off the top of your head?"

Having suspected this was his game, I waved over my foreman, Joe, for a quick conference. As we started the back-and-forth on numbers, I heard my cell phone ringing in the car. Recognizing the ringtone, I motioned that Joe should finish up with Mr. Lee, excused myself, and sprinted for the car.

Yeah, yeah, business before pleasure, but Miss Jewel and I had been phone tagging for two weeks. E-mail, voice mail, text message, we'd exchanged plenty of those. I wanted to hear her voice, I wanted to see her face, I wanted . . . well, lotsa stuff I wanted to do with Miss Jewel.

Word on the vine was she had been on a date or two with Demetrius. D was all right but ya know a brother wanted a shot of his own. The final ring sounded as I opened the door. "Dammit." By the time I reached the BlackBerry, the voice mail icon was up.

"Hey, Roman, it's Jewellen Capwell returning your returned call. Tag, you're it. By now you've got the numbers. I'm stepping into a meeting but try and catch me. Bye."

I hit SAVE and responded with a text message: *Trying to catch U girl.*

Joe came over and handed me a clipboard. I looked at the number he'd written down and shook my head. Reaching in the truck, I pulled up our estimate worksheet and started plugging numbers in. "Add labor to this and get him to sign and date." The phone started vibrating as he walked away.

Maybe U R using the wrong bait.

Tell me what U want to nibble on. I'll put it out there. I paused a minute, wondering if that was too much, too soon? To hell with it; I hit SEND.

Her answer came back shortly: *Partial to chocolate.*

My brows went up. Oh, it was on. *U the kinda girl to go straight for dessert?*

Life is short, player.

Damn straight. I smiled and typed back: *Tell me about it. Y U think I'm chasing?*

Careful, what happens when U catch me?

I'd like to find out.

Maybe U will.

Trying to. Got time to see me tonite?

Not tonight. Gotta date.

D?

Wow, grapevine. Yeah.

What's up with that?

Just friends.

Really.

Really. He's not you.

Glad you noticed.

Ha! What R U doing right now?

I looked up to see Mr. Lee shaking his head and Joe headed toward me, neither one looking very happy. *Dealing with client drama. U?*

Ditto.

Talk later?

Hope so.

Peace.

Her reply came quickly: *Peace.*

Tucking the phone into my back pocket, I reached for the clipboard again. "Mr. Lee, let me walk you through this." Exchanging glances with Joe, we walked together to the proposed Zen garden site, explaining costs one more time. Nothing truly worth having came easy, doncha know? That included unrealistic clients and classy women.

Jewel—Friday, June 19, 8:10 p.m.

"I don't get it either, Roni Mae." I looked at the clock. We'd been on the phone for forty minutes now, thirty-five minutes too long as far as I was concerned. "Yes, she told me." I'd already gone through the whole drama with Renee, and now here was Roni Mae rehashing it again. Personally, I didn't see what the big deal was.

Renee said everything was great between her and Gregory before they decided to break out the freaky-deaky, so if the sex was great as well, doesn't that just make the relationship more great? Or "mo' better" as Denzel once said. Great guy, great sex—where was the problem again? That I should suffer such a fate! I know, I know, I tended to oversimplify. It was now becoming clear to me that Renee had never had mind-altering sex before. She had always been too busy planning, scheming, and setting up the perfect seductive aura that she never allowed herself to just be straight seduced. She had never let down the guard enough to just be taken by someone who knew how to take her there, outta control and mindless.

I shivered a little just thinking about it. But really, this absolutely slayed me. Just between me and you, it cracked me up that here I was, "Little Miss Can't Be Wrong" as Renee called me, and I already did my turn at the ultimate physical relationship. No strings, no ties, no expectations, just me and this incredibly talented brother getting down and dirty at every opportunity. That had been five years ago, and according to all who knew me, it was totally against my character, whatever the hell that means. Be that as it may, I had a slamming no-holds-barred, all-out, go-for-the-gusto, purely physical fling that lasted for six months. To this day, I still regarded it as the best sex and most honest relationship I ever had.

Everyone could be manipulated and weakened by sex in certain circumstances. I allowed myself to be a slave to it for a minute until I realized that's not what motivated me or held my interests for a long time. We had to get up sometime, and then what were we gonna do? Could we hold a conversation, get a common interest, something?

Anyway, there was Renee, "Ms. Sophisticated Woman of the World" (or so she wanted us all to believe), with this string of men who she had fallen in and out of what she called love with, and not once had she experienced multiple-orgasmic bliss? No wonder the poor girl was in a tizzy. To a complete and total control freak like our Darnella Renee, this kind of situation had to threaten all of her carefully laid out plans. Someone else with any kind of power over her, and it was not career-related? The one I felt for was Gregory. He had to deal with all that intense game playing, dig through all the bullshit to get to the actual relationship. Whatever—too much maintenance for me.

Personally, I was betting on Gregory. Unless he turned out to be a total undercover dog or something just off-the-hinges drastic happened, I think the two of them might have a shot at it. "It" being that nebulous promise of a happily-ever-after together, if that even truly existed anymore.

It had been about three weeks since their first little episode, and he was sticking to her like skin on a grape. Smart boy, Gregory. I don't think I'd seen him leave her side except to go to work. That boy had her on such a merry-go-round, I knew her head was spinning too fast to scheme and plot. I say, why not enjoy the ride?

I finally noticed that the line had been silent for a while.

Roni Mae asked, "Did you hear a word I said?"

I tried to play it off. "I'm on this old cordless, and it keeps going in and out. I heard most of it. What'd you ask me?"

"I asked how things were going for you in the big love triangle."

"What love triangle?"

"You, Rome, and Demetrius." She was practically salivating for the details. Always looking for drama where there was none.

"Please, Demetrius is a nice guy, but he ain't It. Does absolutely nothing for me. I've talked to him a few times, and we had dinner one day last week, but I just don't feel any sparks, any clicks, any tingles, any any*thing*!" Nothing worse than apathy between a man and a woman from my point of view. When you were hanging out with someone just to have *anyone* sitting across the table from you . . . not a good sign. But I was attempting to "get out and about." Hanging with Demetrius was better than sitting home alone waiting for Rome's next voice mail . . . but not by much.

"Oh." She sounded so disappointed. "What about Rome?"

Now *I* sounded disappointed. "Roman and I have a steamy game of phone and e-mail tag going. He started out leaving me rated G messages, and I'd say after three weeks of calling each other at home and work, we've worked our way up to that thin line between PG-13 and R."

"You haven't talked directly to him at all?"

"No, but I tell you, I'm almost intimate with all of his technology now." I had to grin, recalling some of the outlandish messages we had been trading back and forth.

"Well, you know where to find him. Why don't you just track him down? Show up on his doorstep."

I rolled my eyes. "Not my style."

Roni Mae clucked her teeth. "And I guess staying at home on a Friday night is."

I refused to be bullied. "Apparently so. Don't you have a date to get ready for?" Hint—go handle your own business and get up outta mine!

I could practically see her smile through the phone. "Yeah, Aaron and I are going to the movies."

"So, how are things with Mr. Paris?" Surprisingly enough, Roni Mae was being very closemouthed about Aaron. Usually you couldn't get her to shut up about a guy.

"Okay, I guess." Her monotone gave nothing away.

"Well, that sounds lackluster. Where's the oomph, the hip-hop hooray?"

"Jewel, I'm doing this thing a date at a time, no more, no less. No lines, no strings, no expectations. By the book, okay?" She sounded defensive.

My eyebrows shot up. This was a whole new Veronica. I decided not to push. "Okay, cool." My phone clicked. "Hold on, it's the other line." I clicked over without checking the caller ID.

"Hello?"

"Is this live, or is it Memorex?" Rome asked with a smile in his voice.

I sat there grinning like a fool. It was HIM. "I don't know. Leave your name after the tone and I'll get back to you. Beep." I couldn't remember the last time the sound of someone's voice made me smile.

He played along. "Ah, Miss Jewel. It's me again. If you don't know my voice by now, shame on ya. It's Friday night, a beautiful night, and I was really hoping we could get together and do a li'l something." He sighed dramatically. "But since you're not there . . ."

I pretended like I just ran in and picked up. "Hello, hello? It's me; is it you?"

"Yeah, it's me and I'm smiling. You're a difficult woman to catch."

I was totally intrigued by how he flashed back and forth from homeboy dialect to Mr. Professional to Mr. Hot Sex on a Platter. "Oh yeah?" I suddenly remembered Roni Mae. "Hold on a sec." I clicked over. "Roni, have a good time tonight. See you for brunch Sunday, right?"

She laughed. "Don't have to tell me twice. Go on, get your chat on, girl. See you Sunday." She hung up and I clicked back.

"Okay, I'm back." I walked over to the sofa and stretched out.

"Okay, I'm here. But you know what?"

"No. What?"

"I'd rather be there, or have you here, ya know?"

I knew. I knew he was the first guy in a long time who made me want to drool and pant just at the sound of his voice. I hadn't even gone out with this guy yet, and I already felt like I knew him.

"I know." Honesty, I liked it. Maybe I should recommend it to Renee.

"Tell me something." Anything.

"All right." Was that breathless little voice mine?

"Someone gonna be pissed if I tell ya I wanna spend time with you?" Nothing like the blunt approach.

"No."

"Ya sure?"

I frowned. "Yeah, I'm pretty positive." Why? What's it to you? Questions I wanted to ask but was too well brought up to do so. Wouldn't I know if I had a hot and heavy romance hiding under the sofa?

"What about D?" he asked.

Who? "D?"

"Demetrius."

Oh yeah, him. "Oh, no. We're not together."

"Does he know that?"

Well now, damn. I answered the first question or so, but what was this? An interrogation? Well brought up or not, maybe he'd be so kind as to answer one very important question for me: "To answer your question, yeah, he knows. And if he doesn't, he should. But, player, since we're playing twenty questions, here's one for you: Does Jaquenetta know she's an *ex*-wife?"

"Ah, that's deep. Why we have to go there?" His tone was pained.

I sat up and grinned into the phone. "Hey, if we're baring it all, let's get down to the undies and examine some labels—what's the deal with you and the ex?"

"We were married, now we're not. I have partial custody and full visitation of Chase. In return, I pay child support and beyond decent alimony to Jaquenetta. I consider it a thank-you for bearing my child and divorcing me before she drove me clean out my mind. Anything else between us is a figment of her overactive imagination. Ya got any other drawers of mine you wanna see flappin' in the wind?"

See? That was what I meant—there went almost a whole statement with no chopped upings, and he even threw the words *alimony* and *figment* in there for good measure; then he closed with the homeboy lingo. One minute he came across like Mr. Corporate America and the next I thought he was trying to get a hustle on. Yeah, I had a question or two.

"Where'd you get your degree?"

He sounded amused. "SMU." Hmm, Southern Methodist, the preppy mecca?

"Bachelor's or master's?" Hey, sister needs to know what she's dealing with these days.

"Both. I could fax you a résumé—don't I sound like I done been educated, Miss Jewel?" he said with a teasing tone.

"So you're a Mustang alum, huh?" I snorted, not having a ton of respect for the most bougie campus around. Having attended the University of Texas, every other Texas school paled in comparison.

"Something wrong with the 'Stangs?"

"We whipped y'all every year."

"Oh, yeah?"

"Fighting Longhorns of Texas, baby!"

"Tired old orange and white ya talkin' 'bout? What else ya wanna ask me? I know you got a list running. You sure you don't want that fax?" He sounded amused.

"I'm trying to get beyond the Google of it all, Mr. Montgomery."

"Ya Googled a brother?"

"Like you didn't Google *me*?"

"True dat."

"So, how old are you?" Damn the niceties, sister was trying to get down to the real.

He laughed. "How old are *you*?"

"Thirty," I answered, hating it. Seems like yesterday I was turning twenty-one.

"You're a baby, Miss Jewel." His voice was pure silk.

"You think so, old man?"

"I got a good four years on ya."

Thirty-four—good, stable age for a man, if there was any such age for a man. "Okay, one last question: Who are you?"

"Huh?" He sounded confused.

"Are you a ruffneck, a professional architect, or a sexy flirt?"

He laughed. "Yes."

Now I was confused. "Huh?"

"Well, lemme ask ya' this—Are you a homegirl, an entrepreneur, or a sexy flirt?"

I got it now and answered accordingly. "Yes." Damn, I liked him. I really did. He had a way about him.

"Bingo, let some folks of African American descent be multifaceted if we have to be. Obama in the White House, babe—it's all about the progressive multitasking blackness of it all. Now, you wanna go out tonight or you one of them girls got rules about how many days ahead a brother gotta call before you'll step out?"

"Not too big on the Rules, player. Whatcha got in mind?" I laid back on the couch in anticipation of his answer.

His voice was rich with inflections when he answered. "We ain't ready for what I got in mind, Miss Jewel. How 'bout if we just start out with dinner?"

I smiled. "Yeah, how about if we do that?"

"I'm turning onto your street right now."

I jumped up from the sofa, damning modern technology and the invention of the cell phone. "What?" I ran to the window and saw a forest green Pathfinder coming up the street. SHIT! I glanced in the entryway mirror. My hair was in a raggedy ponytail, I wore no makeup, I was in bare feet, and I was wearing a ripped up T-shirt and shorts my mother told me to throw out six years ago. Too late. He was pulling into the driveway. "How'd you get my address?"

"You're not the only one with Internet search skills." He braked to a halt. It was getting dark, and his windows were tinted, but I could tell he was turning his head to look at the house. "Nice crib."

"Thanks. How'd you know I'd be here?" In other words, I couldn't believe he rolled up when I'm looking like who done it and why'd ya let them?

"I didn't. I was prepared to sit outside 'til ya showed up."

He searched the front windows until he found the one I was standing in front of. You could say I felt the heat of his gaze. Did that make sense or was I gushing like a fool? No need for an answer—I knew I was skying big time.

"Oh yeah?" Damn but I was eloquent this evening.

"Yeah, three and a half weeks of suggestive e-mails and phone sex with your voice mail is my limit."

"That was phone sex?" I teased.

"Well, phone foreplay."

"Hmm." He gave good foreplay. I stood at the window with the phone in my hand, watching him watching me.

"Miss Jewel?"

Pardon the pun and color me sappy but his deep voice was putting me in the mind of rich maple syrup. And I was seriously contemplating becoming the buttermilk pancake on his plate. Seriously.

"Roman?"

"Ya think I can come in?"

I took one last look at myself in the mirror. Poor boy. He was going to have to take me as I was. I dragged the hem of my shorts down an inch and yanked my T-shirt back onto my shoulder. Walking to the door, I swung it open. "I don't know, can you?"

He hung up the phone, turned off the car, hopped out, and was standing in front of me in record time. He stepped around me and into the house, closing the door behind him. "I'm in."

Yes, he sure was.

The phone hung in my limp hand, and I hoped my mouth wasn't hanging the same way. Hot damn, the boy was *fine*! Finer than I had remembered and my memory had served me well. Black jeans, black polo shirt, black tennis shoes. I loved a black man in all black clothing. All molded to that body. And those eyes! Um, the lips. Lord, the thighs. I took my time looking him up and down and back. A cat-with-the-canary smile spread slowly across my face. Um-um good.

He grinned at me and held his hands out to the side. "Ya like?" No false modesty there.

I grinned right back. "Come into my parlor." I walked into the living room and put the phone back in its cradle. I tried to be smooth as I tugged my shorts down a little.

"You the spider, I'm the fly?" He followed me and stood in the middle of the den looking around. I was rather proud of my place. Everything was antique cherry with brushed nickel accents. My love of tropical colors showed through with hints of turquoise and raspberry. I offset it with chocolate brown for a calming base color. The artwork was mostly beach scenes and seascapes. The ceilings were high, and there were lots of windows, giving the illusion of a lot more space than I had. But, it was all mine. "I like it, Miss Jewel." He looked me over just as intensely. "Yeah, I like what I see."

So, he was diplomatic, along with being smart, funny, successful, and sexier than was fair. "Wanna tour?" I asked politely, already turning back and heading toward the hallway.

"You or the house?" It was the Mrs. Butterworth's voice again.

I stopped in my tracks and actually considered that pancake thing again! *Chill, Jewellen.* I knew it had been a while, but I needed to keep it together. Knowing I had never been a headlong-dive-into-the-deep-end kinda girl, I silently cautioned myself, *Why not stick a toe in to test the water and wade in the shallow end for a little bit?* I looked at him over my shoulder; he was looking at my legs. I looked down and yanked on those damn shorts again. Mom was right about tossing them. "Down, boy," I told him, ignoring palpable chemistry in the room.

He raised his eyes slowly to my face. There wasn't a trace of apology in his expression, and a grin played around the sides of that sexy mouth. Those eyes were the eyes of a lion, king of the jungle, lethal, predatory. He felt it too. "I'd love a tour of your home, Miss Jewel." His innocent tone contradicted the message in those eyes.

I rolled my eyes and led the way back to the front door. I showed him the kitchen, which, thankfully, I had cleaned today. Nothing tackier than showing someone your home with dirty dishes piled up everywhere.

Downstairs was shaped like a box cut in half, with the kitchen, living room, and dining room to the left, home office, guest bed, and bath and utility room to the right. Garage, yard, small (very small) pool out back. I walked back toward the living room, showed him the staircase tucked away behind the bookcase, and led him up to the master suite, which took up the entire second floor.

"Hey, now, Miss Jewel, this is something!" Predatory gleam in full effect.

Large open room, bathroom with attached dressing area and closet. I had a heavy cherry four-poster bed on the far wall between two huge windows. A curl-up chaise was in one corner, a dresser along a wall, and a TV and two speakers connected to the downstairs stereo sat on a credenza and took up another wall. There was a balcony that ran along the back of the house. The door to the bathroom occupied the last section of wall space. Again, cherry, brushed nickel, and bright colors.

"Now, what does this room tell me about you?" he asked, walking around and peering at things. A picture of Mom and Dad on the dresser, a steamy paperback on the floor, my tacky LOVE ME OR GET THE HELL OUT T-shirt I slept in last night draped across the bed.

I picked up a shoe here, a sock there, flung the covers back in an attempt to make the bed, and looked around. "I don't know. It tells you I'm no good at housekeeping?"

"Nah, nuthin' like that. You like your space, you like music, you know how to relax, you got a sense of humor, and a streak of romance in your soul." He was right on the money, but how did he know that from looking around my room?

I stared at him. "They teach you that in architect school?"

He smirked. "School of life, baby." He was cocky, but I could work around that. Truth be told, I liked a man with a healthy ego. Couldn't stand the brothers you always had to be pumping up all the time; the arrogant ones just needed a stroke now and then.

"Listen, why don't you go back downstairs and put on some music while I change?" I couldn't stand around looking like this too much longer.

"Why do you need to change?"

Why do men think that as long as your privates are halfway covered, you're dressed to go anywhere? "I wouldn't hardly go out looking like this!" I yanked the ripped sleeve of my T-shirt back onto my shoulder for what seemed like the millionth time.

"Ya look fine to me, Miss Jewel. Take your hair outta that thing, throw on some shoes, and let's roll." He truly thought it was just that simple.

I pointed at the staircase. "I think not."

He shrugged and trotted downstairs, giving me a nice view of his rear.

I heard Ella Fitzgerald singing about blue skies as I picked out an outfit. I was surprised at his choice. The more I found out about this guy, the more I wanted to know. Suddenly in a hurry, I swished mouthwash, refreshed the deodorant, spritzed on some perfume, slapped on some lipstick and mascara, lotioned the legs, and brushed my hair out, trying to resurrect a curl or two. I tucked a teal stretch V-neck tee into a khaki miniskirt and slipped my feet into some wedge sandals. Added dangly earrings, Y-necklace, bangle bracelet. I grabbed a belt and headed downstairs. Roman was sitting on the arm of the sofa, reading my CD titles. He looked damn good sitting there.

He glanced up at me as I stepped forward. There was the look. That gold-eyed what-have-we-here sweep.

"Nice." There he goes with the killer smile. One word and a smile and I was putty.

I took a breath and tried to sound businesslike. "Ready?" I finished with the belt, snatched up my purse, and threw it over my shoulder.

He took my hand as we walked toward the door. "Oh yeah, I'm ready."

8

Catch a Vibe

Roman—Friday, June 19, 9:30 p.m.

So this was how it was supposed to go. This was what "great date" felt like. . . . I could get used to this. Jewel and I fell into a little dinner lounge with some live music. The food was off the chain, the atmosphere was just right, and the conversation was smooth, smooth, smooth. I would say something; she would pick it up and throw it right back. We discovered we thought alike about a lot of things—politics (middle of the road), child-rearing (nuthin' wrong with a good ass whippin'), church (faithful believers if not faithful attendees), and music (no school like old school).

There were no awkward pauses, no fumbling around, just vibin'; this was nice. We were sitting in companionable silence as the band finished up their set. We clapped and smiled at each other. I picked up the wine bottle. "You want some more?"

She raised a brow. "Trying to get me tipsy, player?"

I put the innocent who-me? look on my face. "Now, Miss Jewel, haven't I been on good behavior?"

She nodded and squinted at me suspiciously. "All right, we'll see how you act. Top it off."

I topped off her glass and mine. I sipped and was enjoying the view and the moment when she said . . .

"So, explain to me how you ended up married to Jaquenetta."

I almost choked on the wine. "Okay, where did that come from?"

She smiled. "You are just a little too perfect, Mr. Montgomery. I figured it was time to dig into the dirt."

"Too perfect? Me? Ya think I'm too good to be true?" I teased. I hadn't heard that one before.

She rolled her eyes. "Let the air out of the ego. Just trying to see what you're coming with."

That statement told me more about Miss Jewel than she probably realized. "Burned before?"

Her eyes met mine. "Scorched."

"Once bitten?" I asked.

"Let me see your teeth," she returned, and took a long sip of wine. Something in her eyes told me she'd been hurt before and didn't want that vulnerability to show. Hidden depths, I liked it. I wanted to take her in my arms and tell her it would all be okay.

Instead, I reassured her in a soft tone, "I don't bite."

"Toothless tiger?"

"Not a tiger at all; basic nice guy."

She tilted her head to the side and stared at me. "Um-hmm . . . I've heard it all before."

"You haven't heard it from me." Had to get my point across. Whoever else she'd known, he wasn't me and I wasn't him.

She looked at me a long time, as if she were trying to decipher my soul. "True."

"Wanna talk about it?"

"I'll give you the first-date short version. Few years back, met a guy, fell in love. He said he loved me too. Thought we were getting married, but he went back to his ex-girlfriend without a backward glance. No reason given."

I wanted to suck my teeth; the stupid things brothers did! I shook my head. "He wasn't good enough for you."

She laughed. "Roman—"

"Nah, shit now, I'm serious. Man gotta good woman and throws her away? No explanation, not even a 'sorry, babe'?"

"How do you know I'm a good woman?"

"A man knows, Jewellen."

"Did you think Jaquenetta was a good woman?"

I winced. "Not at all."

She quirked the brow again. "Oh?"

I sighed and topped off both our glasses before I continued. "First-date short version?"

"Sure."

"Got caught out there. Was in it for a little hit-'n'-run. Was on my way out when she told me about Chase being on the way."

"You think she did it on purpose? Not that you couldn't have been more careful, player."

I shrugged. "Who knows? Anyway, how I was raised—you do the right thing. But Netta and I were not a good fit. Different values, different goals. One of us would have killed the other emotionally or physically. We wrestled and wrangled over all the nasty divorce details, but I knew if I ever wanted to be the man I thought I could be, I had to get the hell out while the getting was good."

"And are you the man you thought you could be?"

"I'm a work in progress, Miss Jewel."

"Aren't we all?"

After that, we settled back into more casual conversation that ranged from sports to current events. Her favorite color was green, and she loved midspring when it's not cold at night but not summer hot during the day. The more I knew, the more I liked.

I asked her to dance during the next set. Miss Jewel was a classy dancer, kinda jazz-club cool with a hint of sex. Nice. I kept the gentleman in me on point and didn't hold her as close as I wanted. I breathed in the scent of the nape of her neck but didn't lick her ear like the dog in me wanted. When the music ended, we stepped back from each other and took inventory. We shared a smile.

"So, Mama like?"

Her smiled widened. "Mama like."

I let out a breath. "When Mama's happy, everybody's happy. You ready to go?"

She nodded.

On the way back to her house, she turned to me. "There's something about you I just can't put my finger on."

"Baby, you can put your finger on anything I have." Oops, the dog jumped out.

"Boy, please, what I *mean* is, you have a vibe about you."

I nodded. "It's *our* vibe. The buzz is about us; it's called *chemistry*, Miss Jewel. Dive on in, water's fine."

Her eyes got wide. "Oh, I'm a baby-toe-in-the-kiddie-pool-first girl."

Poor thing looked like a deer in the headlights. "Ease up; no hurry, no worry. Let's just try and spend some time, catch the vibe."

She didn't respond, and we rode in a vibe-filled silence until I pulled into her drive.

I hopped out of the car, walked around to her side, and extended my hand to help her out. Keeping her hand in mine, I strolled along to her front door. I held out my other hand for her key.

"You're a gentleman." She seemed stunned as she handed me the key.

"Should a brother be insulted?"

"You keep surprising me; one minute you're all round-the-way homeboy, and next you're all Billy Dee."

I opened her door and stepped aside so she could key in her alarm code. When she turned around, I took a step forward. "I'll take that in the spirit you meant it. Lookie here, I wear a coat of many colors, babe. I flow like I need to as need be."

She looked up at me with a bemused expression on her face, mouth slightly open. Too good an invitation to pass up. "I try to be a gentleman, but I'm only human, Jewel." With that, I leaned down and set my lips against hers. Mmm, her lip gloss was some kind of fruit flavor. By holding her beneath her elbows, I could pull her upward and closer at the same time. Not wanting to take too many liberties, I didn't probe around. Just explored those soft lips of hers with mine until I heard that little hitch in her breath. She strained closer, and her mouth opened a little wider. Boom . . .

I beat down my inner dog, took one last taste of her, and took a step back. I slid my hands from her elbow to grasp her hands. I gave them a squeeze before letting go and taking another step back. Her eyes blinked open.

"Good night, Jewellen. Thanks for coming out with me."

A slow smile lit up her entire face, and it was all I could do not to lean back in for seconds. She answered, "Good night, Roman. I had a lovely time."

Grinning like an idiot, I waited for her to close the door before I turned to get back in my truck. Pulling out of the driveway, I allowed for one Tiger Woods fist pump. "Yes!" before lecturing myself. "First date, incredible, yes, but a long way to go yet. Stay chill, stay chill. She just a girl—"

My phone cut me off midrant. "Speak to me."

Jewellen's voice was soft. "So, chemistry, huh?"

"Yes, ma'am. Ya scared?"

"Cautiously optimistic."

Baby was deep and nervous. I'd have to tread careful. "I'll take it. Hey . . ."

"Hey?"

"Red apples. I just realized that's what you smell like. Red apples."

She laughed. "Be Delicious."

"Pardon me?" Mind out of the gutter.

"The name of my perfume is Be Delicious."

I just bet she would be delicious too. "Of course it is. When's your birthday?"

"December. Yours?"

"August."

"Good to know. Call me tomorrow?"

"Definitely."

"Call me tonight and let me know you made it home?"

"You going to bed?" The thought of her in a nightgown (or not) crawling in between some sheets completely shut down the gentleman and let the dog out.

"Yep, but I'll wait for your call."

"Phone sex?"

"Don't start nothing you can't finish, boy."

"Oh, I'll finish. If you want, I'll turn this car around and make sure you finish too."

"Rome, you were being a gentleman!"

"I can be whatever you need." Okay, that slipped out. Kinda aggressive. I waited for her response.

"I just bet you can. Call me back, Romeo."

I laughed. "Peace."

9

Fussin' and Fightin', Giggles and Gossip

Gregory—Saturday, June 27, 6:40 p.m.

This shit was deep. This thing with me and Renee, it was all that and then some. I knew it when I first saw her, I knew it when we first went out, and I was positive after that first episode with the teddy—Renee was *it*. Problem was, now she was tripping. On the surface it was all cool, like we were still hanging out, going out, and going at it. Really going at it—we were burning up some sheets. And that bed of hers, without getting into it, just know, it was *proper*.

But every once in a while, like when there was a lull in the conversation or in the morning when we first woke up, she would eye me with a look that scared the hell out of me. It was a look like, "Who are you, why are you here, what do you want from me, and when are you going to jack this up?" Like she expected me to bolt any minute.

So I asked her what she was thinking or what might be wrong, and she said, "Nothing." Yeah, right. I've had to prod and push her into every little step. Simplest things like her keeping a pair of jeans and toothbrush over at my place. She looked like she was going to cry when I put my spare shaving kit in her bathroom and hung a suit in her closet.

I tried to get serious and tell her how I was starting to feel about her, but she didn't want to hear it. I was in danger of turning into the woman here, trying to express a feeling and getting the cold shoulder! I mean, I wasn't going to use the L word or anything, but hell, I didn't want her thinking we were just having a sexfest here and then I was out. I mean, don't get me wrong, she was good and all, but if that was it, I'd have been long gone when she first came across with the game playing.

Like this weekend, first she acted like she didn't want to see me. I had to go over there last night and coax her into coming over. We got back to my place and all of a sudden she was Suzy Homemaker. She cooked, changed the sheets, washed a load of my clothes, and set the table, complete with candles and linen stuff I had used only twice. Then she turned into Jenna Jameson. She served dinner in this long blue sheer nightgownlike thing. Baby should have stock in Victoria's Secret. Anyway, dinner was a long, drawn-out Playmate of the Month fantasy that ended with her getting carpet burn on that ass.

This morning, I was persona non grata again. She was holding me at arm's length, literally. We cleaned up the mess in the kitchen, got dressed, and went to the rec center for my game. She said not two words to me the whole way there. We got there, she saw her girls, and all of a sudden she was all over me. "Gregory and I did this," and "Gregory and I did that." She turned into Super Cheerleader, jumping up and down, blowing kisses and shit. After the game, we went for pizza and to the park with Jewel; Rome; and Rome's boy, Chase. Damned if she wasn't a mom for all seasons. Got on the swing sets with the child, hit the jungle gym—I had never seen her like that.

We got in the car to go to her place, and she was moody again. Not PMS—she got hyper during PMS. Went into overdrive. Cleaned the whole house, cooked huge amounts of food, packaged it and froze it, worked out for hours, and on top of all that, her sexual appetite went through the roof.

So I had to wonder, was she playing games to keep me on my toes? Was she the moodiest manic-depressive alive? Had she no idea of what we're doing together? Or was she just so unsure of me that she was running scared and dealing with it the only way she knew how? I was beginning to think it was a combination of all of the above. And I couldn't figure out why I was hanging in there putting up with all this shit. It was exhausting.

I heard her coming out of the bathroom, so I turned down the volume on the baseball game I wasn't really watching anyway. "Renee," I called to her, and turned sideways on the sofa.

"Yeah?" She was back in her room.

"Come here for a minute, will you?" Now, I had to be smooth about this, or she would freeze up on me again. If she isn't the touchiest woman I've ever known.

She came into the living room wearing a silk paisley robe I hadn't seen before. Vicki's summer catalog, no doubt. She smiled at me. A good sign. "What's up, Greggy?" Another good sign—I was Greggy when she was sure she liked me, Gregory when we were in public or she was looking at me like I was the boogeyman from her childhood nightmares.

I patted the space beside me. "Come talk to me for a minute." Uh-oh, there was the look. That deer-caught-in-the-headlights look. "Come on." I held my hand out and smiled in my most reassuring way.

Slowly, very slowly, she came over, took my hand, and sat down. She wouldn't look at me. She stared at the pattern of her robe as if it was the most fascinating thing she'd ever seen.

"Renee, look at me." Of course, she wouldn't. I had to do the macho thing and take her chin in my hand and force her to look at me. "What are you so terrified of?"

She shrugged. "Whatever it is you're going to say." Well, at least she was honest.

"Why? What could I possibly say that's so terrifying?"

"That it's over." This honest answer stunned the hell out of me. Was the woman blind? Did I look like I was going somewhere?

I dropped her chin and her hand and jumped up. I was mad—no, pissed. "Renee, do I look like someone on his way out the damned door?" I hold my hands out to the side. I had on a pair of sweatpants and nothing else.

She shrugged again. I hated that shit. What was that shrugging shit? I clenched my fists in frustration.

"Renee, what is it you think we've been doing these past three months?" She started to tilt her shoulder. "You shrug that one shoulder at me one more good time and I'm gonna lose it, and we don't want to go there today, sweetheart." Sometimes you had to get strong.

She stood up, put her hands on her hips, and raised her brows. "I beg your pardon? *You're* gonna lose it? Kiss my ass, Mr. Samson. I've been losing it for weeks trying to figure out just what the hell kind of game you're running around here. And you think you're losing it? Boy, I could smack you but good." Peaches came trotting out of the back room. It was the fastest I'd ever seen that lazy hound move. She looked at me, then at Renee, barked once as if to say, "What's all the noise?" before dropping down for yet another nap.

I wanted to smile but thought it best if I didn't. Back to the familiar ways around here: Peaches was napping, and Renee was speaking her mind. At least this was a Renee I knew and liked. One with grit, backbone, and purpose. A direct, no scheme, no scam Renee. Still a disillusioned Renee, but I liked her nonetheless. "Just because *you* always got a game running doesn't mean everyone else does, Ms. Nightingale." Sidestep that one.

She opened her mouth and closed it before frowning. "Whadaya mean?" Typical evasion.

I took a step toward her and pointed my finger in her face.

"What I mean is, I thought we were in a relationship here. You know, I relate to you, you relate to me. *Relating*. Having *relations*, us two, together. Your problem is, you're too damn insecure and concerned with being played. What would I be playing you for now? I got your ass."

She slapped my finger away. I'd never seen her this mad. "You *got* my ass? I don't see a ring on my finger. I haven't heard any promises outta you. I can x your ass anytime I see fit. Listen here, I didn't even know you this time last year, and I got along fine without your sorry black ass. Just because you sleeping with me doesn't mean you own me. Matter of fact, I'm pretty sure I was getting sexed up this time last year too. And let me tell ya one last thing—last I checked, I'm a free woman."

Well, now I was really pissed. How did we get here? I stepped right up to her. "Slow your roll and check a calendar, sweetheart. It is NOW, here, today that I'm trying to talk about. I see two people in this room, and that's all that concerns me. I don't give a damn what you did last year, and you needn't ever, ever bring up old dick to me again. If any of them was worth a shit, you wouldn't be standing here right now, now would ya? I'm talking about the here and now and the today and tomorrow. You wanna know who you gonna be with? That would be me."

"Who in the hell do you think you are?" She took a step back.

"I think—no, I *know*—that I'm the best damned thing to ever walk into your life, so don't even go there with me." As soon as I said it, I realized how arrogant it made me sound, but it was too late to take it back. Besides, the shit was true. My program was solid and she knew it.

She stepped forward again. "Oh, like I'm not the best thing that's ever happened to you in your preppy little bourgie, buppie life? You act like I'm supposed to grateful to be with you. I'm not some ghetto bitch trying to make the rent. I have, can, and will get along without you. Carry your ass on." She turned around to walk off, and I caught her arm.

"Dammit, Renee! You're making me crazy. I don't know why I take this shit from you."

She waved an arm toward the front door. "Don't let the door hit you on the ass on the way out." She backed up again.

I dropped her arm and put my hands on my hips. "Know what, I'd go if I thought you really meant that shit."

"Now you can read my mind too? You got to be the most arrogant asshole I've ever met."

Suddenly, I wasn't mad anymore. Somehow, I let her goad me into this argument even though I knew she had been spoiling for one for a while now. Any excuse to prove I was really an asshole and not worthy of her time. Something to lump me in with whatever dicks and dogs she'd known in the past. It was a different tactic but still just another one of her little games, little tests.

When I spoke, my voice was deep and sincere, in a way I knew would hit a nerve. "Renee." Boom, she looked at me suspiciously, but she quit inching backward. "Somewhere, we got off on the wrong track with this conversation. I'm trying to tell you how much I care about you."

"Oh yeah? Is that what you were doing?"

I was starting to get pissed again. Let a brother try and be nice, for God's sake! "Renee, chill for a minute and listen to me. I'm not running a line or playing a game. I *like* you." I put my hand on her cheek. "Do you hear me? I *like* you."

"Listen to what I'm saying. I . . . like . . . you."I knew this would mean a lot more than telling her she was special or crazy fine or sexy as hell. I watched her face, wanting her to understand how much I was laying on the line by saying that.

She blinked for a second and looked me straight in the eye. Then she nodded. "Okay."

So far, so good. I took a breath and pushed on. "I want you to live with me."

Her mouth fell open. "What?"

"Or I could live with you. I like your place better than mine anyway."

"What?" She was still standing there with her mouth open.

"Well, it seems to me like that's the next logical step for us. I don't want to be with anyone else. I spend all my time with you, and this is a good way to see just how right we are for each other before I ask you to marry me. Hey, I'm thirty-three years old. I think by now I know what I want when I see it." There, I said it.

"Marry me? What?" Now she was starting to scare me.

I started backpedaling. "Unless, of course, you don't feel the same way, in which case I should just pack up my stuff and get the hell outta here."

"Oh." She sat down and put her elbow on her knee and her head in her hand.

"Uh, Renee?" She looked up at me with the most perplexed expression on her face. "You kinda leaving me hanging here, honey. Could I get some feedback?" I was trying not to sound anxious, but damn, was a brother wanted or not?

She jumped up and put her arms around me. "How soon can you move your stuff in?"

Whew! I wrapped my arms around her and relaxed. It was cool. I wasn't wrong. Damn, I was the man. I was in control. All was as it should be. "We'll start tomorrow, but I'll keep my place in case you show me the door again."

She laughed into my chest before tilting her face up. "I guess you're all right to have around."

I grinned down at her. "Aw, baby, don't love me like you do!"

There was a lot of other crap I could and probably should say right now. We still had a lot of shit to get straight around here—her moods, her suspicions, her feelings. But with her smiling up at me like I just hung the moon especially for her, I kinda thought of something else I'd like to do. Like celebrate this cohabitation thing. I slid my hand down her ass and pulled her flush up against me, a kind of nonverbal question asking, *Do you wanna*? She went up on her toes and snuggled closer, planting a kiss on my chest, a nonverbal answer: *Yeah, let's.* With a move I perfected my sophomore year of college, I eased her backward onto the sofa and stretched out over her. "Let me see if my buppie, arrogant, preppy, bourgie self can figure out what to do here." I couldn't resist teasing her.

She caught me by surprise by sliding out from under me. When I turned to reach for her, she climbed on top of me. I laid back and smirked up at her as she got comfortable straddling my hips. "Greggy, I'm *really* sorry for most of the things I said." She didn't sound too sorry as she slipped out of her robe, wearing nothing underneath. She leaned forward. "Let me see if my insecure, scheming ass can think up a way to apologize."

"Yeah, why don't we apologize each other to death." I grinned; she grinned back. For now, we were on the same wavelength for once.

Renee—Sunday, June 28, 2:30 p.m.

These once-a-month Sunday brunches were my idea, so I had to show up. Truthfully, I was thinking about Gregory over at his house packing up his stuff. I needed to be at home making closet space. I was thinking I needed to call my mom and tell her Greg's moving in. I was thinking I didn't wanna be here. But it was my idea. All six of us, a whole *Waiting to Exhale* sisters' circle thing. I looked around the table and wondered how we've all remained friends.

I knew Keisha from the hood days; Jewel knew Stacie from prep school. Jewel, Roni Mae, and I met Tammy at orientation at UT. Somehow, we're all still hanging in there. Maybe it's because we're all so different. I liked to think we complement each other.

I was the planner, the schemer, the let's-get-organized-and-do-this person. Stacie was the wide-eyed innocent, even now at twenty-nine. She had had a horrible family life and had been through three absolutely disastrous relationships. This time, she was engaged to be married (to a white boy; Jewel says she thought Stace just gave up on black men altogether). Somehow through all this, the rose-colored glasses never fell off her face.

Keisha's rose-colored glasses self-destructed years ago. She was the hard-edged cynic, but every once in a while, the hard shell cracked and you could see that she was a really sweet, sensitive girl inside. Jewel, God bless her, was the middle-of-the-road, practical, stable, feet-on-the-ground mediator. The one you counted on, dependable and reliable in crisis situations. Jewel was the voice of reason, the one who saw solutions when no one else did; she could also diffuse a volatile situation by injecting a sneaky sense of humor you didn't expect from her.

Roni Mae was the flaky artist. She bent with the wind, changed personality with the weather. The only thing you could be sure of with Roni Mae was that she would always be there in your corner, no matter what. Tammy, well, she had a heart of gold, but she was a flat-out ho. I knew it sounded harsh, but she would tell you herself: her favorite pastime was "getting some."

Take, for instance, this one time, about four years ago, back when we were all into the club scene. It was a girls' night out, and the six of us went over to the Safari Bar. Aptly named, the place was a zoo. Anyway, Tammy spied a little cutie up at the bar and sidled over. She sat down next to him and said, "Listen, I just want you to know that I think you're sexy. I'd like you to come home with me." When he had the nerve to look hesitant, she told him, "Look, I don't want you to love me; I just wanna get laid." At that, she left with him. Shocking, okay, but the worst thing was, it had been her turn to drive. We were stranded at the Safari Bar. Classic Tammy.

I looked over at her; she was starting a story.

"So I had this dream."

We all groaned. Her dreams were always weird and generally X-rated.

"I was at this carnival riding along on this white horse."

"Tammy, stop!" Jewel begged.

"What? I wanna hear it!" Stacie said with a sip of her champagne cocktail.

Tammy grinned. "And up comes Emmitt Smith on a big black horse," she said, naming a former star football player for the Dallas Cowboys.

I had to laugh. "Imagine that. Up rides a Cowboy on a horse." Roni Mae and I exchanged a look.

"Anyway, he rides up and we're laughing and talking about horse stuff when all of a sudden, we're on the same horse."

"You don't know anything about horses! Or football!" Roni Mae looked disgusted.

"You two are on the big black one, of course," Keisha interjected.

"Of course. We turned away from the carnival and start riding into the night. Then as the horse starts to gallop, our clothes melt away—"

"No shit? In one of your dreams, you get naked with a man?" Jewel interrupted to tease.

"Naked with an extremely rich man," Roni Mae added.

"The only kind to get naked with. Y'all want her to tell the next part or not?" Keisha lectured.

"Not! Was there a tunnel you had to go through?" I asked laughingly. "A humid pink one?"

"No, but he *was* carrying a small box that kept opening and closing." Tammy grinned. "Anyway, so there we were, naked on the horse and—"

Stacie interrupted, looking very confused. "What in the world could you do naked on a horse?" We all died laughing, and her mouth fell open. "No way! On a horse?"

Tammy shrugged. "Why not?"

"Have you ever done it on a horse?" Stacie asked the table at large.

"Why the hell would I be on a horse?" Keisha asked while the rest of us shook our heads.

"What's the wildest place you ever did it?" Tammy asked us, a mischievous grin on her face. We waited while the waiter placed our food in front of us.

"The radio broadcast booth," Roni Mae announced, and I looked over at her in surprise. She had changed a lot over the past few weeks. The weave was gone, and her hair was styled in a short, flattering cut. The colored lenses were gone, and her nails, while still acrylic, were natural length and painted a natural shell pink. She looked like she had lost weight, and her outfit was solid cotton separates, no rainbows or kaleidoscopes. I made a mental note to call and ask how things were with her and Mr. Paris.

"You did it in the booth?" I asked her. "Were you on the air at the time?"

"Yep." Her expression said that she'd relayed all she planned to reveal.

"Isn't that against somebody's regulations?" Tammy asked.

"FCC," she replied, "and what they don't know won't hurt 'em."

"Unfortunately, you all know about my fling at the Laundromat," I said. They all nodded solemnly, remembering the time they walked in and caught me getting busy on top of the Kenmore. When they said those washers were heavy-duty, they meant it.

"I once did it in the bathroom at Jack-in-the-Box," Stacie confessed.

"Men's or women's?" Tammy asked.

Stacie giggled. "Women's, of course."

"You?" Jewel laughed. "I can't believe it."

"Well," Stacie parried, "I'm not going to tell about you and you know who at Memorial Stadium at UT during halftime of the Baylor game in the locker room!"

Jewel shot her a look. "Yeah, thanks for keeping that to yourself."

"Wait a minute, how did I miss that one?" I asked Jewel, trying to remember who that could have been. Just couldn't picture Jewel letting it all out in public like that.

"Had to be Richie, the Boy Wonder," Roni Mae volunteered helpfully.

"Yeah! The Boy Wonder!" I laughed as Jewel scowled at all of us. We had secretly nicknamed Richie the Boy Wonder for his amazing sexual prowess. He was a football player, notorious hound, and pretty damn near irresistible . . . or so he kept telling us. Jewel called him her "freshman folly." After her, he managed to work his way through a good chunk of the female coeds before flunking out his second year.

"I guess my li'l time in the back of a police car is nuthin'," Keisha piped up.

"Hold up, I wouldn't say that!" I asked her. "Were you under arrest at the time?"

"Yeah."

We all stared.

"No way!" Roni Mae said.

"What about the guy—was he under arrest too?" Jewel asked, as if she couldn't stop herself.

"Nah, he was the arrestin' officer." Keisha smirked.

"Did he read you your rights before, during, or after?" Tammy asked, and we all laughed.

"Can you imagine?" Stacie laughed.

Jewel chimed in, "Yeah. You have the right to raise your hips. And he thrusts." She was laughing so hard, she had to wipe tears from her eyes.

"You have, thrust-thrust, the right to bite my neck." I cracked up.

"And pow! You have the right to yell my name, baby," Tammy crooned.

"You have the right to birth control." Roni Mae giggled.

Keisha finished, "In the event that you do not have birth control . . ."

We all completed the sentence: ". . . some will be provided for you!"

It took us a minute to compose ourselves. I shook my head and spoke up again, "Well, so far, if this was a contest, I'd have to say Keisha wins. Of course, we haven't heard from the Nympho Queen over here."

Tammy smiled. "The wildest place? I'd have to say in church."

"Church?" we all shrieked at once.

Jewel put a hand out. "Now, I mean it, Tammy. I don't wanna hear another word, not a single detail! To think I could've sat on the pew where you . . . No! I don't wanna know." She looked over at Stacie threateningly. "And neither do you!"

"Okay, okay! But speaking of church, I saw you with your man today, Miss Renee." Tammy segued into that neatly.

I looked up from my plate to find all eyes on me. "Yeah, that was Gregory." I smirked. Let 'em wheedle the information outta me.

"Nice-looking guy," Tammy probed.

"Yeah," I agreed with a smile before shooting her a look. "Hands off!" Tammy would try to take your man, if only for a night. Unapologetically a man stealer. I sometimes think she needs professional help. Beyond that warning, I said nothing else and sat eating quietly.

Keisha gave in first. "So, what's the scoop? Two days ago, you were calling everybody up talking about how it's over and now ya paradin' him into the Lawd's house like he's the hottest thing since Taye Diggs."

I laughed. Keisha always had a colorful way of putting things. "You could say we came to an agreement."

Jewel leaned forward and raised a brow.

"Well, what? What!" Roni Mae gave in first.

"He's moving in."

"He's what?" Tammy cried.

"Did ya tell yo mama yet?" Keisha asked.

"Good for you, girl," Roni Mae cheered.

"Why don't you just marry him?" Stacie asked.

Ignoring them all, I looked at Jewel. A slow smile spread across her face, and she nodded her head up and down. "You know I ain't one for the shacking, but if it's cool for you, it's cool for me. High five, sister. You're rolling now," she whispered.

We slapped palms. "You ain't doing too bad either, homegirl."

"Yeah, what up with you and the Roman god?" Keisha asked in her typically brash way. "I never thought I'd see the day when you messing around anything this close to thug life! And old boy got a kid too! And I done met that Jaquenetta he used to be married to! Girl, he may be fine, but with all that baggage, he's trouble. And I'll tell ya another thing—he's got a sweet old house he fixed up over in the Cliff, girl. Southside boy, girl. Almost his whole family lives over there. You moving south? I can't see it; no, I can't see it at all." I wanted to reach over and smack her. She would have to point out all the negatives.

"What I wanna know is, when ya bringin' him round?" Tammy asked. "Is he fine or what?"

"Hands off him too," I told Tammy.

Stacie chimed in, "He's not from North Dallas? Jew-Ro, are you dating thug nation? Hood rat, round-the-way boy? How exciting! Does he have any money?"

"He's not hardly thug nation," Roni Mae chimed in. "Y'all back up off the sister."

Jewel shot them all one of her don't-mess-with-me looks before ignoring them all. She kept right on eating. I sure wasn't going to be the one to volunteer any information.

"Where these guys been hidin'? I been looking for a decent guy for years, and y'all swing by the rec center and snap some up in a day!" Keisha added.

Roni Mae's voice filled the heavy silence. "Get off the girl's back. Rome is a nice guy." She turned to Jewel and asked quietly, "So, how are y'all getting along? Solve that communication thing?"

"We cool," Jewel answered serenely, her tone brooking no further discussion. An absolutely classic Jewel answer: responded to the question but gave up no info or insight. Hated her business in the streets, never made a scene, rarely volunteered the scoop.

"So, what happened to the white horse?" Stacie asked, referring to Tammy's X-rated Emmitt fantasy.

"Who could pay attention to the horse when I had Emmitt's naked body pressed up next to mine?"

"Now, in your dream, girl, was he as muscled up outside of that blue and silver uniform as he is in it?" Keisha asked.

After that, as far as I was concerned, the conversation went downhill. Another half hour was spent speculating on Emmitt's body proportions and how well they could be put to use on horseback and in other athletic pursuits. When Tammy said something about Wesley Snipes and spurs, I quit listening altogether.

I thought about Jewel's calm phrase throughout the rest of the extended brunch and on my way over to Gregory's. I envied Jewel her composed acceptance of everything. She never thinks, What if he leaves? What if we don't work out? What if this is my last chance at a good guy and I drive him away? What if my family hates him? What if he doesn't want kids? What if . . . what if . . . WHAT IF?

Instead, faced with all the uncertainties of a new relationship with a guy she'd been out with only once, a guy with an ex-wife, a kid, a house in the hood he won't leave, and ruff-neck tendencies, what does she say? "We cool."

As I pulled into his parking lot, I looked up at Gregory's building. He had a U-Haul attached to the Beemer already. He, Aaron, and another friend of his, Marcus, were hauling boxes down the stairs. He looked up, saw my car, and smiled. I waved. For today, we cool too.

10

Equal Time

Rome—Wednesday, July 1, 12:30 p.m.

I reckoned that this slow-'n'-easy, taking-it-light, one-day-at-a-time style just ain't me. I was a go-for-it, see-what-happens and suffer-the-consequences kinda guy, ya know? A gambler, you could say. Go for broke, bet it all on black, dive in the deep end, jump first, look later—that was me.

It was how I ran my company and how I wanted to run my love life.

What I was saying was, the date with Jewel was real nice last Friday, and we had a great time with Chase Saturday. It was nice to see the two of them hanging out. Chase liked her, and she was good with kids, always cool to see. Did my heart good for a little minute.

But I played it cool the whole time, a little teasing but not really pushing to get some play. All of which was tight and all but I don't want it to be another two weeks before I get to hold her hand again, know what I'm saying? We been on the phone every little spare second. I was putting the puzzle of Jewellen Rose Capwell together bit by bit.

So, I figured, couldn't hurt to get a look at another side of

Miss Jewel, check if I liked it as much as the others. I wanted to take a look at Ms. Capwell, the career woman, in action. Little free time today, so I decided to roll by the J and take a look-see.

I pulled up to her office building. Nice. Five-story building off Central Expressway. Covered parking, a little landscaping with a contemporary feel. Sounding like a tour guide, right? Hey, I got an artist's eye. I noticed things.

Her office was on the fifth floor. Classy, discreet brass sign by the door. I walked into the reception area; two people were filling out forms, one guy was looking real bored, and there was a little white girl behind the desk.

"Hi, can I help you?" She flashed me that polite what-can-I-do-for-you smile.

I leaned up against the desk. "Yeah, is Miss Jewel in?" She blinked at the name. I guess no one else calls her Miss Jewel.

"Do you have an appointment, sir?" She gave me the once over, sizing a brother up. Ha! Just came from a meeting, had my Italian silk suit on. Navy with a gray pinstripe. Bruno Magli black lace-up oxfords, purple custom-tailed shirt with French cuffs and links, Kenneth Cole paisley tie. By the look on her face, I knew I passed her test.

"Nope, I wanted to surprise her, take her out for lunch." Her eyes opened way up like I was speaking Greek or some shit. Damn, the woman never went out to lunch?

"Oh, well, one moment." She picked up her phone and hit a button. "Miss Capwell, sorry to disturb you, but there's a gentleman here who says he wants to take you out to lunch?" She listened to the reply and looked up at me. "Yes, ma'am, he is . . . yes, he does . . . I can't tell from this angle, but I'm sure that describes him. Yes, ma'am, I'll tell him." She looked back at me. "She says you sure are one for surprise visits and will you please go on back." She pointed. "Take a left here; it's the last office at the end of the hall."

I grinned and looked at her nameplate. "Thank you, Suzanne.

You've made my day." I took off down the hallway, glancing round some. Gray and mauve, cool and sophisticated, yet another side of Miss Jewel. I came up on the last door and knocked.

"Come in."

I swung the door open. Now this was something else. Rich mahogany furniture mixed with navy and burgundy leather, lots of plants everywhere and with a few art pieces thrown in. I saw a Monet print and an African figurine. Now, I had only a second to take all of that in, 'cause right about then, Miss Jewel swiveled round in her chair. Nice! Be damned if baby didn't look good. She was on the phone, but she looked up at me and waved me forward. "Sit down for a minute," she mouthed, and motioned to one of the chairs in front of her desk.

I wasn't having any of that. I came around the desk and took her hand and pulled her out of the chair. My girl was sharp! Had on a navy suit with one of them short skirts that wrap around and some sort of bright blue silky shirt with a V in the front. Now, I done told ya how I feel about those Vs on this girl. Lord have mercy, baby got the high-heel pumps working. With some kind of ankle strap. Hair all curly, falling down round her face. And makeup! She liable to hurt somebody looking this good. I twirled her around and she laughed.

She talked into the receiver in her hand. "Listen, Renee, I understand what you're saying and all, but I don't think you have anything to worry about. Tammy is always gonna make a play for anything with pants on. No, really, she tried to make a play for my dad once. You gotta just ignore it. Besides, Gregory wouldn't touch her with a pole. Don't start inventing shit. You and Greg are hanging in there just fine. Listen, Roman's here so . . ."

I loved the way she called me Roman. Just her and my moms. I sat down in her chair and pulled her down into my lap. She curled right up like she'd been there a million times before. Damn, she was sweet. I took the phone out of her hand.

"Renee, this is Rome." Jewel just smiled and leaned farther into me. The things I could do with this little honey. Umm, made *me* wanna holler!

Jewel flicked on the speaker so she could hear. "Hiya, Rome. Whassup?"

"Ain't nuthin' going on but the rent; you know how it rolls. Uh, listen, Jewel and I fittin' ta jet, right? So, could she like get back to ya?" What I wanted to say was "Quit trippin', manage ya own neurotic life, and let Jewel have one of her own." But I chilled. I liked Renee (sort of), but she was too damn mood swingy for me. And needy. She needed Jewel, she needed Greg, she needed to be fly all the damn time, she needed attention— she needed a lot o' shit.

"You trying to corrupt my girl?" She sounded like she was sorta teasing and sorta not.

"Renee!" Jewel rolled her eyes.

Renee tried to play the innocent role, like she wasn't trying to start some shit. Enough she was trying to jack up her own love life, she had to mess up Jewel's too? "What?" Renee sounded all hurt and shit. "I gotta right to know! You don't ever take time out in the middle of your workday! I just wanna know what the occasion is."

"Seems to me like she was taking time out to talk to you." No one said shit for about a minute. I looked right at Jewel the whole time. I could tell she understood I was trying to set the rules straight up. If we were gonna do this thing, I deserved at least equal time to what she spent hanging with the girls. At the very least.

Finally, Renee came across with a fake little laugh. "Yeah, I guess that's true. Well, y'all have a nice time. I'll call you at home later, girl." She hung up the phone . . . abruptly.

Jewel reached over, flicked the speaker off, and settled back. "You trying to tell me something, player?"

I wrapped one arm around her, and she rested an elbow on my shoulder, bringing her hand up to touch the side of my face. Miss Jewel had a nice touch. She tried to play all tough, but she was a cuddler at heart. I liked that.

I tipped her face up to mine. "Yeah."

"Yeah?" Her voice was kinda quiet and sexylike.

I tilted my forehead forward so it leaned against hers. "Equal time, baby." Her eyes met mine for a second before drifting shut. I couldn't resist; I brushed my lips against hers. "Ya understand?" I brushed again, very softly. Then I leaned back.

Her eyes flew open, and she looked at me, seriously. "So we're gonna do this dating thing?" Her fingers traced along my face, my jaw, my neck. She really was a toucher. Almost like she couldn't help herself from exploring. Cool how a simple touch could move something deep inside.

I answered her. "Oh yeah, we gonna do this thing."

"Like exclusively or are we still playing the field?"

I frowned. I didn't like the way she said that. Like she was going to have to clear out a whole bull pen of brothers for my ass. Before I could ask her what the hell she meant by that, she traced a finger, then her lips across my forehead.

"Quit frowning, Roman. I was asking to be sure of *you*. I haven't played the field in so long, shit, I forget how to get to the ballpark! And I doubt I remember how to get from base to base!" She laughed. Her laugh was a rich sound, like chocolate bubbling on the stove.

I smirked; it was too good an opportunity to pass up. I grabbed her face and brought it close again. "Batter up." I laid one on her. I guessed those kisses on the cheek and little teasing kisses today had her thinking I was kinda slow in *this* field. Not this boy! My lips told her I meant business, and she kinda gasped in surprise. The minute the mouth was open, I was in for the prize. I was in this kiss to find out a little about the sensual side of Miss Jewel and to let her understand a little about where I was coming from. What I was bringing to the table, ya know?

I slid my tongue in and out in slow, deliberately unpredictable strokes. Then I'd pause for a minute and lick round those lips, take a nibble here, a nibble there. I was hitting her with some of my best tricks. She made a sorta kittenish sound in the back of her throat before she dove into the kiss with enthusiasm. Go 'head, Miss Jewel. We had a little thrust-and-parry action going on for a while there.

Going on instinct, I shifted her round so she was kinda straddling me and leaned back. The chair tilted back, and the change of angle pressed her pretty tight up against me. I wrapped both arms round her to bring her closer and settled back into the kiss. She smelled good, like something tropical. Her chest felt real good against mine. For real, I didn't know whose hips started grinding first. Okay, maybe I started a second before she did. What I did know was that one minute I was going slow and easing along real cool, and the next minute I was rock hard and ready to rumble. Time to chill.

Damn. I let out a groan of my own. I sure didn't wanna stop, but our first time together was not going to be in this damned chair in her office!

I ordered my hips to quit moving and put my hands on hers to stop her. Immediately, she lifted her head and took a deep breath. I lifted her chin so I could see her face; I liked what I saw. Flushed cheeks, eyes bright, lipstick smudged—little pleasure, little struggle for control, no regrets. "That was at least first base, Miss Jewel."

She let out a quick laugh. "Yeah, it started coming back to me." She blinked. "If you hadn't stopped, I'd planned on rediscovering home."

I really groaned this time. "Don't say that. I came to *take* you to lunch, not *have* you for lunch." I looked away from her before I changed my mind. The message light was blinking on her phone. "Your light's blinking."

"What?" She turned and almost fell out of the chair before

I caught her. I tilted the chair back up, and she hopped out of the chair. "Damn, boy, you're dangerous!"

"What?" Now I was confused. I been called a lot of shit but *dangerous*? Never.

She shot me a look as she tried to brush wrinkles from her skirt. Silk was nice but it sure did wrinkle all to hell. "Yeah, dangerous. One kiss and I forget I'm running a business here." She smiled at me. "You ought to bottle whatever it is you've got, boy." I reached for her again to show her exactly what I *did* have, and she sidestepped me with her hand out. "Stay over there for a minute now; don't play."

She picked up the phone and hit a button. "Suzanne, what's up?" She listened for a sec. "Okay, send him back; it'll only be a minute." She hung up and reached for a folder on her desk. "Potential client dropped by," she explained to me.

"Lunch another day?" I asked her. I knew what it was like trying to run your own place.

She looked over at me in surprise. "No way, unless you're in a hurry. This'll only take a second."

"Why ya think I'm not in a hurry, Miss Jewel?"

She opened the folder and smirked. "You didn't kiss like a man in a hurry."

She had me on that one. "You want I should make myself scarce while you do your client thing?"

"Nope. I suspect you came to see me in action. Why don't you hang out and watch?" She shot a little smile in my direction.

"You think you know it all, doncha, Miss Jewel?" I teased.

Her tone was real serious when she answered, "No, but I do hope to find it all out, Roman LaChayse." She looked back down at her folder.

Ya gotta like a girl like this, huh? I walked over to the conference table in the corner and sat down to watch her. I sat back to enjoy the view.

Suzanne walked in. "Mr. Collins to see you, Miss Capwell. Can I get anybody anything?" She looked at me, and I could tell she was wondering who the hell I was.

Jewel and I shook our heads as the guy walked in. When he cleared the door, I stood up. He looked over at me. "Roman? What the devil are you doing here?" William Collins and I shook hands.

Jewel smiled and looked back and forth between the two of us. "William Collins, this is Jewel Capwell . . . my girlfriend." Miss Jewel didn't blink when I said it, just extended her hand for the shake. "William and I are working on a golf community planned for North Plano. His company is designing the houses, and Montgomery Design is doing the landscaping and plotting the golf course," I explained to her, and went into a brief detail of what the housing community was going to be like.

"Small world," Jewel said. "Pleased to meet you, Mr. Collins. What can the Capwell Agency do for you?" She motioned for him to sit down before moving back round her desk. I saw her glance at the chair for a sec before she glanced over at me; we exchanged a quick smile. We were both thinking about what could have been happening in that chair. She sat down pretty quick.

William caught the look and smiled. "Am I interrupting something? I realize I dropped in unannounced."

Jewel actually blushed. Didn't know women still blushed. But her face turned red, and she looked flustered as hell—that's a blush, right? I thought I'd better save the day. "Jewel and I are going to grab a bite to eat, William. Would you care to join us?"

"No thanks, I really just came by to ask if Ms. Capwell could round up a few people for us to use out at the North Plano site. We need a receptionist or two and at least three administrative assistants with Microsoft Office skills. Oh, I guess in all, we'll need twenty people out there helping us get set up, handling the administrative side, and showing people around."

My baby had recovered her composure and sounded like a real professional. "Of course, we'd be glad to help out. Tell me, how'd you hear about the agency?" She had a pen and was writing notes.

"Truthfully, we're trying to use a lot of minority contractors on this project. So I got your name off a list." He smiled over at me. "The same list I got Roman's company from. I must say, you two have sterling reputations in your individual fields." William was such a good ol' boy.

Miss Jewel smiled. "Thank you, that's nice to hear. Let me work on getting a good group of people ready for you. Would you like to have final screening?"

"No, I'll go with your judgment. Already I know you have excellent taste in boyfriends." He chuckled at his joke. White folk and they humor, man.

"Yes, well"—she shot me a look—"I'll call you tomorrow morning, and we can finalize the details. I assume you have our package with the basic rate structure and billing procedures?"

William stood up. "I sure do, and I look forward to hearing from you." He turned to me. "Roman, I'll see you at the meeting tomorrow afternoon. Y'all have a good lunch now." He left.

The door barely closed behind him when Jewel threw down her pen and glared at me. "Don't you think it's a mite coincidental that Mr. Collins came to see me the very same day you came to take me to lunch? I can get my own clients, Roman." She got up from the chair.

I shrugged. "Don't go drawing conclusions, Miss Jewel. It's a small world; I didn't have shit to do with it. The fact that we both have a stake in the same project means I'll get a chance to see you more than once every two weeks. Equal time, remember?" Women! They sure could put two and two together and come up with nine. I stood up and walked over to her.

"And what's all that damned 'girlfriend' stuff?" When she was angry, she gestured with her hands. Waving 'em all over the place.

Now she had my attention. "Well, aren't you gonna be?"

She frowned. "Gonna be what?"

"My damned girlfriend!" I never been long on patience.

"I wouldn't call it that! And why you have to say it like that?"

"Like what?" I took another step toward her. "And what would ya call it?"

"Uhh . . . a friend? We're friends?" Her shit was lame and she knew it.

"Ya think I kiss my *friends* like I kissed you?" We were standing toe to toe; I was getting all up in her face. I wanted to make this point clear.

She shrugged. "We've only been out twice. I haven't known you that long."

"There's a time limit we gotta stick to? You gotta rule book?" Not another one with the damned timetables.

"Well, no, but—"

"But what?"

"You don't know me!"

"I like what I know so far. What about you?"

"You seem all right so far." We'd have to work on her ego stroking.

"Aw, shucks, Miss Jewel. You'll turn my head with all them flowery words."

She looked real exasperated. "What if I don't like whatever happens next?"

"Dump me." I planned to make sure that didn't happen. This was one boy she wasn't gonna dump easy. Just to irritate her, I added, "And if I decide I can't stand ya ass, I'll dump *you*, how's that?"

"Yeah, fine. You make it sound so sexy." Her face was all tight, like she swallowed something real sour.

"Hey, listen, if it's there, it's there. I think between us, it's there. Two weeks, two months, two years, what's the difference? Why ya gotta kick up drama where there is none? Why make things difficult when they can be real simple?" Poor thing—she looked like she really wanted to believe we could be something, and this wasn't another tired little episode to be pissed about later.

"I guess you're right." She neither looked nor sounded sure.

"So?" I was losing patience with the conversation again.

"So, let me let it marinate for a minute."

I sighed.

"What?"

I shook my head. "It's about you women and your li'l insecurities. I figure, hey, if I'm here, I'm here for a reason, right? If I don't wanna be here, I'll leave. Simple."

"Simple." She tilted her head to the side and assessed me as if checking my overall mental health.

I met her gaze and held it. "Why not?"

"Why not, indeed?" She smiled some.

I reached out and captured her hand. "Indeed." Sometimes ya just gotta smooth shit out. "So we're doing this thing, you and me, okay?"

"Okay, then." She smiled some more. "But, Roman, know this—I don't share."

My eyes narrowed. "Uh, me either."

Jewel nodded. "I notice you don't shy away from the tough conversations, a little bit of an in-your-face style."

"I notice you have a bit of a temper there," I countered.

"I notice you gave as good as you got." She smiled, pleased with herself.

I sighed. This one was gonna be a handful. I looked at her and grinned, but whatta handful! "Since ya noticing everything, did you happen to notice I'm starving?"

She picked up her purse and smiled. "Yeah, let's roll."

I couldn't help but glance back at that chair as we walked out. Another time, no doubt.

11

His Turf

Jewel—Thursday, July 17, 7:35 p.m.

I turned left and knew I was terribly lost. I was also scared shitless.

I was rolling through South Dallas, right? Roman was all hung up on this equal-time concept, so I said I'd come over to his place tonight. I had been doing well too. But somewhere I messed up the whole Colorado/Sylvan Road thing, and now I was in deep shit. The sun was about to set, and believe you me, this was nowhere to be lost after dark! Not like gunshots ringing out or anything, just not necessarily your safest neighborhood—hence all the damn crime-watch signs. Drugfree-zone signs. Curfew-for-kids-under-eighteen signs. Friendly little signs reminding us no guns were allowed within twenty feet of certain establishments—not so much of this on the Northside. It was generally assumed that guns should be left concealed and at home.

I passed two more streets, and there was no doubt about it—I was lost. I made a U-turn and headed back for the expressway. But somewhere this road split, and now I had no idea what direction the damned interstate was. Not a good time to realize my sense of direction was for shit. I really meant to get GPS as one of the options in this car. Well, wait, I could use my cell phone. Uh-oh, terrible time to realize my cell phone was dead, and I had no car charger.

Thank God, a gas station. Looked pretty deserted but probably safe. I was pulling in.

The front door was bolted, but I could see someone inside. I pulled up and read the sign: USE SIDE WINDOW AFTER DARK. Ah, hell, not a good omen, not good at all. Here I was, rolling a brand-new Lexus and I gotta get out and talk to some man through a side window?

Okay, act grown, girl, buck up! There was nothing to freak about, just get out of the car, set the alarm, and go ask the man for directions. I got out, clicked the alarm button, and jogged up to the 2' x 3' bulletproof glass pane that they called a service window. Service, my ass. An Middle Eastern guy was inside watching a *Seinfeld* rerun. A plaque made with Marks-A-Lot and toilet paper proclaimed him to be Ahmed Davi.

"Hi." I paused. The man never looked up. I noticed a red button with a sign, PUSH HERE TO USE SPEAKER. Lord have mercy, grant me patience. I pushed the damn thing. "Hi!"

He looked over. "'Ello, need gas?"

"No. Can you tell me how to get to Harlowe Lane?"

"Barlawn Main?"

Ah, shit. You tried not to get down on the whole America-as-a-melting-pot theory until you had to deal it with it face-to-face two minutes from sundown in the middle of the hood. Then you'd really rather have someone a little less, uh, ethnic behind the bulletproof glass.

"Haaaar-lowe Lane," I repeated.

"Darling Gate?"

"HARLOWE! H-A-R-L-O-W-E LANE!" Patience and I, we were never all that tight. I tried to strive for it, but even Job would've wanted to choke this guy.

"I can tell ya how ta get there, sugar." A real smarmy-looking dude was standing a little too close to me. He must've been in the bathroom 'cause he came out of nowhere and he smelled like a gas station bathroom—rank and foul. He was in ripped-up jeans, an oversized T-shirt, and a long jacket. It was a trifle warm for a coat. It was over eighty degrees! I started backing away ever so subtly. Jacket seemed more of a concealer than an article for warmth, and I wasn't trying to find out what he was concealing. I had watched enough crime drama in my day to be wary of army-coated, white-T-shirt-wearing strangers.

"Ah, no thanks. I'll find it." I smiled prettily and backed away a little quicker.

"Harlowe by Colorado." The man behind the glass volunteered. Shit, I knew that. I just couldn't figure out how to get back to Colorado.

"You sho, sweet pea? It can be real dangerous out here for a li'l girl like you. You ain't from around here, huh?" Brain surgeon too. I was asking directions at the most decrepit gas station in town, and he thought I might not be from around there?

"Thanks for your help." I tried to smile wider and turned away.

"That your car?" he asked, and inched closer to me. "That a real nice car. That one of those new Benzos?"

Ah, shit, now I was petrified. I didn't want to open it and get in—what if he tried to jump me once I got the door open? Then again, if I stood out there, he could just jump me, take the keys, and get the car anyway. I looked over at Ahmed. He'd gone back to *Seinfeld* and was going to be no help at all.

What the hell, if he jumped me, I'm jumped. I strode back to the car as quickly as I could without running. Hit the button, climbed in, slammed the locks, started it, and peeled out with tires screeching. I was so freaked, I ran a stop sign and a red light. Where the hell were the cops when you needed one?

Right about now, I was debating about just trying to find my way home and Roman be damned. But then again, I was so lost I couldn't get home if I wanted to. Why, oh why did I not charge the phone last night? Wait a minute, was that what I thought it was? It *was*—Golden Arches dead ahead. Thank you, Jesus! Oh, and thank you, McDonald people, for having a restaurant on damn near every corner.

I turned into the lot. Of course, this wasn't the ritziest Mickey D's I'd ever been to. Matter of fact, it looked worse than Ahmed's station. But, at least there were people inside and a pay phone. Pay phones were a rarity these days; everyone ELSE had the sense to keep a charged cell phone at their disposal. Anyway, this should take me five minutes tops. I got out, clicked the alarm, and stepped inside.

Looked left, looked right; the damn pay phone was right by the playground. There was a ragged-looking crew out on the playground. Kids, not children, but teens. With my imagination, I was immediately thinking gang. Of all the McDonald's in the world, I stumbled into a gang hangout. I was not in the mood to tangle with today's disenfranchised, disillusioned youth ruffnecks.

I went straight to the phone, picked it up, and wiped it down the front of my jeans. Then I regretted doing it because now everyone's going to think I was a snob. Okay, so I kinda was. I didn't look at anyone, hoping that meant they wouldn't look at me either. Renee always said you couldn't be scared of your own people. However, you could be cautious, right?

Not wanting to flash even a quarter, I dialed Roman using my calling card number.

One ring. Come on, baby, pick up for Mama.

Two rings.

"Yo, you 'bout through with that phone?" Dammit, if it wasn't for bad luck I wouldn't have any at all. Three rings. I glanced over my shoulder. A big hip-hop hardhead was staring me down. Do-rag on his head, jeans hanging low. Big baggy plaid shirt (plenty of room to hide a gun, I was thinking), tattoo of a bullet on the side of his neck, and a little skull-and-crossbones earring dangling. Classy.

"Yeah, I'll just be a sec." Four rings, where was he?

Five ri—"Hello?"

"Roman!" I almost sobbed with relief. Salvation was only a telephone wire away.

"I need that phone for my bi'ness; you tyin' up my line." The hardhead was getting louder.

I turned around. "Really, I'll only be a minute. I'm sorry." I tried a smile, but out of the corner of my eye, I noticed that the youngsters were all standing in the doorway looking at me. I looked around and one of them was making his way to the Lexus. Wouldn't you know, the damn car was like a gangster magnet. He started circling it. I think *casing* was the correct verbiage.

"What you lookin' at?" Some little fly girl asked me. I hadn't even gotten around to checking out her bandana, combat-boot-wearing ass yet.

"Baby, where are you?" Roman asked me. "Baby?"

I looked down, ignored them, and talked quickly. "Rome, I'm lost. I'm at a McDonald's somewhere near Colorado and Sylvan, I think." I tried to sneak a look toward my car, but the little mobsters were blocking my view. Absently, I wondered how long it took to strip custom hubcaps off a Lexus.

He groaned. "Okay, listen. Take a left out of McDonald's and keep straight through four lights and you'll be back at I-30. Take Thirty west back to Sylvan and turn right, and then follow the directions I gave you. You turned the wrong way on Sylvan last time, okay? Jewel?"

"You gonna give up that phone or I got to make you?" the leader of the pack spoke.

"I still don't like the way she looked at me with her siddity ass," the bandana chick piped in.

I was so scared, I didn't realize that I had nodded and

Roman couldn't hear that. "Yeah, one second." I lowered my voice and turned back around. "I got it. But, Roman?" My voice was cracking. The little hoodlums weren't moving.

"Yeah, baby. You okay?"

"No, how do I get out of here?" I didn't know proper ghetto etiquette. What did one do when you've tied up a ruffneck's telephone line? Give him a quarter? Apologize? Run like hell?

"Calm down, baby. Just don't say anything and walk fast. Hang up the phone and walk to your car. Wait till you have your hand on the handle before you open it, all right?"

"Okay." My voice sounded small and pathetic, and he sounded so safe. Lord, I hated being out of my element. Made me feel really weak, silly, and dependent—three ways I tried never to feel.

"You want me to come get you, honey? You want to wait there for me?"

"No!" I almost screamed before lowering my voice again. "I don't wanna sit in here by myself. I'll make it." Besides, how wimpy was that? Was I some sort of delicate Northside belle who had to wait on her big strong man to come rescue her? Couldn't go out like that . . . even if I really, really wanted to.

"Okay, baby, I'm waiting for you. If you're not here in ten minutes, I'm coming for you, okay?"

"I'm there." I hung up, straightened up, and turned around. I raised my head and without looking left or right, I started for the door.

"Where you going?" The head O.G. stepped in front of me.

Damn. What to do now? What would Renee do? Bluff! "I'm leaving already, all right?"

"You was tyin' up my line. I coulda lost bi'ness 'causa you!"

"Sorry." I started forward again. He stopped me again.

"Uh-huh, now, my girl didn't like the way you was lookin' at her."

I didn't look over at her. "What girl?"

"You didn't see my girl?"

"That bitch saw me, even with her high-yella nose in the air; she seen me."

"Didn't see her. Gotta go." I stepped around him and took off. Two of his homeys were blocking the door.

"That your car?" another fly girl asked me.

"Leave her alone," a man behind the counter called out. "I done told y'all I don't want no mess up in here. Let the lady go."

They obviously respected the man, because they parted like the Red Sea. Feeling in control now, I wanted to stop and take a moment to tell them that if they focused their energy toward school and education instead of all this bullshit, maybe they could buy a Lexus of their own someday with legally obtained funds. I thought better of it, doubting they wanted to hear my public service announcement. Would probably gain a bullet in my "high yella" ass for my trouble. It was time to be out. "Thanks!" I said in general, and in record time was in the car and out the lot.

Six minutes later, I pulled up to a tall, Victorian-style house. Roman was pacing up and down a long redbrick walkway. I barely had time to swing open my door when he grabbed and hugged me as if I were going to disappear. Far from protesting, I held on for all it was worth.

"Ah, babe." His voice was deep and ragged. "I been freaking out. I imagined all kinds o' shit."

"Yeah, well." I tried to make light of it now that it was behind me. I kicked the door shut with my foot and hit the remote button. "Show me the house."

He pulled back and shot me a look. "Damn the house; we got some talking to do." He dragged me up the walk, across a lovely enclosed patio, through the front door, down a hallway, and down some stairs to a big living area. He shoved me down onto an overstuffed brown leather sofa, stepped back, and began to pace back and forth in front of me.

"Where was your cell phone, BlackBerry, GPS—something useful?" He spoke slowly with enough emphasis to let me know he was not happy.

"What? I hate BlackBerries, I forgot to charge the cell, and somehow I don't have a car charge. GPS is a waste of money—I'm *from* Dallas," I protested. GPS, indeed. Even though I'd longingly wished for one not twenty minutes ago, when it was his idea, it suddenly seemed a waste of money when you were just getting around the city you'd lived in all your life.

He stopped pacing and frowned down at me. "You know better than to roll out of the house without a charged cell phone. Why don't you have a car charger? And, yes, you may be from Dallas, but it's clear you had not a clue in hell of where you were driving. With a GPS, you would not have had to stop and get out of your car—your expensive luxury car, I might add. You hear me?" His voice rose with every syllable.

I laughed at him. "Rom—"

He cut me off. "No, Jewel. Listen. That McDonald's where you were is a major gang hangout. They deal drugs and guns through there; it gets raided all the time! Do you understand me? It was on a nationwide report as one of the few McDonald's in the nation that actually loses money. NO one goes in there for a Big Mac and fries. Are you feeling me?"

I jumped up. "I knew it! See, this is why I hate coming over here. A simple McDonald's and you have to be scared for your life!" I whirled on him. "Damn this equal-time shit. You wanna see me, bring your ass to North Dallas." As soon as it was out, it seemed like the wrong thing to say, but shit, I'd been traumatized this evening—couldn't always be reasonable, right, and politically correct. It was my ass standing smack in the middle of gangland this evening.

"You think you're safe over there in Yuppieville? Gangsters live round there too; you just don't see it on the news. Shit,

Jewel, crime is everywhere. Whatcha gonna do? Live in a fortress and never come out? Your neighbors commit crime, too, you know." He was mad. I don't think I had seen him mad before. "I can't stand a narrow-minded stereotyping hypocrite."

My eyebrows shot up. "I beg your pardon?" Hypocrite, me?

"Beg what you want. That's exactly what you sounded like. Besides, that's not the point. The point is, if you had your cell charger or a GPS unit, you wouldn't have had to stop at that McDonald's at all. You can afford it, Jewel, and it's just good sense."

I tried to defend myself. "If the guy at the gas station spoke English, I would have gotten directions from him." Okay, it was a weak argument, but I'm not one to admit wrongness easily.

He looked like he was going to be sick. "Not that dilapidated Exxon up the street from the McDonald's?"

I suddenly felt a little queasy. Ah, shit, what now? "Well, yeah."

He fell backward onto the sofa and put a hand over his eyes. "Ah Christ, Jewel, that place is mostly a crack house. Do you watch the news at all, Jewellen Rose? *Dallas SWAT, Dateline*, truTV, anything to give you a clue of the criminal element present in the city you live in?" He made me feel very stupid and very small.

Well, now I was getting mad. Was it my fault I didn't know the hood hot spots? "Yes, I watch the damn news! I just don't happen to chart the latest vice squad investigation zones or watch truTV! What the hell is truTV anyway?" Now I was pacing. When I thought about how many things I had done the absolute wrong way, I sat down next to him.

He turned to me. "Let's chill for a sec, chill, chill. I'm going off 'cause I didn't realize how naive you are 'bout shit like this. And you are just starting to realize how close you came to being a stat on the ten o'clock crime watch. Okay? Let's ease up." He took a deep breath. "First off, you gotta get a charger and a GPS. I'm not playing, Jewel." He tilted my chin up and stared me down. That look with those eyes meant no argument.

"Okay, okay." When a man like this looked at you like that, you'd pretty much agree to anything.

"Second, I want you to start spending more time around here."

"No way in hell." Okay, so I wouldn't agree to *any*thing; I had my limits.

"Yes. During the day at first, driving around, getting familiar with the streets around my house. We'll work up to nights, branching out so you'll at least know what's safe and what's not."

"No," I repeated stubbornly. I could be pretty darn stubborn. I just flat out wanted nothing to do with it. Shit, we didn't have safe/not safe spots on the Northside. At least, none that I bothered to know about.

"Equal time, Jewel. Your turf, my turf. Or nothing at all. I ain't playing." So, he was stubborn too. Great, two hardheads determined to have their own way.

"I don't want to. My turf doesn't have danger zones."

"Oh, yeah? Not two months ago, a guy in a complex four blocks from your house got raided. He was selling all kinds of shit to you uptown folk. Your precious Willow Bend Mall has recorded more crime in the last six months than any other area of town."

How did he know this kind of shit? "Oh yeah, well, those were rare cases."

"Why? Because you didn't know anything about it?"

I decided not to answer. He was right. For all I knew, there could be a meth house down the block from me.

He continued. "You know what else you get out in the burbs?" He didn't wait for me to respond. "You get the crazies:

the serial killers, the axe murderers, the psycho rapists, the kids who kill their parents, and the wives who run over their husbands. Over here, the crime is out in the street where you can see it; over there, you never know where it's lurking 'til it becomes a Sunday night movie of the week. Over here, we can roll down the street and at least I've got a good idea of which house ya best not trick or treat at. Now, which do you prefer?"

He got all intelligent at the damnedest times. Every word he said was true enough; every point he had was valid enough. But I was struggling with this embrace-the-hood thing.

"Why do you have to live over here anyway?" I tried not to whine . . . but I wanted to. I was out of my comfort zone, and I didn't like it. Never considered myself set in my ways or closed-minded, but damn, I was having growing pains with this shit.

"It's where I was brought up. It's where I'm comfortable. I like to live among my people."

I rolled my eyes. "Roman, even though you rushed me along, I got a decent look at this house, this block. This is that renovated area of Oak Cliff, isn't it? This house is huge, three stories, you said? You can't tell me that the homeys are all living this large up and down the block."

"Actually, some of these houses are owned by whites and rented out to blacks. But you're right— there is a lot of diversity around this section of the Cliff. This isn't really the hood. It's in the midst, though. I go to the grocery store and see black faces. The bank up the street is black owned; the shopping center around the corner is black owned and operated. We're working on getting another black country club off in the old Redbird area, and you know how prosperous that predominantly black area is. I like being here with black folk, Jewel."

I sighed. He made it sound so pleasant, like a community working together for the good of the race. I just sent checks to NAACP and the United Negro College Fund twice a year and figured I was doing my part. Plus, I tried to hire the sisters and brothers to work through the agency. Of course, I never tried to get clients out here on this side of town. Matter of fact, I had very few black clients. I sighed again. Just when you thought you're doing something, you found out there's more you should do. Damn, sister starting to feel a little shallow for a minute. His arms slid around me while I sat there thinking it over.

I leaned into him, knowing I was about to give in. The long and short of it was, if I wanted to keep this boy around, I had to give in on this, because it was obvious he was not going to. Granted, I wasn't sure yet if he was worth all of this changing, but at this point, I had a lot more to lose than gain by being stubborn. I would concede this point—not graciously, but I would concede.

"So, are we on? Equal time?" he whispered in my ear.

No fair for one man to be this likable, this sexy, this . . . everything. I had a sudden vision of Jaquenetta snuggled up here on the couch with Roman, and I didn't like it, not one bit. "Jaquenetta ever live here?"

He frowned at my change of subject. "Naw, she barely been beyond the front door. Maybe as far as Chase's room. I told ya, I don't cotton to having her difficult ass round much. Why?"

I smiled at him. "No reason. And, yeah, we're on. Equal time."

12

Do You Know What Today Is?

Gregory—Tuesday, July 22, 9:00 p.m.

"Where the hell have you been?" Renee was screaming like a banshee. Not a new occurrence, nor a pleasant one.

I almost stepped outside and checked the apartment number. "Mom, is that you?" I asked before walking in. One look at her made me want to turn around and go back out. She was standing in the middle of the living room in what can best be described as a paramilitary stance. She was armed with a wicked-looking spatula and a damp dishtowel. I stifled a sigh. *Welcome home, baby. How was your day*? Not gonna get any of that this evening, huh?

"Very funny, asshole. I asked you a damn question." The mood was tart.

Well, damn. I took a second to close the door, lock it, and set the alarm while trying to figure what I'd done to piss her off . . . this time. "What's wrong?"

"Now, if I have to ask you again, we gonna be in trouble. I done told you and told you how I feel about this shit. If you're playing off on me, you can just pack your shit and get to stepping." She stormed into the kitchen and started slamming dishes around.

Best strategy, I learned, during these misunderstandings with Renee was to focus on the root of the outburst and not get carried away on one of her tangents. The issue was not where I had been or if I was playing off. I had to find out what the real issue was and address that. I walked around the corner and noticed she had set up a romantic dinner for two. "Ray, I told you I had late meetings today! Why'd you go to all this trouble?" Normally, if I work late, she orders something in.

"A late meeting that lasts till nine p.m.? You must take me for a damn fool." She almost threw a crystal wineglass into the sink, and she was very careful with her possessions, me being one of them for now. It came from not having too much as a child, I think. This obsession with possessing and being possessed, so to speak. But back to the thing at hand.

"Ray, I told you! Rome got the bank involved in this new development, and the board assigned me to it, remember? I was with him at this planning meeting for hours." Establishing a firm alibi never hurt, even when you had nothing to hide!

"Uh-huh, is that right? So how come I just got off the phone with Jewel and Rome is already at Jewel's for a late dinner?" She stopped and glared at me. I felt like a trapped animal. And I was innocent!

Lord, the insecurity of this woman. You'd think since I had to come home to face her damn mercurial moods every night, just once I'd get a break. Nope. Night after night, I practically tiptoed in here, never knowing who I might find. Penthouse Pet of the Month or Doris Day or Attila the Hun or Medusa. Tonight, it was the jealousy theme again. Ever since her little friend Tammy came over here attempting to throw her stuff in my face, I have been treated to this delightful possessive side of Renee's personality. At first, I had to admit, it kept things exciting.

That air of mystery, that fascination with figuring out all the facets of her personality. Fighting madly, then making up wildly, that kind of thing was a high for a minute or two. Now I was just about at my limit truthfully. I gave anyone, especially a woman, the right to be moody from time to time, but from hour to hour? So why was I still hanging in here?

I had a couple of reasons. Valid, well-thought-out reasons. One, the down times. Those times when she was open and sweet and just plain Renee. At those times, I felt like she understood me and I understood her better than any other two people in the world. I felt like we fit. Two, the sex. Weak, I admitted to myself. It wasn't as if we invented it and I couldn't get it anywhere else. Just that it was perfect. Okay, not 100 percent perfect, 100 percent of the time. But if it was 200 percent damn near 80 percent of the time, I didn't mind if it was 75 percent the other 20 percent.

The same thing that drove me crazy about Renee out of bed was the same thing that drove me out of my mind in bed—those rapid mood changes. There was something about slipping under the covers with the good girl only to find out she was a porn star in disguise or vice versa.

And the other thing keeping me here? Me. Renee still made me feel something I had never felt before. You might notice I hesitated to call it love. That was only because I wasn't sure I had a good concept of what that truly was supposed to be. Women have said they loved me, but I never felt loved by them. Some of my boys said they had fallen in love, but I never noticed anything loverlike in their actions. In my parents, I saw that affection and mutual respect and an overall sense of ease with each other. But I thought you'd get that with almost anyone you spent forty-two years day in and day out with, right?

Some people said that when you meet the Person, the One, you would just know. Well, when I met Renee, I knew I had to get with her, but I wasn't thinking forever. Then we started spending time together, and I stopped thinking short-term and starting thinking long range. Like instead of days, I thought weeks. Now adjusting to months. But forever? Till death do us part? I wouldn't swear to it.

What I did know was that whatever I felt for her was strong enough for me to stand here and take this shit. So here I stood, trying to answer her stupid question about why Rome made it to Jewel's before I made it here. After a long day like this one, I was all out of witty comebacks. "I guess he drives faster than I do."

She tossed the spatula in the sink. "You just full of little jokes tonight, huh?"

I tossed my briefcase in a chair and took off my jacket. "If you say so, honey. What's for dinner?"

The look she sent me would have frozen water at twenty-five paces in August. "You didn't eat?"

I shrugged. "They served sandwiches at four-thirty or so. I'm starved. Any calls?"

She threw her hands up and stomped back to the bathroom. I could hear her running water into the tub and muttering under her breath. I decided it was best to let her cool off. I dialed up the voice mail and listened to a message from my mother, her mother, my brother, Tammy, and Aaron. Nothing that could have set her off and nothing that had to be returned tonight. I opened the fridge to scan the leftovers. Hey, shrimp and pasta? A cheesecake from my favorite bakery and champagne? What was the occasion?

Oh shit! I went over to my briefcase and took out my BlackBerry. I flipped through the calendar to today. Damn! Three-month anniversary of our first date. Renee was hell about anniversaries like this. Anniversary of our first date, first time we slept together, day I moved in . . . it was never-ending.

But see, I was actually prepared. I figured, this one was a pretty big anniversary for us, seeing as I wasn't sure we'd make it three days. I thought the big day was tomorrow, though. If we go by day of the week, it *was* tomorrow. But if we counted numerical dates, like actual ninety days, damn—today.

I walked back to the bedroom. She had a navy teddy laid out on the bed. Oh yeah, I had to redeem myself. She was bringing out the big guns, and I wasn't here to cock 'em, so to speak.

As I said, though, I was prepared. Flowers are going to be delivered tomorrow to her office, and the present was in my briefcase. Maybe if I broke out the present now . . . I stood in the closet plotting, seriously. What to do, what to say? Within seconds, I had a plan.

I stripped down to my boxers before grabbing the champagne and two glasses from the kitchen. On my way back to the bathroom, I put the *Best of Luther* CD on repeat, took the phone off the hook, and doused the lights. I lit a big candle and stuck it in a holder. I grabbed the present—hadn't wrapped it yet anyway—and headed to the bathroom. I reached in and clicked off the lights.

"What the—?" Renee called out from that huge tub. "Gregory?"

"Who else would it be, Ray?" I walked in, leaving the door open so that Luther could be properly appreciated. Luther never fails as a wingman. I put down the lid of the toilet and set the candle down. I placed the champagne and glasses beside the tub, tossed my boxers aside, and climbed in.

"Greg!" How she could sound shocked after all we had done to and with each other was beyond me. Of course, we'd never done the tub before. And it was plenty big enough for the both of us.

"Um-hmm? Man, you think you got this water hot enough?

Trying to boil a brother up in here." I eased down behind her and pulled her toward me. She was stiff and resistant, but I ignored that. When she was flush against me, I reached over and picked up her present. I put the thin platinum chain around her neck and adjusted it so that the diamond heart hung properly. I fastened it in back and kissed the side of her neck. "Happy anniversary, baby. I love you." Damn, but I'm smooth and I'm almost sure I meant it!

She went absolutely still for a second before looking down at her chest. I gotta say, diamonds look good by candlelight on my baby. "Oh, Greggy." She sighed and relaxed against me.

Ha! I'm Greggy again. Tell me I didn't know women . . . this woman! And here came the ultimate follow-through: "Sorry I didn't call and tell you how late the meeting was gonna run." Sometimes you had to man up and apologize even when you've done nothing wrong.

She shimmied around in the water and wrapped her arms and legs around me. "It's okay." She leaned forward and kissed me in one of those slow and sexy ways she had of telling me it's about to be *on*. "Wait a minute," she said when we came up for air.

"What?" Why did women always want to talk at the weirdest moments? Listen, I was in a hot bubble bath with Luther singing, candles flickering, champagne chilling, and a crazy fine woman wrapped around me, I had nothing more to say.

"I got you something too," she whispered, backing away for a minute.

"Oh yeah?" I smiled and pulled her back.

"Yeah."

"Well, why don't you give me a little something right now and the other thing later, hmm?"

"Oh, Greggy." She giggled. "I love you too. You're so crazy."

Crazy like a fox. Maybe I understood this love thing after all.

Times like this made you forget all the others. I knew it was going to be a while before we drank that champagne, and the candle was a goner. I'd have to heat up the pasta thing later on. Luther was singing "Here and Now" as she pulled my lips back to hers.

13

Love (or Something Like It) Is in the Air

Jewel—Saturday, July 26, 8:10 p.m.

After spending every spare minute of the last month and a half with this boy, I thought I knew him pretty well. Not intimately, but well enough to feel his vibe. Which was why I knew something was different today.

Something had been off with Roman all day. Oh, he was still Roman and all, but different. Haircut this morning—he didn't tease the old barber like he usually did. Just sat down, got the cut, and left. During hoops at the gym, he didn't slam dunk or sky hook, not once. No Air/Shaq/KG moves at all. Didn't talk any trash. At lunch with the gang, he let Renee get away with all kinds of little snide comments he usually never let slide. Didn't tease me for ordering a fried chicken salad with diet dressing and a diet drink.

Then we went to the mall and I tested him. Dragged him into the bookstore and read the backs of at least twenty romance novels before just picking one. He usually hated that! He just stood there, no comment.

And the weirdest thing, he actually offered suggestions in Victoria's Secret! Normally he walked over to the sports store while I bought more underwear that I didn't need. (Mom always said you can never have too much!) Anyway, he came alive and starting picking out stuff. Racy stuff too. Purple lace teddies and hot red garters and a scandalous sheer black nightgown. He actually asked me my size and bought that sheer black thing. We weren't even sleeping together yet and he bought me this thing.

I wished he could have seen himself. This big, tall man dressed in denim from head to toe standing around in Vicki's flipping through negligees as if his life depended on it. And before you ask why we weren't sleeping together yet, I didn't really know. Wasn't like I was being prudish or saving myself. We had the new millennium talk about being protected and AIDS-free and all that, but that was it. I assumed we were waiting—for what, I didn't know, just waiting! It was actually kind of refreshing. One less thing to worry about for now, if you asked me.

Now back to this mall scene. After we left Vicki's with two hundred bucks' worth of truly recreational lingerie, he lapsed back into this apathetic state he had been in all day. He had been social but quiet. Preoccupied, almost like he'd rather be somewhere else. Almost like he didn't really care.

At first I thought it was Chase. Jaquenetta took Chase with her on vacation, so Roman had to skip this weekend with him. But I asked him and he said he was used to Jaquenetta changing the schedule on him, and he'd get three extra days with Chase over Labor Day weekend.

The last straw was the frozen yogurt stand. He hated frozen yogurt. Said you should just eat ice cream and be done with it. But when I walked him over there, he ordered a double scoop of chocolate in a waffle cone! I walked to a booth and sat down, not believing he was actually going to eat it. He dug right in like it was the finest Häagen-Dazs available.

So I just came straight out with it. "What's wrong with you?"

"Nuthin'." He finished the cone in record time, never looking at me.

"Something's wrong; you've been strange all day."

"Oh yeah? Hmm." He reached over and tossed the napkin in the trash.

I rolled my eyes and came to the point. "Almost like you don't want to be here."

He looked at me finally. "I'm cool."

"Roman, you hate yogurt," I persisted.

"So?" He picked up a section of newspaper someone had left at the table.

"So. you just wolfed down a jumbo cone of it."

He looked surprised. "Ah, well, it was all right, I guess."

"Roman, you can bullshit anyone else you want, but come straight with me. If something's up, just let me know."

"Jewel, ya know you're the woman. Quit trippin'." He flipped a page.

"What's that *mean*?" Sometimes, I swear, we had a whole conversation where he meant one thing and I thought another.

"Ya know, you're definitely the woman. Like implying, ya all right with me. We cool and all." He folded the paper in half and kept reading.

That sweet way he had of laying things out clearly just warmed me right up inside. So warm I wanted to snatch that paper out of his hands and smack him right across that chiseled jaw. "Roman LaChayse." I learned that tone from Mom. That no-nonsense, I've-had-quite-enough-of-this tone.

Now he rolled his eyes. "Just got something on my mind. Let it go." He put the paper down.

Well, now I was insulted. If I had a bad day, he would wheedle and cajole and nag until I shared every tiny detail of it with him. Now I was supposed to just let it go? Uh-huh. That was how we gonna work this relationship now? Okay, then, maturity gone. I could play this just as cool as the next person. "Fine. Ready to go?"

He frowned at me. "Now what's wrong with you?"

I smiled at him. "Nothing, you ready?"

Still frowning, he shrugged and stood up. "Sure. Did you get everything you came for?"

"Most definitely," I lied, but I wasn't staying there another minute. I stood up and took off walking.

He caught up to me and grabbed my arm. "Thought you said you needed a new outfit to wear somewhere?"

I tugged my arm away. "Did I? I really have enough clothes. Let's go." I kept walking. When we got outside, I stopped to shove on my sunglasses even though the sun had set. Mid-July and it was hot as hell. I hated to see what August and September were going to be like this year. Roman stood silently beside me, watching me. "Where'd we park?" I asked without looking at him.

He sighed deeply, as if pained, and started forward without a word.

I didn't care. I was still peeved at this double-standard bullshit. If I have a problem, it was, "Talk to me, Jewellen. Share with me, Jewel. What's on your mind, Miss Jewel? We in a relationship; we should be able to *talk* to one another." The lecture was on in full effect.

Today, he had an obvious case of the ass, and all I got was, "Let it go." What happened to the "equal time" he was always going on and on about? As if it wasn't hot enough out here, now my temper was boiling too.

We got into the car and he drove the five minutes back to my place. I got out quick, not really expecting him to come in. So, of course, he did. I went upstairs to put my stuff away and, of course, he followed. I opened one of my drawers to put away the socks I just bought when he tossed the Victoria's Secret bag at me.

"Wanna put that somewhere?" He stood there with some sort of amused look on his face.

I could think of a place I'd like to shove it, I thought. Instead, I opened the bottom drawer and dropped the whole thing in, bag and all, before kicking it shut. I stood by the dresser tapping my nails on the surface. Ever just want someone to be gone from you? Just away. Not in your space right at that minute.

"Gotta problem?"

Brilliant deduction, player. "I'm cool." I smirked at being able to throw his words back at him.

He came over and yanked off my sunglasses and tossed them on the dresser. "I can't read your expressions with these things on."

"I can't read yours either!" I yanked off his and tossed them right alongside mine.

He looked at me for a second and smiled. "I'm going to the video store." He turned away and headed for the stairs.

"So you're coming back?" I asked him.

"Where else would I go, Miss Jewel?" he answered on his way down the stairs.

Home, I thought evilly. Take your sometimey attitude and roll on back to where you came from.

"Want me to pick up something to eat for later?" he called from the hallway.

I looked at the clock on my dresser. It was already close to nine o'clock—how late did he plan to hang around in this present mood? "I'll probably just snack, but you can pick up something for yourself,"—paused—"if you're going to be here that long."

He laughed and shut the front door.

I guess he was planning an extended visit. He'd stayed the night before, and I'd stayed over there a time or two, but never when he was acting this funky. Besides, this sleeping together without actually *sleeping together* was getting on my nerves.

I took a long, hot, soothing shower and changed into shorts and a T-shirt. Calm again, I was pulling my hair up into a ponytail when the phone rang.

Thinking it was Roman calling from the video store, the calm fled and I punched the speaker button and answered rudely, "Yeah, what?"

"Jewellen?" Stacie's voice was confused.

"Hi, Stace, sorry. What's up?"

"I was calling to see if you were going to make church tomorrow? You sound like you could use a little religion." She laughed.

"Yeah, girl, I thought I'd try. Why, what's up?"

"Well, I'm trying to get everyone together so we can go over the wedding plans."

"Ah, it's about that time, huh?" Nobody but Stacie was enthused about this damn wedding.

"Yeah, we got the church for the second Saturday in August. Lucked out, really—someone else canceled."

"How sad. I wonder who." How horrible to cancel a month before the big day. I knocked on wood that something like that never happened to me. Course, at the rate I was going, I needed not worry about marriage plans anytime in the near future.

"Yeah, well, whoever's loss is my gain. Can you make it?"

"I'm back!" Roman bellowed from the front door before slamming it shut. *Goody, His Moodiness returned. Let the peasants rejoice.* My, I really was testy this evening!

I switched over to the handset and headed downstairs. "I'll plan on it." The phone beeped. "That's my other line, Stace. See you tomorrow." I stood in the kitchen and watched Roman unloading all kinds of junk as I switched over. "Hello?"

"Jew-Ro, I'm in love," Roni Mae sang across the line.

I smiled. "Is that right. Who's the lucky man?"

"Who do you think? Aaron Too Fine Paris, that's who!" she squealed, and launched into a lengthy explanation of how this love thing came to be. While she chatted, I hit the MUTE button and glared at Roman.

"What is all that crap?" He had about four bags of groceries.

He smirked at me. "Thought I should keep some stuff I like to eat over here. You know how I hate all that nasty fat-free, low-calorie shit."

Now he was moving food into my fridge? An hour ago, he told me to "let it go." Now our food was cohabitating. I switched the MUTE button, "Girl, I'm happy for you."

"Thanks, girl. You know what else he did?" she started up again. Muted her again.

"So, uh, you're moving food in all of a sudden?" I asked suspiciously.

He ripped open a packet of microwave popcorn and looked at me. "Got another problem?" I didn't care for his tone. At all. Shit, I could have an attitude if I wanted. It was my house, my kitchen, and . . . shit!

"Maybe I do. Hold on a sec." I held the phone back up to my ear and unmuted. "You know, girl, this all sounds so good—why don't you tell me again tomorrow at Stacie's thing." I listened for a second. "Uh-huh, tell me that too. I gotta run; something's about to boil over up in here. Okay, bye."

I slapped the phone down on the counter. "Seems to me you sure are making yourself at home up and through here."

He took out a bowl and two glasses and set them on a tray before answering. "Yeah, that's true. But, hey, I want you to do the same over at my joint, okay?"

Here he goes with the hip-hop again. Before I could think of something else to say, the damn phone rang again. I started to ignore it when I noticed how irritated he was about it, this being the third call in a matter of minutes. Just to be contrary, I snatched it up. "Hello?"

"Jewel?" A male voice I didn't recognize was asking for me.

"Yeah?" I glanced at the phone screen: *Private Number.*

"Hey, how are you doing?" The voice was more familiar, but I couldn't place it yet.

"Okay, how about you?"

"You have no idea *who* this is, do you, honey?"

Only one person ever called me honey like that. Almost like an afterthought. "How could I forget you, Patrick?" I laughed at my ex-boyfriend, okay, seriously, ex-fiancé. Don't they pick the darnedest times to call? Patrick and I were real tight back in the day. I thought he was it. I was sure he thought I was it, too. That was before his ex-girlfriend came along and he realized she was it . . . still. Everyone said I should have fought harder for him, and maybe I should have, but that was not my thing. I was knocked out of the ring the minute the ex turned up with that I'm-so-sorry-I-miss-you-so-much mess.

To my way of thinking, if a man was into you, he was not going to be into anybody else. You know, kind of that whole Bernie Mac philosophy: "Who ya with?" I was not about to go all *Grey's Anatomy* and tell Patrick to "pick me." He tried to play the both of us off each other, and when he realized I wouldn't play, he went back to what was easy. And I was left alone and more than a little disillusioned.

In the long run, I think my mom was far more broken up about it than I was. Lord knew my mother loved him as if he was part of the family. Hey, the way I figured it, what was for you, was for you. Speaking of which, I couldn't help but think Patrick's timing couldn't possibly be worse.

"You know, I was thinkin' that very same thing about you, darlin'." That Georgia drawl hadn't faded one bit. Typical man—call up all out of the blue like they hadn't done you wrong without a "sorry" or a "my bad." *AND* expect to have a nice civil conversation with you like nothing ever happened. Well, I could be a mature grown-up (sometimes). Patrick was once very important to me. I could at least see what he wanted. With Roman acting any old kinda funky way and currently staring me dead in my mouth, I couldn't resist playing along a little bit.

I laughed softly. "Oh yeah?"

"Yeah, I was thinking about that time I brought you home with me and we spent the weekend holed up in that hotel in Atlanta before going up to Valdosta. Remember that?"

"I remember lots of things, Patrick." Couldn't help but let that edge slip out. Wouldn't pay to let a brother think he got off scot-free. There were still reparations to be made.

"You never did beat around the bush, honey. Susan's gone, been gone for a while, and I was wondering . . ." He trailed off hopefully. Of course he was wondering.

Decided to ignore that whole slippery slope. "Where are you?" I asked out of curiosity.

"Wingin' my way back to you, of course. I'm in the Atlanta airport on my way to Dallas for six months or so. See if I still have a chance at a few things." Did he say six months? A chance at what?

I stood there with my jaw open until the microwave timer went off. I jumped and looked over at Roman, who was still looking all up in my face. Hands on his hips, scowl on his face. It occurred to me that this was not the best time to play this game. I had a good idea of what Patrick wanted and needed no witnesses. Might want to keep Roman on his toes, but I was nobody's fool!

"Really, you don't say?" I answered, trying to be cool, turning my back on Roman. I heard him snatching the popcorn out of the microwave and pouring it into a bowl. He slammed the bowl onto the tray and went into the fridge for something.

"Would I lie to you, sweetheart?" Patrick drawled.

I snorted. "Don't go down that road, Patrick. You really don't wanna go there." I heard them announcing flights in the background. "Listen, you've got somewhere to be, and I've stuff to do . . ."

"So why don't I call you when I get settled in and everything. Probably Monday, okay, honey?" Mighty proprietary for someone who left skid marks on my heart as he vacated the relationship with alarming swiftness.

"Yeah, you just do that." I didn't add more. For one, I didn't want Patrick to read much into my words, and for two, I didn't want Roman to read much into my words!

"Lookin' forward to seein' you, Jewel. I really, truly am." No doubt.

"Bye-bye now." I hung up the phone in a hurry and clicked the ringer to OFF. I twirled around to face Roman. His expression said it all. I shrugged. "What?"

"Patrick?" He raised a brow and set two wineglasses onto the tray with a tad more force than was absolutely necessary.

"An ex." I could be as short and unrevealing as he was any day. I tossed a couple napkins onto the tray. Oh, I was so not in the mood to have this conversation with him tonight. The trip down Memory Lane of Significant Others Past was always fraught with pitfalls.

"And?" He glanced up from opening a bottle of chardonnay.

"That's it. Ex." I couldn't let the opportunity pass. "Like Jaquenetta, right? Ex."

He laughed. "I gotta hand it to you, Miss Jewel. You do know how to get your li'l point across." He looped a plastic bag over his arm and picked up the tray. "Course, when I mean ex, I mean as in no longer an issue, you follow?" He turned toward the living room.

"I'm right behind you," I quipped.

"You know what I mean. Let's watch these upstairs." He headed for the stairs. I clicked off a lamp and followed him up.

He set the tray down on the chest at the foot of the bed and extracted three movies from the bag on his arm. "Take your pick," he said, and extended the movies to me, a funny look on his face.

I hoped he wasn't going to turn moody again. I took the DVDs and read the titles. My head popped up and I stared at him. "You trying to tell me something, player?" The movies were *Let's Make Love, Wild Orchid,* and *She's Gotta Have It.* I sensed a theme. Of course, I'd be a damn fool not to.

He put his hands out innocently. "What? That day when we talked 'bout movies, ya said ya liked Marilyn Monroe, Mickey Rourke, and all of Spike Lee's movies. And the video store was out of all the good new releases."

"Um-hmm." I had never seen *Wild Orchid,* actually, but I'd heard a lot about it. I noticed that this was the unedited version as I took it out of the case and pushed it in. Roman clicked off all the lights, and I swirled around to look at him. What were we playing now?

The arms came out again. "What? It's better to watch movies in the dark, Jewel." *Better for who? Better for what?* I wondered as he took off his shoes and stretched out across the bed on his stomach with his head toward the TV. He reached over the foot of the bed and grabbed some popcorn with one hand. With the other, he patted the space beside him. "Come on over, babe. Get comfy." It suddenly occurred to me just what had been on Roman's mind all day.

"Um-hmm." I picked up the remote and stretched out beside him. I had just gotten to the point where I could be around him without my hormones jumping up and sprinting away from me. I was just settling into this "let's wait" mode, and here he went changing the script.

Don't get me wrong—the hormones still jitterbugged around a lot. But I felt like I had them under control. As long as he was over there and I was over here, I wouldn't disgrace myself by drooling over his body.

I distracted myself by picking up the remote controls. TV, audio, DVD—I clicked everything on and waited for the movie to roll. Fifteen minutes into the film, I knew I was in trouble of disgracing myself. A big Brazilian man was having his way with some exotic-looking woman, or maybe she was having her way with him, but however you call it, it was hot. Very hot. The heroine of the movie came across these two people in the midst of a freak fest against the wall of a dilapidated building and couldn't tear her eyes away. I knew how she felt. Finally, it was too much for her and she ran away. Again, I sympathized.

Lord, was it warm! Roman had inched closer to me (or had I inched closer to him?). The heat coming off his body didn't help. The minute the scene changed, I sat up and yanked the cord to the ceiling fan to start that baby whirring. Then I reached forward and grabbed the wineglass Roman had put on the tray for me. I took a long, deep swallow.

"Too hot in here for ya, baby?" Roman asked in that maple-syrup voice.

"A little toasty," I answered without even cutting my eyes in his direction.

"It's a hot night." He glanced over at me. I could feel him giving me the old once-over with those eyes.

"Yeah, hotter than normal," I murmured, still never taking my eyes off the screen. The poor girl kept having flashbacks of what she witnessed. Before she could get it under control, along came Mickey Rourke. She was a goner. I slurped down that wine in no time flat.

During the next steamy scene, Roman's hand rubbed up and down my spine. As if it wasn't already tingling. He touched me and that was it—I was ready. More than ready. Mighty ready. It had been a hell of a long time for me. We're talking over a year. I thought back for a minute— yeah, over a year. It was Patrick, speak of the devil. Anyway, all I knew was, if Roman was ready, I was ready. Truth be told, I'd been ready and willing since he fell on top of me two months ago.

I shot him a glance out of the corner of my eye. Yeah, really ready and shamefully willing. This time, it was me who inched closer. He shifted to lay on his side facing me but kept his eyes on the screen. I did the same. He trailed a hand down my arm; I trailed mine along his neck. He traced the outline of my thigh; I traced a bicep. He took the barrette out of my hair and fanned his fingers through it. Thank God it was clean and manageable today.

"Want another glass of wine?" he whispered as they tried to stuff a vague plot in between the sex. I did notice that Roman had used that whisper as an excuse to inch closer. There weren't too many inches left.

"Hmm? No, thanks." I could barely speak. The next steamy scene came too quickly. I had no recovery time from the last one.

Roman and I had run out of relatively neutral zones to trail and trace. The scene was a wild one, with the heroine watching Mickey urging and coaching a couple on lovemaking in the back of a limo. I imagined the cut version was short and sweet. This version left nothing to the imagination and the places those zoom lenses could go.

Roman reached beneath my T-shirt and unsnapped my bra. It was a front snap, and my poor breasts had been crying for freedom. They practically jumped into his waiting hands. I bit down on my lip as he skimmed his thumbs back and forth across the tips. Wouldn't do for me to start howling at the moon. My fingers grazed along his chest, and I started opening his shirt buttons.

He tugged at the T-shirt lightly. I could take a hint. I whipped it over my head and pitched it aside. The bra was just as quickly disposed of. His shirt followed along. Still, both sets of eyes remained on the movie. The heroine was having a little fling with some guy who thought she was a prostitute. Hey, Mickey told her to go for it. I was pleased to hear Roman's breathing get a little louder. I did hate to pant alone.

He slid his hand down my spine to the small of my back and applied subtle pressure until my hips were pressed against his. My hips were intrigued. They pressed forward curiously.

His belt and the button fly were in the way. I shifted back for a minute and fumbled around till I undid the belt.

"Don't ever wear this complicated thing again," I teased, and was surprised at how breathless I sounded.

"It's history," he muttered. His voice was deeper than I'd ever heard it, almost gravelly. I loved it. He tossed the belt aside.

I undid one button. It was hard to do this stuff without looking. But it was an interesting sensation relying on the sense of touch alone. I paused because Mickey and the heroine were having a little tiff. That was okay; Jacqueline Bisset in a supporting role was going to entertain us with a naked nubile native she just picked up. After the second button, I couldn't resist reaching inside to cop a feel. Silk boxers. Packed and straining silk boxers—wow. I was so impressed, I lingered for a while, rubbing, cupping, squeezing, stroking, teasing.

"Jewellen, just finish up with the buttons, hmm, babe?" His voice was strained.

"Oh yeah, those." I grinned in the darkness and made short work of the last buttons.

"Find anything down there you like, Miss Jewel?" He growled the words deep in his throat as he pulled the jeans off and flung them over the side of the bed.

"Nice drawers," I teased, snuggling up closer to him. He lifted one of my legs over his and wrapped his arms around me. I couldn't help it. I had to groan a little. My breasts came up against that solid chest, and every impressive inch of him was so very close to exactly where I needed it. Did I mention that I was really ready?

But Roman was still watching the damn movie, so I watched too. Finally, Mickey tells the heroine his life story and she's so moved that, lo and behold, her clothes melt off and they get their share of bed-time aerobics going. Good Lord, when they said unedited, they meant it.

"Look, baby," Roman said. As if I could take my eyes away.

Color me naive but it looked to me like they were really doing it, no movie magic involved. Especially, right . . . there! Roman shifted against me, and I had to bite my lip again. "Whatcha thinkin'?" he asked.

It must be my cloistered upbringing or my inner prude, but I just couldn't bring myself to say that I wished he'd do to me what Mickey was doing to her. And I wished he'd do it quick. So I said nothing at all. The movie finished and the credits started rolling.

"Maybe that looked pretty interesting, huh?" He rolled us over until I was on my back, and he was above me. He held my arms out by my head and leaned down as if to kiss me. Instead he flicked his tongue across my lips. Over and over. I made a muffled little sound and tried to pull my hands free, but he held fast. "I wanna hear it, Jewellen."

"What?" My brain was struggling, what with my oxygen going short and my blood rushing around to a hundred other places.

"Every li'l sound, every li'l moan, every li'l demand you make."

I stared up at him blankly. What was he asking me?

"You're gonna totally let go with me; I'm gonna totally let go with you. Good manners ain't got no place in this bed. Two people who love each other ain't got shit to hide." He returned my stare.

Total silence. Then the DVD clicked and started ejecting with a mechanical whine. I shook my head. Did he say *love*?

He squeezed my hands. "I just said I love you, Miss Jewel. Whatcha gotta say about it?"

Whatever well-bred restraint I had broke free. I ripped my hands from under his, dragged his head down to mine, and kissed him like my life depended on it. Hell, maybe it did. I rolled over until I was on top and kissed him until I ran out of breath. Long, deep, and sloppy. Finally, I lifted my head and looked down at him. He looked dazed.

"Christ Almighty, I love you, too, Roman. It's really soon, I mean quick, but . . ." I shook my head. Damn, I guess I've gone and fallen in love with the boy. "I'll be damned if I don't love you, boy." I leaned down and kissed his neck, his chest, and was working my way down to those silk boxers.

He grabbed me and lifted me forward. He held me so that my breasts hung right over his mouth. When he took one in his mouth and started to suck, I not only moaned, but I wailed as well. I tried to dodge away, because I knew I wasn't going to hold out long, but he held me suspended in the air like a rag doll. When he switched to the other breast, a thousand points of light simultaneously burst inside me. I flung my head back, shrieked for all it was worth, and went right over the edge.

He laid me down on the bed and rolled back on top of me. "Aw, babe." He sounded tender.

I was still all aquiver, but I opened my eyes and smiled lazily. "You *did* tell me to let go." Like I said, I was really ready.

He grinned that proud I've-satisfied-my-woman smile. "You took me literally. I love it—I love you."

He leaned down to kiss me, and I yawned. "Sorry, I'm all done in."

He rotated his hips against mine, and my knees came up automatically. "All done in, huh?" He kept that light circular pressure going.

I groaned again. "Maybe not."

He shifted back and slid a hand down into my shorts. "No drawers? All them drawers ya always buying and ya don't wear 'em?" His index finger was searching, searching . . . um, he found it and he was killing me softly.

"I just don't"—I gasped as he changed the rotation of that long, thick finger—"wear them to bed."

"So tell me something, Miss Jewel." His other hand slid back up to my breast.

"Um." My hips were doing the twist. He was a talker. I'd

heard about these guys but never been with one who wanted to chat while conducting sensual warfare.

"Do you prefer li'l swing bys or deep circles?" There was a wicked glint in those amber eyes.

"What?" What the hell was he talking about?

He stripped my shorts off and inched my legs apart. He placed his finger back where it had been and started a truly devastating staccato cadence. Back, forth, back, forth, really quickly. "Li'l swing bys, Miss Jewel."

"Oh, my." Sorry, it was the best I could do. My mind was melting along with the rest of me.

Then he switched to a pressurized rotation. "Deep circles." He paused for a second. "So, which is it?"

"Both," I ground out. I was going to have to retaliate for this out and out assault of my poor sex-starved body. Later.

"Let's try something else." Before I could ask what he meant, he bent his head to me while at the same time inserting a finger inside. The minute his mouth touched down, it was all over for me.

"Roman!" I screamed, and went down for the count again. This time, instead of drifting back down, I was in an agitated high. Enough of playtime, I wanted him, inside, now. As soon as I had enough breath, I yelled at him, "Okay, let's hit it."

He looked up in surprise. "Huh?"

Working on adrenaline and over a year of deprivation, I literally flipped him onto his back and stripped the shorts off of him. Reaching over to the nightstand, I pulled out a condom and quickly got it on him. Wasting no more time, I climbed aboard, took him inside, and commenced to rocking.

"Jesus, Jewel," he ground out, trying to catch a hold of me and slow me down.

I wasn't having it. I scratched his chest, nibbled at his lips, tickled his inner thigh, anything I could think of. Soon he was moaning along with me and bucked his hips up with each one of my downstrokes.

He wrapped his arms around me, and we tumbled around so we could take turns being on top.

"Do you feel it, baby?" he asked me during a stretch when he was on top and making me crazy with impossibly slow and easy movements.

I felt every blessed inch. "I feel it."

"So tell me something."

I moaned. "Oh God, Roman, not now."

He stretched out full length over me, still buried deep. "Short, quick thrusts or long, deep strokes?" He went on to demonstrate both.

"I'm going to kill you, boy." I rolled back on top and swiveled my hips around, clenching down a little.

"Ooooh, Jewellen Rose. At least I'll go with a smile." He grabbed my hips and moved them the way he wanted. Good thing I agreed.

Finally he shut up for a second so I could concentrate on the business at hand or wherever. My hair was plastered to my head, and sweat was streaming down his brow. I could tell I was about to go off again. I whispered to him, "Go with me this time."

That did it. He managed a kind of jackhammer hip flurry before we both peaked.

It was long, long moments before we could move. I was sprawled across him in reckless abandon, listening to his breathing.

"Good choice of movie, honey," I whispered, and listened to his laugh rumbling up through his chest.

"Yeah, but I didn't get to use any of my props."

I lifted my head and looked at him. "What props?"

He grinned. "I planned to rewind the movie and rewatch it. I was going to seduce you into acting out some the better scenes with a few variations."

"Variations?" I slid off of him and sat up.

"Yeah, I brought some whipped cream, some honey, and some jelly beans up here."

Now, I was fully sated, mind you. It was only my curiosity that was aroused, really. "Jelly beans?" Where had the boy picked this stuff up? He was only four years older than me.

His grin was wickedness incarnate. "You gotta lotta catching up to do, Miss Jewel. Might as well start tonight." He picked me up and held me while he stripped the comforter off the bed. Then he laid me out, hit the PLAY button on the remote, and reached down for his bag of tricks.

"Oh yeah?" My breath quickened just looking at his fingers wrapped around the can of whipped cream.

"Oh yeah, and, uh, Miss Jewel?" He started shaking it.

"Hmm?" He sure was one for conversation.

"I don't think you're going to make early service at church tomorrow." He popped the top and took aim.

14

Clearing the Air

Roman—Sunday, August 8, 4:00 p.m.

I should have said, "No thank you, baby—you handle that." But when asked by Jewellen if I wanted to come to a lunch with Patrick, I was thinking with my testosterone and not my gray matter. So what came out of my mouth was, "Oh, I'll be there. You just tell me when and where."

So now I was stuck. Sitting in an Italian spot with Jewellen by my side and Patrick walking in. I was a really uncomfortable spectator to a tragic scene that should've played out years ago.

Patrick Waters was, by my first impression, an overgroomed pretty boy badly in need of having my size 12 shoe placed squarely in his hind parts. He strolled in fifteen minutes late, wearing a pink polo shirt, khaki pants, loafers, and a smirk that I was looking for an excuse to wipe off. He was light-skinned, under six feet, and wore a watch on his arm that cost more than my first car.

He walked straight to Jewel, sparing me a half-assed glance, and kissed her on the lips. My girl's lips. To her credit, she dodged him and he hit mostly cheek. "Jewellen Rose, you're as lovely as ever." Georgia drawl. "Mother sends her love. She always thought highly of you." Mama's boy. "You brought backup?" He finally acknowledged my presence.

"I brought a witness." She smiled at me. "Roman Montgomery, Patrick Waters."

He extended a hand. "Pleasure to meet you."

I stood up and shook his hand. "What's up?" Tightened my grip just a touch before releasing and sitting back down. Casually, I threw an arm across the back of Jewel's chair. Watched his eyes take in the whole scene, the body language and the vibe. He raised a brow; I nodded slightly. He heard me, mouth tightening a little as he sat down across the table from us.

"So, Jewel, I guess you're comfortable saying what it is we have to say to each other in front of your friend here."

Uh, uh, uh. Boy was starting off on the wrong foot. Jewellen's slight smile disappeared, and her head tilted to the side. Uh-oh.

"Patrick, I don't have anything to say. You are the one who wanted to talk. So, yeah, you can say it in front of my man."

He exchanged a look with me. I remained expressionless. Brother was on his own.

"O-kay . . . let me start with an apology."

She smiled without humor. "Only two years late but, sure, what are you apologizing for?"

He shifted in his seat. "Treating you so poorly."

"And?" she prompted.

"And lying to you," he acknowledged.

"And?"

"Leaving the way I did?"

She pounced. "So you're not even sure what you're apologizing for?"

I held my face in check and winced inwardly. Girly was clearly not in the slack-cutting business.

Patrick looked down at the table. "Jewel, I know I made a lot of mistakes with you. I deserve your wrath. I'm sitting here in front of you and your new man. Can you just let me say my piece?"

She looked at me, and I shrugged. "Go for it," she said.

"I loved you, Jewel. I wanted to marry you."

"Uh-huh," she drawled.

"I was just so overwhelmed by what I was feeling for you that—"

She cut him off. "Let me see if I understand. You gave me an engagement ring and went back to your ex-girlfriend four weeks later. Now, nearly two years later, the best you can come up with is the old I-was-scared-so-I-sabotaged-it routine? Seriously?"

"Saying my piece, Jewel?"

My brows went up. I had to give the brother a little credit. Here he was, wrong as hell, and he still wanted to be strong about it. Not the smartest move but he had brass ones. Jewel gave the go-head-on motion with her hands.

"When I realized I had made a mistake, I tried to come back. I tried to make it right, but you weren't even answering the front door. The next time I came by, you had moved out and no one would tell me where you'd gone. I figured you didn't care enough to put it back together, so I gave you up. But now . . ."

My head popped up. Say what now?

Jewel said, "I'm sorry, what about now?"

"I'm ready for you. I still love you."

Before I could even flinch, Jewel put a hand on my arm. "I got this, babe." She fixed a stare on Patrick that I never wanted to see pointed at me. "Okay, Patrick. I met with you because I wanted to see if you were sincerely sorry for the raggedy shit you did, if we could just agree to let bygones be bygones and move on. Thanks for the memories and all that. Anything else is non-negotiable."

"I am sincere. I'm sincerely sorry, but I'm also sincere about wanting another chance."

Okay, the boy had *big* brass ones. I, for one, had heard enough. "Jewel, may I?" She nodded and I leaned forward. "Um, lookie here, friend. You had a shot, and you blew it. You want another shot? Stand in line. It forms behind me. Good luck moving up. We're out." I stood up and held my hand to Miss Jewel. She took it and stood with me.

Patrick said, "Jewel? Is this what you want? You want to just leave it like this?"

She didn't even pause in her stride. "You heard Roman—get in line."

I squeezed her hand . . . my girl.

15

Less than Twenty-Four Hours Away

Renee—Friday, August 13, 7:00 p.m.

Friday the thirteenth, wouldn't you know. Trust and believe, this marriage felt doomed from the get-go. First off, Oliver Salisbury was just about the whitest white boy I had ever seen. And Stace? Oh, she liked to act like she was on the vanilla side of the black scale, but deep down, I believed she was more ghetto fabulous than the rest of us. On the surface, she was the first one to talk about reverse discrimination, the Rainbow Coalition, and equality for all. But peel back a layer and there beat the heart of a little Black Panther in the making.

Just wait until one of his friends slipped up and called her something slap-worthy. Or started a sentence with, "Black people always . . ." Oh yeah, just wait for that. I guess I sound prejudiced, huh? No, no, not at all. I got along with white folk well enough. I really did. I just thought a black man should be with a black woman and vice versa and that was that, period. I mean, come on. We came in all different shapes, sizes, and shades. If you want a white girl, why can't you just find the lightest sister with light eyes out there? You want something exotic? How about a sister from the Caribbean? Or Brooklyn?

Same goes for the women—they could find what they wanted right here within the race.

But as if all of this wasn't enough, here it was, the night before the wedding and it was raining. Supposed to rain all weekend long. Now, I didn't go for that voodoo stuff, but this was a bad omen. Even I understood the omen of torrential rain on your wedding day. Hardly seemed like God's way of smiling on you, now, did it?

On top of all that, Oliver had only one friend close enough to be in the wedding, so Stace had to come up with the groomsmen for him. So here we were: me; Greggy; Jewel; Rome; Roni Mae; Aaron; Tammy; Stace's brother Kenneth; Keisha; Arthur, a real cute little white friend of Oliver's; Stace's little sister Marie; and of all people, Patrick . . . as in Jewel's *ex*, that Patrick. Of all the people in the world, that was who Stacie picked to be the extra groomsman. She said she couldn't think of anyone else on such short notice. Shit was gonna get funky up in here, you mark my words.

This was the rehearsal dinner from hell. The bride and groom argued all through the rehearsal, the minister had a nasty head cold, Aaron and Roni Mae weren't speaking to each other for some reason, and Roman was about to commence to swinging on Patrick. Keisha had already blamed Arthur's ancestors for keeping hers in bondage. Kenneth, recently divorced after a whopping eighteen months of marriage, was hardly pleased to be here, reminded of all things matrimonial. Stace's dad still wasn't speaking to her for marrying a "milktoast with no ends" (translated to "white boy with no money"), and her mom had been nervously hustling us through dinner so we'd be gone before Pops got in from league bowling night.

"So, we don't have to stay long, right?" Gregory asked me for the fourth time in as many minutes. Why men always get so nervous at weddings? Looking like disciples at the Last Supper and shit.

"Till the bitter end, baby." I grinned at him. "Besides, things are just getting interesting, don't you think?"

Gregory glanced around the room. "Remind me, baby—we're eloping."

Hold up! Eloping? As in marriage? My eyebrows shot straight up. "Did I miss a proposal?" My expression said "Gotcha!" and I waited for his answer—eagerly awaited. Marrying Greggy fell right into my scheme. Here was one discussion I was ready to have.

He was saved from replying, because at that moment, Stace burst into tears and ran from the table.

"Lord have mercy, what now?" Jewel, the maid of honor, sighed, speaking my thoughts aloud. She looked over at me and I got up. As if choreographed, all the girls got up from the table and followed Stacie. Jewel stopped at the door and looked back at Roman. "Don't do anything to embarrass me while I'm gone, player."

Roman rolled his eyes and reached for another corn-bread muffin.

Stace must have felt like a cornered turkey on Thanksgiving morn. We were all circled around her in the living room. She stood in the middle of the room weeping, and we hovered about her like vultures circling an expiring carcass.

"So, what's the problem?" Jewel questioned, cutting to the chase as usual.

"So, do ya love 'im, girl?" Keisha asked.

"Really love him?" I repeated.

"Like you can see yourself with him for the next thirty or forty years? That's what I'm trying to find out," Jewel pressed.

"Does your mouth water looking at him?" Tammy added.

"How could her mouth water looking at Oliver?" I couldn't resist. Like I said, he looked white, he talked real white with a British accent, he walked white, and worst of all, he thought white—no flavor whatsoever. Still asked things like, "Why don't you want your hair to get wet?" So unacceptable.

"What's the mouthwatering got to do with any damn thing?" Roni Mae asked. "Your mouth can't water for the next forty years. Shit." Roni Mae and Aaron must've had a big fight. She was sounding a wee bit bitter.

"And mouth water don't pay no bills," Keisha added.

I tried to put it plain. "I guess what I'm asking is, are you sure you're doing the right thing?"

Stace looked scared shitless. "I think so." She was wringing her hands and refused to look any of us in the eye. Poor Marie was only fourteen; she looked kind of shell-shocked by this conversation. Let it be an early lesson to her: men were hell. White, black, purple—hell, every one of 'em. But then again, they did have their uses.

Jewel got that I-can't-believe-this-shit look on her face and took a step closer to Stacie. "What do you mean, you *think* so? Listen, girl, if you've gotta single doubt, speak NOW. Tomorrow at three it's 'til-death-do-you-part time."

"Shouldn't be no *I think so's* this late in the game, girl," Keisha argued.

"I know, I know!" Stacie shouted. We all jumped. Stacie never raised her voice. Ever.

Jewel took her arm and dragged her over to the sofa. She pretty much threw Stacie onto the cushions. "What's the problem?"

Stace finally looked up. She looked like she was going to cry . . . again. "I guess I love him. He treats me like a queen most of the time. No one has ever treated me like he does."

"So?" Roni Mae prompted.

"So, I still feel like something is missing." Her voice was so faint; we had to strain to hear her.

"What?" Keisha asked. "He's got some money, right?"

"Keish," I scolded, "not everything comes down to dollars and cents."

She snorted. "Easy for you to say, Ms. Moneybags." Keisha thought anyone who made over $10.00 an hour was rolling in it.

"He's not rich, if that's what you mean," Stacie answered. "Probably never will be, but we'll get by."

Inwardly, I cringed at the thought of going into a marriage thinking we'd just "get by." Hell, if I wanted to just "get by," I'd stay single.

"Can he fu—" Tammy caught herself as she realized we were in Stacie's parents' house and a minor was present. "There are no sexual problems?" she edited tactfully.

"Tammy, please," Jewel snapped before sparing a smile for Marie. "Hey, Marie, can you run upstairs and look for the Extra Strength Advil?"

She fled like a death-row inmate granted a reprieve.

After she left the room, Stace laughed. "Sex is all right. I've had better; I've had worse."

Again, I mentally winced. *Sex is all right*? What the hell was the point of marriage if not finding all your fantasies wrapped in a bow and tying them to you for life? If she was only getting all right sex, at least the boy should have some bank behind him.

"Well, what about the next forty years? Do they look good with him?" Roni Mae had shaken off her mood to ask an intelligent question.

"I guess so, but he's not sure he wants kids." Leave it to Stacie to break out the major revelation less than twenty-four hours before the nuptials. Damn.

"You once told me you would be happy with a man who just loved to travel and wanted tons of kids," I reminded her. Someone had to point out the obvious.

"Lemme guess, he don't wanna travel neither?" Keisha asked snidely.

Stacie put her head down again. I guess that meant no. I

glanced at Jewel, who looked alternately pissed off, then worried as hell.

"Let me see if I can get this right. All this time you've been with Oliver, all we've heard about is how right, how perfect he is. Now, almost eighteen hours before you are divinely connected in a holy ceremony with this guy, what am I hearing? What's so right, so perfect about him? He wants no kids, the sex is so-so, you're not sure you love him, he doesn't wanna travel, and y'all are going to get by on your public school teacher's salary and whatever it is Oliver wants to be when he grows up? Am I missing something?" Jewel snapped out impatiently, giving in to the irritation.

Stacie jumped up. "He treats me like a queen, I said! Like everything I say is important, like I'm the most important thing in the world to him."

"You are the most important thing in the world to him—you're his food and shelter for the next forty years." It came out before I could stop it. Everyone looked at me, and I refused to take it back. That's how I read the situation and that was that.

Stacie started to cry . . . yes, again.

"Aw, shit," Tammy said, and put her arm around Stace.

Jewel rolled her eyes. "Stace. I hear what you're saying behind all of this. Your parents have done a good job of ignoring you for the past twenty-nine years, and all your major relationships have left you feeling like you weren't important to anyone. Deep down, I know you know that's not true. Now, if you're only marrying Oliver because he puts you on a pedestal, don't do it. If you're only marrying Oliver because black men have trampled you and you don't trust them anymore, don't do it. If you're only marrying Oliver because you don't want to start all over and look for someone else, don't do it. But if you really love him, can't imagine not spending the rest of your life with him, feel absolutely comfortable with having him as your lover and best friend forever more, go for it and to hell with everything and everyone else."

Stace had stopped crying, but she still looked scared as hell. "How long do I have to decide?"

Jewel visibly bit her tongue and shot me a look. I shrugged back at her. I figured I'd already said too much, but I was dying to say that she'd had the last year and a half to decide.

Roni Mae smiled. "Seems to me like you got 'til tomorrow at three."

Roman—Friday, August 13, 11:40 p.m.

Stace and Ollie brought the wedding party out to a club instead of doing separate bachelor/bachelorette things. Personally, I didn't think Stace trusted his ass . . . couldn't say as I blamed her. Bad enough that a fine sister was hooking up with this little white boy, but he ain't 'bout shit neither! I could see it if he had a little something on the ball. My guess was he must be putting it to her pretty good, 'cause otherwise I just didn't see the appeal. Boy was bringing nothing to the table as far as I can tell. Program was raggedy, not the most thoughtful or well-bred dude, the résumé was tired, and he had NO game—he *must* had to be knocking it out the box.

Anyway, we'd been here since eleven, and I was just 'bout ready to call this evening a night. First off, it was old-school jam night. Their idea of old school was songs from the early nineties! Now I got this damn Patrick yanking my chain. We met a couple weeks ago, and I felt it was my place to pull him to the side and hip him to the real, ya know? Let him know that, ah, whatever little plans he had for him and my Jewellen Rose, he could deep-six 'em. I thought he was feeling my vibe, but the brother just seemed to wanna step incorrect on this.

Here we were at the club, and whatcha think was the first thing he did? Goes and grabs Miss Jewel from right under my arm and waltzes her out on the dance floor. I wasn't one to play that shit. I'd've called him on it, too, but he'd been jocking every girl in the joint, even Stace. So I said to myself, *Okay, Rome, chill. Brother just activating his little player card, nothing personal.*

Now I look up during the last little step he cut with Miss Jewel, and what did I see? His hand wandering a little farther south than needs be. Some negroes just made you act a damn fool. Now here I had to go handle business.

Soon as they came off the floor, I grabbed Miss Jewel, went back on the floor, and wrapped her tight. Soon as she relaxed against me, I leaned down and let her know, "Okay, so you either put him in check or I'ma shut it down for you."

"He's just trying to stir up something. If he comes around again, I'll back him down, big boy." She smiled up at me.

"Um-hmm, 'cause I'm done with the nonsense now." I just wanted to be clear. Like I said, not possessive but I had my limits.

Miss Jewel tilted her head back and laughed. "That your way of saying you've had all you can stands and you can't stands no more, Popeye?" She slid her hand around to the nape of my neck and started doing a little tickling thing she knew gets to me every time . . . every damn time.

Forgot what I was kinda pissy about and grinned down at her. "You tryin' to start a li'l somethin' somethin' out here, Miss Jewel?" I slid my hands down to her hips.

She arched her back some and looked up at me through her lashes. "And what if I am?" She slid a hand up my thigh. This was one of the little things I really dug about Miss Jewel—she came across all proper and serious, but truly, baby had a wild side! Always teasing, playing, and joking. I never knew when she would just break loose with something semi-scandalous. I liked that.

"Oh, you wanna play now, huh?" Damn some Patrick. Started thinking it was really time to rise up outta here so me and baby could have a party of our own.

"Ready, willing, and able, player." Hey, I didn't have to be asked twice. As I was scouting quick escape routes to the parking lot, she leaned forward and kissed—naw, licked—down the side of my neck and back up.

Oh, it was on. It suddenly occurred to me that Miss Jewel had imbibed a few glasses of bubbly. I began to wonder how many. 'Cause, Miss Jewel was kinda reserved in public. She didn't like to draw too much attention, wasn't really one to advertise her relationships. A little hand-holding, a peck on the cheek. Pretty much minded her own and expected everyone else to do the same. So imagine my surprise when the beat picked up and Miss Jewel took a step back, threw her hands over her head, and commenced to jammin'.

"Seriously?" I asked her with a smile. Were we getting down like THAT tonight?

She flung her head back and smiled. "Seriously."

Not her regular style of dancing, which was more like a sedate Sade sway with a neck bop. Naw, Miss Jewel was cutting loose. The song was Ludacris's "Money Maker," and she was doing it justice. She stepped to me, turned around, backed her butt up against me, and shimmied all the way down to the ground. Hot damn, did she just drop it like it's hot?

She turned and went to bumping and grinding on me. She tossed her hair, threw that chest out, and looked straight at me. "Can you keep up, player?" Well, hell. What was a man to do? I grabbed her hips and we started rocking.

"Get it, girl!" Keisha came out on the dance floor with Arthur, quickly going into her video-girl mode—not PG-13. Jewel and I stopped for a second to watch before getting back into it. Arthur was actually keeping up, which was no small feat. Considering Keisha had called him a "limey cracker" earlier in the night, they seemed to be getting along real well. Arthur was a lot more down than Ollie, who was sitting in the corner sucking on another beer. Nothing says classy like getting quietly sloshed at your prewedding party.

Patrick came out on the floor with Stacie, and if I were Oliver, I'da ganked his ass. I thought Jewel and I were gettin' a little nasty, but it was nothing compared to Stace and Pat. They were downright raunchy. I never knew little Stace had it in her. She did some move where she kicked her thigh up while gyrating her hips forward.

Jewel snickered. "Oh my!"

Renee came out with Greg, took one look at everyone, and leaned over to Jewel. "You all right, girl?" She started doing a quiet little side step. Yeah, right.

Jewel grinned at her and turned her head back to me. "Renee ain't foolin' no damn body—she's about the wildest dancer you've ever seen. Skipping and jumping all over the place with that ass stuck way out. I guess she's trying to hide her wilder side from Gregory."

I looked as Greg put his arms out on either side of Renee and started to rocking up against her. "Greg's got her number."

"Oh yeah? 'Shake, shake what ya mama gave ya.' " Jewel was singing along to the music.

I thought I'd sing a verse too. " 'You lookin' good in them jeans. Bet you'd look even better with me in between . . .' " Granted, the lyrics weren't Shakespeare, but the beat was slamming.

"Is that right?" She sent me one of my favorite smiles. The one that says it was about to be on and popping.

The song changed to an old Jay-Z tune, so we kept dancing. For an uptown girl, she got some ghetto taste in music. We danced the next three before they played something random, and we headed back to the table. I threw an arm around Jewel as we sat down. "We leaving soon, babe?"

She swigged the last of the champagne in her glass and smiled at me. Leaning toward me, she whispered in my ear, "Got somewhere else you'd rather be?"

Times like this when I just wanna wrap this girl up, take

her home, and never let her out. I tipped her head up and dropped a swift kiss on her lips. "Yeah, definitely got somewhere else I'd like to be."

She pulled my head back down and laid one on me. We were still going after it when Renee and Greg came back.

"Hey, black people, get a room!" Renee said.

That girl sure knew how to spoil a moment.

Jewel pulled her head back and smiled. "Romeo and I are . . . Wait a minute, what's the phrase? We 'bout to rise up outta here." I grinned down at her, she was so cute when she was trying to be hip.

Renee's eyes went wide. "You can't leave now. The bride is still here. You're the maid of honor. We need to stay with Stacie! And God knows, someone's gotta watch her."

I started to say something, but Jewel put a hand on my arm. "Damn, Renee. She's got a fiancé, an older brother, and quite a few friends here; she can do without me for the rest of the night."

"Oh, and he can't?" Renee motioned to me. She had a real funky-assed habit of talking about me as if I wasn't two feet from her fake ass.

Again, I wanted to say something. This wasn't the first time that Renee's raggedy 'tude got on my nerves. Greg must've sensed that I was getting ready to get on that ass, 'cause he looked at me and spoke up. "Ray, baby, chill out. Let a black man and a black woman be in love, huh?"

She spun around to look at him. "But, Greg, she's the maid of—"

He looked her straight in the eye. "Ray, sit down and leave it."

She sat. I ain't lying—my mouth fell open. So did Jewellen's. We both looked at Gregory with a new respect. He winked at us and sat down, offering Renee a glass of champagne as he dropped an arm around her.

"He's got her ass in check and on lockdown, don't he? That's what I'm talking about. Handle your woman, bruh!" Aaron said from the table behind us.

I winced. I may have thought it, I might even have applauded it in my mind, but would I have *ever* uttered the words aloud? Hell, no.

Jewellen and Roni Mae turned to Aaron at the same time and said, "What did you say?"

Poor Aaron sat, trapped by the angry beams of their glares. I tried to look as invisible as possible. Times like this when women turned on men as a species. I was trying to disassociate.

"What did he say?" Renee tried to jump on the bandwagon. She was ignored.

Roni Mae went off. "See, that's why I've 'bout had it with yo' triflin' ass, Aaron Paris. What kinda shitty thing is that to say? To think? Like you tryin' to keep somebody in check round here? You tryin' to run somethin'? You think *your* sorry ass got *me* in lockdown?" Ah hell, some shit was about to jump off.

Aaron looked nervous. "Veronica, don't front. Chill 'til we get home, babe. And we'll talk about it there."

"The hell we will." Roni Mae got up and dug some keys out of her purse. She looked at Jewel and Renee. "I'm out. One of y'all see that Mouth Almighty gets a ride to his own damn apartment." She looked out toward the dance floor, then over to Oliver. "And, Oliver, could ya please put that damn beer down, get off ya apathetic ass, and peel ya fiancée off ya groomsman?"

Oliver jumped and looked up to see that Stace was indeed wrapped around Patrick. Like I said, beatdown would have been in full effect twenty minutes ago. He walked over to the edge of the dance floor with his beer still in his hand.

"Roni—" Aaron started, but she threw a hand out.

"Do not go there with me, boy. Later." She rolled outta there in no time.

"Let's shuffle, doll," I told Jewel, and she nodded.

"Renee, do something about that." She waved a hand toward her ex and the bride-and groom-to-be. They were all in heated discussion in the middle of the joint. I noticed that Patrick still had an arm around Stacie. See? Just wrong.

"Later, G." I shook hands with Gregory as we walked past. "Renee." I nodded politely. Madere raised me well, as I truly wanted to shoot her the finger.

Jewel and I waved at Tammy, who was off in the corner with some dude she just met. When we walked outside, I grabbed Jewel's hand and sighed. "Glad to be outta there, baby. Bad shit was fittin' ta happen."

She nodded. "Ain't it the truth?"

We strolled in silence for a minute before coming to a standstill. Leaning all up against my car were Keisha and Arthur. Had their tongues deep in each other's throats. Hands all over unmentionable parts. "Ain't this some raggedy shit?" I muttered to Jewellen. Jungle fever all over the damn place. Folks wilding out in public places.

"Hey, wanna ease up there for a minute?" I raised my voice.

Arthur lifted his head. "Oh my God." He was gasping for breath, and his face was bright red.

"He can't do nuthin for ya right now, Artie. You and the fly girl carry that on to another car so Miss Jewel and I can roll on to the crib." Arthur took Keisha's hand and started dragging her away.

Keisha looked at Jewel. "Girl, don't tell no one whatcha seen, swear?"

Jewel shrugged. "Shit, girl, I'm not your mother. You've been over twenty-one for a while now, huh?"

"I mean it, girl. I'll never hear the end of it."

Jewel looked at Arthur, who wasn't about to let go of his newfound chocolate treat. "Whatever, girl. Go on and handle your business like you want."

"Yeah, but—"

I had to nip all this in the bud. "We got shit to do. Y'all keep it real. Let's move." I damn near lifted Miss Jewel into the Pathfinder.

"Tomorrow at one, your place?" Keisha called.

"Yeah!" Jewel said as I slammed the door shut. I started the car and backed out of the lot quickly. "You're driving like a man with an agenda, Romeo."

" 'Shake ya money maker like somebody 'bout ta pay ya . . .' " I reminded her of the Ludacris lyrics with a little grin.

"We're gonna have to do more than that, player." She was working that tone of voice.

I almost ran a red light. "Oh, yeah?"

"Might have to break out some props." She grinned.

My foot got real heavy on the accelerator.

16

Holy Wedlock, Batman!

Jewel—Saturday, August 14, 3:08 p.m.

You know how in a movie you get a sense of impending doom? That feeling that something was about to go horribly, terribly wrong? I glanced around and felt the tickle of unease again. A director could not have set the scene better.

Suspense was building as Stacie refused to tell anyone what happened between her, Patrick, and Oliver last night. Today, she was quiet, subdued, and ill at ease. Beyond a terse, "Let's do the damn thing," she hadn't had much to say. Personally, I think that approaching your wedding with a let's-do-the-damn-thing attitude was less than optimistic, but I was keeping my mouth shut.

Renee had been cheerful to the point of annoying, Roni Mae was practically catatonic with depression, Keisha seemed more nervous than the bride, and Tammy was Tammy, gleefully sharing the details of last night's conquest with anyone who would listen. Unfortunately, the only person listening was little Marie. This weekend alone will probably scar the child for life.

As for me, I'd like nothing better than to forget this whole wedding thing and go home. Hey, sister girl was in need of some serious nap time. Roman and I might have topped our personal best as far as the sexual frolicking scorecard went. True, I had been a bit tipsy, but, really, that just added to the experience. Came home, put my old-school Chante Moore's "Sexy Thang" on repeat, lit some candles around the living room, and had a funky good time. Last I thing I could remember, he carried my limp body out of the shower at around 3:00 a.m. That boy could do things that I never . . .

Sorry, off track. I was explaining the scene here. The first thing I should have said was that while I was doing all this thinking, I was standing in the vestibule watching everyone walk down the aisle. Arthur and I were set to go next, then Stacie and her trifling father. I hated to speak ill of anyone's folks, but he had been argumentative, hardheaded, bitter, and difficult from the day I met him over twenty years ago. Sad to say, today was no different.

The rain that let up a little last night was back with a vengeance. So strange for August, when we're usually begging for rain. Didn't I read somewhere that rain on your wedding day was like God crying for you or something?

I've always had this fairy tale in my head of what my wedding day would be like. Simple, elegant, everyone smiling and happy. Sprays of flowers. Me in a beautiful dress with some beautiful groom at my side. Family and friends welled up with joy. Sunshine beaming in—you know, that whole Cinderella-glass-slipper thing Disney messed up our heads with. Looking around—this wasn't it.

Anyway, it was my turn. I turned to Arthur and smiled. Since I saw him plastered against Keisha last night, we've been real at ease with each other today. He was a good-looking guy, a little pale but tall and well built, with curly black hair and the same little British accent that Oliver has, however, on him, it sounds natural, not affected. You would think I didn't like Oliver. Well, shit, I kinda didn't but if he was what Stace wanted . . . Actually, that wasn't even it. Basically, it wasn't going to be me waking up next to his plastic, superficial ass, and it was way too late to change Stacie's mind. I was a friend to the bitter end, damn it. As she so eagerly said not so long ago—let's do the damn thing.

Okay, we're walking. I looked up the aisle and saw Roman grinning like I was walking for his entertainment purposes solely. I grinned back. He winked and mouthed, "You go, girl." Straight stupid, just as crazy as a loon. Just the other day, I was thinking that he might just be it for me. Yes, IT. Could be the One. Let me put it like this: If he's not IT, I really don't know what it is. Sorry, my mind keeps wandering!

I turned, stepped into place, and looked. Music cued up. Audience rose to feet. Bride entered. Audience oohs and aahs. She did look gorgeous. Was it normal for her to be shaking like a leaf? So much so that she looked ready to pass out. Residual hangover maybe? I looked over at Oliver. He looked pretty sickly too. She stopped before him and a loud ominous clap of thunder rolled above, shaking the church. I was waiting for the creepy organ music to pipe in. Jesus, was this happily ever after or a horror flick?

I glanced over at Roman. He smirked and shook his head. Reverend Moss cleared his throat. Did I mention the good rev was sick? Caught some cold bug and had been wheezing and sniffling all over the place. Before the rev could instruct the father of the bride, Stace's dad lifted Stace's arm and shoved it at Oliver before stepping back to his pew.

"Lord have mercy," Renee muttered behind me, and I had to resist kicking her.

Reverend Moss frowned, coughed, and began. "Friends, we are gathered together in the sight of God and man to witness and bless the joining of Stacie and . . . *achoo!* Oliver in Christian marriage. The covenant of marriage was established by God, who created us male and female for each other . . ."

I tuned him out. I had been to so many weddings, I could recite the ceremony verbatim. This was my second time as maid of honor, though. First time was for my sister. Now, she and her husband had a "love thing" if ever there was such a thing, and they still struggle to make it work.

That was probably one of the reasons why I was so concerned about this marriage. If I really thought it was the best thing for Stacie, I'd be overjoyed. But I've seen marriages fall apart that had a whole lot more going for them than these two.

And that whole Patrick thing last night? Unbelievable. When Patrick came back to Texas, he hit the ground running in dogged pursuit of me. But Roman was no dummy. I don't know how he did it, but I've been so wrapped up in him, I couldn't think straight, let alone think of any other guy. Didn't really even want to. Why blow a good thing? The grass was *not* always greener. Particularly grass I had already trod upon.

When Pat saw that it was nothing doing, he slipped into this "good friend" role. Fine by me. Of course, Roman didn't like it, but what could he do what with Jaquenetta popping up like the proverbial bad penny every time I turned around? I've spent some quality time with Chase, making sure he understood that I wasn't a threat to his time with his dad. Not trying to take his mom's place but hopefully establishing a role that balanced friendship and authority. But try and explain it to Jaquenetta's threatened ass. It was worse than trying to talk Stacie out of marrying this joker.

I wanted to say that last night and all the soap-opera-like shit that went down was just a wild and rare episode with everyone overindulging in champagne and overcome with prewedding jitters. But I still had this feeling. And it didn't bode well at all.

"In the name of God, I, Oliver, take you, Stacie, to be my wife, to have and to hold, from this day forward, for better, for worse, for richer, for poorer, in sickness and in health, to love and to cherish, till death do us part. This is my solemn vow."

All eyes turned to Stacie. In a shaky voice, she repeated her vows. The pastor signaled me and Arthur to step forward with the rings.

"These rings are the outward and visible sign of an inward and spiritual grace, signifying to us the union between Jesus Christ and his church."

Stacie and Oliver swapped rings with more vows and walked over to the unity candle. Oliver picked his up and it went out. Stacie lit his with hers, and they lit the big one in the middle. When they turned to come back, thunder rolled again, a blue-white streak of lightning zagged directly over the church, and the air went still, then thick, humid, and staticky. An angry thunderclap boomed, shaking the entire structure and rattling stained-glass windows and wall hangings. The large middle candle tumbled off the holder onto the carpet. Renee gasped audibly as we stood watching.

The meager flame must've brushed a flower petal on the way to the ground, because the entire silk arrangement of white roses and purple irises was blazing. Naturally, a flame-ridden flower fell to the carpet where the candle wax was pooling and ignited another fire. In fascination and horror, we all stood and watched the fire jump onto the long train of Stacie's gown. Funny how you never think of flame-proofing a wedding gown until an instant such as this.

"Stacie, look out!" I managed to gasp out.

She whirled around as the fire swept up the train. She screamed and started spinning around in circles. Which only caused the material to wrap around her, bringing the flames closer. The audience saw the bride running around like a Roman candle and commenced to shrieking and panicking. Gregory was closest to her, so he threw her on the ground and started stomping on the dress and rolling her around. Roman ran to take care of the sparking flowers, and Patrick grabbed the urns of ceremonial water and starting dousing her with them. Oliver stood there with his mouth open.

Stacie looked up at me from the floor with wet hair falling

into her eyes, her veil askew and a charred, and her dripping train wrapped around her. Our dazed eyes met for a brief eternity before I saw it coming. I snickered, couldn't help it. She put her head down before throwing it back to roar with laughter. After a brief moment, when I was sure everyone thought we were crazy, quite a few people joined in. The reverend shifted from foot to foot, torn between concern for Stacie and concern over his scorched pulpit area.

"Have you ever seen the like?" Roni Mae asked me.

I tried to answer but I was still laughing. Finally, Stacie put a hand out. It was Patrick who helped her up. She flashed him a charming smile, despite the circumstances. "Thanks, Trick." My eyebrows flew up. Trick? I shot Tricky Rick a narrow-eyed look and he shrugged.

Stacie unraveled the train, brushed her hair out of her eyes, and faced Oliver. She smirked at him. I knew the smirk—it meant trouble.

"Are you okay?" he asked belatedly.

"Peachy." She rolled her eyes. She looked down at the band on her finger and pulled it off. "Here, baby, this ain't gonna happen."

A collective gasp from the audience. Sighs of relief from the bridesmaids. Grunts of disgust from the groomsmen. Muttered prayers from the pastor.

"Stacie Ann!" Her mom was flabbergasted.

"Mom, God sent me floods, a burning bush, and baptism by fire and water. Do I really need another sign?"

I giggled again. It did sound downright biblical.

"I say, what God has put asunder, let no man join together." She laughed. "But I do feel in the mood for a party." She looked at me and raised a brow.

I stepped forward, reading her mind. "No need for all that food and entertainment to go to waste. Why don't we all go over to the Westin and celebrate the . . . uh . . . the . . . ah . . ." I looked at Stacie.

"The first day of the rest of my life." She snatched the veil off and tossed it to her mom. "Save that for me, will you, Mother?" She put an arm out for Patrick. "Trick, shall we?"

She recessed out with Patrick, and I followed with Roman. Renee and Gregory were fast on our heels. Would you believe that the sun was shining when we stepped outside? Yeah, I thought you would.

17

Do NOT Burn the Ribs

Roman—Sunday, September 8, Noon

Miss Jewel slammed the wooden spoon down and turned to glare at me. "What're you implying, Roman LaChayse?" She put one hand on her hip and tapped her left foot impatiently.

She sounded just like Madere with that tone. Even worse, I've heard her take that tone with li'l Chase. Still, I stood my ground. "All I'm saying is, seem to me like you ain't too happy 'bout Stacie bringing Patrick. I'm wondering why that is?" Truth be told, homegirl has been tripping over this whole Stace/Trick thing. The two of them have been a duo since the wedding-from-hell weekend. In the beginning, Jewel was like, cool, whatever it took for Stace to get through. Then, when they kept hanging tight, her attitude started getting a little tart.

She looked at her watch. "My mother is going to be here any minute and you want to talk about Stacie and Patrick?" She went over to the refrigerator and took out some barbecue sauce. She could get real busy when she didn't want to talk about something. She already had two bottles of barbecue sauce out.

"Yeah, I happen to think now is a perfect time." I stepped around the counter and began seasoning a platter of chicken.

"Did you start the coals?" She stirred the beans on top of the stove.

"Are you jealous 'cause Stacie's sleeping with the love of ya life?" There, I threw it out in the open. Let her break that on down.

"Who said he was the love of my life?"

"Overheard Renee and Tammy talking to you. Yeah, I started the coals, and I noticed you didn't answer my question." Now, I hadn't thought Patrick was that big of an issue. Was there something I needed to be worried about? What was really going on?

She turned and looked at me. "Love 'em though I may, Renee and Tammy aren't the best sources of truthful information. Want to put out the ribs first?"

Jewellen Rose was a master in the art of verbal tap dancing. I really wasn't trying to have it today. Particularly hated it when she ignored me like I was stupid. "Jewellen, don't push me."

"Pardon me, player, but I've got twenty people due here any second. Could I get some help?" She turned her back on me like she was dismissing a damn servant. "Check and see if we've got enough chairs around while you're out there. And check the heat in the pool, could you?"

"That's how we're getting down today?" I turned away, went outside, and slapped a slab of ribs and some chicken quarters on the grill. Because I was still too pissed to continue the conversation, I poured the bags of ice into the two igloos and started loading 'em up, one with sodas, the other with beer and wine coolers. I was pouring potato chips into a big bowl on the back porch when Jewel came out.

"I'm doing it again, aren't I?"

"Doin' what, Jewel?" I was going to man up on this one.

Cut her no slack. Be ruthless. Don't let her get to you. Stoic, silent, let her do all the talking.

"Treating you like—"

Stoic went out the window and I cut her off. "Like I'm your amusing li'l playmate from the ghetto? Yeah, you are. Acting like I won't realize you can't answer a direct question? Umm-hmm, you are. Pretending that my concerns aren't valid? Definitely. Let me set some shit straight here, Miss Jewel. If all you wanted was some corporate thug for stud services, a li'l excitement, you really shoulda said something a lot sooner. So, what, is it like a bonus 'cause I'm what you consider respectable? Gotta degree, a business, little bank, house of my own. Am I supposed to be honored you giving a brother the time of day? You gotta know it's not gonna work that way."

"Well, damn, Rome, where's all this coming from?" She looked confused. "Is this all about Patrick, because if so—"

"Did you love Tricky Rick, Jewellen?" I stepped closer to her. I wanted to see every expression cross her face.

She looked away. "At the time, I guess—"

I wasn't having *that* half-assed shit. "Either you did or you didn't—don't give me that North Dallas psycho shit. Come clean with a straight answer for once, for Christ's sake."

"Okay, I did. I did, okay? It has nothing to do with you and me. That's in the past. " She walked over to me.

"Is it?" We stood toe-to-toe.

"Is Jaquenetta?"

I scowled at her. "Now, every time we get in an argument and you get into a tight spot, you throw Jaquenetta up in my face. Okay, I was married and I have a child. I won't start apologizing for that. I never said I was a perfect knight in shining armor. I'm just me—either it's enough or it isn't."

She waved her hands all round the place when she was angry. Right now, she looked like she was directing traffic. "And I never said I was a damsel in distress. I'm supposed to just ignore the fact that Jaquenetta exists, is that it? She had your ring, your name, and your child, Roman. I can't forget that."

"You're jealous? Of Jaquenetta?" This was new. Never occurred to me that she'd be jealous of something I considered history.

"I'm NOT jealous. I just find it hard to ignore, that's all."

"I never asked you to. But I divorced her. I told you where I stand with her. Can you do the same?"

"She was your *wife*. Patrick was just a *boyfriend*."

I look right at her. "He was a *fiancé*. Someone you considered spending the rest of your life with. I'm *just* a boyfriend." Bingo, baby.

She huffed in frustration. "You know what I mean."

"No, I don't. Whadaya mean? Help a brother understand." The way I saw it, six months from now, she could be having this conversation with some other brother talking about me. I needed to know what was different now than with Patrick. Why was she still all secretive and flustered about this boy? What was it I didn't know? What was it about me that made it different? Yeah, a brother was trying to find out where he stood. Been around too many times before to take things like this for granted.

"What're you getting at? What're you asking?"

"All I ever asked was to be with you and have you be with me." Simple.

She threw her hands out. "I am with you!"

"One hundred percent, Miss Jewel. I want all or nothing." Mind, body, and soul.

"But you know I love you!" She was missing my point—deliberately, I thought.

"You love me like you loved him? 'Cause you let him walk away without a fight or a look back. You say you love me, but I wish I knew why and for how long. Hell, I wish *you* knew why! You act like you are surprised to be with me. Like you are just along for the ride."

Her mouth fell open and she looked scared. "Roman!" she whispered in a shaky little voice.

Anger or no, I couldn't help it. It was the Y-chromosome knight in me, reaching out to that damsel in distress. I wrapped my arms around her and drew her close. "What, Jewellen?"

"You're scaring me," she mumbled into my neck.

"You're scaring *me*, babe." I ran my hand down her back.

"This is the first time we've talked about this stuff, and it sounds like you're leaving me." She clutched my shirt and looked up at me. "Are you leaving me, Roman?"

I took her chin in my hands. "No. But I'm not sticking around for some bullshit. Let me be clear. I love you. Either you know who or what you want or you don't. And if I feel like you don't, I'm out. Out. Do you hear me?"

She shook her head. "I hear you. But we're okay, right?"

"We're okay for now, baby. Sooner or later, you're gonna have to answer the hard questions." I pulled back and started to turn away. "I've gotta finish setting up out here." This was obviously as much as we were going to get settled for now. For the most part, I liked to just go with the flow, you know? Like Madere says, "Let go and let God." But other times, like today, I needed to know whether I was standing on shaky ground or not. We might not have completely settled anything, but she knew where my head was at and I'd learned a little bit more about her insecurities too.

"Wait a second." She pulled me back and stood on tiptoe. She wrapped her arms around my neck and kissed me. It was different, searching and kind of desperate. I pulled back as she tilted her head away, and I opened my eyes. She blinked her eyes open, and my breath caught in my throat. Swear to God she had tears in her eyes. My Jewellen, always so strong, practical, together. Nothing broke this girl down.

I stared as the tears started running down her face. She was crying over *me*, a regular brother from the other side of town. Not that I thought I wasn't worth a tear or two but not from this lady, who always kept her head high and her fears hidden. Opening up was something she did rarely, usually late at night or if she'd been drinking. To see this . . . this hurt, to know I was the one to cause her this pain. And it kind of threw me, just how much I cared.

"Aw Jesus, Jewel." I groaned and kissed the tears off her face.

"I don't want to lose you. Don't let me mess this up," she whispered.

"You're not losing me; you're not losing me, babe," I whispered back.

"I'm sorry. I never cry." If anything, the tears flowed faster down her cheeks.

"Then stop." I kissed her. "Stop. You're killing me, baby, stop." Next thing I knew, I was kissing her like there was no tomorrow. She groaned deep in her throat and matched me, kiss for kiss. Something about this girl likely to drive me right over the edge one day. Right over. I lifted her up and she wrapped her legs around my waist. I backed over to the porch and set her down on the patio table before settling in between her thighs.

Both of us forgot about ribs on the grill, friends and family due any minute, Patrick, Jaquenetta, the world. In this moment, none of it was as important as this, nothing was as crucial as the validation of us. She shifted forward and rubbed that chest against me. I slid my hand up her thigh. "Jewellen?" She knew what I was asking.

"God, yes," she answered, sliding her hands down my chest to my belt buckle, unfastening it and shoving my pants down just enough so she could reach me.

When her hand wrapped around, she squeezed twice and I winced with the sensation. "Ah jeez, okay."

I bent down to kiss her again as I flipped her skirt up over her knees. Skipping all preliminaries, I shifted her panties to the side and thrust deep.

"Mmm." We both groaned. The emotion and the passion were running so high, I knew it was going to be quick. Didn't realize it was going to be so hot. The first time I pulled back, she growled in her throat, grabbed my ass, and yanked me back.

I looked down at her and we shared a damn-this-is-good moment. "Hard and fast?" I asked.

"Quick and dirty," she answered before I braced my hands on either side of her head and got down to business. This was not finesse sex; neither of us was patient enough for that. It was hot and sloppy, both of us straining as we slammed against each other. I knew I wasn't going to last long.

"Baby?" Gritting my teeth, I wanted to see how close she was.

"Yes, now, that's it—ah!"

Feeling her convulsing around me, I let go. It was always better with Jewel, more intense, more everything. I lay on top of her, getting my breath back. "That was nice."

She arched a brow. "Okay, player, calling that nice was like saying Hurricane Katrina was just a storm."

Laughing, I rose up off of her and agreed. "True dat. Okay, off the chains, Miss Jewel. But you know this."

She pulled me back down and placed her mouth next to mine. "I know this." She was doing this crazy tongue thing when a voice came out of nowhere.

"Jewellen Rose, what are you doing?" I went absolutely still. Pulling back, I looked down at Jewel. She blinked up at me before looking over my shoulder. My girl's mouth fell open.

"Mom!" she shrieked. I yanked her skirt down, pulled my pants up, tucked a few things in, zipped, and jumped back. Whirling round, I saw an older version of Jewel standing just outside the back gate with a nervous-looking guy, another older woman I didn't know, Tammy, Aaron, and my brother Beau with Chase.

Jewellen's mom spoke first. "We've all been standing out front ringing the doorbell for God knows how long, Jewellen." Shit—great first impression here.

I stepped off the porch and walked over. "I'm sorry, Mrs. Capwell-Williams. We were—"

"I think we all saw what you were doing, young man. Might wanna buckle your belt," she said.

Tammy snickered behind her. Jewel handed me a wet wipe.

I decided to play it off, buckling said belt and wiping my hands with the wet wipe. Smiling, I cleared my throat. "Yes, well." I thought about extending my hand before going with a nod. "A pleasure to meet you, ma'am. I'm Roman Montgomery."

"I should certainly hope so. Might as well call me Cleo," she retorted, returning my nod and raking me up and down with a look that could have cut glass. If it weren't for the look she was giving me, I would say she was still a nice-looking woman. Pretty. Still looks nice in a cotton shirt and denim shorts.

"Mom." Jewel had recovered her composure and walked over. "Leave him alone and come sit down." She hugged her mom and turned to the man. "Vince." She reached up and kissed his cheek. "I'm glad you could make it." She reached a hand out for me, and I took it. "Roman, this is Vince Williams, my stepdad."

I smiled and shook his hand. "Vince." Lord have mercy. What a way to meet the folks!

She smiled at the other woman and leaned forward for another hug. "Roman, this is Trudy Capwell, my stepmom. Trudy, where's Dad?" I shook Trudy's hand too. She was very fly. Long hair perfectly done up, nails on. Nice outfit, sandals that matched her belt. Makeup just so. Wonder how she looks so cool when it's already ninety degrees out here. She reminded me of an older Renee, always styling and profiling.

Trudy smiled. "He'll be back; he went round to the liquor store. You know your father—said you never keep good scotch around."

Jewellen laughed. "If he means hundred-dollar bottles of Chivas, he's right!"

Cleo shook her head. "That sounds just like Claude."

There was a brief lull in all the meeting and greeting. Wouldn't you know that Chase saw it as an opportunity to speak his mind?

"Daddy, I saw you kissing Miss Joo-well! But Uncle Beau told me never to interrupt a man when he's getting some. Getting some what, Daddy? Hi, Miss Joo-well." Little Chase didn't have a shy bone in his body. Tammy snickered again.

I knelt down to catch the little badass as he ran forward. But instead of running to me, he launched himself into Jewel's arms. Well, damn, I guess I saw where his loyalties lie.

She caught him with a smile, and they shared a kiss. "Hello, LaChayse. Meet my mommy." He wrapped his arms around her neck and stared at the new people. "Y'all come on out to the deck. Roman, check the ribs, honey." Halfway over, she threw a glance over her shoulder and smiled. "Hey, Tam, show Aaron where everything is. Oh, and hello, Uncle Beau." She sent him an I'll-get-to-you-later look.

Beau smirked. "Hey, *chère*."

I grabbed Beau by the neck and dragged him over to the grill with me. "So, what else did Uncle Beau share with my four-year-old son?"

"Teachin' *mon neveu* man thangs, ya know, bro?" The thought of Uncle Beau teaching his nephew anything struck a little fear in my heart.

Beau was one inch taller than me, ten pounds heavier, and three and a half years older, and still I thought of him as a little brother. Beau had more of the Cajun in him than I did, played it up for all he was worth, and he was real big on *Laissez le bon temps roulez*. That "let the good times roll" attitude was his way of life. He wove Cajun French in and out of his conversations, just enough to be charming or exasperating, depending on how you took it. Real good with charm. 'Til I started a company and gave him a job, his primary occupation had been seducing beautiful rich women and living off of them. Women loved Beau. Everybody loved Beau. Hell, I loved Beau, even if he was a pain in the ass. And Beau loved himself that much in return.

Beau was the life of the party. When the party ended, Beau disappeared. I looked at him smiling what Madere called his "corn pone" grin. You knew it was no good for you, but you had a big old helping anyway. I shrugged. Beau was Beau.

"Want a grab a couple beers out of the cooler while I turn these?"

"Yeah, brother, *pas de problème*." He pivoted toward the back porch and stopped dead in his tracks. "*Qui est cette jolie fille, mon frère*?"

"Who is what pretty girl, Beau?" I turned and looked. "Tell me you ain't talking 'bout Renee?" Renee had just walked in with Gregory. She was fly, as usual. Who the hell wears silk to a barbecue? Soul Sister Fly Girl, dat's who.

"Renee, hmm? Think I'll go get that beer now." He walked away like a man with a plan.

I watched the women watching Beau approach, and I shook my head. Whatever it was about a man that made women stop and stare, Beau had it in abundance. Beyond the 6'4" 230 of it all, Beau just looked like a man who loved women, and women responded to it . . . repeatedly and with enthusiasm. The only one who ignored him was Jewel, God bless my baby. From the moment they met, she saw right through what she called the "yada-yada" of Beau. She told him straight out, "Don't even shovel it this way, playboy. I've heard it all before."

I watched as Jewel opened the Igloo for Keisha and Arthur. Then she came over to me with Chase on her hip. When she reached my side, she handed me a beer. "He's got nothing on you, player."

"Oh, yeah?" Baby was starting to get to know my moods and read my mind a little bit too well.

"Except maybe that sexy way he has of sliding those French phrases off his tongue." She grinned mischievously.

"Comme ça, ma petite douceur?" I let the simple sentence roll from my throat.

She almost dropped Chase. Her eyes went wide and she flushed. "I didn't know you spoke like that."

"Ya all right, Joo-well?" Chase fanned her face with his little hand.

"Just a little warm, sweetheart," she reassured him before turning her attention to me. "What did you say?"

"I said, 'Like this, my little sweetness?' " I grinned at her expression. Women were suckers for a foreign language. No need to tell her that for Madere and Pops, bayou French was their first language; English was secondary. Let her be dazzled by the patois every now and again.

She shifted Chase and looked me up and down. "Standing there with sizzling pork in your hand, talking that talk, mmm, we are gonna need an encore of that patio table action, player."

I smiled at her. "You liked that, huh?"

"Oh yeah, I liked it a lot. Right up until the woman who gave me birth was a spectator."

"Definite buzz kill." She and I shared a laugh.

"When we eating, girl?" Roni Mae had arrived. She ignored Aaron and sat down next to Jewel's mom.

"Soon," Jewel said with a smile. "We'll talk again later, Frenchie." Jewel set Chase down and sent me the Look. You remember that time-to-get-wild-and-loose thing I told you she does.

"Patrick, I didn't know you were in town!" Cleo's voice carried across the yard. The joy in Cleo's voice was obvious.

It immediately set my teeth on edge. Talk about killing the mood.

"Okay, he was SO not invited," Jewel reassured me.

"I know." Sooner or later, I was sure I would get over the need to put my fist in Tricky Rick's face.

Jewel and I turned to look. Sure enough, Patrick stepped out on the porch with Stacie on his arm and Kenneth right behind him with a twelve-pack of beer in his hands.

Cleo sprang up and I watched while she and Patrick hugged like long-lost relatives. I sent a look to Jewel. "Yeah, we'll talk again later."

We both sighed deeply. As Beau would say, "*Laissez le bon temps roulez.*"

18

Not Gonna Sweat It

Gregory—Sunday, September 8, 1:12 p.m.

Yeah, I spotted Captain Trouble when we stepped out onto the porch. Believe it or not, I'd met Beau a time or two before. Back when I was into the club scene, Monsieur Montgomery was a regular. If I hadn't seen him here, I'd never have connected him to Roman. As different as night and day. Though seeing them side by side, I suppose they did favor each other.

So what was my problem today? Why did I give a damn about the Bayou Romeo?

Hell, I got problems enough with Renee without dropping this zero into the equation. I knew Renee. I might have her wrapped up now, but the first hint of trouble, she would get those eyes to roving again.

Beau was most definitely her type. Type her roving, restless eye would land on. Pretty boy with a little bank behind him.

So what if it described me too? At least I possessed some substance, some sense of responsibility. Look, I was at the point in life where swinging and flinging was a thing of the past. Much as I resisted it—hell, I was tired of the game—I needed to settle my black ass down, start working on the wife and kids angle.

Hey, I had been around enough women to know—Beau was a fantasy come to life for most women. He was 6'4", light brown skin but not too light, easy smile, and that damn accent. I had witnessed him and that accent in action. He stared right into a woman's eyes when he talked to her (a little trick I actually use now and again), made a woman think she was the only thing on his mind. But tell me how *he* had an accent and Roman didn't. Help me with *that* fake-assed shit, if you can?

He had that poor-boy-done-good thing down. Didn't bother him a bit that it was Roman who put in the years and the sweat. He was happy enough to ride along in his wake, collecting a paycheck for whatever he did at Montgomery Design.

And that bad-boy-looking-for-a-good-girl-to-come-save-me act. We had been here only five minutes and I was beyond ready to beat him down. I sighed and decided not to sweat it so hard. Renee walked over to the pool to talk to Jewel, so I turned to talk to Jewel's mom.

"So, you're Renee's beau?" I winced at Mrs. Capwell-Williams's terminology.

"Yes, ma'am." I sat down next to her and watched Tammy strip down to her bathing suit. If you could call it that. More like a few carelessly placed triangles of fabric connected with string.

"Call me Cleo, Gregory."

"Okay, Cleo."

"How long have you known this group, honey?" We watched as Aaron sidled up to Roni Mae, and she walked away. Besides trying to run shit and act like Mr. Big, Aaron had been cold busted with some little hottie. Roni had kicked him to the curb two weeks ago. Heard her saying she forgot to rescind the invitation or he would not have been here.

I sighed. "Seems like a long time, Cleo. But it's only been about five or six months."

"My, my, my! Who are all these beautiful grown-up women in my daughter's backyard?" A tall man with salt-and-pepper low-cropped hair came in through the back gate.

"Daddy!" Jewel got up and ran over to him, greeting him with a hug.

"Hi, Mr. Capwell!" Stacie, Roni Mae, and Renee called out.

Cleo looked at me. "Gregory, let me tell you something. With some people, one minute seems like an hour. An hour seems like a day. And every day lasts a month and a half."

I took my eyes off Renee, who was now lounging in a chair with Beau crouched by her side like a leopard waiting to pounce. She wasn't hardly objecting to the attention.

"Care for a drink, Cleo?" I volunteered, sensing a kindred soul.

"Cleo, is that you up on the veranda?" Jewel's father belted out.

"Feel I'm gonna need one, Gregory?" she asked me, ignoring her ex-husband's exuberant greeting.

"Can't hurt." We shared a smile. I reached over to the Igloo and handed her a wine cooler before getting a cold beer for myself. I've never been a heavy drinker, but that beer sure felt good going down my throat. I had a feeling that one or two wasn't going to cut it. I was thinking about how to play this whole scene here when Cleo spoke again.

"I like you, Gregory. If things don't work out with you and Renee, you keep my Jewellen in mind." She patted my hand.

Rome stepped onto the porch. "I think Jewellen'll be pretty much tied up for a while." The expression on his face was grim. I sympathized but I wasn't getting in the middle of all that mess.

I threw both hands up. Last thing I needed was Roman for

an enemy. "Hey, I've got my own woman to worry about. Wanna call off your brother?"

Rome quirked a brow. "Beau's his own man. Besides, Renee's no fool."

I refrained from snorting as I watched Beau brush something off Renee's bare shoulder. I decided to play it cool. Hell, she still had to come home with me, right?

"Hey, Romeo, which one of these ladies is your Juliet?" a smooth female voice said from behind me.

I damn near dropped my beer in my lap. The most beautiful woman I'd ever seen in my life stood in the doorway. She had on a halter swimsuit and a long silky thing wrapped around her waist. Her hair was long and glossy. Not a weave either. Her eyes were a haunting shade of gold. She was a six-footer, sleek and gorgeous. She glided forward and hugged Rome. She moved sinuously like a . . . "Kat. You must be Kat, Rome's sister. I'm Gregory." I stood up and took her hand.

She smiled up into my eyes. "If I must be, it's a good thing that I am, huh, Gregory?" My God, she was aptly named. Soft and feline, sexy as all hell. I forgot all about Renee's difficult ass cooing over Beau. I was too busy being dazzled by a Montgomery of my own.

"My, those Montgomerys are a handsome lot, aren't they?" Cleo was murmuring to her husband.

"She's damn gorgeous, that's for sure," Vince answered. I agreed.

Roman smiled. "Katrina, let me introduce you around." He took off down the steps with her, and I sank back into my chair.

Cleo looked over at me. "You all right, dear? You look like a hit-and-run victim."

I came out of my trance and smirked. "She must be the model Roman's always talking about."

"Has to be."

"Cleo, old girl, weren't you even going to say hello?" Jewel's dad came up on the patio with his arm around Trudy.

"Hello, Claude." Cleo inclined her head. "You remember Vincent, don't you?"

Claude stuck a hand out, "Vince, how's Mile High City?"

Vince shook his hand. "Mighty fine. How's the Crescent City?"

I sat and watched the two couples, wondering what it must feel like to be them. Married and divorced with grown kids and new spouses. They seemed amicable enough. Of course, according to Renee, the divorce had been years ago, and they only had to see each other once or twice a year. No reason not to be pleasant. I looked up in time to see Renee throw her head back and laugh at some mighty hilarious thing Beau said.

"Mr. Capwell, I'm Gregory Samson. Nice to meet you." I shook his hand before turning to Cleo. "Cleo, it was nice talking with you. Will you excuse me?" I took my beer and headed over to the pool, determined to break up the cozy little duo. I mean, damn, I was cool, not invisible.

"Jewel, I need a tray for these ribs, baby," Rome called out. "And bring out the chicken when you come back."

Jewel got up. "Yessir! Right away." She took a look at my face and slipped her hand around my elbow. "Greg's gonna help me."

She shanghaied me inside, pausing on the porch to say, "I want no trouble out of you four today." Her dad burst out laughing.

"We're grown folk, girlie. We know how to behave." Claude winked at us.

"That's what worries me—how you'll behave." She smiled at him fondly before pushing the back door open.

When we reached the kitchen, she pushed some spices and a pan of chicken in front of me. "Can you sprinkle those with some seasoning, Gregory?"

"Sure." I picked up the first container I saw and started sprinkling.

We worked in silence for a minute.

"What's wrong?" I asked her.

She looked up in surprise. "Nothing, why do you ask?"

"You don't usually single me out, Jewel. Matter of fact, I get the feeling you don't like me much." It was true. She always looked at me like she knew something I didn't. Hell, maybe she did.

She laughed. "Gregory, I like you well enough; I just don't trust you. There's something a little too slick about you. But I like you."

Too slick? Me? I'm the original Mr. Low Profile. And I said so. "Jewel, I'm strictly low pro." I turned the chicken over and went on sprinkling.

She smiled. "Exactly. Now, you gonna chill out over Beau or do I have to make you peel potatoes?"

I laughed. "I'm chill." She was good people.

She picked up an empty tray and motioned for me to pick up mine. "I don't usually jump into Renee's business, because, truthfully, I don't want her too close up in mine, but let me give you a word of advice, Greg."

I raised a brow. "I'm listening." My ears were wide open. I doubted anyone knew Ray as well as Jewel. I sometimes suspected Jewel knew Renee better than Renee knew herself.

"Don't give her an inch. Don't relax your guard. Renee is a restless and greedy soul. I love her and I hear you say you do too. But when something in Renee's life blows up, she's usually the one with her finger on the explosives, you feeling me?"

I nodded, having always suspected this about my baby. Not surprised to hear it confirmed. "I hear you, but I can't stay on her twenty-four-seven. I won't."

"And I hear you, but she needs twenty-five-eight. You take the risk." With that, she swept out the back door. What choice did I have but to follow?

Handing the tray over to Roman, I went over to the pool. There was an empty lounger in between Roni Mae and Aaron. I took it. Roni Mae flashed me a smile of gratitude.

"Hey, Greg, how's it going?" Roni Mae asked me.

"Can't complain." I smiled back at her. Roni Mae was a little flighty but just about the sweetest girl I'd ever met. Just plain good people. I liked her; she was a straight shooter. These days I could appreciate that. I flicked a glance over to Aaron. He was in an argument with Arthur. "How about you?"

She grinned. "I could complain, but why bother?"

I glanced over to Renee and kept my gaze on her until she dragged her eyes off Beau and looked up. My expression said, "I'm watching you, girl. Don't slip up."

"A little constructive complaining every now and again never hurt anyone," I told Roni Mae. "By the way, I've been meaning to tell you how great you look lately." And she did. She'd lost a lot of weight and was really putting herself together.

She looked surprised that anyone noticed. "Thanks, Greg."

"So tell me, how are things at the station?"

I had one eye on Renee and Roni Mae had one on Aaron, but we managed to navigate a decent conversation anyway.

19

It's Just a BBQ, People

Renee—Sunday, September 8, 7:00 p.m.

Stacie's parents came and left early. Roni Mae's mom only stayed long enough to visit with Jewel's mom. Roman's folks only came to get a glimpse of Jewellen, then left. She charmed the hell out of them, of course. Tomorrow, she's going over there for the Montgomery Labor Day celebration. The rest of the parental types left two hours ago. Which was good because there were things that might need to be said out here that didn't no parent need to hear. Greggy been sending me these looks. Jewel shooting me little glances. Saw Roman eyeballing Patrick. Aaron looking at Roni Mae. Jewel looking at Roman. And Beau looking at me.

I can't believe Jewellen hadn't said anything to me about Beau before. He said he met her way back in June. Now I wondered where she had been hiding him all this time. My homegirl been holding out! This boy was *something*. Don't get me wrong, Greggy wasn't chopped liver and I loved him and all, but *this*? This was the kind of man every woman wanted a shot at once in her lifetime. The guy every other woman wanted. Not only pretty, but tall, intelligent, well bred (how he and Roman are related, I'll never know), funny, spontaneous, *fine,* and sexy as all hell with those light eyes and that Cajun thing he did. Did I say fine?

I felt bad for thinking this, but to tell the truth, Greggy was bread and butter, chicken and rice, my everyday-great-for-the-long-run man. The one I wanted to build a life with, have a future with and all that. Beau . . . Beau was dessert. Mocha chocolate cheesecake with café au lait on the side, you understand? Beau was a fling waiting to happen. Just right there, patiently waiting for your resistance to drop and temptation to take over.

Thing of it was, I didn't wanna risk my thing with Greggy for Beau. But I still wanted Beau. Have you ever had this, oh, let's call it wild sexual curiosity about someone? Like, you just had to know if it was as good as it looked, at least once before you missed your chance and ended up rocking on the front porch with your grandkids, still wondering about it? This was terrible; Gregory had been nothing short of perfect, emotionally, psychologically, and definitely sexually. Nothing could possibly be better than what we had. I glanced over at Beau. He was getting out of the Jacuzzi. Water rolled off of that body like a liquid caress. My God, 6'4". I took a sip of my drink to moisten a suddenly dry throat just as he looked up. He caught me staring, and a slow, sexy grin spread across his face. He only looked away when Kat called his name.

This was Jewellen's fault. If she hadn't kept Beau hidden away like some forbidden fruit, I wouldn't be in this predicament now. I wouldn't have met Beau right in front of Greggy. God knows he was watching me like a hawk, probably reading my thoughts right now.

I slanted a glance over at him. Damn, he knew. I don't know what he was all pissed about; he had been salivating over Kat since she got here. I was surprised he didn't have eye strain trying to keep his eyes focused on the both of us at once.

I just wanted to spend a minute with Beau just to see if he

was really "as advertised." So if I could get Jewel to take me with her to the Montgomerys tomorrow, then I could . . . no, I couldn't. I was going over to the Samsons. Wished I didn't have to but as it was, his mother didn't like me much. No need to give her another reason to dislike me. His father I got wrapped around my finger. But for some reason, Moms was still pretty cold toward me.

Maybe if we go early and leave early . . . I commenced to scheming. Looking over, I saw Jewel. She had come back out after putting Chase to sleep. She was curled up in Rome's lap, and he was stroking a hand down her back. If you had told me three months ago that the two of them would still be together, I'da laughed you outta town. He was not her type at all. Good for a drop-'n'-roll but a relationship? Please! She was so much into the well-bred, yuppie, take-him-home-to-Momma type . . . like Patrick. He was perfect for her. I could tell there was still something there between them. If Rome would ever give her an inch of room to breathe in, she would see it herself. And Cleo? Cleo didn't make no bones about who she preferred for her daughter. Made me wonder what my mom will think when she comes up to meet Greg in a few weeks. I'd love for her to see Greggy and Beau in the same room and tell me what she thinks. Not that Beau was really an issue . . . yet.

"Jewellen, come here for a second," I called over to her.

She looked at me. "Girl, I just got comfortable."

I frowned. I hoped Rome didn't have my girl whipped. "Your man ain't going nowhere, girl, come here."

I could tell from all the way over here that she was rolling her eyes. She leaned into Rome and whispered something in his ear. He looked over at me and laughed before standing up with her. He walked over to Beau, and they headed inside the house with Kat. Jewel came over and sat down.

"What is it, child?"

"Nice day, isn't it?" I wanted to lead into my pitch.

She shot me a look. "So far so good. Why?"

"Naw, I'm just saying. Food was great, weather held up, folks acted like they had sense. Look around, everybody's all nice and friendly."

We looked around. Greggy was sitting at a card table playing spades with Arthur, Keisha, and Roni Mae. Kenneth, Aaron, Tammy, and a couple of Rome's boys were playing a loud game of dominoes. There were other people around, some from Jewel's office, some from Rome's, a few guys I recognized from the rec center, some girls from church. There was some dancing going on by the pool, a Scrabble game was going on inside, and there were still people eating.

"Yeah, it's nice," Jewellen answered.

"So, you looking forward to going to the Montgomerys' tomorrow?" I looked as innocent as I could while I asked.

She turned her head until her eyes met mine levelly. "No, Renee. No, no, and hell to the no. And don't go there." Damn, she was always trying to get inside somebody's head.

"What?" I blinked at her.

She shook her head. "I got eyes, I got ears, and I got good sense in my head, which is more than I can say for your stupid ass. Lord, I can read you like a book." She pointed a finger in my face. "You wanna jack up your thing with Gregory, go ahead, but do it without involving me. You will not be joining me at the Montgomery party tomorrow, nor will you be invited to anything I think Beau has a chance of attending."

I leaned in close. "Jew-Ro, you 'spose ta be my girl! Come on, catch my back on this."

"Jew-Ro my ass, Renee. You want Beau? You wanna sneak behind Greg's back? Do it behind mine too." She got up and stormed off.

Shit, I hated it when she got all up on her high horse like that. Worse still, she was right. I should just forget about it. After all, I was finally in a position to get everything I wanted. Why jeopardize that?

"*Bien-aimée*, want some dessert?" My eyes traveled up the

long length of Beauregard Montgomery, who was standing by my side offering me, of all things, a slice of cheesecake. He was psychic. My eyes met his; then again, maybe that wasn't all he was offering.

"Thank you, I'd love some." As I took the plate, I felt the weight of at least two sets of angry glares. Me being me, I ignored them and smiled. "Sit down, we can share."

He felt the eyes and ignored them too. "*Merci*, Renee, if you're sure?" He sat on the chaise next to mine.

"It's only dessert, right?" I shrugged and smiled.

"*C'est vrai*, only dessert." He looked up from the plate and straight into my eyes. Right then, we both knew. It might not happen today, tomorrow, or next week, but it was gonna happen. Consequences be damned.

20

Seriously, Go Home

Jewel—Sunday, September 8, 10:00 p.m.

I hated to be the hostess from hell, but I was ready for all these folks to rise up out my house and be gone. What did that comedian say? "You don't have to go home but ya sure gots ta get the hell up outta here!" I was feeling that.

It had been a long day, especially with Roman scaring the shit out of me with that talk. Granted, I had been a little weirded out seeing my ex-fiancé slobbering up on one of my best friends, but it did not detract from what I felt for Roman! I really needed to make myself clear on that. For a second today, I thought he was gonna walk, thought he was done. Felt like someone was ripping me apart slowly into small pieces. How quickly you can get used to someone in your life.

Shit, I was not ready to be single again; I was not ready to be without him. I was not prepared, period. Couldn't recall ever letting anyone matter to me this much, this fast before. Had to get a handle on this thing.

"Miss Joo-well?" Chase's little voice came down the hallway, reminding me that I had yet to go in to check and see if he was sleeping. Apparently not.

I went into the guest room, and there was Roman's son, bouncing up and down on the bed like he was on the playground.

"LaChayse!" He stopped instantly and crawled under the covers. I sighed, children and their little tests. I pulled the cover up to his neck and leaned over him. "What's the problem, Little Montgomery?"

"Don't wanna sleep." His eyelids were drooping as he got the words out.

"Why not?"

"Wanna stay up and play with you, Miss Joo-well. I never gets to just stay with you. And you know lotses of games and stories and stuff."

I smiled. At least I didn't have to worry about Roman's child liking me. We had become pals early on, and I finally got him to the point where he respected my requests and rules. We did have this one conversation quite a bit, though. "Well, Chase, you have to stay with your parents. They love you and want you with them."

His eyes went wide open. "Don't you love me?"

Kids can sucker punch you with the emotions, damn! Thought I was gonna tear up for the second time today. "Of course I love you."

"I love you too. So why can't I stay here sometimes like I stay with Dad sometimes and Mom sometimes?"

"Chase, I'm not your mom or your dad."

"If you married my dad, you'd be my set-mommy."

"Set-mommy?"

"Yeah, Ricky's dad got remarried and he got a set-mom, so that's what you'd be; then I could stay."

"*Step mom,* Chase. And I don't know if I'm marrying your dad."

"You don't?" He looked hurt. "Don't you like my daddy? He cooks pancakes and drives a fun car and makes his own money." Chase broke it on down to the least common denominator.

I was trying to come up with an answer when Roman spoke from the doorway. "Yeah, don't you like his daddy? He's potty trained, too, you know."

Chase giggled and I tickled him a little. "Daddy is housebroken, huh?"

"Better than a puppy!" Chase said.

"I can paw, growl, and lick with the best of them," Roman said in an all-too-adult tone.

"Guess I'll have to keep him," I told Chase. "Did I tell you the story of the little dog that lost his spots?" I launched into it for a few minutes before he fell asleep.

Roman and I closed the door and went back to the living room. I looked around; it was empty. "Is the party over?"

"I chased most of them away; you still got some diehards out back."

I sank down onto the sofa with a sigh. "They'll get the hint when I turn the lights off in a little while." Roman sat down next to me and started massaging my shoulders. "It was a nice day, huh?"

Roman quirked a brow. "Overall, yeah. But if you looked at all the damn drama going on, it was *Days of Our Lives* up in here."

I turned to look at him. "What about us? Are we a drama too?"

"I guess we'll see. As long as it's just about you and me."

I nodded. Yeah, him and me . . . I put my head on his shoulder and relaxed. "So, Chase wants me to be his set-mommy." I felt Roman go absolutely still beside me. Interesting.

"That's what he said, huh?" His tone was the most guarded I had ever heard it.

"Yep, any comments?"

"Ah, not sure I'm very marriage inclined."

My head swiveled to the side. "Seriously?"

"My first marriage was such a nightmare, Jewel."

"No doubt. So you don't plan to try again?"

"Not without really looking before I leap. I don't want to go into another marriage without knowing where all the skeletons are buried and the land mines are hiding."

Whew, marriage with land mines and skeletons, this was good to know. It was also a topic to explore later, not today. As I said, it had been a long day. "Well, Roman, that's some romantic view of marriage you have there."

"It's real, baby."

"Is that why you are so crazy about Patrick?"

He shot me a look. "First off, I'm not crazy—I'm cautious. Second, based on my experience, when something feels like it might be trouble, it usually is. So, yes, I am sensitive to potentially bad juju."

"Juju, huh? Your Cajun is showing, player." I leaned up and kissed him on the cheek.

He put his lips next to my ear and whispered, "I can show you more than my Cajun, baby."

I hopped up and stalked to the back door. "Lights out, people. Anyone not off the property in ten minutes gots to start paying rent."

As the last person skittered out the yard, I turned back to him. "Let's see what we can do about that juju, hmm?"

21

Turkey Day

Jewel—Thursday, November 24, 2:15 p.m.

"Mom, I hear you." How could I not? She'd been screaming into the phone for the better part of a half hour. Okay, not screaming. Cleo Williams did not raise her voice. She spoke forcefully with a raised inflection that really felt that screaming when you were on the receiving end of it.

"And I understand but you've gotta understand that it's all settled. Roman and I are walking out the door as soon as I hang up. Listen, we'll see you at Christmas. Roman's really looking forward to Cancun." I looked over at Roman. He threw his hands up and went over to pick up his keys. Cleo was having trouble understanding why I wasn't coming to New Orleans at all this Thanksgiving. Every year it was the same argument. Usually I spent Thanksgiving with Renee or Stacie or my sister so I wouldn't have to choose between going to Mom's or going to Dad's. But this year had been . . . unique, to say the least. I didn't feel like flying all the way to my sister's in Alaska, Renee was going to Gregory's house, and Stace and I weren't as tight as we used to be.

No big thing. I had been wrapped up in my job and

Roman. She had been wrapped around Patrick . . . Oh, sorry, he was called "Trick" now. No, I wasn't jealous. As I explained and explained to Roman, it was not jealousy. It was the principle of the thing. Okay, I would never admit it to Roman, but there really was a time when I felt Patrick *was* the love of my life. The fact that she was dating him now pissed me off. It went against those unwritten rules in the girlfriend handbook. Like dating your third cousin's ex-husband—it simply wasn't done. Wasn't so much like he was mine once and so he was mine forever. But if he was mine once, he should be hers never. They should etch it in stone somewhere: Once a man had been with a relative or close friend, he became absolutely *off-limits* to all close friends and relatives. Amen.

When their relationship goes rocky, what then? Could Stacie come to me and say, "Why didn't you tell me that Patrick was like this?" No, she could not. Not to mention the tacky fact that we now had *intimate knowledge* about the same man. Did she use something that I said against him or maybe to entice him in the first place? Or did the two of them discuss some habit of mine? See how messy it could get?

"Jewellen Rose, are you listening to me?" Mom's voice had taken on that no-nonsense tone.

"Yes, of course I am! I always listen to you, Mother." Was it something to worry about when a lie rolled that easily off your tongue? Roman was making gagging sounds across the room. I shot him a look and he tapped his watch.

"Well, I'll let you go. I'll call you after the Cowboys game." I paused for her response.

"Mom, no, I'm at Roman's. I'll call you tomorrow. What? Of course I'm going home for the night! Yes, alone!" Roman snickered and I shot him a look. He thought it was ridiculous that at thirty and even after the Labor Day patio episode, I was still lying to my mother about where I spent my nights. Hey, they say a son's a son till he takes a wife; a daughter's a daughter for the rest of her life. As far as I was concerned, my mother didn't have to know I was sexually active (blocking out the Labor Day episode!) until the day I got back from my honeymoon. Not that she thought I was still a virgin, but we need not advertise otherwise (still blocking it out!). "Love you, too, Mom . . . bye now." I hung up and picked up my purse.

Roman was jingling his keys around like there was a fire somewhere. The worst thing about great guys is that underneath all the great stuff, they were still just guys. Pity that Y chromosome was always getting in the way. Like the key-jingling thing was going to make me walk faster. "I'm ready." I smiled at him. Guy or no guy, mother or no mother, it was the holiday season. Made me feel charitable all around.

"Let's roll."

Now, we had a pleasant fifteen-minute ride over to his parents' place. Wouldn't you know the boy waited until we pulled up in the driveway to tell me, "Did I tell you that Jaquenetta's gonna be here?" My charitable feeling was starting to evaporate some.

I turned my head slowly to look at him. "Ah, good, the ex-wife. No, Roman, I don't believe you mentioned that. To what do we owe the honor of her presence?"

He shrugged, as if it was nothing. "She always spends Thanksgiving with us."

How cozy, I thought. "Really? You don't say?" I spoke casually, as if this was no big thing. In truth, I hated damn near every minute I had to spend in that woman's company. Beyond the obvious reasons for not liking each other, Jaquenetta and I had never attempted to bond or establish common ground. We tolerated each other for Roman's and Chase's sake. I didn't want to get to know her better, and she made it real clear she felt the same way.

"Now, Miss Jewel, she got nowhere else to go, you know? I can't just uninvite my baby mama just 'cause I gotta girlfriend, right?"

"Umm." Baby mama drama. He had a point. I hated it, but he did have a point.

"So, we straight, babe?" Sometimes he had a way of putting things that just set my teeth on edge. That cocky so-are-we-all-clear-on-this? attitude. But what could I do? Sitting there in the driveway of his parents' house on a major holiday with his family, ex-wife and child inside? Who was I to make waves? I was just the girlfriend. Still, I wasn't going to put up with any of Jaquenetta's crap. My philosophy is *don't start none, won't be none.* That's where I was coming from and I said as much.

"Not having it out of her today, Frenchie. If she plays nice, I'll play nice. Otherwise, the gloves are coming off."

He looked at me to gauge my seriousness and finally shrugged. "You got to be you. Do your thang. Let me know when to duck. We cool?"

"Yeah, we cool." He leaned over and kissed me. One of those come-on-you-know-you-love-me-baby kisses. He was cute, but he wasn't that cute. Okay, so he was.

"Come on, *chère*, Madere's been asking about you. She really likes you." He must have known I was displeased or he wouldn't have whipped out the French on me. Brother was no fool; he knew the weaknesses and just when to push those buttons.

Now, did he sound surprised when he said his mother liked me? Why wouldn't she? Just when you think you understand a guy. Or was I overanalyzing again?

"You two comin' in or are you sittin' in the car all day?" Beau called from the front door. We exchanged a look, got out of the car, and headed up the walk.

Renee—Thursday, November 24, 3:15 p.m.

"Renee, why don't you help me carry these plates out to the formal dining room?" Mrs. Samson (she hasn't given me permission to call her Fiona yet) asked me. Though why she asked, I would never know. It wasn't as if I could have said, "No, I'd rather sit here with the guys and watch the football game," now, could I? I got up and headed for the dining room.

I was getting yet another good glimpse of life in the Samson household, and I had to say, it didn't bode well for the future. Greggy helped out around the house and did his fair share, but looking over at Garry, Greg's dad, I had to wonder if he didn't start out the same way. Maybe Fiona went into it the same way I did—happy and smiling, thinking she'd found an equal and loving helpmate for life. Here it was, thirty years later, and she was cooking and setting tables while they watched the football game. And here I thought we'd come such a long way, baby.

Sure, she had a maid. Old Eugenia was in there cleaning pots as we spoke. But looking around this seven-bedroom palace they call a home, I was thinking it took more than a seventy-year-old maid and a fifty-year-old housewife to keep the place spotless, which, of course, it was. Fresh flowers in almost every room, carefully laid-out snack trays, pressed linen tablecloths and napkins—even at the breakfast bar, for Christ's sake!

Yes, I always said I wanted to live high on the hog, but the hog was starting to look like a pain in the ass. Who kept all those flowers fresh and linens pressed?

"Don't forget to lay the soup spoons, too, dear." Yes, there was enough silverware laid out to eat six meals. And I had no idea where the proper place to lay soup spoons was supposed to be. My Emily Post was rusty at best. Now, I considered myself pretty damn worldly. I'd eaten in some of the best restaurants across the nation, but never had I seen such a daunting display of flatware and cutlery.

"Hey, girl, let me help you with some of this stuff." Cassia, Greg's sister-in-law, came in. Cassia was married to Greg's only sibling, Geoffrey. They had twin boys aged three (Godfrey and

Garrison) and had a girl on the way. It was clearly a "G" thang for the Samson offspring. Geoffrey was a little on the snooty side (he must have taken after Fiona), but I liked Cassia.

I smiled at her. "Thanks, girl. I was beginning to think this was a test I was about to flunk."

She laughed. "Honey, the first time I came here for Thanksgiving, she did the same damned thing. Had so many different kinds of forks and mystery utensils, I wanted to cry. 'Cause you're right—it *is* a test. I call it the silver spoon test." She grinned.

"Oh yeah?"

"Yeah, if you can properly place the spoon, I guess she figures you're deserving of her son. God knows they were born with 'em in their mouths."

I looked at her in surprise. "You weren't?"

She let out a peal of laughter. "Girl, hell, I was born in a little shit-kickin' town in Georgia."

My mouth fell open. Cassia seemed so at home in these surroundings. "No shit, girl?" I watched while she laid out forks on the left, knives on the right, then the teaspoon. She laid the soup spoon horizontal above the plate, then stacked the salad plate and soup bowl. Water glass, champagne flute, and dessert plate were no problem for her. She finished by rolling the napkin, stuffing it into a ring and laying it across the soup bowl. I was in awe and set about copying her. She went on talking as we worked around the table.

"Yeah, girl, I just happened to bump into Geoffrey at a basketball game. Georgia Tech was playing Duke, and there we were."

I shook my head. "World is small. So what did you do?"

"Hell, I married him and never looked back." She grinned.

"No, I mean, how did you pass the silver spoon test?"

"Oh, I rolled all the silverware in each napkin and set them to the side of each plate, just like they do at Denny's. It looked neat, so Fiona couldn't say much, but you could just tell when she unrolled it and fifteen utensils came rolling out . . ." We laughed together.

"I guess you won her over in the end, though, huh?"

She raised a brow. "Not really. It's not like we're best buddies or meet for lunch or anything. The kids are what really keep us friendly."

I shook my head. "Why can't a relationship just be about one girl and one guy and what they feel for each other?" I could almost hear Jewellen in my ear telling me to get real.

Cassia smiled. "Never happens. You've always got family, friends, coworkers, somebody. It's a nice dream, though—that deserted-island fantasy."

"Renee, could you come stir the gravy, dear?" Fiona called out.

Cassia and I exchanged looks. I'd have to fantasize later; I had another test to take. Gravy, at least, was something I knew about.

Jewel—Thursday, November 24, 4:45 p.m.

"Okay, *mes petites. Allons, nous mangeons!"* Madere Montgomery called us to come eat. There was a general stampede. Beau, as usual, had some little bimbo on his arm. I cut her off rounding the corner from the kitchen and outmaneuvered two cousins for sixth place in line. There were a whole bunch of Montgomerys, and they could all eat like Hoovers. The aunts and uncles alone numbered over fifteen without counting in-laws. I learned on Labor Day not to be shy and retiring around this bunch. Good manners were nice, but in this crowd, manners would get you an empty plate and hurt feelings.

Pops Montgomery (yes, everyone calls him Pops or sometimes Avery) grabbed me around the waist. "*Viens ici, petite fille!"* Though the way he spoke, it sounded like, "*Vi'ci, 'tite fille!"*

" 'Come here, little girl,' he said," Roman whispered in my ear. Still translating for me even after I brushed up on my

French. Sometimes with the bayou dialect, it was hard to catch, but I got the basic idea.

"I've got it, babe." I smirked at him before looking up at Avery. "What can I do for you, Pops?"

"Chu need to eat, little girl! Put some mo' flesh on dose bones, eh, Rome?"

"I don't know, Pops. She looks plenty curvy to me!" Roman laughed as he cut in front of me in the buffet line and started piling his plate up.

I looked at him as I picked up a plate. "You just make sure you don't get too curvy yourself, eh *petit garçon*?" I was catching on to this Cajun thing. I grinned as everyone hooted and hollered. Pops gave me a squeeze and walked away.

"Who you calling little boy, Miss Jewel?" Roman frowned down into my face.

"Eh, *chère*, you no take no mouth from LaChayse, ya hear?" One of the uncles called out to me.

Roman grinned, leaned closer, and kissed me. We got a few more whistles. I was trying to get used to these public displays of affection. Like I said, this was a tough crowd to try to be proper and polite in.

"That's the only kinda mouth to take! What you say, *Bijou*?" Kat called out, and I laughed into his mouth. Kat and some of the others had taken to calling me *Bijou,* which, appropriately, means "Jewel" in French. It amused me to hear how the Montgomery children used their Cajun background. Beau played his up, making it a charming accessory to his already happy-go-lucky personality. Katrina switched back and forth from earthy bayou woman to sophisticated cover girl. And Roman? God bless him, he used the Cajun like he used the hip-hop—when he felt it was appropriate and to help him play whatever role he was into that day. I was starting to get used to that mercurial, multifaceted thing he did. This boy took moodiness to new heights. Whoever said love was easy?

"Hey, Romeo, ya holdin' up the line!"

"Let *l'enfant* up for air!" That was Aunt Yo-Yo. She called everyone *l'enfant*, or child, even Grandmere Montgomery, who was pushing ninety-five.

Roman released me and gave me one of those cat-with-the-canary grins before turning back to the buffet. Just then, Jaquenetta came in. Did the woman own anything other than black Lycra? She had maroon-colored curls cascading down her back (bad weave) and flying saucer silver hoop earrings on. Without sparing me a glance, she stepped in between Roman and me with Chase at her side. "Ya don't mind if we cut, do ya, Juliet? Romeo's child is hungry." She bared her teeth in what was supposed to be a grin, no doubt.

I'd been having such a nice time that I'd almost forgotten she was there. And how clever of her to use Chase as an excuse.

I grinned back, just as sincerely. "I would never deprive this child of anything, honey. You just go right on ahead."

"Are you sure, Miss Joo-well?" Little Chase blinked up at me, almost as if he knew his mama was up to no damn good.

I leaned down to kiss his cheek. "I'm sure, sweetheart." I looked back at his mother. "Go ahead, I can wait."

"As long as you don't mind coming behind me. You might have to settle for what I leave behind," she said, and turned her back.

Oh, like I wasn't supposed to know what that little dig meant? Two could play these little word games. "Well, no, I don't mind at all. They say timing is everything, don't they? Sometimes you just gotta save the best for last."

"Some people happy wi' sloppy seconds."

"A real diamond always sparkles; cubic zirconium loses its luster pretty fast."

"Uh, babe, I got enough food for you too. Come on and let's find a place to sit. The game'll be coming on soon." Roman, the little peacemaker, spoke. He dragged me into the family room and onto the love seat closest to the TV. "Meow, meow, Miss Jewel."

I sank my fork into an interesting-looking dish on his plate. "She scratched first, player." I took a bite. "Oh my God, that's heavenly. What is it?"

"Oh, that's Aunt Yo-Yo's oyster and crawfish stuffing. Good, huh?"

"Um-hmm." Talk ceased as our forks battled for position on the plate.

Madere and Pops walked in and stood watching Roman and I eat off the same plate until we got self-conscious and looked up. Madere was a tiny woman with dark skin, a beautiful face, and a petite figure. Avery was a light-skinned giant of a man with rough features and beautiful eyes. Oddly enough, they looked perfect together.

Madere smiled. "You happy, you two?"

"Yes, ma'am," we answered in unison.

Madere nodded and nudged Pops. He cleared his throat and looked down at me seriously. He was a tall man, still very charismatic, and he had an almost regal air about him. When he looked down at me with that expression on his face, I have to admit, I felt a twinge of apprehension. "Question, Jewellen."

I put the fork down. "Yes, sir?"

"When you gonna marry my boy here?" Funny, marriage was the one topic we have avoided like the plague since Labor Day weekend. After Mr. Cool-About-Everything-Else looked like he was ready to flee at the mention of the "m" word, I damned sure wasn't bringing it back up. God, you just had to love parents, didn't you? Just break a question like that out, no buildup, in the middle of a holiday thing.

"Pops!" Roman handed me the plate and jumped to his feet.

Once I closed my mouth, I had an answer ready. "It's early days yet, and to be truthful, he hasn't asked, sir. And I'm an old-fashioned kinda girl. I do believe the woman should wait for the man to ask." Ha! Let him take the heat.

Pops shook his head. "Alanna, we raised him wrong. In my day, a man see what's good in front of him, he makes sure he gets to keep it for himself. How he let this get away?"

Madere reached over and yanked Roman's ear. *"Tu ne demandes pas?"*

I interpreted that as, "You haven't asked?" I took a bite of food so I wouldn't break out laughing.

"Madere! No, I . . . well, we're not . . . I mean, we don't . . . Jewel?" He looked over at me for help.

I was fascinated. It was the first time I'd ever seen the boy at a loss for words. What was it about the word *marriage* that freaked a brother right out? I shrugged and sat back to enjoy it.

But Pops wasn't having it. He pointed at me. "*Tu l'aimes?"*

Did I love him? Easy question, easy answer. "*Oui.* I mean, yes." Now they had me doing this French thing.

He turned his stern gaze on Roman. *"Et vous, l'aimez retour?"*

Roman blinked. "Do I return this love?" He relaxed and grinned. "Pops, I multiply it."

I rolled my eyes and shot him a look that said "Good answer, Slick." He could be such a corny poet when he was trying to impress me. But I could tell from the expressions on his parents' faces that they loved his answer.

Madere threw her hands out. "*Ça va. Ça suffit. Temps et que Dieu nous dira. Allons,* Avery." They turned and walked out.

I raised my brows and looked at Roman. "I missed that part. What was that?"

Roman sat back down. "She said, 'Okay, that will do. Only God and time will tell. Let's go, Avery.'" He shook his head. "I wonder what brought that on?" He looked like a man who had just been granted a stay of execution.

I shrugged. " 'Tis the season, I suppose."

He looked over at me. "Uh, you wanna talk about this some more?"

I raised my eyebrows and grinned at him. He was so uncomfortable; he looked like he wanted to crawl out of his skin. I decided to let him off the hook. "Maybe another time. The game's about to start; people are coming to watch." Besides, I had no idea what I'd say if he asked right now. I loved Roman, but marriage . . . that meant forever and ever, didn't it? Something about that was far more serious than leaving my toothbrush and fat-free cookies at his house.

He looked around and tried to disguise his sigh of relief. "Yeah, yeah, another time."

I smirked at him. "You can exhale now. Happy holidays, player."

22

'Tis the Season

Renee—Thursday, December 22, 11:35 p.m.

Greggy and I were on our way to the airport when I had to ask him, "What's the problem here?" He'd been edgy all day, and it was making me nervous. Bad enough that we were spending Christmas apart. But with my mom in Arizona and his still not all that warm about me, what could we do? My mom, on the other hand, adored Greg. Couldn't shut up about him. Fiona still barely gave me the time of day.

"Just missing you already, Ray. That's all." I shot him a look. That was all, my ass. He could be so slick sometimes. I still didn't 100 percent trust his cute ass.

"Greg, it's me, huh? Don't bullshit me, boy."

We stopped to pull a parking ticket before he answered. "Ray, don't trip. You're going to be gone for a few days; leave on a good note."

I snorted. "If you wanted me to leave on a good note, you would have given me my present last night when I asked for it." I was still good and peeved about that. Really, what was with all the drama? Truth be told, this was our first time spending more than a day or two away from each other, and I didn't like the feel of it. Not that I didn't trust my Greggy to be faithful; that I had no qualms about. Then again, 'tis the season to be jolly, as they say. Old girlfriends popped back into town. All them damn tidings of joy start swimming around, ya know?

It would be just like Fiona to wait until I was away. I would lay odds that she had called all of Greg's old skanky hos. Knowing his mother, she's had this planned for months. I tell you, no matter what people say, a black woman's worst enemy was another smart black woman with an attitude and an agenda of her own. And I had to say, that described Mrs. Fiona Samson to a tee.

"Renee, for Christ's sake, I can practically see the steam coming out of your ears. What are you boiling up in that mind of yours? Whatever you're thinking, baby, quit." He leaned over and kissed me on the cheek.

He parked the car and popped the trunk. He grabbed my suitcase, I grabbed the carry-on, and we headed inside the terminal. We were standing in line, and I kept sending him these little ya-better-not-slip-up-while-I'm-gone looks. Greggy being Greggy, he read me like a book.

"Ray, where are we without trust?"

"Phoenix and Dallas," I answered wryly. My mama didn't raise no fools.

He smirked. "That's cute, baby. Real cute."

I had to make just one last effort here. "Just promise me one thing, huh?"

He rolled his eyes. "Anything within my power, baby." Always the perfect comeback.

"Promise me you'll hang up on any of your ex-hoochies when they call."

"My ex-*hoochies*? Ray, I never dated any hoochies."

"You know what I'm saying, boy."

"Yeah, I just resent like hell the way you put it. And I'm getting a little pissed off at your implication. Like, the minute your back is turned, I'm gonna go hit the streets or something.

If anyone around here should be anxious about someone playing off, it's me."

Now what did he mean by that crack? "Greg, I haven't so much as looked at another man while I've been with you." Well, almost. Unless you counted Beau. And since Jewel had made good her promise to keep an entire city between me and Beau at all times, I didn't think that one night of harmless flirting over three months ago counted.

He hit me with that look. That don't-make-me-call-you-out-girl look. Oops, I guessed it counted.

"What? Who? When?" I just wanted to see if he'd have the nerve to bring it up. He'd never said anything to me about what I called the Labor Day Incident. I guess I wanted to see if I could push him a little bit.

We stepped up to the counter. I checked my baggage, and the woman stapled the claim stubs to my ticket. "That's gate twenty-four, sweetheart. Happy holidays, y'all."

We smiled at her and went and sat down near the security gates in silence. I waited for Greg to speak.

It appeared I was waiting in vain. He just reached over, took my hand, and we just sat. I looked at him questioningly. He smiled and said nothing. Five minutes. Ten. Fifteen. And he knew how silence drives me crazy.

They began boarding first class. I stood up and started toward the screening tables. He stood up and watched me. The silence was unnerving. I was about to break down and apologize when he stepped over to me, pulled me close in a hug, and spoke in my ear.

"We're not ever going to talk about Beau and whatever that thing was, okay? Not ever. If you ever want me to leave, you just let me know and I'm gone, no questions asked." I pulled back to protest. Damn but brother got strong on me all out of the blue. One minute I was teasing, next he was all tough guy. I opened my mouth to say something, anything, when he hit me with one of those sneak-attack kisses he was so damn good at. The kind of quick, in-out, heart-thumping, panty-soaking tonguing that left me kind of misty. Beau who?

He stepped back and cleared his throat. "Okay now, baby, I'm gonna miss you." He reached into his coat and pulled out a wrapped package. "Take this with you. Call me when you get there. I love you, baby. I know sometimes I bullshit around and say what I need to say to get what I want, but I really mean this. I love you. Merry Christmas." He started backing away before turning with a wave and walking off.

Dammit. Just when I was being cool and in control, playing the role, he had to come correct with something like this. Now I was standing in the airport crying like a fool with my hormones raging. "Gregory!" He stopped and spun around. I just looked at him for a second. He really *was* fine and good and sweet, and did I already say fine? And God bless me, he was all mine. He arched a brow at the way I was looking at him, and a slow grin spread across his face. He started back toward me slowly.

"You love me too? Is that what you want to say, Miss Nightingale? Don't know how you'll get through the next five days without me? Praise the Lord for the day you met me?"

Outrageously arrogant and obnoxious, that's what he was. "Dammit, Merry Christmas." Shit, since he knew me so well, he knew what I meant.

He kissed me again and wiped my face with his thumb. "I hear you. I even hear what you didn't say." This time when he spun away, he didn't look back.

I was the last person to get on the plane, and the flight attendant had an attitude about it. I gave a damn and took my time stashing my carry-on in the overhead compartment. I fumbled around with my book and the gift from Greg before settling into the seat. She shot me a look as I finally sat and buckled my belt.

I ignored her as she started in on the safety bullshit they always told you. I tried to read my book, but that present just kept winking at me. I really should wait till Christmas. Then again, he wouldn't have given it to me if he wanted me to wait. We were airborne when I gave up the struggle and ripped into it. It was one of those box-in-a-box things he knows I hate. They're so irksome, and I was not close to being patient enough for these things. The old white woman next to me clucked her teeth as I opened the sixth one.

"He's really making you work for it, isn't he, honey?" She reminded me of my grandmother.

I thought, *You don't know the half of it, Grammy*. That boy made me work for everything. It could never just be simple with him. But instead I answered politely, "I guess he thought this would draw out the suspense." I came to the last box, and my heart started to beat a little faster. It was a little Tiffany blue box, and to me, that meant only one thing—jewelry. Yes, I loved that boy!

I was thinking tennis bracelet. Then I remembered when we went to the mall the last time and stopped in the jewelry store. "I'll bet it's those diamond studs I wanted!" I told Grammy next to me. She looked as excited as I felt. When I popped open the enclosed gray velvet box, my mouth fell open.

"Oh my God!" the woman next to me said, and all I could do was nod. I was staring down at the most beautiful diamond solitaire ring I'd ever laid eyes on. It was a flawless, simple, marquise-cut rock set into platinum. Simply perfect, had to be between three and four carats. There was a note jammed into the back of the case. I pulled it out, expecting beautiful words of love. It said, "Let's cut the bullshit, quit with the games. Enough already. I want it all or nothing. Marry me. Gregory."

"Lord, he's an arrogant asshole even when he's proposing." I felt the tears starting back up again. I couldn't believe it. Here it was, the day I'd been waiting on for thirty years. And I couldn't believe it, just was not absorbing the reality.

"Try it on, honey!" Grammy was still leaning all over into

my business. I started to hand her the note, since she was having a hard time reading it from her angle. I picked up the ring, and my hands were shaking. Jesus, I didn't want to drop it. I finally slipped it on the proper finger, and of course it fit perfectly. Fault him on some things, but he knew his shit.

"It's beautiful," a young girl across the aisle breathed. I looked up to realize that the whole section of the plane was watching me. I smiled at them smugly.

"It *is* beautiful, isn't it?" I flashed it around some so all their poor asses could get a good look. That's right, baby. Sister done landed her a good man. Strong, black, fine, and paid! And mine . . . all mine, forever and ever! I wanted to close my eyes and send up a prayer of thanks, but I couldn't take my eyes off the rock.

"You gonna marry him?" a guy in the row back and over an aisle asked. "You gotta marry a guy who buys you *that*!"

I grinned a little wider. Hell, yes, I was gonna marry him, and Fiona could kiss my entire black ass. "You bet I'm going to marry him." I cleaned it up a little so as not to shock the folks. The attendant came by to see what all the excitement was, and I flashed the rock and explained. Then I asked her to take the trash from the boxes away for me. Her look clearly said "You stuck-up bitch." I just smiled at her and whipped out my credit card for the air phone. I took the phone and went into the bathroom, as there was no hope of privacy at my seat. I dialed up his cell phone number first.

He answered on the first ring. "Hi, baby, how's the flight?"

I laughed. Of course he knew it was me. "You're an asshole. I love you. Yes."

"Like the stone, do you?" I heard the smile in his voice.

"Think you know me, huh?" I grinned right back.

"If not, I guess I've got till death do us part to find out."

"You bet your sweet ass, you do. You stuck with me now, Mr. Samson." I hung up on him. In the mirror, the ring winked at me. I winked right back. "Merry Christmas to me."

Jewel—Friday, December 23, 1:10 p.m.

Roman's voice was low and urgent. "Come on, baby, come on. Give it to me. Come for me now, baby. Now!"

"Sweet Lord." I gritted my teeth and begged for mercy.

"Jewel, now, baby."

Since the boy had me plowed up against the wall of some employee lounge at the airport and was loving me senseless with impossibly deep strokes at an incredibly fast pace, I had to comply with his demands. I let the climax slam across already jingling nerves, seep into tingling muscles. I felt his immediate response surging within me and bit my lip to keep from crying out.

I sighed and sagged back against the wall. We'd done quickies before but never quite this quick and frenzied. *Hot and sloppy* was the phrase I was searching for. We had been sitting in the gate area listening to my mom go on about the hotel she booked for us. She told Roman he'd be getting a chance to know Ross better, as they'd be roommates for the duration of the trip.

Roman and I looked at each other. For some reason, it hadn't occurred to us until just that minute that we wouldn't be sleeping together for a few days. Now, don't get me wrong; sex wasn't everything. But, uh, we're still in that haze, you know? That cloudy place where great sex was yours for the taking so you took it, often—more often than that if you could get away with it.

Anyway, Captain Cajun Fine Ass hit me with the smolder. The let's-get-it-on smolder. Next thing I knew, Roman told Mom that he and I were going to grab a snack. Five minutes later, we were down the terminal in some employee lounge. No idea how we got in or why it was empty. All I knew was it was about to be on. He grabbed me and lifted me, pressing me against the wall. Just like that, we were ready to rumble. Panties tossed, my skirt hiked up, legs wrapped around his waist. Zip, snap, drop, and he was in. And now here we were. Amazing how the thought of being deprived of something makes you instantly ravenous for it.

"That was a snack?" I teased, wheezing for air. I loosened my death grip on his hips and let my feet slide to the ground.

He grinned. "It sure wasn't a full-course meal, Miss Jewel." He stroked a hand down my back before backing away to put himself back together.

I looked for my purse before I noticed it was still on my shoulder. I dug my mirror out and looked in it. I was shocked—very little was out of place. God knows I felt completely disheveled. I dug out some Kleenex and did some quick cleanup work before picking up my drawers and shaking them out a little before pulling them back on. I sprayed a little perfume in some strategic places and planned to stay upwind of Mom and Dad for a little while.

He zipped up and checked his watch. "Let's shuffle."

"This how it's gonna be the next few days, player? Wham, bam, thank you, ma'am?"

"I didn't hear you complaining a minute ago, sugar." He grinned real annoyingly.

I wrinkled my nose at him. The damn male ego. Sometimes I forgot to tiptoe around it. "I was outta my mind a minute ago and you know it. All I'm saying is, if we can't do it well, let's not do it at all."

He spun me to him so quick I dropped the purse. "You saying I didn't do it well, Miss Jewel?" He wrapped his arms around me and put his hands on my rear, pressing me to him.

"You did it well, just not right, player. Sex without foreplay is like food with no flavor. It satisfies the hunger but lacks the visceral enjoyment."

He smirked. "All that groaning and quaking you just broke off? I got your visceral enjoyment."

I stood on tiptoe to kiss his jaw. "Idiot. I'm trying to say that I'm going to miss being with you. Being *with* you. You know you make me wanna do things . . ." I trailed my tongue from his ear to his jaw.

His eyelids dropped down a little. "What kind of things? Things we haven't done yet?" His breath caught on the word.

I grinned a little grin; men are so easy. "And in the tropics with the rum drinks—you know how I get after a drink or two, baby."

He groaned. "You get hungry . . . for more than a snack." He turned his head to capture my lips with his.

"Um, for more than a snack."

He lifted his head. "You better try to work out something with Heather, then, huh, baby?" Heather was Ross's new and very white girlfriend. Jungle fever all over the place these days. We were going to be roommates according to Cleo's little plan.

I shook my head. "But then Ross would know."

"Your brother thinks you're a virgin?" Roman looked at me skeptically.

"No, but I—"

"See no reason to prove otherwise, right?" Roman sighed. He'd heard it all before. I understood that this was a concept that he, as a male, wasn't going to be able to grasp. As the baby girl in the family, I had a certain image. I was the young, sweet, unspoiled child until the night of my wedding. If my parents or older brother suspected otherwise, we never spoke of it. Ever. My sister and I knew the real deal.

"You know how I am about stuff like this." I shrugged.

"A puritan in public and a wild woman against the wall?" he teased.

"I don't see why we have to break it on down like that."

" 'Cause, baby, you gotta decide if your brother's image of you is gonna hold up. Like you said, the sun, the sand, the sea. You and me cocoa buttered up with a rum drink or two? Hmm, I can hear the Bob Marley sound track in my head."

Be damned if he didn't have a point. Shrugging, I reached over and picked up my purse. "I'll have to see what I can do. Let's go; I'm ready."

We looked each other over before he took my hand and led me back to the gate. They were all there looking at us. Mom and Vince, Dad and Trudy, Stefani and Lamar, and Ross and Heather. I felt like they all knew. Hell, maybe they did.

"Did you eat?" Stefani asked with a gleam in her eye.

"Just grabbed a quick snack," Roman answered, perfectly straight-faced.

"Oh, a little something to tide you over, huh?" Ross asked.

I looked him straight in the eye, knowing my image was blown. "Yeah, you know how that is."

"I do indeed, little sister." He grinned at me and winked. "We'll have to work on being mindful of those hunger pangs while on vacation. Hate for my little sister to be deprived."

I blinked at him innocently. "And since you've been known to sit down and enjoy your meals at leisure, big brother . . ."

Heather looked between us and whispered to Ross, "Are y'all talking about the buffet schedule or the sleeping arrangements?"

We all exchanged glances.

"Kids, we're boarding," Cleo called out.

Roman and I let the others go ahead of us. As I picked up my carry-on, he leaned over to me. "Looks like it's gonna be a very merry Christmas after all, huh, babe?"

I grinned. "Yeah, and to all a good night, player."

23

Paradise Lost

Roman—Monday, January 9, 6:15 p.m.

The bitch of it was, we were actually minding our own damn business. I mean, I could count on one hand the number of times Beau and I went out to lunch together. This year, maybe two, three times tops. And coming downtown? Forget about it. Almost never happened. In a way, it was my fault. I suggested we swing by and see if Greg wanted to join us. It was when we were leaving the frigging building that it happened. Out of nowhere she came. Broadsided us, really. One minute I was talking Italian or Chinese food, next thing I knew, Beau started skinnin' and grinnin', dropping Cajun endearments like pennies into a fountain.

It was Renee. No hello or shit to me. Went straight for the kill: "Beauregard, you are a sight for sore eyes." She had squeezed her ass into some midthigh-length clingy dress with sky-high-come-and-get-me boots on. I'll say one thing—it was possible to be fly with no class at all.

Beau turned the grin up fifty watts. "Eh, *petite chou,* 'tis you that's a vision." *'Tis?* I didn't think anyone used the word " 'tis" outside of a Dickens novel.

"Ah, that's sweet to say," she cooed. On her way to see her damn fiancé, a big rock weighing down her finger and she was cooing at Beau. Made *me* wanna holler, throw both my hands up, you know?

"Sweeter to see, *ma belle*." He stepped closer. I rolled my eyes. The mack was in full effect.

I'd had enough. "Hello, Renee." The tone was like, remember me?

She flashed me a look. "Yeah, hi, Rome." I didn't know exactly when it was that Renee and I decided to dislike each other. It probably started the first time she commenced to perpetrating a fraud in front of me and I called her phony ass on it. Yeah, maybe that was it. All I knew was that it was kinda like a habit now. Which was too bad, 'cause I thought Greg was all right. At least when it came to business and shit like hanging out, he was okay. Didn't seem like the type to catch your back in a crisis, though, from a casual impression. Funny, 'cause Renee seemed the type to need a lotta catching over the years. I sent another look at that rock and shook my head. A woman oughta live up to a ring like that. She saw me looking and flashed it in the light a little bit.

Her mercenary ass, almost made a brother feel sorry for Greg. Hoped a brother knew what he was getting into. I turned and walked away a few steps. I didn't want to be part of it. But the whole thing started me to thinking about sneaking and cheating and such things. And I had to wonder, at what point did this kinda thang cease to be a harmless flirt and start easing into mental adultery? Glancing over at the two of them, I'd have to say right about now.

I stepped back to 'em just in time to hear Beau say, "We were going to take Gregory out to lunch with us, but he said he had another engagement. *C'est vous, oui?*"

She blinked up at Beau as if he'd just sung all of Luther's greatest hits. "I'm having lunch with Greg."

"That's what he just said, *chère*." I told her in a nasty voice, knowing I was being nasty.

She ignored me. "Why don't we all lunch together?"

Beau started to answer. "Sounds—"

I put the hand up to cut him off. "We gotta shuffle. Beau?" He might be older, but he recognized when I'd drawn a line. I wasn't going for that shit, no way. How was a brother supposed to get his grub on with all the drama flying round the table? Naw, wasn't gonna be me, not today. Renee sent me a look that could've dropped me at twenty paces.

"Perhaps another time, Renee?" He smiled at her with a perfect mix of regret and eagerness. I swear, if I wanted to be King Dog of the pound, I'd have to start taking lessons from big bro.

"Of course." She extended her hand to him like she was freaking royalty. Of course he kissed the back of it with all his charm oozing like hot syrup. She went for it in a big way. Ten to one, Greg skipped lunch and did a little office quickie with Aunt Jemima here. I pitied any man who had to eat Beau's leftover waffles, know what I'm saying?

I headed for the door. "We out, Beau." In that good old peripheral vision that came in handy, I saw her hand Beau her business card. I kept walking. When Beau caught up to me, I started in on him. "Beau, you saw the rock on her finger."

"And the gleam in her eye, little brother. I distinctly saw the gleam in her eye. Did you not SEE the boots she had on? My God."

I gave it up.

Jewel—Tuesday, January 17, 11:07 p.m.

I hung up the phone with a sigh. Renee had called Roni Mae on a tear about Roman and how she didn't think he was good enough for me. What was I, royalty? Roni felt it was her place to call me with the heads-up. With friends like these, well, you know what they say.

"So, what'd she want?" Roman asked. He was sprawled out in the bed playing with the remote control. His bedroom was like a shrine to bachelorhood, I kid you not. Black, brown, and some cream thrown in to lighten it up a little. Big heavy ebony pieces, king-size bed with black leather headboard. I didn't have to wonder about what he did before he met me. I knew. He had got this room hooked up for solid seduction. The light switch had a dimmer that was conveniently located both at the door panel and beside his nightstand. The universal remote, or should I say control panel (by far the most complicated piece of machinery I had ever seen), operated the stereo, the TV, the DVD player, and his iPod-playing alarm clock. If he tried, I'm sure it could set the microwave too. And he was a rabid TiVo guy. Oh, heaven forbid we should miss a sporting event or an episode of *Heroes* or a single freaking rerun of *The Sopranos.*

During football season, he not only watched the games, but he also TiVo'd each Cowboy game along with the pre- and postgame shows, the ESPN (a moment of silence for what has got to be the man's favorite channel) wrap-ups, the NFL channel previews, and any other show that might have some subtle insight we might have missed.

But I was rambling again, huh? If you hadn't noticed, I rambled when I was trying not to think about something.

I went into the bathroom for my brush, came out, and sat on my side of the bed. Something we fought over routinely. We both slept on the right. So when we were at his house, he slept on the right and vice versa at my house. But we still talked about it like one of us was going to change our minds. I looked over at him, sprawled in what I called his king-of-the-castle pose. Propped up against the headboard with all the pillows around him, legs sprawling over a big chunk of the bed, his control tucked just out of my reach, a soda in one hand and the other working on devouring all the popcorn. *Letterman* was on. What was it about men and David Letterman? Personally, I'd like to slap the cigar out of his smug little late-night mouth. But that was my opinion.

I grinned over at Mr. Wonderful, who was just tickled over Dave's latest top ten list. "Honey, you gonna save me some corn?"

He looked down and lifted his hand out of the bowl. "Got a little carried away."

"Wanna spare one or two of those pillows?"

He tossed two over. "Yeah, sorry, babe."

I was brushing my hair up into a ponytail when I finally asked him, "What the hell did you do to Renee?" That got his attention. He turned down the volume and looked at me.

He looked guilty as hell all of a sudden. "Nuthin'. Whatcha mean?"

I put the brush down and climbed over where I could get a good look at his face. "What I mean, player, is that you have somehow made an enemy of her, and she is now determined to free me from your evil clutches."

He put the soda down and sat up, suddenly alert. "Say what? What'd the bitch do?"

I frowned. Renee had her selfish tendencies, but there was no reason to call her a bitch. Only I could do that—homegirl prerogative. "Roman," I scolded.

"Sorry, what'd li'l sweetness do?" He didn't even try to sound sincere.

I had to laugh. "Nothing yet. She told Roni Mae she had a plan to show me the error of my ways. That was Roni Mae calling to tell me."

Roman scowled for a second, then shrugged. "Renee don't wanna start shit with me. I got her scheming ass cold."

"Oh yeah, why is this the first I'm hearing about it?" I didn't like the idea of him not telling me things. Not that he had to tell me every detail of his life but, well, hell, you know what I mean.

"Don't get spastic on me, Miss Jewel. I didn't tell you

'cause I knew you didn't wanna hear it." He looked like he was satisfied with that answer. I was far from it.

"What else haven't you told me that you thought I didn't wanna hear, hmm? You keeping secrets, player?" I tried to play it light, but I was not liking the way this conversation was going. Me being a naturally suspicious person and that little history with Tricky Rick started rearing its ugly head and suddenly I was looking at the boy like I didn't know who he was.

He sighed deeply and put his head down. "Let's not get into a big thing here. I ain't keeping shit from you that's important."

Wrong answer. "And which of us gets to decide what's important?" Now, I knew he probably didn't have shit to hide, but you couldn't be too careful these days.

Like I said, times like this reminded me of Patrick coming to me, telling me he had been seeing his ex-girlfriend and was going back to her. There I was, thinking everything was fine and dandy and he had the ex on the side. I was dreaming about bridesmaids' dresses and he was thinking up his next lie. And when it all came down, he told me, "I didn't tell you before because I knew it would upset you." Like I wasn't upset in the end? Like I wasn't still upset just thinking about it, the no-good two-timing son of a bitch. I blinked. This was now. This was Roman. He was different. He was *real*. He could be trusted . . . couldn't he?

Damn that Eddie Murphy. What did he have to do with anything, you ask? Lemme tell you. Remember that movie *Raw*? The live one in which he basically said all men sleep around no matter who they are or who they had. He messed up a lot of us with that one. Just jokes, or a little too true? And then you look at history—Patrick cheated on me, all my girlfriends had ex-boyfriends who cheated on them, couldn't think of too many married couples I knew that haven't had the whole fidelity-infidelity issue come up. The numbers didn't look good. Yeah, yeah, I know, it was just a *movie*. And you tried to be cool, like not all men were like that—there WERE some good brothers out there. Then you prayed and prayed that the one you found was one of the GOOD ones. But every once and a while, that doubt reared its head and here we were.

Roman snarled and threw his hands up. "Baby, what we fighting 'bout? I ain't cheating or sneaking or even looking, okay?"

Then, honestly, I don't know where it was lurking, but it just popped out of my mouth. "So why do you get so nervous every time someone brings up marriage?"

His jaw clamped shut. " 'Cause I been married, baby. I know it ain't all that holy an institution."

To say I was insulted didn't even begin to say it. "I'm not Jaquenetta!" Whether I wanted to get married or not, he should want to marry me. He should be giddy I would even consider it, damn!

"You really think you gotta tell *me* that? I know who you are, thanks much. You know who I am?"

I rolled my eyes. "I know you're not Patrick, if that's where you're going with this." Again with this shit.

He jumped off the bed and started into the bathroom. "Just remember, you brought his name into this bed. I didn't." He slammed the bathroom door behind him and slammed the toilet lid up.

What? Brought the name into the bed? Was that some sort of Cajun curse or something? I hopped up and swung the door open. He was standing there taking a pee and turned his head to look at me in amazement.

"Do you mind, Jewellen?" Oh, now we're Jewellen; brother wanted to get proper. I knew when he started talking slowly and properly that he was good and ticked off.

I shrugged. "Mind what? I've seen it before, player. Reckon I'll see it again before too long. And watch your aim, could you?"

He finished and flushed the toilet. As he tucked himself

back in, he sent me a look. "Naw, Miss Jewel, ain't gonna be no dick tonight." He dropped the lid and walked over to the sink.

My mouth fell open as I watched him wash his hands and pick up the toothbrush. "Whadaya mean, 'ain't gonna be no dick tonight'?"

He finished brushing and spit into the sink, then reached for the mouthwash and nodded at me. "You heard me."

I laughed; I couldn't help it. I'd never heard of the man holding out before. "What am I, on restriction?" I walked up behind him and wrapped my arms around his waist.

He stepped away and peeled my hands off him. He was serious and he said so. "I'm serious, Jewellen. You can splay yourself out spread-eagle on that bed buck naked with whipped cream and I won't touch you."

Well, now I was mad. What the hell was going on in here? "Oh, yeah?"

"Yeah, until you apologize for comparing me to Tricky Rick and bringing his name up in my bed, you can just go without." And with a cocky little grin, he went back into the bedroom.

Pretty sure of himself, wasn't he? "Who says I'll go without? Plenty of fish in the sea, player," I said silkily as I followed him. I had an irritating smirk plastered on too. Knew I was crossing the line but was too damn mad to care.

He stopped dead in his tracks and turned to look at me. "We don't seriously wanna go boating down that river, do we, Jewellen?" I actually felt a twinge of fear when he looked at me like that. Not fear that he would hurt me or anything like that. It was a gut feeling, fleeting and quick. His was a no-nonsense, don't-jack-with-me look you really couldn't ignore. I backtracked a little.

"Uh, no, we don't." I might have been mad, but I wasn't out of my mind.

He nodded once and climbed into bed. Methodically, he started clicking off appliances.

I crawled in on my damn side, too pissed to argue about which side I was on. So pissed in fact, that I got back up and headed for the door.

"Where you going?" he asked.

"To sleep in Chase's room."

"Don't trust yourself not to pounce in the night, huh? *Je comprends, chère, notre amour, cette passion . . . c'est puissant, non*?"

He was stooping low to whip out the French on me. He said, "I understand, darling, our love, our passion . . . it's powerful, no?" I really wanted to smack him. Really. But I didn't feel up to losing another fight tonight. Besides, I did have my pride. I turned around and got back under the covers, staying well on my side of the bed. "You might want to know that I've gone without before and can again. For as long as it takes."

He chuckled softly. "Of course, during that time, you were angry at all men, you built up a business that required all your spare time and energy, you bought and furnished a house, and had no one around to tempt you. Now, the memory of how we are together is fresh in that fertile mind of yours. And here's a warm body, not four feet away from you with nothing but a few measly words keeping you from getting what you want, for as long as you can stand it. You already know how it is between us. You wanna live without it for the sake of pride? *Eh, Bijou*?" He eased a little closer to me. He ran his tongue along the side of my neck in a way that drove me crazy, and don't think for one minute he didn't know that. He slid one hand down to rest on my hip and started rubbing in little circles. "*Eh, Bijou*, you have something to say to me?"

I reminded myself that there was more to our relationship than sex. Okay, great sex. Okay, mind-altering sex. I reminded myself that I had to be at work in the morning, looking well rested and professional. I reminded myself that he was going to have to go without too. Didn't take much to remind me how pissed I was at the boy and wouldn't have him if he begged right now. I refused to apologize. I was *not* sorry. What we had here was some sort of childish power play. What, I couldn't say certain things in his bedroom, but he could say whatever he wanted, whenever he wanted? Bump that. And let me get this straight—if I didn't toe the line and do what he wanted, I was cut off? So now we had this sex game, who could hold out longer? Damn the nonsense. I know I can sometimes be stubborn merely for stubborn's sake, but in this instance, I'd done nothing wrong. "Good night, Roman," I said firmly.

"So that's the way it's gonna be?" he said softly, and ran a finger down my spine. His breath was all up on my neck.

I jerked forward out of his reach and snapped out, "Sleep well, player."

"*Ah, bon nuit, Juliet.*"

It was two hours later as I lay in the dark listening to him snoring away like all was right with his world while I was literally stewing in all my own juices that I remembered something. He never did tell me what he had on Renee.

24

Just Messy

Renee—Thursday, January 19, 7:46 p.m.

I was on the treadmill in the cardio area next to Jewellen. God I hated coming to the gym. Half of these damn girls didn't need to be here no way. Pencil thin, not an ounce of fat on 'em. This was one of those new state-of-the-art gyms. Every damn thing was computerized and high tech. I slid my card into a box on the side of the treadmill, and it greeted me and automatically set my pace. After I was done, it was set to remind me to get on the thigh machine. God, I really hated it. But you had to stay fine. This world was all about packaging, no lie. Jewel was on the StairMaster, cursing up a storm. Now, even though my hair was getting nappy and sweat was rolling off me in rivers, I had to smile. You know why?

'Cause my shit was straight. Finally got the career hooked up, bank account smiling. I was looking good, got the good man hooked and reeled. Nothing left but the net. June 7, I would land that fish for better or for worse. Better be better.

Now that my ducks were in a row, I had to get Jewel to come correct. Couldn't have my girl going out like this.

I've thought about it a lot, and all I could say was, Rome

ain't the one for her. He got too much baggage, too much ghetto in him, too much attitude. Just too much shit, period. She didn't need that. That hip-hopper-done-good, street-smart-turned-savvy shit had to wear thin on her ass sooner or later. No matter how down she tried to be, Jewellen was an uptown girl through and through. Let me put it like this: she was croissants and mimosas, he was Wonder Bread and Kool-Aid.

Now what about me and Greggy? Couldn't the same be said of us? No. It was totally different. Everyone knew that women adapt to their surroundings a whole lot better than men; I could *be* croissants. Rome would always be, at best, toasted Wonder Bread.

We switched to the Nautilus machines, and I took a good look at my girl. She didn't look happy. Not the regular unhappy look that you get trying to push fifty pounds of resistance with your upper arms. A deep-down unhappy. Something wasn't right.

"Wanna knock off and go to the snack bar?" I asked. Any excuse to avoid that thigh thing.

"Yeah, sounds good."

We walked upstairs, sat down, and ordered strawberry protein smoothies. After they came, I started in. "So, girl, how's Rome?" No use beating around the bush.

Jewel shot me a suspicious look. "He's fine."

I smirked. "Yeah, he is that. But how y'all doing?"

"Why are you asking, Renee?"

I raised my brow. Homegirl was tense and defensive. Was there trouble in paradise? "Girl, what's up? Y'all seemed so happy after Christmas." Matter of fact, they came back disgustingly happy, all sunkissed and shit. I went over to flash my rock and could hardly get a word in with the two of them all cuddled up and slobbering on each other. Sick the way that boy kept her wrapped up. Hope she ain't whipped; brother did look like he knew how to throw it.

Jewel rolled her eyes. "Who wouldn't be happy after a great vacation in Mexico? The weather was perfect. My mom finally gave up on the idea that Patrick and I will ever get together again. Once she got over it, she actually allowed herself to like Roman a little. After he bought her the ugliest straw hat I'd ever seen, she couldn't say enough good things about him. Hell, one afternoon, I caught him and Dad doing tequila shots by the hotel pool. Another night, we all went out dancing." She smiled to herself. "Yeah, it was a good time."

Right off, I noticed that she stressed *was*. But I decided not to press her on it. I went another direction. "Talked to Trick the other day."

Jewel grinned a funny little grin, like there was a private joke I wasn't getting. "Oh, yeah?"

I pounced. "Have you talked to him?"

She laughed shortly. "Not hardly. How are he and Stace?"

I threw the bait out there. "Oh, not so great."

"Hmm, too bad." She didn't even nibble.

"He's still not over you, you know." Dangle, dangle. I was doing this for her own good.

"He said that, huh?"

"He sure did, girl."

"Figures."

"What?"

Jewel shrugged. "I'm surprised to be the only one to figure this out, but Patrick's always in love with the one he's left, not the one he's with. If Stace wants to keep him, she should leave him before he leaves her."

"I think he really loves you, Jewellen."

She stopped swirling her straw around and looked straight at me. "Can't resist, can you?"

I blinked innocently. "What?"

She sighed. "Renee, I'm sorry you and Roman don't get along, but I'm not leaving him for Patrick. Truth be told, unless something drastic happens, I'm not leaving him, period." Her expression turned thoughtful. "Yeah, if we split up, he's gonna have to walk, not me."

For some reason, that really pissed me off. I mean, how could she be so secure about it? Drastic things happen all the time. What made her think she was immune? No relationship was ironclad. Apparently I had a nasty expression on my face, 'cause when she looked up, she grinned at me.

"Don't look so fierce, Renee. What's he got on you anyway?"

"Huh?"

"Did he catch you in a compromising position with Brother Beau or what? Come on, girl, what's really going on?"

Now, why she had to bring Beau into it, I didn't know. Whatever I decided to do about or with Beau was my business and mine alone. Roman didn't need to put his nose in it and neither did she. But that would be like admitting I was planning on doing wrong. So instead I said, "Jewellen, I'm marrying Gregory."

She laughed outright, her first genuine display of humor all day—wouldn't you know it was at my expense? "Yeah, six months from now. And in the meantime, what happens?"

"I haven't even seen Beau," I lied smoothly.

She shrugged again. "You will."

"Jewel!" I protested. It was true, though. It was just a matter of time.

"Renee, I know you. You want that man so bad, you're probably wearing poor Gregory out night and day. Beau is that pretty boy you've talked about wanting since freshman year of college. Everyone has a personal fantasy weakness, girl. Yours is that tall, fine, part corporate, part thug pretty boy with just enough exotic sex appeal to make everyone in the room want him but he's with you. Beau is that fantasy come to life for you. And here he is, oh so available. Kid Greg because you have to, kid yourself if you feel you need to, but remember who I am—you ain't fooling me."

She was right on the money. Nothing was more irritating than to have someone tell you about yourself. "You totally misunderstand the situation. I love Greg. I'd never do anything to hurt him."

She snorted. "You love what Greg is, not who he is. And aren't you the one always saying 'what they don't know won't hurt them'?"

I pushed my drink away. "That's a shitty thing to say, homegirl. Really shitty." It was a sure sign we've been friends too long if she could so easily throw my own words back against me.

She laughed again. "What? You want me to apologize? Join the club."

I had no idea what she was talking about, and I didn't want to know. She didn't sound remorseful any damn way. She made me sound so shallow, like I only loved Greg for what he could do for me and what we could have together. It ain't even like that. If you took away Greg's money, position at the bank, good family name, excellent breeding, and the BMW, I would still . . . I would . . .

Damn, I would never have given him the time of day. Well, I might have had to swing a little episode or two, 'cause the brother was horizontally talented. But then again, those were the things that make up who Greg was, right? So I did love him, and that was why I planned on marrying him. I mean, you think he would have given me the time of day if I was plain and overweight, working at the gas station with no ambition to do otherwise? Not hardly.

Besides, how'd we get onto this? I was talking about Rome. Man, I hated it when she turned shit around on me.

"What I was trying to say before all of this came up is that you don't seem happy with Rome."

"We're fine," she snapped, reticent again.

"You were happy with Patrick. Just don't miss the forest for the trees, girl."

"Uh-huh. And what about Stace? I suppose I just trample over her to get to him, hmm?"

I shrugged. "Hey, I like Stace, but she wasn't worried about your li'l feelings when she jumped on him like the first boat outta Timbuktu. You hear me? You gotta give as good as you get in the world, girl." Shit, it was tough out there; sometimes you gotta let the rules go, make your own. Long as you got yours.

"One good turn deserves another?" Jewel asked.

Now she was getting it. "Exactly."

"What about two wrongs don't make a right?"

I shook my head. "See, girl, you always take shit one step too far."

"Uh-hmm."

"Listen, just do this. I told Patrick to call you so y'all can talk. When he calls, can you be open and receptive?"

"I can."

"Will you?"

"Like I was open and receptive when he ripped my heart out and flew back to Georgia without so much as a good-bye?"

"Jewellen, let the past go, girl." She was still real bitter about that.

"Renee."

"Hmm?"

"Leave it be, girl."

"But, Jew—"

"As long as we've been friends, through all of our ups and down, are you really going to try and run game on me now?"

"I'm not running game, Jewel. I'm up in your Kool-Aid because I believe this is what's best for you."

"No, really. To coin one of your clichés, whatever will be, will be, okay?"

True enough, but who was to say that we couldn't nudge

things in the direction we wanted? I pretended to let it drop. "Fine, let's talk about the plans for the wedding."

Gregory—Friday, January 27, 1:29 p.m.

I was in a state of confusion. Some shit was funky. As I sat in the restaurant waiting for a waitress to notice me, I reflected on the fact that despite the declarations of love, the great sex, and the impending wedding, something was wrong between me and Renee. I had tried looking at it as objectively as I could from all angles. I had to conclude that whatever it was, it wasn't me and there was nothing I could do about it. The worse thing was, I couldn't put my finger on it. Was hard as hell to find a solution if you're not sure what the problem was.

Of course, it could just be that I was in a foul mood because they were going to announce the promotions at the bank this afternoon. I was up for regional director of special projects. Not only would it mean a hefty pay hike, but it also meant a step closer to the vice-president position I hoped to reach before age forty. That was why I took off for a solitary lunch. I couldn't sit in the office, waiting and thinking. I hated it when things are all up in the air. It made me uneasy. With a sigh, I reached for a menu.

"Gregory?" I looked up from the list of lunch specials to see Roni Mae standing beside my table. I blinked once or twice, because I'd never seen her look like this. *This* meaning, this together. She had on a navy suit with high-heeled sandals. The skirt was short, and I was shocked to notice that Roni had legs. Nice legs. Her hair was in a normal style, and she had subtle makeup on. Roni Mae with clear lip gloss! It was new but it was nice. She shifted uncomfortably as I scanned her up and down, and I grinned. She was going to have to get used to men giving her the once-over.

"Sorry, Veronica. You look nice." She looked stunned that I knew her real name. Looking like she did, she looked like a Veronica, not a Roni Mae. "So what brings you downtown?"

She grimaced. "Meeting with my lawyer; it's contract-negotiation time."

I nodded. "A necessary evil." I knew I was making her uneasy with the way I was looking at her, but I couldn't believe how much she'd changed from the catsuited blond woman I met about nine months ago. I wondered how much weight she'd lost. I couldn't remember her having a waistline before. Roni was . . . well, shit, she was fine! And it wasn't just the weight—she had a pretty face now that I could see it.

She cleared her throat. "Well, don't let me keep you from your lunch. I'll just grab a table over there." She turned away, and I reached out and grabbed her hand. Her skin was soft and smelled of peaches and vanilla. Now why would I notice something like that? I *had* been under stress lately, and weird shit has been in my head.

"Veronica, I didn't mean to make you uncomfortable. You just look so great. Why don't you join me for lunch? The waitress hasn't asked for my order yet anyway." I flashed the grin at her for good measure.

She smiled a genuine smile for the first time. "Well, if you put it like that . . ." She eased into the booth seat across from me. "So, how's the great house-hunt coming?"

Ray and I had been casing all of Dallas for a house, and it was not going well. "It would go better if your homegirl didn't expect to live in a castle," I answered with a scowl. That girl had more styles. "I want a pool, Greggy. I need a double oven, Greggy. We need bigger guest rooms, Greggy." All this after she told me the mortgage would be my responsibility and she'd take over the utilities and groceries. Already it looked like the wedding was going to be mostly on me. Except her dress and those of the bridesmaids. How generous of her. Like I didn't have a car note or anything else to pay? And I just knew it was going to fall to me to come up with the extras. The vacations, the little gifts, the nights out. My wallet was having chest pains just thinking about it. I could only hope that my promotion comes through. Otherwise it looked like I couldn't afford to be married to Renee.

Roni Mae nodded. "Yeah, I told her she was being unrealistic, but you know how she is. Renee wants it all and then some . . . and then some more on top of that." She flashed me a surprisingly pretty smile. "She should just be happy she's got a good man and take the rest as it comes."

I stared at her. That was it. Right on the money. Within half a minute and without fanfare, she managed to get right to the crux of the problem. No matter what I did or bought or said, Renee would always want more. That's who she was. I shook my head. "Amazing."

Roni Mae looked confused. "What?"

I laughed shortly. "Just that quick, you managed to solve a mystery that's been eluding me for months."

She shrugged. "Sometimes you see things more clearly from the outside looking in."

We fell into a contemplative silence for a few seconds before the lethargic waitress appeared.

"Can I get y'all something to drink?"

Roni Mae looked at me and rolled her eyes. "Actually, honey, we're ready to order. I'd like iced tea and a grilled chicken salad with your house vinaigrette." If I had been with Renee, she'd have cussed the poor girl out and then ordered something complicated just to torture the waitress.

"I'll have a club sandwich with curly fries and a Coke," I ordered. After the waitress left, I sat there smiling at Roni Mae.

She frowned. "Why do you keep grinning at me?"

I tilted my head. "I guess it's because you look so different."

"Hmmph, I'm still the same person," she said crankily, but she couldn't hide her wide grin.

"Well, then, I'm sorry I never got the opportunity to get to know you better before this."

We lapsed into a steady, comfortable stream of conversation throughout the meal. I was shocked from time to time to realize that this was the first nonbusiness conversation I'd had with a woman in a long time that didn't involve some master plan on my part. I didn't stop to analyze how I was saying things or why. I was having a simple, enjoyable conversation. We talked about Aaron, and she forgave me for ever introducing the two of them. We talked about my promotion and how anxious I was about it. I glanced down at my watch after she told a hilarious story about one of her call-in contestants on the radio show.

"Veronica, we've been here for an hour and a half!" I couldn't believe it—I never lose track of time. Especially not during the workday!

She looked shocked. "Damn, I've got to hurry over to the station for a meeting."

We both stood hurriedly, reaching for coats, wallets in hand. "I've got it," I protested as she grabbed the check.

She sent me an amused look. "You're going to need it marrying the cash queen, darlin'."

I winced and let her take the check. Hell, she spoke the truth. I was just shocked she'd offered to pay. Renee never offered to pay for shit.

As we walked to the register, a colleague of mine waved at me. "Now that you're the boss, you can take long lunches, huh, Samson?"

Veronica and I stopped dead in our tracks and turned toward him. "What did you say, Klingman?" I asked slowly.

He grinned. "Haven't heard yet? You got it, man. Congratulations, Mr. Regional Director."

Veronica squealed beside me, and without thinking, I turned and grabbed her up in a big hug. I swung her around in a circle before setting her down. I smiled down into her face. She grinned up at me. "Congratulations, Big Man." She said it in her best Veronique voice, and I just went with the moment. I leaned down and kissed her. Not lightly either. Hell, I was caught up in the moment and she was there. What surprised me was that she kissed back . . . with enthusiasm. I dropped my coat, pulled her closer, and started acquainting myself with Veronica Mae Jackson's mouth. I liked what I discovered. She was sweet, natural. No snazzy technique, maneuvers, or manipulation. Just pure, honest sensation. Basic chemistry, man to woman. It was hot, it was wild, and I couldn't get enough. She sighed into my mouth as I slid a hand behind her neck to change the angle. The kiss went on and on until I was hard as a rock and she was sagged up against me, grasping my jacket for support.

"Way to go, boss!" Klingman called out, effectively splashing the moment with an ice-cold reminder of where and who we were. I stared down into Veronica's face and saw passion, longing, and surprise. I felt the same way.

Immediately, Veronica lowered her lashes and took a step back. For some reason, I didn't want her to retreat. If this wasn't the damnedest thing! This was Veronica—hell, Roni Mae—for Christ's sake.

"Veronica—" I started, and she put a hand out.

"No, no need to say anything. It was just a spur-of-the-moment thing." She looked up at me and smiled a fake little smile. I could tell she was embarrassed as all hell and was trying to be brave. Hell, I was the one standing there with a hard-on like a lead pipe caused by my fiancée's bridesmaid.

I nodded. "Okay. Thanks for a nice lunch. And a nice, um, celebration." I groaned inwardly. *Quit talking, Samson.* But what could I say? Hell, what was there to be said?

"Uh-huh, congratulations again. See you around." She backed away before turning and practically running out of the restaurant. I leaned down to pick up my coat and noticed the check lying where she had dropped it during our little, um, celebration. I paid it and headed back toward the office.

So, I started thinking. I knew about the job—that was set. I knew what was wrong with Renee, but what could I do about that? But what the hell was that thing with Veronica?

Christ! Roni was sexy as all hell; didn't know why I never saw that before. Aaron must've been a damn fool. If she was my woman—stop right there, Samson. Had to get my head together and get with the program. To think I went to lunch hoping to ease my confused brain. Next time I got confused, I'd order in.

25

Getting to the Party

Jewel—Saturday, February 4, 2:57 p.m.

We were hidden between the produce and the dairy sections, partially camouflaged by a Nabisco display. I peered over the Wheat Thins and around the Triscuits to the butcher's corner.

"I can't believe you're doing this," Roni Mae whispered to me.

I spared a withering glance in her direction. "Shut up, Roni. I know what I'm doing." I sort of had a plan. Roman and I were still on the outs. I hadn't laid eyes or anything else on him in two and a half weeks. I was too proud and stubborn to apologize, and he was too proud and stubborn to give in. It was a foolish standoff, and neither one of us would back down. But enough was enough. I was afraid that the longer we stayed apart, the harder it would be to get back together. Desperation was just around the corner, and I *hated* feeling desperate. I needed an ally. Someone who could give me a little insight into how to solve this thing without either one of us appearing to give in. Like an accidental reconciliation, that's what I needed.

Alanna Montgomery was my target. I was going to casually bump into her and see what happened. If this didn't work, I would have to go to plan B. The *B* stood for "begging," and I really didn't want to go there. So here I was, at the supermarket, waiting for Alanna to come in and do her weekly grocery run. I knew exactly what I was doing . . . sort of.

Roni Mae snorted. "You're stalking Roman's mama; that's what you're doing." She rolled her eyes. "Why didn't you just call the woman up and ask what you can do to get her son back without groveling? Ain't she gonna wonder why you're shopping in a grocery store way 'cross town from your house?" Her voice had risen dramatically, and I hurriedly shushed her.

"Shh! That's why you're here. I'm going to say that you wanted to come to this store. She doesn't know you don't live over here. Okay, there she is." Alanna Montgomery pushed her cart up to the butcher section and began an animated discussion with the man behind the counter. "Let's get ready to go. Grab some stuff." Roni and I shoveled some items into our cart and plunged forward. I circled the produce section while Roni convincingly sniffed and fondled fruit. Slowing down, I glided toward the meat counter.

"Eh, Bijou, is that you, *chére*?" Alanna sang out, and I smiled. Perfect. She came over and hugged me.

"Mrs. Montgomery! How are you doing?" I hugged back. What a great woman; hopefully she'll make this easy for me. I really didn't want to have to beg.

"How many times I tell you call me Alanna, huh?" she scolded good-naturedly.

I smiled wider. "Alanna. You remember my girlfriend Veronica?"

Alanna narrowed her eyes at Roni. "You get thinner since I see you last, Roni?"

Roni Mae nodded with a grin. "Yes, ma'am."

Alanna shook her head in resignation. "*Les jeunes filles aujourd'hui*!" I took that as "you young girls today!" She looked into our cart. "You diet on Teddy Grahams and Triscuits, *chére*?"

Roni sent me a suffering look. "Actually, these are for the station. You never know when low-fat snacks will come in handy." I gave her a mental high five for improvisation skills.

"Um-hmm." She sent Roni a last dubious look before pinning me with her gaze. "So, we miss you at *le diner Dimanche, Bijou.*" Sunday dinner. The last Sunday of every month, the Montgomerys got together for dinner. This was the first month I had missed it since September. Just this moment, I realized how much I had missed it. Come to think of it, I'd spent the past Sunday cleaning out my pantry . . . hold back the excitement, please. It was pathetic. You think I was going back to that every weekend?

I shifted uncomfortably, and Roni spoke up. "I'm going to check on that new protein granola bar. Be right back." She took off, practically leaving skid marks.

Before I could speak, Alanna continued. "And my Roman, *le 'tit chou*, he has the grim look in his eyes even when he smiles, *Bijou*. You fight, no?"

I sighed. "We fight, yes."

She shrugged. "So make up, chile."

I squirmed a bit. "Well, it's not that easy. See—"

"*Bijou*, please." She cut me off. *"L'orgueil et la jeunesse ne faisons pas bien ensemble, tu entends?"*

Frowning a bit, I tried to translate. "Pride and youth don't do well together?"

"Exactement!" She was pleased, but I wasn't. What she was basically telling me was that I was going to have to give in. Damn.

I really wanted to stand on my principles. Of course, that appeared to mean I would stand alone.

"Listen, *Bijou, je comprends* how hard it is to let go of the stubborn pride—the female ego has size too! Ah, when I think of the *mêlees* Avery and I used to have. Ha! We still fight, *chére*!

But tell me, is your pride so *importante* that you want to lose my Rome over it? Eh?" She rushed on. "Kat has a fancy soirée tonight to celebrate her new contract. It's at the Anatole. Seven o'clock. You come. You look good and show that boy of mine what he's missing. Let him sweat *pour un moment,* then snatch him up, chile." Roni Mae was easing her way back over to us. "And you bring the shrinking Roni, no? We feed her better than crackers!" Alanna laughed.

I'd heard about the party from Renee. Her company, Royal Mahogany, was sponsoring the event. Kat had just signed an exclusive modeling contract with them. Renee said invitations were impossible to get. "We don't have invitations, Alanna."

She dug into her purse, whipped out two envelopes, and handed them to me. "These are my last two, *chére*. You and Roni put them to good use." She smiled at me. "Now, I'm going to do some grocery shopping. And next time you want to talk to me, try the phone, eh, *Bijou*?" She laughed in hearty amusement at my expense and started off down the aisle.

"She knew all along, huh?" Roni asked.

I watched Alanna disappear around the aisle. I could only pray that I had it that much together when and if I reached her age. "Yeah, I guess she saw right through me." Same as her son did. I ditched the cart and we started out of the store.

Roni peered over my shoulder at the invitations. "So where we going tonight?"

"The Royal Mahogany Presentation Ball, baby!" I grinned, absolutely pleased with myself. I looked over at Roni. She did not look quite as pleased. "Don't you want to go? This should be a great little party! Think networking. Work the room, scout for men?" I loved stuff like this, and Roni Mae usually did too. Well-to-do, influential, and up-and-coming blacks from the Dallas area and beyond all gathered together in one room. She should be in heaven. This was a supreme networking opportunity. I unlocked the doors and climbed in. After a minute she climbed in too.

"Renee and Greg will be there?" she asked uneasily, fiddling with the seat belt.

Something in her tone worried me. I started the car before speaking. "Of course! Most of this campaign will be directly under Renee's jurisdiction, and I'm sure she'll have Gregory on her arm as the ultimate trophy date. Can't you just see them? Her in some skintight number flashing that rock all over the place and Greg power-brokering the hell out of the room, Armani tux in full effect, no doubt. The ultimate buppie couple at the ultimate shindig. I can hardly wait to see it."

"I'm not going," Roni said.

I stared at her. "What? Why not?" Ah, damn, there was a story here. Did I want to hear it?

"I'm just . . . no, I just can't, that's all." She turned to look out the window.

"What's going on with you? You've been irritable and nervous for the past week. Who are you dating that's doing this to you?" Roni Mae only got this unsettled over a man. God, if I had a dollar for every man who could send and had sent this girl swinging. Like a pendulum from glad to sad in a heartbeat. Silently, I thanked the Lord for blessing me with a calmer disposition. Then again, I just finished stalking a man's mama from behind the Nabisco display. Who was I to talk?

She laughed nervously. "No, no, I'm not dating anyone right now; you know that."

I sighed. "Well, then, bring it on. What's up, girl?"

"Well, I'm starting to have feelings for someone I shouldn't."

My eyes went wide, and I made a point of turning the corner and easing into the slow lane before I looked at her. My mind was going a mile a minute. Who? God, don't let her say Roman. My relationships with two of my girlfriends are strained enough because of men; I couldn't afford another. Stace tripping over Trick, Renee all in my face about Roman . . . What was this going to be about?

"Well?" I prompted.

"It's Greg," she whispered so softly, I had to lean over to hear her. Still, I thought I couldn't have heard her properly.

"I beg your pardon—did you say Gregory Greg? Greggy Greg? Renee's Greg?" My voice had gotten louder until I was sure I had shouted the last word.

She winced. "Yeah. That's him."

Ah, shit. Women could get along if it weren't for men; I swear we could. Of course, we'd be cranky and there'd be no one to kill bugs and take out the trash. But at least we could eat ice cream without worrying about fat grams, stop and ask for directions without being mocked, and watch TV without the channels being switched every thirty seconds. Rambling again . . . sorry, flustered. I attempted to be calm. "So, when did all this come about?"

"It started the night of the barbecue at your place, you know, Labor Day?"

"Uh-huh." I had no idea what she was talking about. I didn't even notice her speaking to Greg.

"Well, he was just so nice. I kept thinking, 'Damn, he's a nice guy.' You know, Aaron could be such an ass about things."

"Uh-huh." It was the best response I could muster.

"Anyway, it's not like I'm doing anything about it. I just really like him. But I'm pretty certain I'd feel funny making little chitchat at him and Renee right about now."

"Roni, you're in the wedding! You can't duck and run from them forever."

She sent me an irritated look. "I know that, Jewellen. But for right now, while everything is fresh, I need my space."

While *what* was fresh? I decided to approach this cautiously, like the ticking time bomb of a situation that it was. "So, you haven't seen him since when?"

"Well, at church and stuff like that. And, oh, at that dinner at Pops Montgomery's ."

I shot her a look. "No, Roni, I mean alone." I just knew she was going to say no.

"Well, uh . . ."

"Veronica!"

"We accidentally met for lunch last week."

To say I was shocked was putting it mildly. Roni Mae was the least deceptive person I knew. If she was sneaking around behind Renee's back, who was left to trust in the world? And Greg, well, I had to know. "Accidentally?"

She put a hand up. "Absolutely, swear to God. I had no idea he was in that restaurant."

"So what happened?"

"Nothing really." She turned to look out the window again.

"Nothing? But you don't want to look him or Renee in the eye tonight?"

"Okay." She turned back toward me. "It was just a kiss. He'd just found out about his promotion, and we got caught up in the excitement and he kissed me. That's all."

"Hmm." I raised a brow. I knew if I stayed silent, she'd spill the truth of it.

"A series of kisses linked together as one, really."

"Really."

"Really."

I thought about it for a second and decided to probe deeper. "This series of kisses, are we talking tongue here?"

"Uh, yeah."

"Heavy breathing?"

"Um-hmm."

Damn, this could get messy. "On your end, are we talking electricity?"

She leaned back against the seat and closed her eyes. "Snap, crackle, and pop." The expression on her face said it all. All at once, I felt worried for her and lonely for Roman. What a mess.

"Snap, crackle, AND pop. Oh my. On his side, any, er, noticeable signs of reciprocal feeling?"

She moaned a little in her throat and whispered, "Rock-solid evidence, you could say."

"So basically if you two had been anywhere the slightest bit private . . ."

"Horizontal bugaloo, knocking boots, the hookup, wild thing, down and dirty, whatever you want to call it, it would've been *on.*"

It was too much for me to take in. Roni Mae and Greggy. "Oh my."

"So you see the problem."

I couldn't hold it back. All of a sudden, I'd had it with all this mess. I let it out. "Roni, I see that Greg was nice to you when you needed someone to be. I see that you two were thrown together in an unique situation and you acted on those feelings. I also see that Renee and Greg are headed for a fall, and maybe Greg wants someone there to pick him up when it happens. I see that you have feelings for someone you know is completely off limits. He's Renee's fiancé, for Christ's sake! That's what I see, Roni. Now let me tell you what I think. I think you need to forget that kiss ever happened. And I think that you need to go to this party tonight, ignore your libido, and look around for a nice guy who comes without strings that could trip you up badly. Put you on a nice dress and dance with a good-looking man. Mind over matter. That's what I think, Roni."

She looked at me, tight-lipped and glassy-eyed, for a long time before speaking. "You're right."

Even though I knew I'd been bitchy about it, I smiled at her. She would do the right thing. Thank God we were close to the mall. My sympathy-empathy quota was used up for the day. I wanted nothing more than to find a killer dress, get to this party, and get Roman back into my life. Slowly but surely, he was becoming the only sane relationship I had left.

Roni Mae smiled. "I'm gonna get me a new dress and a new man."

I patted her hand. "That's good, girl. You're doing the right thing."

"I know. I just needed someone to tell me."

"That's what I'm here for. Besides, you hid behind Ritz crackers for me today, girl. I owe you for life."

We grinned at each other as I turned into the mall parking lot.

26

Let's Get the Party Started

Renee—Saturday, February 4, 8:17 p.m.

Finally got a minute to chill out and catch my breath. Nothing has and nothing will go wrong this evening. Put plain, I was the shit. No, really. I looked like a million bucks—got a sweet deal on this leave-nothing-to-the-imagination, electric-blue, off-the-shoulder sheath cocktail dress with a killer slit up the back. Sexy ankle-wrap peep-toe pumps in silver. Ring just a-winking and a-blinking in the light. Greggy was looking fly as all that in the *GQ* tux. Company president came over to me and congratulated me on putting this shindig together right. YES! I felt like breaking out in a Hammer dance and singing "Can't Touch This," but that would age me in this crowd.

And that wasn't all—Roman was here with some little hoochie on his arm. Guess he and Jewel were splitsville. Like I didn't see that shit coming! For the icing on the cake, got Beauregard Montgomery standing not two feet away from me. That boy was hot sex on a silver platter and damned if he didn't know it. Greggy was somewhere networking the crowd, so I could just take this minute to gaze my fill at the black Adonis here. Um, um, um. Good to the last drop. I was about to take a step toward him when a familiar voice spoke from behind me.

"Hey, girl, whatcha doing?" That couldn't be Jewellen. No way. I turned slowly. Hot damn. This girl showed up in the damnedest places. She looked good too. Bright purple halter evening dress in satin with the cleavage going on and a slit right up the thigh of that long, tight skirt.

"Hey, girl! Whatta surprise!" In other words, why you here? Out of the corner of my eye, I saw Beau move away. Another chance blown thanks to Jewellen Rose. Buster! Always saving me from myself—even when I didn't want a life preserver!

"I ran into Mrs. Montgomery, and she gave us tickets." She was speaking to me, but her eyes were scanning the room. From her expression, I knew the instant she laid eyes on Roman and his companion.

"Us?" I shifted a little so she could get a better look at Romeo and the fly girl.

She looked behind her. "Roni was with me a minute ago." We searched the crowd for a minute, but I didn't see Roni anywhere. "Oh, there she is," Jewel said in a funny tone.

"What? Where is she?" I couldn't see her anywhere.

"Over there dancing with Greg." She looked out at the dance floor with a strange expression on her face before turning to look back at Roman.

I scanned the dance floor, and it took a moment to place her. Roni looked great. Had on a sequined black minidress. "Wow, I hadn't noticed how much better she's looking. That's sweet of Greg to spend some time with her." Greggy was a good guy. Not only did he love me, but he was also considerate of my friends. He knew Roni had been having a tough time of it since the thing with Aaron went up in flames. She looked at him and laughed. At least she was having a good time.

"Yeah, he's a saint," Jewel said drily before turning away. "You will excuse me, won't you?"

I caught a glimpse of Beau out of the corner of my eye. He was holding up two glasses of champagne with a questioning grin on his face. Brother was wearing all on that tux. Looked like an ad for something sinful.

Quick survey: Greg with Roni, Jewel headed for Roman, my boss was drooling over Kat. All clear. "Yeah, girl, catcha later." Jewel and I parted and headed toward our respective Montgomery men.

Roman—Saturday, February 4, 8:23 p.m.

I didn't see baby 'til she was fifteen feet in front of me. Carla was going on about something, and I was just thinking how much I missed intelligent conversation. I looked up and BOOM! Like a vision, she came sailing toward me in a dress meant to make me beg. I started from the high-heel CFM shoes with the strap wrapped all around her ankles and worked all the way up to the curly do. Christ Almighty, baby fine. The look on her face was serious. But I was determined to play it cool. I slid a hand in my pocket and watched her approach.

She stopped a foot in front of me and stared right into my eyes. Without blinking, she reached out and put a hand on Carla's arm. "I'm really sorry to do this, honey, but you're gonna have to excuse Roman. I'm afraid he's already taken."

Carla's mouth dropped open. "Now wait a minute . . ."

Still, she looked straight at me. Sending me the look that drove my temperature straight through the roof. When she spoke, it was in that husky let's-get-it-on tone. "Much as I hate to treat a fellow sister girl like this, trust me, it's better this way. Look at it this way—now you have the whole rest of the night to land another fish. This trout is on my line. It's time I reeled him in." She took her hand off Carla's arm and took my hand in hers. "Dance with me?"

I let her pull me onto the dance floor, and we began a reserved side step. "So what brings you out, Miss Jewel?"

"Had a few things to say to you." She stepped in a little closer, meeting my gaze.

I looked down and caught a truly applause-worthy view of the cleavage. Um, I had missed this girl in so many ways. Lifting my eyes back to hers, I joked, "You thought that dress would get you listened to tonight?"

She smiled. "I needed to get your attention."

"You succeeded." The music turned slow and sultry. She slid her hands up my arms to my shoulders.

"Shall we?" It was then I saw what I was looking for. That slight uncertainty that showed she was a little nervous, vulnerable but putting herself out there . . . for me.

I nodded and placed my hands on her waist. I lowered my head and said in her ear, "You came in here like a woman on a mission. Wanna tell me what's up?"

"Came to get my man."

"Your man, huh? Is that what I am?"

"Not gonna make this easy, are you?"

"You walked away a little easy. Think I should let you walk back in the same way?"

"I didn't walk away; you shoved me."

"I had a reason." At the time I did. I really did.

"You had a grudge."

"Is that what you think?"

"No, no, I'm doing this wrong." She wrapped one hand around the nape of my neck.

I needed to focus. "Yeah ya are."

"Will you give me a chance to explain? Make it right?"

"Think you can?"

She sighed. "God, I hope so. I want you back. I missed you."

"I missed you too." I pulled her in a little closer.

"Will you come home with me?"

I stepped back and raised a brow. "Brazen girl, I ain't easy. We are deeper than the sex, babe."

She flushed and shook her head. "I meant, come home with me so we can talk, Roman."

"You wore that dress to get talked to tonight?" We shared a laugh. We both knew that the way we were feeling, the heat we were generating just standing next to each other, there would be a lot more than talking going on.

She swayed her hips a little bit as she stepped backward. "You coming, player?"

I swallowed and forgot all about playing it cool. "As soon as you want me to, baby."

She grinned. "I hear you—let's go." She turned around and headed toward the exit.

I was fast on her heels; it never occurred to me to do anything other than follow.

27

The Party Is Over . . . So Over

Gregory—Saturday, February 4, 9:34 p.m.

"Greg, where's your fiancée?" Veronica asked me.

I jumped back a little, startled at the reminder. I hadn't seen her in a little over an hour. I laughed. "Do you know I have no idea?" I figured she was off impressing some company bigwig.

"Do you care?" she asked in that Veronique voice. Veronica and I were sitting at a table in the corner of the room. When she came in, I could immediately sense that she was uncomfortable, so I asked her to dance and pretended like nothing ever happened. No easy task on my end. This girl can wear a minidress. I was engaged, not dead. Who'd've thought it? Roni Mae with a set of killer legs. Roni Mae, a sex kitten?

Anyway, soon as she was a little more at ease, we worked the room a little. I was surprised at how many people listened to her show and had complimentary things to say about it. By this point, she was completely comfortable with me, so I shuffled her over to a corner for a little chat. I did something I rarely do with a woman—I was totally honest with her. I told her that I wasn't going to pretend we never kissed and that I was both surprised and unnerved that I was attracted to her. I told her I knew she was attracted to me. I said there was no reason to rehash all the reasons we couldn't do anything about it. It was best just to acknowledge it once and then shelve it. She agreed, then asked me a messed-up question like that.

"What do you mean do I care? Didn't we just have that discussion?"

She didn't flinch at my tone. "All I'm saying, Gregory, is that your fiancée has been invisible for the last hour, and you never once stopped to look around for her. Usually you keep an eye on the person you came with, fiancée or no. Nor did it even occur to you to wonder where she was. *I* brought it up. That's all I'm saying."

When she put it that way, I felt less than committed. So I went on the offensive. "Well, what about Jewel? Do you know where she is and what she's doing right now?"

Veronica smiled. "Jewel is not my fiancé, but to answer your question, I can pretty much guess that she's somewhere with Roman getting wild and loose right about now."

"Oh." I hadn't even noticed them leave. "How're you getting home?"

"I drove; I'm fine." She looked at her watch. "As a matter of fact, I need to go and get ready for my show." She picked up her purse and stood up.

I checked my watch and stood too. "You don't go on until midnight on Fridays."

She smiled at me as if I were a dim-witted child. "I know that, Gregory, but I want to go home, change, get to the station, and look over tonight's playlist . . . that sort of thing."

For some reason, I didn't want her to go. "Well, come with me to find Renee and then you can go."

She gave me a long look before shrugging. "Okay."

We circled the ballroom a few times before someone said they thought they saw her going into one of the hospitality suites. Riding up in the elevator, I stood close to Veronica. With her sexy high heels on, we were eye-to-eye. She smelled like some sort of exotic tropical flower. I reached over and touched her hand. "Hey, Roni."

"Hey what?" She looked down at our fingers as I linked them.

"Thanks for tonight; it was nice. Did I tell you how lovely you look this evening?" I didn't know where it came from—just fell out of my mouth.

She looked at me. "Aren't you supposed to say that to person you came with?"

"Veronica . . ." I stroked my thumb over the back of her hand.

She shrugged and smiled. "Okay, okay, I'll leave it alone. Thank you—it has been nice. I think we'll make great friends . . . but, Greg?"

"Yeah?"

"Do you hold hands like this with all your friends?"

"Oh." I dropped her hand. *Good going, Gregory.* "Sorry about that."

"No harm done, friend." She placed emphasis on the word *friend*.

We arrived upstairs and looked through the two suites. No Renee. I was about to give up when Roni turned down another hallway. "Isn't this room reserved for Royal Mahogany too?"

It was the executive suite. "Yeah, but I don't think she'll be in there."

"Well, won't hurt to look." Roni walked over to the door. She swung it open, stopped short, and shut the door quickly but quietly behind her. When she looked at me, her eyes were wide and her mouth was kinda hanging open. "You're right; she's not up here. Let's just go downstairs and look some more."

I laughed at her expression. "Well, okay, but what'd you catch a glimpse of in there? One of the executives getting busy with someone from the modeling agency?"

Veronica looked flustered as all hell, and she laughed shortly. "You know how it is at these things. Let's go down." She slipped her hand in my arm and started easing me back toward the elevator. Her hand was shaking, and she was out of breath.

"Hey, what's up with you?" I stopped and tilted her chin up so I could examine her expression. She was really freaked out. "What? Is someone dead in there?" I turned back toward the room, and she grabbed my arms.

"Gregory, don't go in there!" She was frantic. "Let's go downstairs now."

Well, hell. Now she had me wondering. What could make her so panicky? I mean, what could be going on in that room that she didn't want me to . . . I pushed her away from me roughly and was at that door in two seconds flat. Without ceremony, I pushed the door open. There, splayed out on the coffee table, was my loving fiancée. Legs wide open, dress hiked up to her waist while none other than a buck-naked Beauregard Montgomery knelt between her thighs, feasting away. Renee was thrashing about and moaning, sounds I'd heard before and was all too familiar with. For a minute, I couldn't believe this was really happening. Not to me!

Nobody played off on Gregory Samson. Nobody. Damn. My heart was in my throat, threatening to jump out and run screaming with pain into the night. My stomach was churning, yet somehow I couldn't rip my eyes away from the scene. This was the woman I was supposed to spend the rest of my life with, and she's giving it up like a common slut to that no-good sleazy-ass Louisiana gigolo.

Veronica came in behind me and tried to pull me away. Beau and Ray never looked our way. I shook off Roni's arm and walked over to them. When I was standing right beside them, they both looked up and froze. Beau made to get up. I put a hand on his shoulder. "Might as well stay where you are." I reached down to Renee's hand and disentangled it from

Beau's hair. I was amazed at my ability to appear cool, calm. I wanted to plunge a sharp object through the both of them. If I was one of the gun-toting brothers, I'd've been spraying lead left and right just then. I wanted to rant and rage and rave. But for what? Nothing would change the fact that I was standing here looking at another man's head between my fiancée's thighs. Nothing. So I did the only thing I could do. I kissed the back of Ray's hand and slid that rock right off of there. Hell, I was stunned, not stupid. "Bye, Ray." I looked at Beau, who had his head turned to the side. Like what was there to hide now? "She's all yours." I thought about taking a swing at him.

"Greg . . . ," Veronica said, and I turned around. Thank God she was there. She was the only thing that kept me from punching the living shit out of both of them. I should've listened to her and gone back downstairs to wait.

"Let's get out of here," I said, and handed her the ring. I didn't want to touch it. Everything felt just a little tainted. We turned and walked out, leaving the door open.

"Greggy, wait! It's not what it looks like."

Now that stopped me in my tracks for a minute. It wasn't what it looked like? I balled my hands into fists and made a quarter turn to look at her. Renee was struggling to get her legs together and her dress in place. "Roni Mae, help me! Talk to him for me! Beau, dammit, I thought you locked the door." Roni put her hand on my arm and turned me back around. Renee's shrieks followed us all the way to the elevator.

When the doors closed, I started shaking. Shit, I never shake. Never. This painful soreness welled up in my throat, and I turned helplessly to Veronica. She put her arms around me and held me. "You come home with me. Everything will be just fine."

Dammit, this hurt like hell. I was in literal physical pain. I laughed shortly. "I guess I should've listened when you said she would always want more. I guess I should've listened." I stood there in her arms, furious. I was mad at Ray for doing this. I was mad at me for not foreseeing it. And I was mad that I was standing there shaking like a punk. I should've hit somebody. I still wanted to. "I'm going back up there."

Roni grabbed my hands and squeezed them. "No, you're not. You come with me. Everything is going to be all right." She put her arms around me again and stroked my back.

Probably because I so desperately needed to believe something, somebody . . . I closed my eyes and believed her.

28

After the Dance

Roman—Sunday, February 5, 3:11a.m.

I let my head fall back against the pillows as Jewellen slid down my body. She was turning me inside out, had been all night long. We pretty much came in and marched straight upstairs to her bed. She stripped me down and said, "I'm only gonna say this once, so listen good. I'm sorry for bringing up the name of an old lover in your bed. I'm sorry for playing games. I'm sorry if I take you for granted sometimes. I'm sorry I get insecure and lash out. I'm sorry. Far as I'm concerned, no one compares to you. You're it for me—past, present, future—you hear me, Romeo?"

"I'm sorry too. I'm sorry I let it get so far. I just wanted—"

"You wanted to be right and have me admit it." She dropped the halter on her dress.

My concentration on the conversation slipped a little bit, but I dug deep for the answer as she raised her leg to unstrap her shoe. "Shallow of me, I know, baby. But I felt like—"

"Like you're always the one who gives in?" She finished with the shoes and starting rolling down her thigh-high panty hose.

I nodded. "Yeah, but it shouldn't be that way; we should talk, not walk."

"If I hadn't come to get you tonight, would you have called me?"

I watched as she shimmied out of her strapless bustier thing. Even though my next words could affect my shot at handling the goodies she was displaying, I decided to be honest. "I'm not sure."

She stood in front of me with nothing but some wispy panties on. "Pride. Hmm. It's gonna break us if we don't learn to bend. Fair enough, at least now I know where I stand and I know what I've got. I've still got you, right?"

"Anyway you want me, *Bijou,*" I replied, and reached for her. Enough words.

We got a nap in round midnight. I kissed her awake a minute ago, and she was taking her time turning me inside out.

"So tell me something, player?"

I groaned as she took me in her hand and started a diabolical stroke. Ah, hell.

"Hmm?"

"You want light licking with teasing nips or strong, steady sucking?" She demonstrated both.

"Ah, that's evil, Miss Jewel." Maybe it was my imagination, but damned if Miss Jewel wasn't getting real good at this. Christ, mighty good.

She lifted her head for a second. "Want that I should stop?"

"Doncha dare," I ground out as she started in again.

"Sure I'm not still on restrictions?"

"Jewel . . . evil," I hissed.

"Just . . . a . . . little . . . quid . . . pro . . . quo, *'tit chou,*" she whispered in between licks. Girl had a mean streak a mile long. As if she sensed my thought, she sped up a little and added a tickling thing with her finger.

"Yeah, uh-huh. Like that right there, baby." I was getting

into the rhythm when I could have sworn I heard a banging sound.

She lifted her head again and I groaned. "Do . . . NOT . . . stop." Not now! Damn, it *was* a banging sound. Like on the front door!

"Do you hear that?" she asked me, sitting up and reaching for a robe.

"Yeah, damn it all. Who the hell is it at three in the morning?" While she went downstairs, I opened the dresser drawer she had given me. My stuff was still in there. I pulled on some shorts and ran to follow her. That time of night, I would be opening the door. I stepped in front of her and looked out the peephole. "I'll be damned—it's the fly girl."

Jewel frowned at me. "Renee's here? Now?" She reached around me, keyed in the alarm code, and opened the door.

The fly girl didn't look so fly. Her hair was all over the place, her makeup was streaking down her face, and her clothes didn't match. She had on purple sweatpants, a bright red shirt, and green tennis shoes. Something had to be real wrong; fly girl didn't step out the crib without matching from tip to toe.

"Girl, what is it?" Jewel asked, and led her inside. I would have let her stand outside and spill the story. Wouldn't you know that Renee's damn crisis had to interrupt my reconciliation? I was just about to apologize the hell out of Jewel.

Renee flung herself down on the sofa and started sobbing. Jewel exchanged a look with me before kneeling beside her. In time, she sat up and extended her hand to Jewel. "It's gone, homegirl. Gone!"

Jewel blinked up at her, not understanding. I got it in a heartbeat. Greg wised up and dumped her phony ass. And look at her, she was more concerned over losing that damn rock. She came up in here busting up my shit and said, "It's gone." Not *he's* gone, but the damn ring. Jewel looked over at me, and we exchanged knowing glances. I shook my head and went upstairs. In my opinion, she got exactly what was coming to her perpetrating ass. Thought it best I didn't stay down there and share my opinions.

Renee—Sunday, February 5, 3:20 a.m.

"Girl, I f'ed this up bad," I told Jewellen.

She sighed and sat down next to me. "Just tell me what happened."

My voice was raw from screaming and crying. Took a deep breath and broke it on down.

"Beau and I went upstairs to one of the suites to have a drink."

"Renee!" Jewellen looked disappointed.

"Don't judge me, Jew-Ro."

She put her hands up. "Okay, okay."

I continued. "We just sitting there drinking champagne. I said it was delicious; he said it probably didn't taste as good as me. I asked him if he wanted to find out, and one thing led to another."

"One thing led to another?! You invited him to—"

"I know what I did, Jewellen." I just couldn't help myself. In retrospect, my timing could have been SO much better. "Anyway, I told him to lock the door but—"

She gasped. "Wait a minute . . . Greg walked in while Beau was—"

"Yeah," I cut her off. "He and Roni Mae walked in. Beau was naked and rock hard, just doing his thing. Girl, that boy . . ." I shivered just thinking about Beau's fine ass. Talented fine ass.

"Renee, focus! Greg walked in with Roni Mae?"

"Yeah."

"What did he say?"

"I don't recall exactly, you know? Couldn't have been good. He took my hand off Beau's head, slid off the ring, and left."

"Did you go after him?"

Okay, this part I felt bad about. I knew the right thing to do was to run after him, but I was in an awkward position and felt it was probably best that he cooled down for a minute. "I thought I'd give him time to cool off."

Jewellen looked at me like I was crazy. Then her eyes went wide. "Darnella Renee Nightingale, PLEASE do NOT tell me you finished what you were doing with Beau before going after your fiancé?!"

When she put it like that, I felt shamed. I dropped my eyes.

She sighed again, deeply this time. "So after that, what happened?"

"After I, um, finished up in the suite, I went downstairs. Gregory wasn't there, and Roni Mae was gone. I went home, but he wasn't there. I just knew he'd be there waiting for me so we could fight it out. I called everywhere. He's not answering his cell. I can't find Roni Mae. I finally changed clothes and drove around looking for him. I can't find him, girl. I can't find him!" I started crying again.

"Let me ask you one thing, Renee," she said softly. "Was it worth it?"

"If you are asking if it was good—"

"Hell no, I'm not asking if it was good! I am asking you if getting done by Beauregard Montgomery was worth losing your marriage to Gregory Samson?"

"Girl, please, did you not just crawl out of your sex sheets with the younger Montgomery?" I had to point it out.

She hopped up. "Renee, Roman is my boyfriend. Neither of us hurt ANYBODY else by being together. Are you crazy or just delusional?"

I hopped up too. "You supposed to be my girl. You supposed to have my back!"

"I am—I do—but that also includes calling your ass on the

carpet when you are wrong. I mean, you DO know you're wrong, don't you?"

I hung my head. It was all starting to sink in. "I know, I know, but I can fix it. Greg loves me. It was just this one time. He'll forgive me. It'll be okay."

Jewel didn't say anything, just looked at me all crooked.

"What? Rome took your ass back!"

Jewellen got angry. And Jewellen angry is no joke. "You have lost your mind! Why do you keep pulling Roman into your shit? Here's the deal: You messed up. Bad. You landed the guy you always wanted to land, but you just couldn't help yourself from wanting a little more. From being a little greedy. What's bad is this: Everybody knew it. Everybody saw it. Everybody, including Greg, warned you. And you did it anyway. That boy probably did love you; he asked you to marry him. Did you even think about that tonight? He wanted to spend the rest of his life with you. You think Beau is gonna give you a ring?"

She wasn't helping. I was tired. My head hurt, and I just didn't want to think anymore tonight. "Just help me get him back. Tell me what to do."

She shrugged. "I can't imagine. I'm tapped out. I got nothing."

Now I was angry. "I come to you with the biggest problem I've ever faced in my life and this is what you got for me. You got nuthin'? Are you shitting me?"

She shrugged again. "I'm sorry. I don't know what the protocol is for begging and groveling my fiancé to take me back after I slept with a guy he specifically told me not to sleep with. They didn't teach this in my etiquette class."

"Oh, you got jokes. I'm in pain here. I'm losing my man, and you got jokes?!"

She put her hands up. "I'm not joking. I don't know what

to tell you. If begging and groveling doesn't work, I hope you can get your deposit back on the church and the caterer."

I felt like she was being bitchy for no reason. "Kiss my ass, Jewellen."

"Alrighty, then, on that note . . . I was actually in the middle of something when you dropped by. I'm sorry about what happened. I'm here for you, but I honestly don't know what to say right now."

Wait a minute—she was blowing me off for Roman? "You in such to hurry to lay under that ruffneck that you would send me back out in the street on the worst night of my life?!"

"Renee, before we say stuff we're gonna regret, you should head on home. See if Greg returned any of your calls. I'm always here for you. But right now, you need to get your head right." She walked toward the door.

"That shit is cold, Jewellen. Thanks for your support." I slammed out of the house. Climbing into my car, I checked my cell phone. No missed calls. It was five a.m. and I was alone.

Jewel—Sunday, February 5, 5:03 a.m.

I shut the door behind Renee and leaned back against it. God, I was tired. What a mess. I walked up the stairs and slid into bed beside Roman. Thank God he was here.

"What time is it, baby?" he asked me. I had missed that voice.

"About five; go on back to sleep." I snuggled up next to him.

Instead, he turned over to face me. "How'd it come down? Was it Beau?"

So, he had known. "It was Renee but Beau helped. A lot."

He winced. "Caught with the pants down?"

I nodded. "Red-handed, or in this case, red-tongued."

"Ouch! Not the oral! Greg walked right in on it?"

"Him and Roni. Right on in."

"Whew, that had to hurt. Bad way to go down."

"No pun intended."

He reached his arm over and pulled me to him. "You got jokes."

"Yeah, apparently." I sighed, snuggling into him as I reached for the phone. I punched in the number and waited.

"Hello?" a wide-awake voice answered, just as I assumed.

"He's there, isn't he, Roni?"

Silence was my answer. Just as I thought.

"I don't have to tell you you're just adding grease to the fire, salt to the wound? Renee just left here. She's been looking everywhere for Greg. She's real broken up."

At this, Roni spoke. "I don't give a shit! I don't wanna hear about her! She can keep looking. God, Jewellen, if you could've seen her laid out on that table."

I winced. "On a table."

Roman clucked his teeth and muttered underneath his breath beside me. He moved in closer so he could hear. I tilted the phone for him.

She lowered her voice. "And didn't even stop when we walked in. Skirt up all over her head—she hadn't even undressed completely! How could she not have seen us? Even when he walked right up to them, you'd think she have tried to get up or . . . or something!"

"Just laid out there, huh?" The story was getting worse with each version.

"That ain't even the worst of it, girl. The worst thing was that she was torn between begging Greg to come back, screaming at me to help her, and asking Beau why he didn't lock the door in the first place. She never got up. Never pulled that skirt all the way down."

Roman shook his head in disgust.

I closed my eyes. "Uh-uh, girl, you're lying."

"I kid you not. No remorse, girl, none at all."

"Well, how is he?"

"In shock. Keeps talking about how he should've seen this coming and so forth. He's all broke down, girl. Talking to himself and laughing, walking around in circles. Shaking like a leaf but he won't cry."

Roman frowned and shook his head, making hand motions. I tried to interpret. "Girl, if he cries at all, it won't be in front of you."

"Oh."

I went back to my original point. "So why's he there, Roni? And how long is he staying?"

"He couldn't go back to Renee's!"

"He kept the lease on his old place, and all his furniture is there. Why didn't he go there? And how long is he staying?"

"He said that was the first place she'd look, and he doesn't want to see her."

It was the first place she'd looked, but that wasn't the point. "*And how long is he staying?*"

"We talked about it, and he said just 'til he gets his head together."

Roman rolled his eyes.

"Uh-huh. Well, I hope you know what you're getting into." The entire damn thing was foul.

"What do you mean?"

"What I mean is this—just today you told me you have feelings for that boy, and now there he is under your roof. Try to remember that he is a man scorned and on serious rebound. Also, you've got a good friend who is going to come looking to you for support. How do you think Renee is going to feel when she finds out Greg's staying with you?"

"I don't owe Renee shit. I'm telling you, girl, if you could have *seen* her!"

"Glad I didn't, thanks anyway. The real issue here is that

you're pissed off that she did this to Greg. If she'd done this to someone else, you'd be laughing about it right now—admit it."

"Fine, I admit it. And as for the rest, thanks but I know what I'm doing."

This time I rolled my eyes. "Fine, I'm out of it."

"Jewellen, you're not gonna take sides, are you? Are you mad at me?" Roni asked.

Roman tucked me in closer, and I laid my head on the pillow. "Girl, I'm not mad, but I *am* out of it. O-U-T of it."

"I take it you and the Roman god are back together? You haven't sounded this chill in weeks."

"Bite your tongue, woman. I got along just fine without him." I laughed when he pinched me. "We're okay. You take care of yourself, and tell Greg to call if he needs anything." Roman pinched me again . . . I was feeling charitable.

"We'll be okay too. Later, girl." She hung up.

I switched off the phone and chucked it off the bed. I turned in Roman's arms, and he wrapped me up.

"So this is what you had on Renee, hmm?" I asked him.

"I knew it was gonna happen, babe. I just didn't want either of us involved. Just a matter of time."

"Water under the bridge now, I guess." I snuggled in closer.

"So . . . got along fine without me, hmm?" He didn't sound like he was joking.

"Truthfully?" I leaned back to see his face.

"Yeah, I need to know."

"Truthfully, I missed you like hell."

He grinned in the dark. "Good, we're even. Chase missed you too; he thought he'd done something wrong."

I winced. "I thought something like that might happen. Let's try not to get to this point again."

"I hear you. By the way, how'd you end up at that party?"

I laughed. "Now that's an interesting story involving Teddy Grahams, your mother, and the butcher's counter."

"Sounds like a story I gotta hear."

"Believe it or not, it all started less than twenty-four hours ago. . . ."

29

Lay It on the Altar

Renee—Sunday, March 5, 1:03 p.m.

"You don't have to confess your sins to me."

"Amen."

"You don't have to apologize to me."

"Preach now."

"You can hurt me, mock me, talk about me to my face, and walk away!"

"Um-hmm. Say it now!"

"But you can't walk away from the Lord."

"Sho' nuff!"

"Tell the truth!"

"Talk to me!"

Reverend Moss was off and running in fine form this morning. He was on a roll, and the congregation was right there with him. Today, the first time I had been back to church since the Loss of the Ring, what do you think he preaches on? Sin, guilt, and confession. Easter's around the corner; why couldn't he do a good rousing He Is Risen speech?

Beau sat next to me, shifting uncomfortably on the pew. I glanced sideways at him and grinned. If I had to face the Lord head-on, at least I had my partner in crime with me. Beau moved in with me the day after Gregory came and moved his stuff out—Valentine's Day of all days. It had been exactly a month and a day since The Loss, and I still hadn't fully accepted it. The fallout had been incredible.

My mother was hardly speaking to me. I reached out to Greg and tried to explain that it was one night, one stupid mistake, the champagne, but he wasn't trying to hear it. He sent me an e-mail making it very clear that whatever we had was history. I found out that Greg had stayed over at Roni's the night of The Loss, and I hadn't spoken to her since. Beau and Roman just started speaking again last week, but Jewel was pissed that I let Beau move in. Well, what was I supposed to do? Sit around and mope alone? Work was tough since all my time was spent with Kat, and she has made it clear that she can't stand me. My boss was thinking about switching me off the account, which was really a demotion in disguise.

I was at a place where I needed some answers. Some direction. I knew what I did was wrong, but was it so major that my whole life had to be turned upside down? Who really suffered? Okay, I feel bad about Greg, but there he was, four rows up and one over, right next to Roni Mae, Tammy, Stacie, and Trick—all *my* friends. Looked like he was over it. Meanwhile, my life was still in chaos. Where did I go from here? And who did I go with? To think, a month and a half ago, I was planning my wedding, looking for houses, scheming a way to get a tennis bracelet to match my necklace out of Greggy . . . Greg.

Okay, Beau was a lot of fun and he could really, well . . . I was in church, but you know what I'm trying to say. He was a nice, fun guy, and in the looks and body department, he was by far the closest thing to perfect I had ever seen, but for the long haul, what did that net me? I didn't see him buying a house, having two kids, and telling me to stay home and give up work. If anything, Beau would be inclined to stay home while I kept working. And just the thought of having to start a whole new thing over with somebody from scratch made me cringe. I'd just gotten Greg to the point where he put the toilet seat down. Truthfully, I was about desperate with despair. I couldn't believe I blew a good thing. I looked inside myself and still couldn't see exactly when I turned the wrong corner. Was it Beau or was it something within me? All I knew was, Greg was gone, my relationships with friends and family were strained, the job was tense, and Beau was here. I came to church for answers, not a guilt trip. I was seriously thinking about getting up and walking out.

I tuned back in to hear the reverend's words: "I *said*, 'You can't walk away from the Lord.' Do you hear me, Church?" He waved his handkerchief at the congregation, and the organist tapped out a little beat. I sighed. So much for the leaving idea.

"Amen!" rose the responses from the congregation.

"You don't hear me, Church! I say you can run, but you can't *hide* from Jesus. You don't have to talk to *me*. Who am I? I'm just a man trying to talk to ya 'bout a thang called salvation this morning. That's who *I* am. I can't save you. Yo' mama can't save you. . . ."

"Ah, watch out there, Reverend," Old Man Jones called out from the front pew. That man had sat in the front pew calling out the same thing since I was a little girl.

"Yo' daddy, yo' boyfriend, yo' wife, yo' doctor, not even yo' lawyer can save you! Can I get a witness this morning?" He stepped from behind the pulpit and started pacing in front of the altar. "You got to come to the Lord with love and reverence. On bended knees, Church!" He knelt down. "You got to bow your head down to the Master." He bowed his head. "And ya gotta say, 'Lord, I'm a sinner!' " He flung his arms out to the side. "I'm a sinner, Father God. I've sinned before, and the devil surely knows I will sin again. But, Father! Admit me to your kingdom."

A string of "Amen!"s and "Preach, Preacher!" ring out as Rev hopped up. "Precious Lord! Forgive me, Master. Admit me!" He turned to the congregation. "Do you want to enter the kingdom, Church?"

"Yes! Amen! Have mercy, Lord!"

"You gotta tell the Lord your sins. Tell him your sorrows. Tell him your joys! 'Cause when the end comes, Church, you don't wanna be left down here. Oh precious, precious Lord, don't leave me down here."

"Don't leave me, Lord!" The masses were in a frenzy. And I was very uneasy. Was I going to burn for all eternity behind Beauregard Montgomery? I began to pray in earnest.

He quieted his voice. "Don't get left behind, Church. Take it all to the Lord in prayer. Plead for mercy and remember his grace, for he is gracious. . . . He is gracious. Oh precious Lord."

"Precious Lord," we all repeated. And the organist began to play and sing.

"Precious Lord, take my hand. Lead me on, let me stand. I am tired . . . I am weak . . . I am worn. Through the storm, through the night . . . lead me on to the light. Precious Lord, take my hand . . . and lead, lead me home."

As she sang, tears ran down my face. I looked over at Beau and was surprised to see that he looked moved too. He reached over and took my hand. It was a sweet thing to do.

The reverend spoke up during a piano interlude between verses. "There may be those of you who have troubles weighing on your mind. Those of you who need guidance. Those of you who have strayed off the path to salvation and are walking down a lonely, dark road. But there is hope, my brothers and sisters. There is light! For the Lord says, 'Ask and it shall be given, seek and ye shall find, knock and the door shall be opened.' If there are those of you among us who want to join our church family or rededicate yourself to the Lord, come forward. Ask, seek, and knock this morning."

The organist began to sing again, and he continued speaking. "I know you've done things that weigh heavy on your heart, your mind, your soul. Let the Lord help you carry that load. Come to Jesus this morning. `Whosoever will, let them come.'"

I'll never understand what happened, but I felt someone pushing me. From the inside, I felt a great pressure. The next thing I knew, I had gotten up and dragged Beau to his feet too. It wasn't until we were standing and I felt the weight of hundreds of eyes on me that I realized what I was doing. I looked at Beau, who looked both dazed and baffled. Next thing I knew, we were walking up the aisle toward the altar.

"God bless these young people," Reverend Moss said as we stood in front of him moments later. He handed me a microphone. "Make your testimony, child."

I froze for a moment. I looked to Beau for reassurance, but he was just as scared as I was. I scanned the congregation. Greg looked skeptical. Roni, Stacie, and Patrick looked shocked. Tammy looked amused. Near the back on the right sat Jewel and Roman. Roman looked blank, but Jewellen, my homegirl, was smiling at me. I held on to that, took a deep breath, and spoke. "I just wanted to take this opportunity to get back on track with the Lord, with my life, with my friends and family. I've taken a few wrong turns, and I've made mistakes. And I'm—" I started to choke up and cry, but I forced it out anyway—"sorry for that. I never meant to hurt anyone. I only hope that with the Lord's help, I can find a way to make it up to everyone. Including myself. I just . . ." I broke down then, and Beau had to take the mike away. He put an arm around my shoulders as he spoke. I couldn't help but think that we probably a real cute picture standing up there together.

"Renee's not the only one who has made mistakes. I never would have come up here on my own, but now that I'm here, I'm glad about it. It's been a long time since I took responsibility for anything, myself included. I can only pray that today marks the beginning of a whole new me. Thank you."

By the time the reverend asked people to come forward

and rejoice in our reaffirmation of faith, I was a little more composed. The first people up to the altar were Rome and Jewel. I couldn't say as I've ever really gotten along with Roman, but when he smiled at me and gave me a hug, I felt he meant it.

"Good for you, girl," Jewellen said as she leaned forward to hug me.

I was still too choked up to do much more than nod. When Beau and I went back to our seats, I felt more at peace than I had in years. Who knows, maybe this God thing was the way to go. I felt cleansed, as if nothing I'd done before mattered. My slate was clean. And I saw the look on Greggy's face; he wanted to believe that I was truly sorry deep in my heart. Hell, in a way I was. I was truly sorry I had gotten caught. I smiled over at Beau. God bless his beautiful hide, he was going to have to move out. If there was the slightest chance I could get Greg back . . . Oh yeah, he'd have to go and soon. Beau grinned back. That grin was the furthest thing from sanctified I'd ever seen.

"Feel better, *chere*?" he whispered.

"Yeah, I really do. Thanks for coming up there with me."

"You can thank me very personally later. Get your prayers in now."

A slow smile spread across my face. Hey, I was dedicated to the Lord, but I wasn't dead. Beau would go, but tomorrow was plenty soon enough.

30

Don't Play

Roman—Sunday, March 5, 4:39 p.m.

We were chilling at Jewel's crib with Stacie and Trick. This was a kinda test both of us set up. Yesterday, we hung out with Moms, Chase, and Jaquenetta. We passed that one. I thought Miss Jewel finally understood what's left between me and Jaquenetta. Chase. Period. Now I needed to understand whassup with Tricky Rick here. Trick and I were in the kitchen doing the dinner thing. Hey, these girls don't play. Women of the new millennium and all that. In other words, if we wanted to eat today, we were gonna have to pitch in with the cooking. Now, I could bake the hell out of some chicken, and Trick looked pretty good on that salad thing. I figured we'd add some baked potatoes and BOOM! Dinner. Funny thing was, we'd been in here for about fifteen minutes and neither one of us had much to say. When we got the food to a stage where all it had to do was cook, we went and joined the girls in the den. They were talking about Renee and her new devotion to Jesus. I jumped right in.

"Think she means it, or you think she's full of shit?" I asked Miss Jewel as I sat down by her on the sofa.

"I think she wants to mean it," Jewel waffled. "But as for Brother Beau . . ."

I laughed. "Oh, I know he's full of shit; you ain't even got to start there. He always means well, but somehow, between wanting to do right and acutally walking that line, he strays from the path of righteousness. No doubt there's a woman out there who can get him to settle down and do the right thing. That woman is not Renee. Partners in crime if ever I saw them."

"Either way, it was still a smooth move on her part. I mean, this way she's left the door open for Greg to come back. She's asked for forgiveness from everyone and basically given herself a clean slate," Stacie added.

I nodded. "Yeah, but I still don't buy it."

Jewel shrugged. "People change."

Tricky Rick piped up. "People do change."

The room went still. Talk about subtle. Nice of him to tack on his two cents right there. So, just to be contrary, I said, "Some do, some don't."

"Roman," Jewel said softly.

"No," Stace said, "let's just get this whole thing out in the open."

"Let's not. I hate shit like this," Jewel said.

Stacie raised a brow. "Like what, like saying to me, 'Stacie, I can't believe you're seeing my ex-boyfriend—sorry, ex-fiancé.' Shit like that?"

I hopped in. "We don't have to go all there." Now *I* was back-pedaling.

"Besides," Patrick said, "Jewel doesn't care who I date anymore."

"How do you know what I care about? As if it ever concerned you much!" Jewel snapped out. She was getting that crease between her brows that meant she was about to go *off*. She stood up and started pacing the room back and forth. Aw, damn, pacing meant bad things were coming. I tried to calm her down before the eruption.

"Now, baby—" I started in.

Tricky Rick cut me off, "So you *do* care?"

Stace jumped back in it. "Why do *you* care if she cares?"

She had a point. I had to ask, "Exactly who still cares about what here?" This I wanted to hear.

"Everybody shut up!" Jewel said in what I've come to think of as her lethally calm voice. Wisely, we all remained silent while baby got it together enough to talk. "Number one, you, Stacie, can just kiss my ass on this whole thing."

We all had our mouths hanging open, and Stace said, "Jewellen Rose!"

"Jewellen Rose, my ass—you knew, you've always known, how I felt about the passing-around-the-boyfriend thing. What, there was no other black man in the whole damn world who caught your attention? It just had to be Patrick?"

"Well, I—" she tried to explain.

"Save it." Jewel shook her head. "This was the man I had planned to *marry*, Stacie, not some one-night pickup I'd never think about again. Did it at all occur to you that I maybe didn't want my philandering ex-fiancé around all the time? Truth be told, your ass was wrong from the get-go. And all you had to do was say, 'Jewel, I'm sorry. I know I'm wrong, but Patrick and I are tight and this is how it is; hope you don't mind.' Personally, I'm still waiting to hear it." She pointed at Patrick. "And you! All I can say is that you sure have your nerve. How do you really think this is going to turn out? What's going on in your fickle little brain? You thinking it's gonna be you and me one week and you and Stace the next? You think I'd give up a good thing just 'cause you came waltzing back into town? Or did you just think I'd wait around and see if the thing with Stace fell through? Have you changed at all? Do you really acknowledge that the shit you pulled with me was *foul,* or are you too busy doing one of my best friends?"

"Now, darlin'—"

"Don't call me darlin'!"

"Don't call her darlin'!" Jewellen and I spoke at the same time. She sent me a look, and I shut up. Besides, I was feeling pretty cool behind that "good thing" statement she made. I leaned back and propped my feet up. Finally, this conversation was going the way I liked it.

She put her hands on her hips and faced Stace and Trick squarely. "I hate to disturb y'all's groove like this, but I'm doing it for your own good. Tell me, Patrick, suppose I was to tell you that as of tomorrow, Roman and I are through?"

I jackknifed up and came to instant attention. "Say what?"

"Stay outta this, Romeo," Jewellen said. "Well, Patrick?"

Stacie looked at him. "Well, Patrick?"

Now I was feeling a little antsy up in here, but my consolation was that Patrick was four times more uncomfortable than I was. Besides, I was hanging on to that new trust thang Miss Jewel and I had talked about since the party. At the very least, I had to trust that she would tell me to my face and alone that we were through and not all out here in front of folks. Couldn't say I was enjoying her tactics for getting her point across, though.

Patrick shrugged. "Now, I can't answer that; you know that."

"Do I know that? Why don't you just tell me?" Jewellen had dropped her voice to that seductive level and had taken a step toward him. Well, hell, what to do? Do I get up and start clocking somebody or stay chill? Trust, I remembered, trust. I decided to wait and see. But somebody was gonna pay hell for this little piece of drama.

Tricky Rick reacted to the tone. "I never thought it was really over between us," he drawled, before catching a glimpse of Stacie's face, "but I accepted that some things are a part of the past. I had to move forward." His shit was weak and we all knew it.

"We were good together once," Jewel murmured, and I about lost it. Trust or no, the last thing I needed to hear was how she and Trick used to burn up the sheets. That trust thang was hanging by a slim thread. Mighty slim. And if this was some sort of game she was playing, I wasn't amused. Not by a long shot.

Trick's ass looked mesmerized. "Yeah, that's true. That's true." He looked over at me. I had my hands balled into fists and was about half a second from pouncing on that ass. "I mean, we had good times and bad times."

"Good and bad." Jewel nodded. She hadn't looked at me once since she started this.

" 'Course, when they were good, they were good." He just couldn't keep himself from adding it.

"I'll be damned. You'd go back to her in a heartbeat, wouldn't you?" Stacie asked. When it took him longer than a breath span to answer, she jumped up and ran outside. He rose and followed.

"Um, guess I'll check on that chicken," I said slowly, then got up and went to the kitchen.

I heard her come in and slide onto the barstool. "Baby—"

"Baby, my ass," I answered, and leaned down to open the oven.

"You know what I was doing in there, don't you?"

"Yeah, losing your mind." I pulled the rack out and peeled back the aluminum foil.

"Ah hell, you're pissed!" She had the damn nerve to sound surprised.

"You de high-class smart one, Miss Jewel. I just de ignant stud from de hood."

"Dammit, don't start that again!"

I had to put her ass in check. "Hold up. You trying to get a case of the ass with me now? With *me*? I just sat in there and watched you offer yourself to Tricky Rick and go on and on about how great it was between y'all, and *you* getting the ass?

Ain't that a bitch?" I spooned some more melted butter over the meat and shoved it back in. Turning, I kicked the oven door up with my foot.

She went absolutely still. "Did you just call me a bitch?"

I sighed. "I said, 'Ain't *that* a bitch.' That's what *I* said; what did *you* hear?"

Her head was going in that black woman's way. "I heard you call me a bitch."

"Then you can't hear."

"I ain't gonna be no bitch up in here!"

I laughed. "Now who sounds like they're from the hood?"

"Kiss my ass."

"Right after ya kiss mine, baby!" We stood across the kitchen glaring at each other for a long time. Finally she huffed and turned her head.

"I can't believe you don't see that I was trying to get Stacie to see the light about Patrick!"

"Why, so you can have him for yourself?"

"Damn, you didn't catch shit of that trust conversation, did you?"

"Same way you weren't paying attention during my don't-play-games speech."

"What games?"

"What was that whole scene out there? A prelude to Pictionary?"

"Now we gonna be smart-alecky?"

"Now we gonna answer a question?" Another glare-off. Dammit, I was in the right here. You don't pull no bullshit stunts like that. Ever. Trust or no, you don't bring up old dick in front of me. Ever. Especially not when the dick in question was sitting in the room.

"I'm only gonna say this one more time—I don't want Patrick. I don't miss Patrick. I wouldn't take him on a platter wrapped in thousand-dollar bills. Okay?"

Like she was getting off that easy? "No, it's not okay, Jewellen. Look at it this way—suppose it was Jaquenetta out there, telling me how great we used to be and if I could just ditch yo' ass, we could be that way again? How you gonna feel?"

"Like kicking her ass and then yours." I wanted to laugh then. Jewellen Rose Capwell ain't never kicked nobody's ass in her life. A little something told me it wasn't the best time to break into a hearty chuckle, you know? Besides, I still had a point of my own to make.

"Uh-huh. Why couldn't you just be understanding? After all, you trust me, doncha?"

"Understanding? Trust? Hell, you don't bring that kind of shit up in front of me and expect me not to . . . oh. I get it." The lightbulb went on over her head.

"You took it too far. Wrong place, wrong time."

She thought about it for a minute, then admitted, "I took it too far; you're right."

I couldn't resist the smug little grin. It snuck out before I could stop it.

"Okay, okay! No need to gloat. I was wrong and I'm sorry."

My poor baby, she hated to apologize for shit. Could be wrong as two left shoes and just hated to force the words past her lips. I was about to take pity on her and go round and give her a hug when she started back up again.

"But how many damn times you gonna bring that ghetto shit up?"

"What ghetto shit?"

"We get into a major fight and next thing I know, you gotta bring up the fact that you came up hard and I didn't. Sue me. I've never said a thing about where you come from."

"Never said anything, huh?"

"No, Roman, I never have."

"And this is, like, a favor you're doing me? Shit, I know where I'm from. I know who I am and where I came from—do you?"

"Oh, so I'm a sellout now. Here we go. I'm light-skinned, live north, and don't talk black enough, so now I'm a sellout, an Oreo. Not real enough for you."

I rolled my eyes. "Ya ass is sensitive; I never said none of that shit."

"And I never said shit about the freaking hood!"

"Except that you hate going over there, don't trust the people there, don't wanna live there, and don't do business with people from there," I reminded her.

"That's not true. You take that back!"

"Which part's untrue?" I really hated having to call her ass on shit like this, but she never wanted to admit when her ass was wrong.

"All of it!"

"Oh, you like rolling through the hood now? Just hanging out when you're not on your way to or from my crib?"

"Well, no."

"And you feel real comfy walking down the street?"

"I don't feel 'comfy' walking over *here,* player."

"And you wouldn't mind packing your shit up and moving into my place?"

"Now, I do have a mortgage to pay over here. Makes more sense to—"

"Yeah, right. And how many inner-city black clients have you added on?"

"Dammit, Roman."

"Dammit Roman what? For someone all gung ho on truth and trust and honesty, you sure don't wanna face facts. Tell me, Miss Jewel, did it ever cross you mind that I ain't exactly enamored of this bougey side of town? The fact that a lot of the other brothers I see are valet parking or pumping gas over this way? So progressive. How every time I run down to the Seven-Eleven to grab something, the li'l ole woman behind the counter keeps her finger near the security button? That lovely way these Northside cops have of following me down your street 'bout once a week? Did you think any of that?"

"You get that anywhere in the nation, Roman!"

"You think so? I don't. I think you get it more in the white neighborhoods than in those that are at least attempting a little integration." I was good and fired up now.

"Why are we on this? What's this got to do with us?"

I sighed. "Well, let me tell you—it all comes down to this. You keep saying that where I come from doesn't matter. But it does. It's part of who I am and who I want to be. If you're thinking that one day I'm just gonna give in, chuck my house, and come over here with White Boy Roy living all up in my face, you wrong. That ain't who I am. So maybe you oughta rethink who and what it is you want around here. You keep asking about the future; did you stop to think of how we gonna live, where, and why?" I took the oven mitt off my hand and started looking for my keys.

"Roman, don't go. Not like this . . ."

"I gotta go. I can't stay . . . not like this. And while you're thinking about this, I gotta son to think 'bout. My child. His mama comes from the hood too. So it's part of who he is. You want me, he comes with me. I can't have him getting mixed signals 'bout what it is to be a black man nowadays. You understand what I'm trying to say?"

I continued. "Listen, babe, if you really buy in to the theory that the world you are comfortable with is the only way to live and that way is somehow better than my way, then maybe you *should* be with Tricky Rick."

"Roman!"

"What? I'm giving you your options. You know what I'm about. I'm tired of justifying my shit. This is who I am. A little bit uptown, a little bit downtown. I don't have to be one or the other, and I'm not trying to getting locked down into that whole buppiefied mentality. Where to shop, where to eat, how to speak, what to drive. You hear what I'm saying?"

She was nodding when the back door flew open, and Stacie came running in. "I'm getting out of here. I just can't deal with this now." She picked up her purse and was out the front door in a flash.

Tricky Rick was standing in the hallway looking at Jewellen. I had to give the man an A for effort, persistence, and out-and-out balls. I picked up my keys and headed to the front door myself. Miss Jewel followed me. She stood in the doorway, and Patrick was about six steps behind. Rising up out of there and leaving my baby, my *heart*, standing there with him was the toughest thing I'd done in a long time. I grinned a grin I really didn't feel. "Hey, like that Prince song says, 'Do you want him? Or do you want me? 'Cause I want you.' It's just that simple." I started down the driveway.

"Roman, I know what I want—I love you," she said.

"Like I said once before, I wish you knew why. You let me know when you're sure."

"Are you . . . are you coming back?" she asked, tears glistening in her eyes.

Swear to God, this was the hardest thing I ever had to do. "Not until you convince me you know what you want . . . who you want . . . and why."

I heard her last words as I climbed into the Pathfinder. "I can't believe you're really leaving."

I couldn't believe it either. But that didn't stop me from closing the door, starting the engine, and driving away.

31

Mother Knows Best

Jewel—Monday, March 27, 8:43 p.m.

"I can't believe you're still at the office, Jewellen Rose."

I reached back to rub my neck. "I know, Mom, but I've got to get this last thing done. Then I'll go home." Of course, home was a pretty empty place to be right about now, but I wasn't admitting *that*. What would I be going home to? My spices were alphabetized, my closet was color-coded, and I had made a database to log my DVD collection. I used to be a more exciting person. Even before Roman, I had to have had other interests besides work and organizing my house, didn't I? Sure, I used to read, surf the Web, go to movies with friends, work out . . . very exciting life. Was this it? Life without a man . . . again?

She clucked her tongue. "Still on the outs with Roman, hmm?"

I winced. "Mom, I don't wanna talk about it." I hadn't seen or heard from him since the day he left me in the house with Patrick. The more I thought about it, the more pissed off I got. How dare he act like I was some sort of possession to be passed back and forth between the two of them? After he left, I unloaded all my wrath on Patrick. He was real clear on where we stand now. Absolutely nowhere together. I talked to Stace last week, and we managed to patch things up. Of course, she took him back. All I could do was sigh over that one. At least Patrick was better than Oliver.

But as for Roman, here we were with the same issue again. Who was in control? Who had the power? It was either his way or the highway? Dammit, I couldn't give in all the time.

Mom broke into my musings. "I don't care if you don't want to talk about it. I'm your mother, young lady. I don't understand what the problem is."

"The problem is, I refuse to be the one to break down and apologize—again. Why is everything my fault? Why do I have to be the one to give in? Why do I have to make the sacrifices?" Point of the matter was, I felt like I'd already sacrificed and changed up my lifestyle to mesh with his. I couldn't see the point of compromising. I wasn't moving to the hood; he wasn't moving north. And that just outlined the geography problems. My head spun every time I thought about the problems we had with trust and compromise. All I knew was that I was determined not to be the one to admit fault again. My reasoning was, if he really loves me, *he'll* make the sacrifice for me. Like Chase was going to lose his sense of black maleness growing up in the suburbs? Roman's view was narrow-minded and unrealistic. His idea of integration was 85 percent black, 15 percent other. For me? I was just happy to get one or two of us in the same five-block radius. What did he want? For me to give up my home, buy some hip-hop clothes, and hang out at the rec center every weekend? Wasn't gonna happen. Course, that sounded kinda like when he said I expected him to put on khakis and loafers and hang out at the Galleria all the time. Problem was, I was confused over which one of us was wrong. Maybe we both were. But I was too stubborn to back down this time. If I kept bending, I'd never stand tall again.

So this was how it was gonna end—he wouldn't call me

and I wouldn't call him, and all of a sudden, all the emotions we feel for each other, all the dreams we harbored for the future are just gone? That was what I couldn't get past. A week ago, I was happy and in love; this week I was alone and depressed. Damn this. A woman could be happy and fulfilled without having to sacrifice her soul for some controlling-assed man. I wasn't going out like that. What the hell was the point of educating myself, building a business, and trying to do something if I was just going to submit to some man's wishes? Shit, I could've done that straight out of high school.

This was what they meant when they said sometimes love was not enough, huh? Well, that sucked. You spend your whole life thinking that if you just meet the right guy and love each other, everything will be fine. Well, apparently it won't! I met the right man and he expected me to re-create myself for him again and again and again. I couldn't live with that shit. Maybe I wasn't meant to be married. All those songs make sense to me now, "What's Love Got to Do with It," "When Something Is Wrong with My Baby," "Since I Fell for You"—all that shit was true. And it stunk.

"Jewellen, listen to me."

"I'm listening, Mom."

"This is what women do, dear. They meet a man and make a few sacrifices. You think Eve wanted to leave the Garden of Eden? No, sweetie, but someone has to be the sensible one and keep the peace, no matter who was wrong and who won the argument. You know what Ephesians Six says, don't you?"

Lord help me, she was gonna whip out the biblical scripture on me. "No, no, I don't, Mom."

"That's because you don't attend enough church, but we're not going to get into that now. Ephesians Six tells us that the wives should be subject to their husbands as they are to the Lord. 'Just as the church is subject to Christ, so also wives ought to be, in everything, to their husbands.' "

I was really too tired and depressed for this speech, but I

forged ahead anyway. Hell, if she didn't say it now, she'd just call back and say it later. "Okay, hold up, Mom. First off, I'm not married to that boy. And second, I didn't see you being subject to Dad when you drop-kicked him out of the house and divorced him."

"You need to read your Bible. The devil is busy." That was Mom's way of saying, "why we have to go there?"

"That he is but I still make a good point."

"Jewellen, I hate to bring this up, but in the eyes of the Lord, you are married to that man. I know you think I don't see things, but I know you spend a lot of time in that boy's house and vice versa. You practically live together as man and wife right now, and you know what I'm talking about. You can't split hairs with the Lord, baby. And on that second point you didn't have to bring up, let me say that the Lord didn't mean for me to act no fool over my husband. You know your father was out there doing wrong and desecrating every vow he ever took. That's why I ceased to be subject to him."

There comes a time in every argument when you know you've either won it or lost it. I gave this one up as lost. "Okay, Mom."

"You're just trying to rush me off the phone because you know I'm right."

"No, no, I understand you're making valid points."

"But you still aren't going to be the one to give in."

I remained silent.

"I know you think I'm just old and don't know anything, but men like Roman don't grow on trees, sweetie."

"I know, Mom."

"Don't you want a strong man? Isn't his strength part of what attracted you to him in first place? You're going to lose that boy if you don't let go of some of those rules you've made for yourself."

I exploded. "He's gonna lose me too! Why doesn't anyone bring that up?"

"Face facts, sweetie—good black men are hard to find. And with the white women out there waiting to snatch them up, you can't afford to blow a good thing."

I hated that argument more than anything else in the world. If one more person told me how there was nobody left for me and I could easily be replaced by a white girl, I was gonna scream. It was time to end this conversation. "Be that as it may, Mother, I'm not making that move."

"I may have had some reservations about Roman, but over time I've come to see him as a good man. He's strong, intelligent, and a hard worker, with good morals overall. He overcame some early setbacks, and he comes from a good family. He's got a solid future ahead of him; anyone can see that."

"You call him and apologize, then."

"You can watch that tone, Jewellen."

"Sorry, Mom. I'm just not backing down on this."

"Okay, what started the argument?"

I wasn't about to tell her that I had propositioned Patrick to prove a point. So I just stayed silent.

"Okay, who was wrong?"

"Well, initially I was, but—"

"Stop right there. You start out apologizing for whatever thing you did. Then work toward a compromise on the other things."

Made sense but I just couldn't get there yet. "Can't do it, Mom."

"Well, if you want to live alone, unfulfilled and childless, it's your life. I can't tell you how to live it. Sooner or later, you have to prioritize. What's really important? What can you really afford to lose, and what do you really want to have in this life? You are given only so much time, you know."

"Mother, I am not calling him—I can't and I won't."

"How do you know that if you just take that first step, he won't meet you in the middle, Jewellen? Are you not willing to risk it?"

"No, I'm not. I put myself out there before. Hunted him down, apologized, and where'd it get me? Right back where I was before I swallowed my pride. No, I'm not calling."

"That's really too bad, Jewellen. You're going to let your stubborn pride stand in the way of something precious and rare. I'll pray for you, baby. Talk to you later." She hung up the phone.

I sat there dazed for a second. It was the first time in a long, long time she had sounded disappointed in me. Doesn't matter how old you get—that sad, let-down tone of voice from your mother could still tear you up inside. For the first time since the boy walked out on me, it really hit me that he was gone. Gone and not coming back. A sexy dress and a come-hither smile wouldn't do.

I'd tried to be brave about the whole thing, but truth be told, I was devastated. I loved him and he was gone. I put the phone back on the cradle, put my head down on the desk, and wept.

32

Gregory and Renee

Gregory—Saturday, April 15, 7:19 p.m.

That day—yeah, I knew it was Valentine's Day—I moved all my stuff out of Renee's, I knew I was never going back. I thought Valentine's Day was a fitting day to celebrate the death of a love affair. The death of dreams.

I went back to my crib and listened to Rahsaan Patterson's version of Sade's infamous "Love Is Stronger than Pride" over and over again for hours before I realized three important things. First was that Sade was way off the mark on that love and pride thing. Love didn't mean much of a damn when your pride was ripped all to hell and back. Either that or Sade was a far more evolved person than me.

Second was that next time I fall in love, it will be with someone who loves me above all else save God. Absolute devotion, that was what I was holding out for. I wanted to know that I was the most important thing in that person's world. I wanted to feel the warmth of that love in every fiber of my being. And I will clearly define what love is, thank you. No more guessing that my idea of love was the same as the other person's. Didn't I just read that common sense isn't common anymore?

And the third thing was that scheming, game-playing, and planning got you nowhere. The only thing to be sure of was that there was nothing in life to be sure of. So why waste the time scheming your life away?

So was I over her? For the most part, I thought so. Every once in a while, I would have what I call a "Ray Flashback," and it would hit me just like it happened yesterday. Like when I saw the new Victoria's Secret catalogue, I went into a rage like you wouldn't believe. You know, the mind played evil tricks on you. You start thinking, "I bet Beau has seen her in that navy sheer thing, or the green teddy with the pumps." And all those thoughts did was make me think about how that woman had the nerve to dog me. ME! She played me like a grand piano. And I ain't never been played before. I stopped and thought. Was I mad because my heart got broken or because my pride got wounded? Then I sunk into a funky little mood indigo for a while.

But I got over those faster and faster each time. Veronica had helped a lot. That girl was a rock. She had absolutely become the best friend I ever had. I'll never forget that second day after the "Big Bang," as I referred to it. I realized that I was going to have to go to Ray's and get some clothes. I can't begin to tell you how much I dreaded it. I really thought that if I had to look that woman in the face, I was going to kill her with my bare hands. Roni took my key, went over there, got some clothes, and was back out without Renee knowing. On the fifth day, she made me go back to my own place. Told me I needed a new outlook, not a new lover. Not like she even let me try anything the whole time I was there. And believe me, a little sexual healing would've been greatly appreciated. I dropped enough hints and made enough attempts. But not Roni, she wasn't having any. Another first for me, turned down. Nicely, but no was no.

I started spending more and more time at work, traveling more often than I needed to, basically living for work instead of working for a living. I came home one night to find Miss Veronica leaning against my door frame. She handed me a brochure on funeral plots and said, "If you wanna work yourself to death, at least be prepared." Then she walked off. I took the hint and eased back on the hours. Spent a little more time with friends and family I'd neglected while being all wrapped up in Ray's world. I started to realize that Ray's world had been a tight space to be in.

Another night, I went to a club with some of the fellas, and I was sitting off in a corner getting good and quietly drunk when I heard Roni's whisky-laced voice saying, "Ain't nothing worse than a bitter man drinking himself into oblivion. I once thought you were a together brother. Hate to be proved wrong."

Roni stayed on me when some of my best boys had given up and told me to call them when I was "ready to roll" again. Long after my hoops partners told me I was acting like a punk and disappeared on me, Roni was still hanging in.

I had a slight setback after that church thing. Ray almost got me with that one. Just wanted to believe again. Thought it could all go back to the way it was and everything would somehow be all right again. I wanted to believe. To believe that she was truly remorseful and that it would never happen again; after all, it's not like we were married yet. And truth be told, that night could've gone the other way. She could've come upstairs and found me and Roni in the exact same position. Well, maybe not the *exact* same one, but you know where I'm coming from. Then again, I'd like to think that Roni and I had a little more moral fortitude than that. I'd like to think we had a better sense of right and wrong, no matter what we were *tempted* to do.

So what stopped me from going back to Ray? Again, three things. The first was that I would never, ever, be able to wipe the image of her laid out on that table with her dress hiked up and Beau . . . Well, I just knew I'd never be able to touch her again without thinking about it. Didn't matter how much we skimmed over it or tried to erase the memory, every time we had a disagreement or I got upset about something—I knew myself—I would bring it up and throw it in her face. Every time she was late, every time she acted suspicious, the image would come back to me like it was yesterday. And I knew it.

The second thing was that I kept remembering how my mother, my friends, and Roni had told me, "She'll always want more." That was a fact, an honest-to-God fact that wasn't going to change about Renee. So what was to stop her from pulling this stunt again the next time some smooth-talking creamy brother with a wink and a smile came on to her? Nothing except her newfound religion, which I found harder and harder to swallow by the minute. I had offered Renee all that I had and all that I was, and it wasn't enough then; why would it be now? I had committed myself to her and meant it. I reassured *her* that I was in it for real. I even proposed and put a ring stating my intentions on her finger and still it wasn't enough. Well damn that.

And the third thing that stopped me was Veronica. It was no lie (maybe an exaggeration) when I said it could've been us that night. Hell, it could be us tonight if she would quit being such a buddy! But she was determined to let me have my "rebound relationship," as she called it. I was into Veronica, not some rebound chick. She was sexy, smart, funny and real. She put me first but didn't lose herself in the process. She has been so concerned I'll never get over Renee.

No need telling her I did the rebound mindless sex-fling thing last month when I went out of town. You know, just to make sure I was still all that. I was up front about it; met a little honey, she was down for a hit-and-run, and we hung out for a few days. Had to try it out on someone I didn't give a damn about first, get that itch out of my system so I could be cool about things. Too old to be out there flinging and swinging. I got in deep with Ray because I wanted a *relationship*, and I still do. I could wait. If I learned nothing else during the "Ray Days," I did learn patience.

I was thinking that in about a month or so, Veronica'll be convinced my head was back together and I was back on track. That's when I'll make my move. Veronica Mae will not stand a chance against me. Now wait, I know you think it sounds like I was planning and scheming again, but really, I learned my lesson. When I stepped to Roni, I was gonna be for real about it. Break down what I was looking for and what I was willing to give up. If it floated, we'll sail. If not, we won't. Amazing how simple things could be when we stopped trying to complicate them.

On that note, I ran into Roman the other day. Now, that was one sad-looking brother there. I tried to relate, but I couldn't see where the big conflict was. 'Course, I was hardly one to be handing out advice to the lovelorn and shit, but I told him straight up, "When you've gotta good thing, and you know it's good, don't let it go. No matter what." Getting deep with it, wasn't I? Ma said I've grown through the pain, whatever that means. I guess it means I recognized the fact that I was lucky to escape Renee's clutches with the few scars I had. Overall, I supposed the whold thing might have just made me a better man all around. Now, if I could just convince one sexy late-night radio personality of that . . . Stop, quit planning, Gregory. Some old habits were hard to give up.

Renee—Friday, April 28, 10:19 p.m.

I was ready. Beau was out the house for a while doing God knows what. I had planned on kicking him curbside, but he smoothed things over for me with Kat. Something told me that unless I eased him out proper, my job was in the tanker. But he was definitely going to have to go. Beau did not share the same work ethic that my Greggy did. He worked when and if he felt like it. Life with Beau was one big playtime. Like being in recess all the time. Wouldn't you know that Rome's ass paid Beau by the hour, so sometimes that boy was beyond broke. Of course, if he didn't spend every spare dime on clothes and good times . . . Well, he did have his uses, but like I said, he was definitely here on borrowed time.

Anyway, today was exactly a year to the day of my first date with Gregory. I took a chance that he'd be home remembering and alone. My confidence was high even though he hadn't contacted me after my public plea for forgiveness. The grapevine said he was licking his wounds in solitude and finally appeared back to normal. I knew it was just his pride keeping him from calling. Somewhere in the back of my mind, I was thinking that if we get this thing ironed out and patched up, we could still make that June 7 wedding. I'd have to think long and hard about letting Roni be in the wedding, though. I run into her at the gym all the time, and though we speak cordially and all, there's this big wedge between us. His name . . . Gregory Samson.

Confidence or no, my hand was shaking as I dialed the number. He picked up on the second ring.

"Hello, this is Gregory."

I heard party sounds in the background. So much for him being alone. It was still good to hear his voice.

For a minute I couldn't speak. I felt a flash of guilt followed by a flash of determination.

"Hello?" he repeated.

"Greggy?" I asked in my best yes-it's-me-baby voice.

Silence on the other end. He was probably all choked up with emotion.

"Greggy? Aren't you going to speak?"

"Hello, Renee," he said finally. "Turn that music down a second, could you?" he said to someone in the room.

Was that his big greeting? Well, not quite what I hoped for but still not too terrible. "Hello. How are you?"

"I'm well, thanks."

I frowned, he was still using his business voice. I decided to dive in. "I was just sitting here thinking about us."

"Us?" He said the word like it was a nasty thing. I started to doubt that this conversation would go well.

"Yes, us. You know, today is a year to the day that we went out on our first date."

"Oh yeah? You always were good for remembering that kind of thing. Seems like years ago."

I disagreed. "Seems like just yesterday to me."

"Hmm. What can I do for you, Renee?"

Immediately, my mind flashed back to that wild day in his office when he said those same words. My response then was, "Come over here and do for me, Greggy." I sensed that now wasn't the best time to bring that up. Instead, I forged ahead with my prepared speech. "I saw you in church that day I stood up."

"Um-hmm, with Beau. I remember that." His tone was wry.

Oops, might've been a mistake to bring that up. I'd forgotten about the Beau factor. "Uh, yeah, I was hoping you realized that I was apologizing to you. I don't know what happened to me. I was a lost soul."

He made a sound that resembled a laugh. "And you're found now?"

I hesitated, sensing a trap in his words. "Well, I recognize right from wrong now, that's for sure."

"You recognized it before, Renee. You simply chose to ignore it."

Ouch. Brother was harsh! "So, you don't forgive me?"

Now that sound *was* laughter. "Consider yourself forgiven, Ray." I took it as a good sign.

I grinned. He was calling me Ray. Feeling confident again, I laid it out there on the line. "I'd like to see you again, Greggy."

"What for?" He sounded horrified. Horror was not good.

"There's still a lot unsettled between us, Greg. Don't let your pride make a terrible mistake."

There was a long pause on his side of the line. When he spoke, his voice was somber to the point of grim. "Don't force me to be ugly to you, Renee. Let's just leave things as they are. Okay? We had our time together, and no matter how badly it ended, there was still a lot of good between us, emotionally and physically—"

I cut in, desperate now that I had an idea where he was going with this. "It could be like that again!" And I truly believed it could be, if he could just get past his pride.

"Ray, please. Let it go." I could tell he was holding back something.

"No! I want to know, what is it? Your ego, your pride? Is it Beau? He's nothing to me, nothing! Another woman? Whoever she is, she can't do anything for you the way I could. Baby, you know how I—"

He interrupted in a quiet but firm tone. "Renee."

"Yes?"

"Don't make me say this."

"Say what?"

"The thing you don't want to hear that will hurt you the most."

I frowned, what could it be? "Just say it."

"Ray, I don't want you anymore. In retrospect, I'm not sure that I ever even loved you."

I felt like all the breath had been knocked out of me. I was literally reeling and had to reach over to grab the edge of the sofa. I couldn't have heard him right. "What?"

"You heard me, Ray."

Yeah, I'd heard him. I just didn't believe him—how could he not want *me*? What did he mean he'd never loved me? We were going to get married! "I'm coming over there. You look at me—look me in my face—and tell me that." How could he *not want* me, *not love* me?

"I will if I have to, Renee, but do you really want to put both of us through that?"

My mouth fell open. He was serious. "You're serious?"

"Like a heart attack."

"And we're really through?"

"Completely over."

I was in such shock, I barely knew what I was saying. "So I guess the wedding's off." Soon as I said it, I winced. Of course it was off!

"Good-bye, Renee. Listen, I'm sure our paths will cross again in the future, since we have, er, mutual acquaintances. Let's try to be adult about this, shall we? No matter what happens?"

I pulled out of my dazed fog of pain long enough to register that. "What do you mean, mutual acquaintances . . . no matter what happens?"

"Enough said, Ray."

"Wait!"

"What?"

"You . . . you really hurt me just now, Greg. I just can't believe it."

"I'm sorry I hurt you. I guess it's ungentlemanly of me to point out that how you feel now, at this very moment, is probably exactly how I felt about three months ago. Here's some friendly advice from one who has been through it—you'll get over it." He hung up the phone.

It took me a while to get up and walk the handset to the cradle. I felt as though I'd been dealt a physical blow to the stomach. I looked around frantically for something, anything, to relieve the pain. Beau chose that moment to walk back in the door. He walked over to me, grabbed me by the waist, and kissed me.

"I'm home, *chére*."

I grabbed on to him like he was a lifeline. "Thank God, I missed you."

He tilted my face up and for once actually tried to see what was going on with me. "*C'est bien, chére?*" He frowned; he was not one for crisis situations.

"No, no, I'm not all right. But I think you can probably make it all better." I snuggled closer.

He grinned. Now we were back on territory he was comfortable with. "I'd say it's more than a probability, sweetheart." He picked me up and headed for the bedroom.

I allowed myself to be carried away.

33

Rome and Jewel

Roman—Friday, May 5, 6:21 p.m.

You know, I could have started getting over the damn girl if people would give me half a chance. It ain't enough that I kept running into folks who asked me, "How's Jewel?" all the damn time. No, last Sunday, I was at Moms and Pops' place. I went into the kitchen, and there was Moms chatting away to her on the phone like she was family or something.

Now I heard Chase downstairs talking to somebody, so I came down to check it out. There he was with the phone clutched in his little fingers. Made me rue the day the boy ever learned to use a phone. I was just gonna hang here and listen in for a minute before I broke this call up.

"How come we never see you no more, Miss Joo-well?"

Oh, I'da gotten up off all my bank to hear that answer.

"Doncha love us no more?"

I'd throw in the house too.

"You do?" Chase grinned. "I told Daddy you loved-ed me. Him, too, Miss Joo-well?"

I wanted to pick up another extension so bad, it was 'bout to kill me.

"I growed up since ya seen me!" He paused to hear her response and then launched into a lengthy description of all his activities over the past two months. When he ran out of breath, he took a deep one and said, "So, whatcha been doin'?"

I perked up again.

"Nothin' at all? That's sad, Miss Joo-well. Oh, you do?" He turned around and saw me. "Daddy, Miss Joo-well says she misses us lots and lots."

I sighed. "She knows where to find us, son."

"He says you know where to find us. Are you lost again? My daddy can tell you how to get here if you're lost again." Ah, the innocence of childhood. There was more than one way to get lost once you got older.

"Well, okay, if you say so. When will I see you again?" His little face frowned. "I don't 'stand it, but okay." He listened intently for a moment. "Love you, too, Miss Jewel. No, I won't forget." He held the phone out to me. "Miss Joo-well wants to talk to ya, Daddy."

"You sure?" I stared at the phone in my child's hand as if it would bite if I touched it.

"Yeah, Daddy, come on!"

I reached forward and grabbed the phone. "Hello?" Chase hopped down and started playing with his toy cars on the floor.

"Hello, Roman." How could she sound the same when everything had changed?

"How ya doing, Miss Jewel?"

"I'm making it, player." Small talk when there was so much to be said.

"Good to hear."

"Listen, I just wanted to say that I hope it's okay for me to keep in touch with your family; they've come to mean a lot to me. I really love them."

"Just my family, Miss Jewel?"

"You know better than that."

"Do I know that?"

"If you don't know I love you, then we don't have a thing to say to each other."

"Just had to hear it."

"Well, I love you."

"And I love you, Jewellen Rose."

She sighed. I sighed. Love don't conquer all, not in the real world.

"Anyway," I said, "it's fine with me if you want to keep in touch with the Montgomerys. No problem at all." Except that it was a punch to the gut every time I heard her name.

"Okay, I guess that's it." She sounded expectant, but for the life of me, I didn't know what she expected me to say.

"I guess so." I rubbed the bridge of my nose. Man, this was tough.

"All right, well, you doing okay?"

" 'Bout as well as can be expected. You know how it is."

"And the office?"

She knew how I hated chitchat. If she had something else to say, I wished she'd come on with it. "Business is good. Yours?"

"Good. You still playing at the center?"

"Yeah, season just started. Greg came with me last week."

"Oh, how's he?"

"Really good. Better than ever, actually."

"That's good. Renee's doing fine."

"Yeah, I know. Beau brought her to Sunday dinner last week." Much to my dismay. The one good thing about not seeing Miss Jewel was that I didn't have to see the fly girl either. Wouldn't you know I saw more of her now than ever before? "She says Stace and Trick are back together."

"More power to them, I say," Miss Jewel said.

"Yeah." This was never really about Patrick but was about whether, through all the nonsense, we were a fit.

"Well . . ." She paused.

"Well . . . ," I prompted.

"I'd better go and let you get back to LaChayse."

I was disappointed. Was this it? All it was going to be? "I guess so." It really wasn't that I was being stubborn. A little stubborn, okay. But I truly felt that if Jewellen couldn't understand what I was about, there was no need to prolong a relationship. Much as I thought we could have something special, I needed to be accepted for who and what I was.

She took a deep breath before saying, "Guess I'll see you around."

"Yeah, you take care." I hung up the phone before we could drag it out any longer.

Chase looked up from his cars. "You didn't tell her to come back, Daddy." He pinned me with an extremely accusatory look coming from one so young.

"Well, ah, no, son, I didn't."

"Doncha miss her, Daddy?"

"Yeah, I do, Chase."

He shrugged and shook his head. "Then I don't get it."

"Well, when you get older, you'll understand."

"How old, Daddy?"

"I'll let you know." Just as soon as I found out.

Jewel—Saturday, May 27, 1:21 p.m.

I was still fuming a bit as I pulled into the parking lot of the rec center. I had gone over it and over it in my mind, and I knew I was doing the right thing for me. It just pissed me off. Why couldn't *he* cave in? Why couldn't he come to me and say, "Look, let's do whatever it takes to make this work. You're too important to me to lose." Hey, that sounded good. Maybe I would use those exact words. Still chafed a little that it had to be me to do this thing. But after plenty of thought, I finally got it. I had played some games with Roman—I had held Jaquenetta over his head, and I basically told him I hated how he lived his life, that I didn't respect the things that were important to him. I wanted him to fit into my world (which he did), but I made little effort to fit into all of his. No wonder he wanted to know why I loved him; I had basically taken potshots at every element that made him who he was. After being taken for granted with Jaquenetta, he wasn't having it. You either accepted him for him or moved on. It took me a while but now I knew. Stubborn pride and humble pie made lonely bedfellows.

You know what else? That was *my man.* No how, no fly girl, hot mama was going to snag my man because I couldn't learn to bend a little. Well, I was here. I was willing to make a few concessions and see where that led. If it didn't work out after this, at least I'll know I tried.

I got out of the car and checked the reflection in the car window. I looked good. Denim shorts, button-front T-shirt with not two but three buttons undone—never hurt to remind the boy what he was missing. I took a last look and swung my hair in the wind a little. Yeah, I was tight today.

I'd deliberately waited until I knew the game would be just about over to arrive. I found which court he was playing on just as Demetrius was coming down from the game-winning layup.

"Looking good, Demi," I called out.

"You too, Jewel." Demetrius smiled.

"Jew-Ro!" Roni Mae called out, and I felt a flash of déjà vu. Matter of fact, it was about a year ago this time that I strolled in here and laid eyes on that boy for the first time. Looking over, I waved at Roni. She looked nothing like that outlandish character from last year. As I walked toward her, I saw Greg come off the court and exchange a high five with her. I was amused by this friendship they had formed. I gave them another two weeks before they gave in and hit the sheets. Funny how things turned out.

"Hi, Greg. Roni." I smiled at them both.

Greg leaned over and gave me a kiss on the cheek. "Good to see you. I guess you're here for Romeo?" He nodded toward the court. Roman was standing there looking at me, still clutching the basketball in his hands.

I smirked at him. Greg had proved himself a man through this past year. I couldn't resist teasing him a little. "So, Samson, you think you found your Delilah?"

He grinned. "Naw, been there, done that. Got the strength sucked right out of me. I'm looking for a more stable sort these days." He looked right at Roni. She hid a smile and turned her head.

I laughed. Who'd've thought anyone would refer to Roni as stable?

"Miss Joo-well! Miss Joo-well!" Chase catapulted himself out of nowhere into my arms. Like father, like son.

I hugged him tight, kissing his little cheek. I missed him as much as I missed Roman. "Hey there, Chase. You got so big. How's it going?" I stood up with him as he started to chatter in my ear. I sent a smile toward Roni and Greg. "Talk to y'all later." I tuned in half of what the little sweetie was saying as I started toward his dad, who had yet to uproot himself from the middle of the floor. When we stood right in front of him, I stopped and gave him the old twice-over. Still made my mouth water and then go dry.

"Lookie, Daddy, it's Joo-well!"

"So it is." A slow grin spread across his face. "Go get Daddy's bag and bring me some water, okay, Chase?"

"Sure, Daddy!" I let him slide down me and watched him run off.

"So, what brings you out?" he asked.

I reached forward and grabbed the ball out of his hands. I was doing an okay dribble action. "I thought we could talk about a little one-on-one action, player." I swiveled and made a halfhearted move toward the basket.

He immediately started to guard me, crowding behind me and trying to reach around for the ball. "Oh, yeah?"

"Yeah, I thought, maybe this time around, we could try to compromise. Instead of playing by my rules or your rules, we could make some up together?" I shuffled to the right.

He followed. "Sounds like an interesting game plan. But why you wanna play at all?"

"I love the game; I love the players. Everything about them, where they came from, how they got here, where they're going tomorrow. It's something I can't do without. I want to be involved in all four quarters. Why are you still on the court, Romeo?" I tried to pivot and he blocked my move.

"Well, now, I always thought this was the only game in town."

"Some things were said and done during the last few little scrimmages," I started.

"Things get said in the heat of competition. Crazy things get done. You can't take it all to heart. Just as long as you're loyal to the team." He was letting me off the hook.

I went for the fast break but forgot you really can't fast break in strappy sandals with cute little heels. I proceeded to trip over my foot and started falling backward. Roman lunged to catch me, but the ball was in his way and he fell too—right on top of me.

I grinned up at him; he smirked down at me. "Right back to where we started, huh, player?"

"Give or take a coupla feet, yeah." He turned serious. "So, we gonna do it right this time?"

"I'm willing if you are."

"Ah yeah, I'm willing." He shifted on top of me. Good thing the gym was just about deserted.

"Ready and able, too, I notice."

"Glad you noticed." He started to lower his head.

"Hey," I said softly.

"Yeah, *Bijou?*"

"We need a twenty-four-hour rule."

"What is that?"

"When we have a disagreement—"

"When we fight, um-hmm. Go ahead."

"We have to reconnect in twenty-four hours, decide if it's gonna be big or something we can work out quickly. What do you think?"

"An updated version of the don't-go-to-bed-angry rule?"

I laughed. "Yeah, something like that."

He smiled. "I like it. And we both have to reach out, no matter who started it."

"I can't promise I'm always going to cave in."

"I don't need you to cave; I just need to communicate. You can't shut down on me. Let's make this promise; we'll trust each other. I won't blow up."

"I won't play games."

"I won't shut you out."

"I won't shut down," I promised. Teasing, I added, "These sure sound an awful lot like vows."

He laughed. "True dat. Check it—I didn't freak out at your reference to marriage."

I was starting to get the good vibe about us again. "So, we'll take it a day at a time."

"A day at a time . . . together."

"Deal," I agreed.

"Sealed with a kiss." His lips grazed mine once.

Chase came running up. "Here's your water, Daddy. Whatcha doin'?"

"Forgetting where I am, son. I could sure use a cool drink." He stood up and pulled me to my feet.

"You comin' home with us, Miss Joo-well? Daddy was gonna barbecue." Chase held his hand out. Roman shifted his stuff to one hand and held out his.

"Now that's an offer I can't refuse." I took both outstretched hands.

"We cool now?" Little Chase had a way of cutting to the heart of things. He got it from his dad.

I looked over at Roman and raised a brow. He nodded. So I answered, "Yeah. We cool."

There was more to say and specifics to be settled, but for now, I was right back where I belonged.

34

Enough Is Enough

Renee—Monday, June 13, 8:08 p.m.

That settled it. I'd just gotten off the phone with Keisha. She said she and Arthur are talking about getting married. I'll be damned! It should have been me a week ago. Oh, I could just scream. I decided to call my homegirl for a little consolation.

"Hello?" Jew-Ro sounded all breathless.

"Jew-Ro, have you talked to Keisha?"

"Uh, yeah. I told her congratulations. What's up?"

"Wanted to see if you wanted to hang out this weekend."

"Roman and I are taking Chase to SeaWorld this weekend, but next weekend is wide open. How are you doing?"

"A little down . . . you know."

"Renee, it's gonna take a little time for you to get back on track with everything."

"I really blew everything the hell up, didn't I?"

"You did it up, girl. Big Willy style," she said drily.

We paused for a minute and then we both started snickering. "Oh shit, I really did. God, it's good to laugh about it. Thanks for hanging with me, girl. I know I'm a handful."

"Two handfuls and some still spills over, girl. But you my

girl. As long as you don't drop the drama at my front door again, you and I are good."

My girl, she'll back your play as long as you stick to her rules. Fair enough. "We cool, girl?"

"We cool. Listen, girl, I'm kinda in the middle of something. Can I call you back?" I heard her giggle and rolled my eyes before putting down the phone. Still didn't think Roman was the guy for her, but I've learned my lesson about getting in other folks' business.

Stacie was all geeked behind Trick's doggish ass and Tammy had whoever the freak of the week was. Roni, well, who knew what Roni was up to, but she looked so damn good lately, it made me sick.

I had to get my shit correct. How could this have come to pass? My program was NOT tight. Mere months ago, everyone was telling me how lucky I was, how I had it all. How far I had fallen. Sitting at home all the time, waiting on the "Cajun broke one" to remember he lived here. What was so great about great sex if immediately after you wanted to kick the guy out of bed and tell him to go away till next time? Oh yeah, something had to give around here. I needed to be back out, on the mac move. I couldn't go out weak like this behind Beau.

"Beau!" I called him from out of the bedroom. "Come here for a minute."

"Eh, Renee?"

"Baby, it's time."

"Time for what, *'tite chou*?"

"Time for all good things to come to an end. You got to rise up outta here."

"Ah, but *douc*—"

"Nah, none of that shit. Pack up your fly gear and roll out. If you'd like, we can still swing a little episode every now and again." I leaned up and gave him a kiss on the cheek. "Bye, Beau. "Yes! I was back in control of my shit. I was strictly looking out for me. After all, if Renee didn't look out for Renee, who would? My problem was that I let that love and lust nonsense get in the way of my goal. Was trying to live large and get paid up in here.

Beau went back to the closet and started getting some stuff together. I already had my organizer out when he came back through with a garment bag and his shaving kit.

"It was real, *chére.* We get together from time to time for old times' sake, no?"

"Sure, why not?" I was scanning the Cs.

"I come back Friday and get the rest. We'll have a *petite* party; I'll bring champagne." He set his key on the countertop and grinned. One thing was for sure—his was a heart you didn't have to worry about breaking.

Ds, Es, Fs . . . Franklin, Jhorry, attorney-at-law. Yeah, I wonder what he's up to nowadays? I sent Beau an absent smile as I reached for the phone. "Okay, baby, but call before you come over."

"Always," he said, and went on out the door.

As I locked the door behind him, the person I was calling picked up. "Hello?"

"Hello, is this Jhorry?"

"Yes."

"This is Renee Nightingale. I don't know if you remember me—"

"Oh, but I do, Renee. I never thought you'd call, though. I heard you were engaged to Gregory Samson."

I laughed. "How do these rumors get started? No, no, I've been spending a lot of time working on getting myself together. I'm free as a bird. Just came across your number and thought I'd give you a call. Hope I'm not interrupting anything?" In other words, how single or need I skip to the Gs?

"No, no, I'm pretty much my own man these days. This must be my lucky night, huh?"

"Could be, Jhorry. Sure could be. So tell me, what've you been up to lately?"

I let brother man ramble on, and I started jotting notes down. You had to have a plan, right? You couldn't chew your cabbage twice and let the grass grow under your feet. It was dog-eat-dog out there, every sister for herself. I was just trying to get mine, know what I'm saying?

35

Takin' a Shot

Gregory—Saturday, June 18, 1:06 a.m.

"Hello, you're on the air with Veronique on the Love Line. What can I help you with this evening?"

I smiled. "Hello, Veronique, I have a problem."

"Okay, what's your name?"

"Well, you can just call me G." I clicked off the lights around the room and lit some candles.

"G." I could tell she recognized my voice by the way she said it. "What seems to be the problem, G?"

"Well, I've got this friend . . ."

"Uh-huh. A male friend or a female friend?"

"Oh, she's very female."

"Sounds interesting, tell us about it."

"Well, see, I've known this lady for quite some time now."

"Um-hmm."

"We started out as casual acquaintances, and then we kind of fell into this attraction thing."

"An attraction thing, G?"

"For lack of a better word. It just came upon me one day

that she was sexy as all hell. Oh sorry, can I say *hell* on the radio?"

"This late at night, you sure can. Say anything you like; it's just starting to get interesting."

"Anyway, I was involved with someone else at the time; the situation was complicated, and we never really did anything about it."

"I still don't see the problem, G."

I grinned. "Well, let me spell it out for you. Since then, we've gone into a friendship-like relationship. She saw me through some rough times and pretty much hung in there for me. Now, I appreciated that, but I need—I want—more."

"More?" Her voice took on that molasses quality. I was gonna have to have this girl but soon.

"Much more. I want to be with her. Physically, emotionally, sexually. But she still wants to be buddies."

When Roni spoke, she sounded kind of breathless. "Well, maybe she just needed to hear you say it."

"Well, if she's listening, let me say it to her directly. I want you; you know who you are. I want you—in every way, as my friend, my lady, my lover."

"Are you sure, G? This seems like a big step, especially based on your past history and all."

"I know what I want. It's time to move on. You gotta either live today or sit thinking about what you missed tomorrow."

"That's, uh"—she stopped to clear her throat—"that's very well put, G. I'm sure your lady friend is listening and appreciates the words."

"I'd do a lot more than talk if I could see her tonight. Maybe she could come over and show her appreciation."

"Maybe she could." I could tell she was smiling by the sound of her voice. "Well, listeners, we're going to have a slight change in our programming for this evening. For the next hour, you will hear uninterrupted love songs for all you

'Candlelight by Moonlight' lovers out there. After that, E. Z. Groove with be here to take you on into the wee hours. Live, love, and laugh, Dallas."

She switched over to music and said into the phone, "Hold that thought. I'm on my way."

"I can hardly wait." I turned up the radio and smiled into the darkness.

36

Meeting in the Middle

Rome & Jewel—Sunday, June 26, 9:31 p.m.

Rome

It was a great day we had today. Went over to Moms and Pops for dinner and on the way home, I swung by this house. It was a big old rambling house, in need of some tender, loving care before it'll be all that. Right off of Central near Walnut Hill. Located almost exactly halfway between her house and mine. Pulled up in front the house and hopped out. Miss Jewel looked at me like I was crazy, so I opened up her door, took her hand, and pulled her out. We walked to the front door and I pushed it open. She stepped inside and stood there with her mouth open. I went on in and she followed behind me.

"It's beautiful!" she said as I showed her around.

"You like?" I asked as we stood in the kitchen, looking at what was once a beautiful hardwood floor.

"I love it. Whose is it?" She smiled at me.

"Ours," I said smugly, and turned away to examine the moldings in the living room.

"Beg your pardon?"

"Ours if we want it, baby. Greg's got the papers ready for us to sign anytime we want." I smiled. "We've been going out for just over a year. You mentioned a few times that I don't seem to compromise. How does this strike you?" With a smile, I headed up the stairs to let her take that in for a while.

Jewel

Did he say "ours"? As in together? I followed him up a majestic, wide staircase, which still had the original walnut banister intact.

"Roman, what are you talking about? I can't live with you." He knew how I felt about that living-together thing. Not down with the shacking. You wanna live with me 24/7? Marry me.

"I didn't ask you to shack up with me, Miss Jewel."

"So what are you asking?" I held my breath.

"Buy this house with me, let's fix it up together. By the time we get it in shape, it'll be a good time to start talking about that marriage thing." He looked shy for the first time since I'd known him. "Whadaya say?"

I started smiling. "Let me see if I get this straight—we're getting, um, engaged to be engaged sometime in the future?"

"We're engaged and married in eighteen months, Jewellen. Word is bond. I know you are not the string-along-shack-with-me girl. That's what I'm saying."

"I see. Now, what happens if somewhere down the line, we fall out and decide it ain't gonna happen for us? What do we do with this house?"

"Sell it and split the profits down the middle. Uh, you planning on cutting out some time soon?"

"Just being prepared, player—you know how it is."

"Oh, I know how you roll, Miss Jewel. Can a brother get an answer?"

Took a deep breath. What the hell. "I accept."

"Yeah?"

"Yeah."

He slung an arm around my neck and pulled me close for a kiss. "You know what today is, doncha, Miss Jewel?"

"Are you going to say something corny like 'the first day of the rest of our lives'?"

"Actually, I was. Let a brother be sentimental up in here."

I kissed his cheek. "Go ahead on."

"I thought about getting you some bling, some of them slinky drawers you love so, maybe a vacation."

"Instead, you've given me a promise for the future and half a house . . . I like it."

"I thought you would. Let's go back downstairs so I can carry you across the threshold. Might as well do it up right."

As we headed downstairs, I had to grin—to think I thought chivalry was dead. Lucky for me, I got the last black Prince Charming on the face of the earth. Bet you half a house I keep him.

A READING GROUP GUIDE

HEARD IT ALL BEFORE

MICHELE GRANT

ABOUT THIS GUIDE

The following questions are intended to enhance your group's reading of this book.

DISCUSSION QUESTIONS

1. How can coming from two different backgrounds hamper a relationship?

2. Do you think Greg should have taken Renee back? Why or why not?

3. Do women have to apologize or back down more than men in relationships?

4. How sensitive are men about their girlfriends' exes?

5. Why do women always get "caught up" by men like Beau?

6. Were you surprised by the evolution of Roni Mae/ Veronica? How so?

7. What do you think Roman learned from being married to and divorced from Jaquenetta?

8. Who is the more sensitive sex when it comes to getting their feelings bruised, women or men? Who recovers faster?

9. How much influence did Jewellen's family and friends have on her relationship with Roman?

CPSIA information can be obtained at www.ICGtesting.com
Printed in the USA
LVOW13s1811041213

363880LV00003B/570/P